D0344302

All Emergencies, Ring Super

Also by Ellen Emerson White

The Road Home
Long Live the Queen

All Emergencies, Ring Super

Ellen Emerson White

St. Martin's Press
New York

For Nick

A THOMAS DUNNE BOOK.
An imprint of St. Martin's Press.

Design by Nancy Resnick

Library of Congress Cataloging-in-Publication Data

White, Ellen Emerson.
All emergencies, ring super / Ellen Emerson White. —1st ed.
p. cm.
"A Thomas Dunne book."
ISBN 0-312-15651-0
I. Title.
PS3573.H4635A79 1997
813'.54—dc21 96-6575
CIP

First Edition: August 1997

10 9 8 7 6 5 4 3 2 1

One

Dana liked to tell people that her ambition in life was to ride down Broadway on the M104 bus, singing "I Have Confidence" out the window. The fact that she was only half-kidding was one she thought best kept to herself.

After all, there was something kind of appealing about an ambition that, for the price of a token and a little personal dignity, could actually be *accomplished.* Somehow—she must have had her back turned at the time—her life had drifted into a holding pattern lately. Flux. Indecision. Uncertainty.

Unmitigated panic might well be next.

Not that she was nervous about pushing thirty. And, okay, pushing damned *hard,* as Peggy, her closest, and most acerbic, friend had put it. She was just sensibly, maturely, reassessing things, having come to the sudden, startling realization that reciting lines someone else had written, and waiting for strangers to clap for her was a fairly banal way to make a living. Doing twenty-six takes extolling the virtues of a mediocre brand of coffee, while an agitated auteur-to-be kept referring to her as "*You,* whatever your name is" seemed even more bizarre. To say nothing of telling young urban under-tippers about specials cooked in lemon-butter sauces with capers, sun-dried tomatoes, and freshly-cracked peppercorns.

Of course, at the moment, she was spending her days fixing faucets, rolling flat white paint onto innumerable sooty walls, and dragging heavy plastic sacks of trash out to the curb after five-thirty in the evening on Mondays, Wednesdays, and Fridays. It was a pretty good deal, since building superintendents got a free apartment, in addition to a salary, but—well, so far, she had held off on alerting the alumni bulletin.

She had a nice red clipboard that she used to hold her worksheets, and every morning, she would put on superintendent outfits, generally including sturdy hightops, army pants with plenty of pockets, a series of paint-stained sweatshirts, and—always—a baseball cap cocked ever so slightly to the left. Well, okay, her sister Janet had said, but how is that different from your *normal* outfits? Since she was older, Dana had just laughed in a very wise and pitying way.

The funny thing was that now, for Christmas and birthdays, apparently purely by coincidence as opposed to discussing it behind her back, people were giving her things like how-to books and carpenters' belts. Little plastic goggles, a *very special* wrench. She wasn't exactly sure what had possessed them—and she kind of missed her normal allotment of sweaters and books—but, hey, tools were nice, too. Lately, she had her eye on a jazzy retractable tape measure at Ace Hardware, and—well, her family had been known to exchange gifts on St. Patrick's Day, so maybe a couple of small, pointed hints were in order.

It was February, it was a Tuesday, and the fourth job on her list was to go unclog the sink in 3D, where, as it happened, her friend Craig lived. Since he liked dogs—not everyone in the building did—she had allowed Bert, her scruffy shepherd mix, to come along with her. Bert was, naturally, delighted.

Then again, Bert was almost always delighted.

Which made him very pleasant to be around.

Craig answered the door, wearing a red headband, bicycle pants, an ancient *Evita* T-shirt, and Capezio dance sneakers. "Hi," he said, out of breath. "Okay if I finish my workout?"

Dana nodded, lugging her toolbox into the cramped little kitchen, while Craig went back to his quest for Abs of Steel. She glanced at the cloudy water standing in the sink, then filled his shiny copper teakettle and put it on to boil.

Bert was already restless, so she gave him a rawhide bone from the right envelope pocket in her army pants, and he carried it happily over to the rug in front of the couch and began chewing. Craig, also on the rug, didn't even notice.

Neither boiling water, nor her plunger, had any effect on the clog, so she crawled underneath the sink with a pail, some pliers, and her ever-useful, straightened-out wire coat hanger. After digging around inside the trap, she was able to extricate a thick clot of unknown, and unattractive, debris, getting only partially wet in the process.

Craig came over after she had replaced the cleaned-out plug and was pouring more boiling water down the drain to flush the pipes.

"There enough left in there for coffee?" he asked, even more out of breath than he had been before.

Dana shook the kettle, and then nodded.

He opened the cupboard, took down a jar of Royal Coffee—yes, the very brand for which she had embarrassed herself in two separate regional commercials—and set it on the counter with a great flourish.

"It's lousy coffee," Dana said.

"It'll make *anyone,"* Craig said, and mimicked the cheery wink she had had immortalized on low-grade celluloid, "feel like a king."

Upon which, the camera had panned up, and—there she was!—wearing a cheesy-looking crown.

Her loved ones had been so proud.

"They made me wear my hair like that," she said defensively. Not that she was ever going to live that damned Alice-in-Wonderland pouf down. The pink ribbon, in particular.

Craig laughed.

"*Made* me," Dana said, and patted Bert, who had become bored by his bone and was now lying on her right foot.

"Well—so you say." Craig fixed their coffee, and then picked up a pack of Marlboros from the counter, lighting one and offering the pack to her.

She hesitated. "I quit."

"Again?" he asked.

Again. She nodded with extra certainty, and tasted her coffee. It was, indeed, lousy.

"Are you really not going out on auditions anymore?" Craig asked.

So far. She nodded.

He blew out some smoke, and sucked in some coffee. "Terence must be pissed."

Her agent. "Yeah," she said. In fact, he was veering between berating her, and suggesting intensive psychotherapy.

"There's a part in the new WPA thing you'd be perfect for," Craig said.

Dana grinned wryly, feeling temptation rearing its ugly little head. "No, I—I think I'm retired," she said. Or, anyway, on sabbatical. Hiatus.

For now.

Craig frowned. "You're not dating some damn banker again, are you? Getting stupid ideas?"

She shook her head, since, to her extreme consternation, she hadn't been dating *anyone* recently. Wildly-inappropriate, or otherwise.

"Well, good," Craig said, but kept frowning. "Actors should never date out of the business."

Dana laughed. "Oh, yeah, you and I have had a *lot* of success dating actors." In fact, on one epic occasion, they had both—briefly—dated the very *same* actor. Fortunately, she had never done more than have lunch with the guy. To the best of her knowledge, neither had Craig.

"Okay," he said, "but you were making it. Talk about a dumb time to change your mind."

So Terence kept telling her. As far as she was concerned, she had, in fact, simply come to her senses. But she just shrugged, and sipped her coffee.

"Frank Rich liked you," Craig said. "*John Simon* liked you."

Not that she read reviews, but—okay—those were two she had cut out and saved. More than one copy. "Well," Dana said, and grinned again.

Craig grinned too, looked around for an ashtray, then leaned over to knock his ashes into the sink.

"I just finished unclogging it," Dana said, impatiently, and pulled the empty Diet Coke can she always used as an ashtray—except that she, of course, didn't smoke anymore—out of one of her pants pockets.

Craig shook his head, indicating the can. "That is *such* a good choice. I mean, it's so authentic."

She had spent most of her adult life having conversations like this. Scary. "I was carrying an empty Budweiser can before," she said, "but Mr. Abrams"—the landlord—"came by, and thought I was drinking on the job." Much as the last superintendent in their building had. Day and night.

"It's such a great choice, though," Craig said. "It says *woman,* it says down-to-earth, it says *super.*"

Was it her imagination, or was that his tongue, deep in his cheek? Although she did have a little tendency to go through her daily life equipped with—props.

But she really didn't smoke.

Much.

"About the sink," she said, and pointed at the drain. "Every week or so, throw some boiling water down. A little baking soda and vinegar couldn't hurt, either. Because I have to go up to 4E now and"—she could hardly wait—"grout."

Craig looked sheepish. "I had a garbage disposal in my old apartment."

So he told her, every time she had to come in here and unclog the thing. She nodded, and bent down to repack her toolbox.

"Um—before you go? Can you, um"—now he avoided her eyes completely—"show me how to time-tape again?"

Without a doubt, the single most common request on her daily worksheet. "Numbskulls," Dana said. "I live in a building full of numbskulls."

Craig nodded, sheepishly, and followed her out to the living room.

After grouting in 4E—Mrs. Bergman fixed her some tea and

vanilla wafers, and then tying up mounds of newspapers for recycling—a feat for which she was given no snacks at all, she had just about enough time to make it up to the alternative school where she tutored every week. In some ways, it was one of her favorite things to do; in other ways, she always dreaded it, because even when things went well, spending the afternoon with recalcitrant inner-city teenagers was exhausting.

The school was very small, and catered to students who had been unable to make it in the public school system—for any one of a number of unhappy reasons. So, they were assigned to this program, which was aptly titled "Second Chance." For most of the forty-odd students, it was just that, although there were a few for whom it was more like a *last* chance.

Regardless, she went up there every week, and helped a fourteen-year-old boy named Enrique with his writing, and a fifteen-year-old named Shawn with his reading. Enrique tended to be sullen, but cooperative, while Shawn was usually jolly, but incapable of paying attention for longer than about a minute and a half. Most of the time, afterwards, she would go up to the makeshift little gymnasium, and shoot baskets—she was from New England; she would feel foolish saying "hoops"—with whoever was so inclined, or swing at a whiffle ball, or something. The boys, like every male she had ever known, were always greatly amused by her prowess. Girls seemed able to take that sort of thing in stride.

That particular afternoon, she ended up throwing around a slightly deflated football with four of the boys, and Ned, the city-appointed social worker, until her arm started hurting.

"Whatsa matter?" Shawn asked, as she retired to the sidelines. "We too tough?"

Dana shook her head, putting on her ski jacket. "Old rotator cuff injury."

The boys seemed dubious, but Ned laughed.

Actually, she had a long history of sports—and stage—injuries. Growing up, she had gotten to know her family doctor so well that she had ended up baby-sitting for her regularly. A mutually beneficial relationship, as Dr. Jennings had put it.

The alternative school was on Amsterdam, in the low 100s, in the middle of what was easily the Upper West Side's worst drug neighborhood. The police would come, and sweep the area out every so often, but the clean-up never seemed to last more than a couple of days before the streets would be littered with depressingly-interchangeable miscreants again.

More and more often lately, there were times when she just wanted to go back to Massachusetts and look at the ocean for a while.

She was walking towards Broadway when a guy came leaping down at her from the front stoop of a seedy-looking building and she almost forgot how cool she was, and started running. Luckily, she remembered just in time, and was able to fold her arms and maintain total aplomb.

"Hey," he said, not sounding friendly.

Travis Williams—everyone's least favorite student at Second Chance. A "Next stop, Rikers Island" kind of kid. All of the boys in the school *looked* tough, but Travis wasn't kidding around. In the four or five months Dana had known him, the extent of their interaction had been him muttering what she suspected were obscenities whenever she walked by. Personally, she preferred people who looked her straight in the eye when they swore at her.

On the other hand, he was just a kid—and she liked kids.

"Hey, sport," she said.

He shrugged, fists in his pockets, shivering slightly in the wind.

God forbid he make any form of human communication easy. "What's up?" she asked.

He shrugged, scowled, and shrugged again.

Right. "Didn't see you in school today," she said.

He—predictably—shrugged, barely looking at her, his White Sox cap down low over his forehead.

Perhaps not the most successful conversation she had ever had. Although it was preferable to his swearing at her. "Well, I guess I'll see you next week then," she said, and headed towards Broadway again.

He came after her, staying a step and a half behind, and if he was trying to be menacing, she was more annoyed than alarmed.

She stopped walking. "Do you want something, Travis, or am I a little confused here?"

He shrugged without answering, looking up and down the street, watching each car—mostly cabs—that went by.

"Come on," she said. "It's cold out here."

He nodded, his shoulders hunched up, and it occurred to her that it was February, and all he had on was a hooded sweatshirt.

"Where's your coat?" she asked.

He shrugged—unhappily, this time.

Second Chance was next to a church, and if she took him back there, someone would find him a coat. He certainly wouldn't be the first kid at the school who couldn't afford warm clothes.

"Look," he said, before she had time to move. "I know I don't know you or anything, but—" He stopped. "Your boyfriend's a cop, right?"

News to her. She shook her head.

Travis frowned. "I saw like, a cop hugging you and all." He gestured in the general direction of the most recent drug sweep. "That time before."

There was only one cop on the face of the earth who ever hugged her. "That's Ray," she said. "He's just a friend." A guy she had gotten to know when he was working in the community policing unit because she was always walking her dog, he was always walking his beat, and they were both prone to making indiscriminate conversation with total strangers.

"Oh." Travis frowned again. "I was hoping you went out with him."

Strange that he had noticed, one way or the other. Dana looked at him thoughtfully. "Because he's a cop, or because he's black?"

"I just—forget it, okay?" he said, his shoulders hunching up more. "It doesn't matter."

Indicating that he was being jittery and urgent for absolutely no reason at all? "If you need a police officer," she said, "we can go down to the—"

He shook his head, checking the street again. "Just forget it, lady. I gotta go."

"Wait a minute." She reached out for his sleeve to pull him

back. "At least tell me what—" There seemed to be something heavy—very heavy—*too* heavy—in the front pocket of the sweatshirt, weighing it down, and she let go abruptly. "I really hope that isn't what I think it is, Travis," she said, keeping her voice calm.

"I need it," he said, his right hand going protectively inside the pocket.

Jesus. A gun. The stupid kid was walking around with a gun. And—clearly, a measured and judicious response was required here, but her mind was a blank.

"I just—" He stopped to watch another car cruise by, his hand visibly tightening inside the shirt. "Can we go somewhere? Somewhere private?"

Exactly what she felt like doing—heading off alone, with a hostile, jumpy kid she didn't even really *like,* who was carrying a gun. "I, uh"—Her mind was being very slow on the uptake here—"I don't think that's such a great—"

"Please?" he said, looking a lot more scared than dangerous, as he shivered in the cold.

Was this the point at which she was supposed to recommend that he go seek out the advice of a kindly, older relative or a trusted clergyman?

"Please?" he said. "I need *help."*

Not the easiest request in the world to refuse. Impossible, in fact. She took a deep breath, and then sighed.

"Okay," she said. "Let's go."

Two

For lack of a better idea, she brought him back to her apartment. Actually, she brought him to the door of her apartment, and then stopped.

"I don't like guns," she said, "and I *really* don't want you bringing that thing inside."

Travis looked sulky. "Bet you'd let that cop guy bring his gun in."

She liked, whenever possible, to maintain ethical consistency. "That's different," she said. "He's a trained professional. Besides, he doesn't carry it around socially." At least—she didn't think so.

Travis just shrugged, making no move to comply.

Okay, a strict teacher voice hadn't worked, so she would pull out the heavy artillery, move straight past drill sergeant, and all the way to the crackling authority of a Mother Superior. "*Take* the gun out," she said, *"unload* it, and then leave it open"—open, or should she have said uncocked? Maybe she'd better double up on the authority—*"right this instant."*

Travis, sulkily, took the gun out of his pocket—some kind of small, ugly handgun—and popped the clip out.

"Good," Dana said. "Now, let me have it, please."

Maryanne, the very tall and pale freelance artist who lived in the apartment next to hers, came down the hall, lugging her bulky portfolio, some dry cleaning, two plastic grocery bags from

Sloan's, and a small pizza. "Hi," she said, sounding very vague.

Dana nodded, moving the gun down by her side, and closing her other hand over the clip. "Hi."

Maryanne felt around for her keys, then handed Travis—who blinked, but took them—her portfolio, the pizza, and one of the grocery bags, searching until she found them in her left poncho pocket. "It's sticking again," she remarked as she opened her top lock.

Dana nodded. "I'll put some WD-40 in there later."

"Thanks," Maryanne said, retrieved her bundles from Travis's arms, smiled—vaguely—at both of them, and went into her apartment.

"That lady didn't even notice you like, have a gun," Travis said, staring at the now-closed door.

Dana nodded. Maryanne was the kind of person who strolled through freshly poured cement, crossed Broadway against the light, wandered underneath rickety ladders—and somehow managed to remain intact on a daily basis. It was amazing.

Anyway.

She could hear Bert fretting and sniffing behind her own door, and quickly unlocked it, lifting her foot to block any possible animal escape attempts.

"Watch the cats," she said to Travis, who looked uneasy, but followed her inside.

Bert was bouncing around, and she held the gun well out of his reach, setting it down cautiously on one of the kitchen counters. Theodore, one of her cats, bounded up to examine this new, very intriguing, metal toy, and she quickly brushed him off the counter and away from it.

"So, you, uh," Travis shifted his weight, his fists in his pockets, "you live here?"

It would be cruel to point out his astonishing grasp of the obvious. "Yeah," Dana said. "Sit down while I feed everyone."

He watched her, remaining standing, while she measured a precise cup and a half of Nature's Recipe for Bert—he was getting a little plump these days—splashed some water and vitamin powder onto it, and then gave Theodore and her other cat, Edith, a pat each and poured some dry CD into their small blue dishes. Finished, she turned to Travis.

"Hungry?" she asked. "How about a sandwich?"

He shrugged uncomfortably.

She decided to take that as a yes, and opened the refrigerator. "Grilled cheese okay?"

He shrugged.

Another yes? Why not. She took out cheddar cheese, a loaf of wheat bread, some mustard, and a tub of margarine.

Travis looked around. "You, uh, read all these books?"

Did people ask that—which they always did—because they thought it was too many books, or because she didn't seem bright enough to engage habitually in literary pursuits? "No," she said. "But I think they look pretty."

Travis nodded, frowned, and shifted his weight some more.

Even unloaded and disassembled, the gun made her very nervous, and she pushed it farther over on the counter, making sure that it was still pointing away from them.

"Why don't you call your mother, or whomever, and let them know where you are, and when you'll be home," she said, turning on the gas underneath a cast-iron frying pan. She had learned, "Hot pan, cold oil, food won't stick," during one of her tentative forays into the world of PBS.

Travis looked confused. "What do you mean?"

She frowned at him. A teacher frown. "Just do it. I don't want anyone to worry about you. The phone's right over there."

He slouched over to the telephone on the desk, and punched in a few numbers. "It's me," he said, when someone answered. "I'm s'pposed to tell you I'll be home later." He listened briefly, then shrugged. "I don't know. This dumb lady from the school just said I had to call." He listened again. "Okay. I mean, I won't," he said, and hung up.

She hadn't been eavesdropping, but— "Won't what?" Dana asked.

He shrugged. "She says I'm not s'pposed to call you dumb."

Oh. Good advice. Dana nodded, swiftly assembling three sandwiches.

"I'm also not s'pposed to call you lady," he said.

Dana nodded, putting a lump of margarine in the pan and swirling it around as it sizzled.

"So, what do I call you?" Travis asked, after a pause.

Anything was a step up from obscenities.

"Like, you know, your name?" he asked. "Or Ms. Coakley?"

She might actually prefer obscenities to "Ms. Coakley." Dana lifted the corner of one sandwich with her spatula to see if it had browned, then flipped it over. "How about Dame Coakley? Or—Ensign. Ensign would be okay."

Travis looked sulky.

If he had a birthday soon, maybe someone would give him a sense of humor. "Dana," she said. "Dana is fine."

He shrugged, sulkily.

By the time, she had finished setting the table, the sandwiches were ready, and she arranged two on his plate, serving them with a pickle and a very generous handful of Doritos. If she'd had a sprig of fresh parsley, it would have been a *perfect* presentation—but this would have to do.

"Okay?" she asked, putting the plate in front of him.

Travis shrugged.

Quel surprise. "That means, 'Thank you very much, looks delicious,' right?" she said.

He didn't answer, but came close to smiling.

"Want some soda?" she asked.

He shook his head. "Can I have a beer?"

That would be pushing it. "No," she said. "You may have soda, or some juice, or seltzer, or—" Did she have anything else? "Tea or coffee."

Travis made a face.

"Cup of bouillon?" she suggested.

"Coke," he said.

Fine. She poured him a Coke, and one for herself, before sitting down. Edith had jumped onto the table to sneak a little taste of grilled cheese, and Dana glanced at Travis, then set her back on the floor.

"Bet if I wasn't here, you'd let her stay there," he said.

Yeah. Dana picked up half of her sandwich, but paused when she saw that he wasn't eating. "What, do you usually say grace?"

Travis shook his head.

"Neither do I," Dana said. "I have a certain amount of guilt about that, but—well, let's just say that it doesn't spoil my appetite." She frowned. "Unless I give it some thought. Which, as a general rule, I would only do *between* meals." She looked across the table. "You're still not eating, Travis."

"You, uh, you don't like me much, do you?" he asked.

Honesty was not always a virtue.

"I mean, mostly I just goof on you, you know?" he said.

She nodded—but doubted it.

"I just—kind of like to scare people," he said. "Rich people, you know? I just gotta walk *by* rich people, and they're scared." He grinned a little. "White people."

Dana nodded. Shawn and some of the other kids at the school who she knew better—and liked more—had told her that even when they were just walking down the street, not doing anything, people—okay, *white* people—would cross to the other side to avoid them. Minority teenagers, sauntering along in baseball caps and overpriced sneakers. A lot of New Yorkers' worst nightmare. Sometimes, admittedly, for very good reason.

She just didn't ever want to be the one to have to admit it. Privately *or* aloud.

"Anyway," Travis went on, "doesn't mean I want to *hurt* people, know what I'm saying? I'm just—goofing."

And his sandwiches were almost cold. "What are you getting at here, sport?" she asked.

"That I got some idea," he said. "You know, right and wrong and all."

Carrying a gun would seem to contradict that, but Dana shrugged politely. "Okay."

Travis frowned at her. "I got, like, not a lot of choices, you know what I'm saying?"

Oh, please. That line of argument always irritated her. Which was probably a sign of incipient Republicanism, but—nevertheless. She preferred to think of herself as a Moynihan Democrat.

"I don't know," she said, more stiffly than she'd intended. "I should think that, at some level, you have to take responsibility for— "

"Hey, that's what I'm *trying* to do," he said, "okay, lady? If you'd just like, *listen* for a minute."

All right. She sat back, folding her arms so that she would look as annoyed as she felt. Clenching her fists would be overkill—and besides, he had already beaten her to it.

"Like, I don't know you, right?" he said. "I don't, you know, know any adults. And my mother's real nervous lately, so I don't want to—I don't know what to do."

For the first time, in the bright kitchen light, she noticed that he was trying, and failing, to grow a mustache—which both broke her heart, and reminded her that he probably *didn't* have all that many choices in his life. And even if he did, he might not *know* that he had them.

"What you do," she said, "is tell me, and I'll— " she shouldn't promise to fix whatever it was, in case she couldn't "—do my best to help you."

He looked at her, then nodded, his fists loosening slightly. "I live in Harrison. Or, you know, I did."

The Harrison Hotel. Low-income, mostly homeless, families and elderly people—and the place had burned to the ground a few weeks earlier. She couldn't remember the details, but the fire might even have been started by the lights on a dry Christmas tree, of all disturbingly ironic things. A number of people—almost all children, but also two firefighters—had been killed, and even more were injured.

"I'm sorry," she said. "I didn't know that. Is everything— " stupid question "—all right?"

"My family didn't actually burn up, if that's what you mean," he said. "Just like, all our stuff."

No wonder the poor kid was walking around without a coat. She sighed. "I'm sorry. Where are you—?"

He cut her off. "Don't worry, I'm not like, about to move in."

"Okay," she said, "but if you need a place to stay— "

He nodded grimly. "Hey, don't worry. We're on a *list.*"

Yeah. Homeless families in New York were always stuck on some damn waiting list or other. "I know my apartment isn't very big," she started, "but—"

He shook his head. "My sisters got sent down to Alabama, to my grandmother, and me and my mother are at my aunt's."

There probably wasn't much she could do, but she certainly had some spare clothes, and—"I'm really sorry," Dana said. "I had no idea you—"

He scowled at her. "Save it for like, you know, *brunch.*"

Right.

"It wasn't any goddamn space heater," he said. "They torched the place."

Dana frowned. "I didn't hear anything about—"

"Hey, you don't have to, you know, *believe* me or anything," he said. "I'm just telling you."

She tried to remember the articles she'd read, but even really terrible city tragedies—unless there was a tawdry sex angle—had a pretty short shelflife. The Harrison Hotel had dominated all of the newscasts—for a day or two—and then the media migrated to some other, now-forgotten, catastrophe.

"*Knew* you wouldn't believe me," he said.

Well, it was hard to imagine anyone would be depraved enough to burn down a building full of children and old people. "What makes you think it wasn't an accident?" she asked. "I mean, with all the coverage the story got, wouldn't someone have—?"

"I know a guy, would've gotten paid to do it," he said.

Oh.

Edith had gotten back up onto the table and Dana broke off a little piece of cheese for her without thinking. Or maybe because she was too busy thinking.

"So, why doesn't he go to the police?" she asked. "People were *killed.*"

Travis looked at her without any expression at all. "Got himself blown away, few nights ago. You know the way us folks is 'bout guns and drugs."

Dana rubbed her forehead, feeling a sudden, terrible headache.

"Don't exactly got a lot of proof," he said, "but my mother didn't raise a fool either."

And he wouldn't make something like this up. Would he? "Well," she said slowly, "what we have to do, then, is get you to the police."

Travis nodded. "Oh, yeah, the police love my guts. 'Sides, how long you think I'd last after that? You know, if like, it's true? 'Bout an hour?" He shook his head. "I figured you could find out, you know, quiet-like, and then you and me'd be out of it."

Sounded good—in theory.

"Hey, no reason you gotta help me," Travis said. "I mean, it's not like people who *matter* dying."

He'd definitely picked up his cynicism the hard way. "It's not that," she said. "It's just—" Implausible. "They've had investigators, and commissions all over the place." Hadn't they? They must have. "I don't see how—"

Travis's nod was very stiff. "Yeah. Just some dumb welfare grandmom with a space heater, trying to keep welfare kids warm." He pushed his plate away, the sandwiches barely touched. "You ever read the paper, lady? A fire on Park Avenue, now that's news. Black folks? That's *good* news."

Made even worse by the fact that it had the unmistakable ring of truth. At least in this city. She sighed, and pushed her own plate aside.

"Don't see you putting up much of an argument," he said. "Hell, the projects can like, burn to the ground and that's, you know, too bad, but let a white lady get looked at cross-eyed, and—stop the goddamn presses."

She had lived in New York for a long time. Listened to, read about, and *discussed* so many horrific events over the years that they all pretty much blended together in her mind. By now, it took something a lot more unspeakable and unexpected than—oh, say, another baby in a dumpster—to get her full attention. She'd thought that the fire in the Harrison Hotel was—very sad.

Unfortunate.

Christ.

Travis was looking at her, his arms tight across his chest, slumped down in his chair.

Okay, he had her full attention.

"I'm going to need details," she said. "Everything you have." She reached for a pen and an unused legal pad. "Start at the beginning."

He didn't have much. Rumors. Hearsay. Guesswork. A guy—now dead as the result of a drive-by shooting—who knew another guy, who had seen a third guy. Nothing resembling evidence, or proof, or even, really, probable cause.

Keeping in mind that the bulk of her legal knowledge had come from *L.A. Law, Court TV,* and the odd courtroom thriller she'd read here and there, generally while being bored by the view from Amtrak's Northeast Corridor.

"Remember, you can't tell that cop guy who I am," Travis said. "I mean, I gotta trust you."

A promise she might not be able to keep. "If there *is* a case here," she said, "they're going to need all the witnesses they can—"

Travis shook his head vehemently. "I wouldn't like, testify or anything. I mean, *no way.* Besides, I just, you know, *heard* stuff."

Police officers loved people who wouldn't come forward. "Well, I'll tell Ray everything," she said, "but the truth is, it's all pretty sketchy." To put it mildly.

"How long you think it'll take?" Travis asked. "For him to, you know, find out."

"At least a couple of days," Dana said. "It'll depend on who he knows, and how much trouble he has pulling the files."

Travis nodded, and they sat quietly at the table.

"Well." He stood up, shoving his hands into his pockets. "I guess I'll, you know, see you later."

There was no point in telling him to finish his meal—since she wasn't hungry anymore, either. "I'll stop by the school and let you know what I find out," she said.

Travis nodded, took a step toward the counter—and the gun—and she shook her head. Firmly.

"Not a chance," she said.

"It's *mine,"* he said.

Tough. She shook her head again. "Forget it."

Travis looked like he was going to argue, but then just headed for the door.

"Wait a minute," she said after him.

He sighed, extra-heavily. "I gotta *go,* lady. I'm late."

The least of his problems. "I'm doing you a favor here, and I want one in return," she said.

He folded his arms, looking wary.

"School," she said.

He frowned at her. "What's that supposed to mean?"

Precisely what he thought it meant. "You're a bright kid," she said, "and the deal is that you're going to start showing up every day and getting good grades."

He laughed. "Yeah, *right."*

"Hey!" Dana yanked him back as he started to open the door. "That's the deal, Travis. Period. No negotiating."

"Cut it out, lady," he said, trying to pull his sleeve free. "You're gonna rip it."

She shrugged, keeping her hand twisted in the cloth. "So try saying something like, 'yes, ma'am, sounds fair to me.' "

"I don't think it *is,"* he said.

Every so often, although she liked to keep it to herself, she felt a slight strain at the boundaries of her patience and goodwill towards others. Rather than betray this, she just looked at him without blinking.

"Okay, okay," he said. "Let go of my shirt already."

She let go of his shirt.

"I don't think I like you, lady," he said, smoothing his sleeve much longer than seemed necessary. "I don't think I like you at all."

She ignored that, taking her army field jacket out of the front closet, and emptying the pockets. It was her favorite coat—one in which she felt fierce and unapproachable; often handy in New York—but it was also, by far, her most androgynous, and she couldn't bring herself to send the kid home in nothing but a sweatshirt. "Here. It's cold out there."

Travis shook his head. "No way."

Was he being difficult, or unpredictably polite? "Go ahead," she said. "I hardly ever wear it." Which was a lie, but what the hell. "And you can't tell me it's not cool enough, because I see guys with them all the time."

Travis hesitated.

"Just take it," she said.

He looked uneasy, but put the jacket on.

"Good," she said. "Now, zip up."

Obediently, he zipped the jacket up. "Um, thanks. I mean—" he didn't quite look at her "—well, just like, thanks and all."

Right.

Three

Once he was gone, she wasn't sure what to do with the gun, but finally, she put it at the very back of her top dresser drawer—and didn't sleep very well.

In the morning, she called the precinct house, found out that Ray was working the eight-to-four tour, and then spent most of the day cleaning and starting to paint Apartment 1E so it would be ready for the new tenants moving in on March first. The previous ones—two Columbia graduate students who had had trouble making the rent—had left the place in pretty bad shape, and scrubbing the bathroom and defrosting the two inches of ice inside the refrigerator made her cranky enough to drink three Diet Cokes, in lieu of going through half a pack of cigarettes. The caffeine made her even jumpier than she might normally be, but it was better than lapsing into the lure of nicotine.

Right before four o'clock, she retrieved the gun from her dresser, put it inside a small brown paper bag, and went over to the police station to try and catch Ray on his way home. She stood near the main entrance to wait for the shift change, very self-conscious about holding an illegal handgun as police officers coming on, and going off, duty, kept walking past her. She couldn't decide what bothered her more—the ones who made a big point of checking her out, or the ones who *didn't.*

After a while, she went inside and politely asked for Ray at the front desk, only to find out that—despite the supposed modernization of the system—he was down at Central Booking for the foreseeable future.

Which left her holding the bag, as it were.

Since she wasn't sure how they would react to receiving a gun from a stranger, and she didn't want to answer a lot of questions, she went back outside and stood around being indecisive for a few minutes.

There was a fire station right next door to the precinct house, upon which, the obvious occurred to her. After all, who knew more about what caused fires? They might not feel like talking to her, but either way, it would only be five minutes out of her life, right?

She walked up to the main entrance, where two brawny, brown-haired firefighters with mustaches were leaning against the side of the building, enjoying the unseasonably warm afternoon.

"Nice day," Dana said.

Both men nodded amiably.

"Real nice," one of them said.

"Nice as can be," the other said.

Were they related, or did they just seem to be? For some reason, firefighters always looked pretty much alike to her. Then again, it might be because the FDNY wasn't exactly notoriously multicultural.

"Either of you guys in charge?" she asked.

They shook their heads.

"You want Lieutenant Saperstein," one of them said.

"Five foot two, eyes of blue," the other guy said.

That, she doubted. She went inside the main station, taking off her sunglasses to see in the dimmer light. There were a number of firefighters doing routine servicing and cleaning of various pieces of equipment, while a few others were gathered around a table, watching a very small firefighter, who was playing two games of chess simultaneously. In the far corner—she had to look twice—another firefighter seemed to be trying to teach an old black dog some new tricks. Without much success.

It was hard to be sure who was in charge, so she took a guess and wandered over to the chess crowd.

"Saperstein?" she asked.

"Check," the very small firefighter said—in a distinctly female voice—to one of her opponents. She made a move on the other board. "Mate." Then, she turned around. "Hi. What can I do for you?"

Five foot two, eyes of blue.

How about that.

"Wait a minute," her opponent who was still in check said. "We're not done yet."

Lieutenant Saperstein turned back to the table and looked at the board. "Is that your move?"

He nodded.

She also nodded, and moved her rook. "Now we're done." She turned back to Dana. "Come on, I just have to sign a few things." She picked up some folders and documents, and headed towards a small office, Dana walking along next to her.

A firefighter came over with a small bowl of chili and a spoon, holding it out to Saperstein, who tasted it.

"What do you think?" he asked.

"I don't know." She looked at Dana. "Care to give us your input?"

Dana shrugged and tasted it. Not as hot as she would make it, but still good. "I think you maybe need some more cumin," she said. "And—cayenne, if you were so inclined."

Lieutenant Saperstein nodded. "My thoughts precisely." She handed him the bowl and spoon. "Otherwise, very delicious." She continued toward the office. "Insurance?" she asked.

Dana blinked. "Do I want some?"

Now Lieutenant Saperstein looked confused, too. "Do you have some?"

Dana nodded.

"Good," Lieutenant Saperstein said. "That's very prudent." She snapped her fingers to get the attention of a guy up on top of one of the trucks. "Make sure you check the suction strainers, okay, Jimmy?"

"You got it, Lieu," he said.

So she ran a tight ship, and a reasonably happy one. But she really *did* seem small.

"Am I not what you expected?" Lieutenant Saperstein asked, with just the slightest edge in her voice.

Dana quickly shook her head. The fact that she hadn't seen female firefighters in New York didn't mean that there weren't plenty of them.

"I got in the year they lowered the standards," Lieutenant Saperstein said, the edge somewhat sharper.

Dana held her hands up. "I didn't ask."

"No, you didn't," Lieutenant Saperstein agreed, glancing at—and then signing—a report someone handed her. "I guess I just like to answer before people do."

Dana nodded, feeling a little cowed. Which was stupid, since this woman wasn't that much older than she was. "Are you really five two?" she asked.

Lieutenant Saperstein looked offended. "I'm five *six."*

Well—maybe. If she were standing, say, on top of a very thick dictionary. Dana started to follow her into the office—it looked like a dispatch center or something—but Lieutenant Saperstein frowned at her.

"We prefer not to have civilians in here," she said.

Oh. Dana stopped, and waited while Lieutenant Saperstein conferred with the firefighter behind the desk, glanced through a small stack of papers, and made some notations. Then, she came out and folded her arms.

"So?" she asked, receptively. "How can I help you?"

Dana hesitated. Since she had only walked in on a whim, she hadn't really taken the time to frame her thoughts first. It would also be nice not to be holding a handgun in a small flimsy bag that might up and rip at any moment.

"Not reporting a fire, I hope," Lieutenant Saperstein said, sounding amused, but looking alert.

Dana shook her head. "I just have a few questions."

"Okay," Lieutenant Saperstein said, shrugging. "Fine."

Maybe she should lead up to it, instead of jumping right in. "Well, I—" Dana paused. "I thought this would be the most logical place to get information, and—" Maybe she should have just jumped in. "Well—"

"Hey! I still don't have your exposure report," Lieutenant Saperstein said—barked, sort of—as a guy coming either on or off duty walked by. "I *want* it."

The guy didn't look enthusiastic, but he nodded.

"Anyway," Lieutenant Saperstein said, and refocused her attention. "You were saying?"

Stammering, actually. "Well," Dana started, "I—"

Lieutenant Saperstein grinned at her. "School report?"

"I'm not as young as I look," Dana said defensively. Although still young enough to be offended.

Lieutenant Saperstein shrugged again. "Neither am I."

Okay. "I guess I just—" Dana stopped, trying to plan a more articulate approach. "About the Harrison Hotel."

Lieutenant Saperstein looked over, her smile disappearing. Swiftly. "What about it?"

The walls had not come tumbling down; they'd *slammed* down. "Well, your, um, unit must have been there," Dana said, "and—"

"What *about* it?" Lieutenant Saperstein asked again, stiffly.

"I just have a couple of questions," Dana said.

Lieutenant Saperstein opened the top folder in her stack and examined it, her face expressionless. "It's all in the public record."

No doubt. Dana nodded tentatively. "I just wanted to get your impressions of—"

Lieutenant Saperstein interrupted her. "Are you asking in some sort of official capacity?"

Dana hesitated, but then shook her head.

Lieutenant Saperstein's nod was brief. "Well, then, you should go through Community Relations, or the PIO, or maybe the Mayor's Office."

Not that the Fire Department had anything to hide. Maybe there *was* a conspiracy going on. "Or, perhaps, visit my local library?" Dana asked.

"Yeah," Lieutenant Saperstein said, without a hint of a smile. "Why don't you try that."

Fine. Dana pushed away from the wall. "I'm very sorry to have bothered you. I just wanted to talk to someone who was there."

"Well, ask someone else," Lieutenant Saperstein said. "I don't have enough time to waste it on some damn reporter looking for news where there isn't any." She shook her head. "You people make me sick."

Did media phobia explain the hostility, or was there more to it? "I'm not a reporter," Dana said.

Lieutenant Saperstein just looked at her. "Oh, really? Then, what's your interest? You want to sue us because you got some water sprayed on your nice new hairdo or something?"

It would be banal to remark that where there was smoke, there was fire. Dana shrugged. "I'm a concerned citizen."

"Oh, please." Lieutenant Saperstein went back to her papers. "I grew *up* in this town."

And, comparatively speaking, she had just fallen off the lobster boat. Dana sighed. Waiting to talk to Ray would have been a much better idea. "Again, I'm sorry to have bothered you. Excuse me."

"That concerned citizen business is pretty lame," Lieutenant Saperstein said after her. "I *know* I've seen you on television. What are you doing, trying to dig up a story so you can get more on-camera time?"

What was funny, was that Lieutenant Saperstein could, very easily, have seen her on television. Often. "A Today cereal, for Today's Active Woman," Dana said, recreating one of her commercial tag lines.

Lieutenant Saperstein looked at her suspiciously.

Okay. She'd have to try another. "I'll never trust my fine washables to that *other* brand again."

Lieutenant Saperstein frowned.

Okay. Royal Coffee never failed. "It'll make anyone," Dana said, and winked, "feel like a king."

Lieutenant Saperstein laughed. "Oh, no. Is that you?"

In the very embarrassed flesh. Dana nodded.

"I'll be damned," Lieutenant Saperstein said, and then went back to frowning. "You're really not a reporter?"

Dana shook her head.

Lieutenant Saperstein looked at her for another long minute, then nodded. "Okay," she said. "Let's start over."

Good. "So," Dana said, and looked at her thoughtfully. "*How* tall are you?"

Lieutenant Saperstein grinned. "Let's start a little further along than that."

Okay. Back to the fire. "I wasn't even remotely insinuating that you all did anything wrong," Dana said, "I just—someone I know was personally affected, and—" She should get to the point. "Was it arson?"

"Once the investigation has been completed, I'm sure that the full results will be provided to the public at large," Lieutenant Saperstein said. Rather flatly.

What a successful conversation so far. "You know, if you ever leave the fire department," Dana said, "you have a fine political career ahead of you."

Lieutenant Saperstein didn't smile. "And my current guess is that you're a personal injury lawyer who's fairly quick on her feet."

Only fairly? "You want a classical monologue, or should I have prepared something more modern?" Dana asked, and looked around at the bustle of activity on the apparatus floor. "The thing is, I'm going to need *absolute quiet* for a few minutes, so I can explore my sense memories and get into character."

Now, Lieutenant Saperstein smiled. "Okay, you're just plain quick on your feet."

Better. Dana nodded pleasantly and slouched against the wall, on the offchance that the Lieutenant might become—garrulous.

"It was a bad night, and it was a bad fire," Lieutenant Saperstein said, "okay? And regardless of the final cause determination, the city should have shut down the damn place years ago. You could inspect it one day, and the next day, the fire doors would be propped open again, smoke detectors smashed, you name it. In the summer, we might get called up there eight, ten times a day. Mostly false alarms, but—" She stopped, her expression unreadable. "Well. It was a bad night."

Continuing to tread carefully would be a good idea. "What's your best guess about what happened?" Dana asked.

"I don't *care* how it happened," Lieutenant Saperstein said. "What I care about, is that people died, including a close friend, probably because someone somewhere was trying to save a few bucks on life safety and maintenance. *That* is the only thing I care about."

Leaving them pretty much on the same page. "I care about the someone somewhere, too," Dana said. "I don't think they should be able to get away with it."

Lieutenant Saperstein narrowed her eyes. "Where are you from, anyway?"

Surely truth, justice, and the American Way weren't exclusively New England notions. "Massachusetts," Dana said.

Lieutenant Saperstein nodded. "And what, your family was part of the gang throwing tea in the harbor?"

Her family only *wished.* "We were still busy planting potatoes in inhospitable Irish soil," Dana said. And, family legend had it, stealing horses and getting thrown out of pubs a lot.

Lieutenant Saperstein nodded again, possibly appeased. "Okay. So were we?"

Hmmm. "Saperstein?" Dana asked, in spite of herself.

Lieutenant Saperstein frowned at her. "Are you familiar with the institution of marriage?"

No, unfortunately. "In theory," Dana said, maybe more grimly than she'd intended.

Lieutenant Saperstein laughed. "Okay, then."

Forget the upper hand, she wasn't even getting an *equal* hand here. "About the fire," Dana said. "Do you think—"

The alarm sounded, loud and distinct amid the constant drone of dispatchers putting out first responder calls over the radios in the little house-watch office.

"Okay!" someone yelled. "Everybody goes!"

Lieutenant Saperstein moved even more quickly than Dana might have predicted, grabbing her bunker gear, helmet, and a computer printout with location information in about half a second, while the other firefighters snapped to action with the same swift grace, leaping into boots and turnout coats and running for the trucks.

"Stay clear until we've gone!" Lieutenant Saperstein ordered.

Dana nodded, backing up instinctively.

"And *next* time, do your damn homework, first," Lieutenant Saperstein said, before jumping into the cab of the engine, both fire trucks screeching away from the station in a matter of seconds.

Off to God only knew what.

Once they were gone, Dana gave the couple of guys still standing around a self-conscious nod and went outside.

Had she accomplished absolutely nothing—or did it just seem that way?

Going home and taking Bert for a walk seemed like a very nice idea.

It was getting colder and she zipped up her ski jacket—briefly missing her beloved army jacket—and looked down at her crumpled brown paper bag, tempted just to drop the stupid gun in front of the police station and run away.

"Hey, it's my favorite actress!" a cheerful voice said. "What are you doing here?"

Ray, just getting out of a squad car, with his usual smile. "I came to see my favorite cop," she said. "Are you in a hurry?"

He shook his head. "Not after I go in and take care of a couple things. Can you hang a minute?"

Dana nodded. "Absolutely."

"Here." He dug into his pocket, coming out with some keys. "Wait in my car, so you won't get cold."

He drove an old blue Datsun, and when she found it parked in the lot behind the precinct house, she let herself inside, holding the paper bag on her lap.

Ray came out about fifteen minutes later, wearing civilian clothes and carrying a gym bag. He was about her age—maybe a couple of years younger—and despite his job, almost perpetually in a good mood.

"I'm supposed to meet some of the C-POP guys over at the Dive for a beer," he said, as she got out of the car to meet him. "Want to come?"

It had been a frustrating day. *Too* frustrating. "Next time, maybe," Dana said.

"Well—you'd *better,"* he said, and unlocked the car trunk, dumping the gym bag inside. "What's up?"

Dana hesitated. "It's kind of a long story."

He shrugged. "Most of the best ones are," he said, and sat down on the car hood to listen.

Although she told it in as cogent and compelling a way as possible, he seemed less than convinced—and *not* happy about the gun.

He checked to make sure that it wasn't loaded, then frowned. "Piece of junk," he said, and looked up. "Think there's any chance the kid used it?"

Slim to remote. Dana shook her head.

He moved his jaw. "With our buy-back program, we're not supposed to run the serial number or anything."

Making it damn near impossible to find out if it was used in the commission of a felony. Actually, turning a weapon in was probably a good way to cover something like that up.

Not that, somewhere deep inside, she had a criminal mind fighting to get out.

Ray sighed. "You want, I don't know, one of our coupons for sneakers or something?"

An enticement that had always seemed sort of simplistic to her—but if it worked, she was in favor of it. "I'll pass," Dana said. Although she *did* love sneakers.

"Thought you might." He dropped the gun into the bag. "I'll get back to you on this, but there really aren't even any rumors going around. It was just—a fire."

A bad fire. A bad night. "Thanks for checking, though," Dana said. "I owe you a couple of beers."

He grinned at her. "And I *will* collect."

She *would* deliver.

Four

When she got home, she called her friend Peggy at work, and was told by an unfamiliar and nervous-sounding secretary—being something of a martinet, Peggy went through them like there was no tomorrow—that she was still in an editorial meeting, but would, the secretary said uncertainly, be sure to return her call.

Dana decided against holding her breath.

Nevertheless, her phone rang at six-fifteen.

"What do you want?" Peggy asked. Well, no—demanded. "You know I hate getting personal calls at work."

"I wanted to know if you have Prince Albert in the can," Dana said, and although she was amused by herself, she heard nothing but silence on the other end of the line. "Okay. I wanted to know if you were free tonight."

"That's a stupid question," Peggy said. "I'm free *every* night now."

Since she was in the throes of a recent, unexpected—and ugly—breakup. As a result, Dana had decided to rise above any testy remarks for the next few weeks. "Okay," she said, making sure she sounded astoundingly affable. "I thought I'd stop by around eight."

"I'd prefer that you didn't," Peggy said. "I'll be right in the middle of wallowing in despair."

Well, biting humor was definitely better than snappishness.

"I'll wear all black," Dana said, "if that would make you more comfortable."

"Try sackcloth," Peggy said, and hung up. Abruptly.

She ended up wearing an oversized black turtleneck, black stretch pants, and the black hightops she used when she was waitressing. She also decided to arrive bearing a gift, which was, in this case, a newly refinished coffee table that had been in terrible shape when the tenants moving out of 2B had left it behind a couple of months earlier.

Peggy answered the door holding a thick manuscript in one hand and a pair of dark brown reading glasses in the other. She had on a faded Smith T-shirt, sweatpants with the drawstring missing, thick ragg wool socks, and—a telling detail—no earrings. Her hair was, as always, up, but in this case, sloppily so, with large blond hunks escaping everywhere.

She frowned when she saw Dana's outfit. "Is that supposed to be funny?"

Yes.

"Can we make it another night?" Peggy asked. "I'd rather be alone, so I can feel free to be ill-tempered and embittered."

Since, normally, she was just ill-tempered. Dana shrugged. "You can be that way in front of me. Just don't get too personal."

"Well, don't say I didn't warn you," Peggy said.

Dana nodded, lugging the table inside. Peggy had an absolutely smashing apartment—penthouse, Central Park West, the whole nine yards—but right now, it looked a lot more sparse and bereft than it had a week earlier.

"Really cleared the place out, didn't he," she said.

Peggy nodded tightly. "Made a *big* production number out of it, too."

Sam had been nothing if not prone to overdramatization. "You knew he would," Dana said.

"Rented a van, brought stupid Vincent along—" Peggy shook her head. "I told him to do it while I was at work, but—he had to go through this whole nightmare scene." She scowled and sat down on the couch. "No doubt it'll show up in his next goddamn novel."

No doubt.

"I know we now heartily disapprove of Woody Allen," Peggy said, "but he was right about one thing. Before you let someone move in, make sure you get your name inside all of your books."

Dana nodded. Peggy was extremely generous—sometimes too much so—when it came to things like money and presents, but God help the person who borrowed even *one* book and didn't return it. Sam, in his emotionally immature way, would have made sure to exploit that.

"And don't ask me why I didn't stop him," Peggy said. "I just wanted him *out* of here."

Dana nodded.

"And *don't* tell me I told you so," Peggy said, preemptively. "I know you never liked him."

No. She had never liked him. But, to be polite, Dana just shrugged, and then looked around at the gaps in the bookcases, and the places where pieces of furniture—including the very mod, and expensive, stained-glass coffee table—had once sat. Apparently, Sam had decided that anything they had picked out together was now his.

"I thought I had—more stuff," Peggy said, her voice rather small. "Only, I was sitting here last night, looking around, and—" She stopped, pulling in a deep, controlled breath. "Well, anyway."

The atmosphere badly needed lightening. "I'll tell you what," Dana said. "I was having a little rest today—because, as you know, I tire very easily—"

Peggy smiled a little.

"And I was thinking," Dana went on, "that your couch would look a whole lot better over *there,* by the window."

Peggy frowned down at the couch, then over at the window.

"I was thinking we should redecorate," Dana said.

Peggy shook her head. "I don't want to."

Dana pretended not to hear that, trying to move the couch even though Peggy was still on it. "I'll have to have some coffee, or a snack. For my flagging energy."

Peggy smiled again. Slightly.

"Well now, you're not much as a host, are you," Dana said.

Peggy got up and moved to an antique rocking chair, putting her glasses back on and resuming work on her manuscript. "Generally, one is a host as a result of having extended an *invitation,* first."

"Yeah?" Dana struggled with the couch. "Go make some coffee already."

"I don't want to," Peggy said.

Embittered, ill-tempered—and also, surly. Dana lifted one end of the couch up onto the Oriental rug so it would be easier to push. "Then, help me with this."

"I don't want to," Peggy said, reading away.

Not unexpected. Dana shoved the couch the rest of the way across the room, and then put the new coffee table in front of it.

"I thought that was the table you were refinishing for your parents," Peggy said, without looking up.

Dana shook her head. "Oh, I'm sure you're mistaken. Must be some other friend, and some other table."

Peggy grinned, and kept reading.

Dana moved the table down a few inches, adjusted the angle, then stepped back to study the arrangement. "Looks *good.*"

Peggy glanced over. "I don't like it."

Grouch, grouch, grouch. "Come on, onward and upward." Dana crossed over to one of Peggy's many heavy, mahogany heirlooms. "Let's move this thing next."

"Credenza," Peggy said.

Dana put her hands on her hips, somewhat insulted. "I know it's a credenza."

"Leave it where it is," Peggy said, and turned a page.

A grouch of unparalleled dimensions. Dana pushed against the side of the credenza, trying to remember to use her legs instead of her back. She stopped, barely able to budge it. "Want me to injure myself, doing this alone?"

Peggy turned another page. "If you were injured, you might go home."

"I might have to *live* here," Dana said. "As an invalid."

Peggy shrugged, writing a note on a yellow Post-it and sticking it in the right margin of the page she was working on. "I'd move."

Hell, she probably would. "Fine," Dana said, and put all of her weight into pushing, managing to move the credenza about a foot. "Play us something on the piano, then."

Peggy wrote on another Post-it. "I don't want to."

Okay, sometimes she *was* an acquired taste. "You're beginning to annoy me," Dana said.

Peggy lowered her glasses enough to look at her. "I seem to recall giving you fair warning."

Even so. Tired of pushing—in every sense—Dana paused to admire the huge room, the bank of windows, and the incredibly panoramic view of the park. "This is such a great apartment," she said. "I can't imagine having an apartment like this."

Peggy shrugged. "Yours is okay."

"Okay" was just about the size of it. "Yeah," Dana conceded, "but—all this space. Swell view. A kitchen with room for a table. Your own—"

"Hey, I used to have trust fund guilt," Peggy said, then paused. "I got over it."

Dana nodded. "I would have, too." She nodded again, for emphasis, and shoved the credenza.

"You're going to mar the floor," Peggy said.

"Well—I have no help," Dana said. Pointedly.

Peggy put the manuscript down, got up—and went straight to the baby grand piano. She held her hands above the keyboard for a few seconds, then began playing a particularly complex Scott Joplin piece.

"Then again, you *are* rich," Dana said. "You can have the floors redone."

"Why don't you just be careful," Peggy suggested.

Right.

Over the next hour and a half, Dana pushed and tugged, and

lifted and arranged, until the entire living room and dining area looked completely different. In the meantime, Peggy played the piano, running through an impressively exhaustive repertoire. Once she had finished moving everything, Dana collapsed on the couch to rest, and listen to the music.

Peggy finished "The Cascades" with a flourish, then stood up. "That *was* a nice way to spend a couple of hours."

"You certainly know your ragtime," Dana said, grimly.

Peggy nodded. "Mother was dismayed." She looked around the room, her face falling a bit.

"Fresh start," Dana said.

Peggy nodded, and straightened one of the paintings. A small, but original, Hassam. "It's never going to make *Town and Country.*"

Was that kind of like a thank you? Dana sat up. "Are you going to move it all back as soon as I leave?" She thought about that. "Never mind, don't tell me."

Peggy just grinned, picked up her glasses and manuscript, and sat down at the other end of the couch to read.

The only thing in the room she hadn't moved was the piano, and Dana studied it for a minute.

"*Touch* that piano, and die a slow and painful death," Peggy said instantly.

Dana looked away from the piano.

"Thank you," Peggy said, and read her manuscript.

Dana watched her for a minute, then got bored. "Want to hear a sordid tale of murder and arson?"

Peggy looked up, frowning at her from over her glasses. "Good Christ, no."

Right. "Want to make me some coffee?" Dana asked.

"No," Peggy said.

Right. Dana sat there, fluctuating between boredom, and irritation. "Want me to go home?"

Peggy looked over and grinned at her. *"Desperately,"* she said.

In the end, they ordered up Chinese food and Peggy made a number of remarks about the paucity of things to watch on television—despite appearing to enjoy all that the Fox network, "E!" Entertainment, and Comedy Central had to offer. Not being terribly picky about such things, Dana ate broccoli in garlic sauce and shredded Szechuan beef with hot chili sauce, and watched whatever channel was on at any given moment.

Late the next morning, she wasn't surprised to receive a large and exceedingly tasteful arrangement of exotic, out-of-season flowers, with a note in familiar tall handwriting that read: *"Thanks. Sorry if I was a jerk. (But I do it so well)—P."* Her cat Theodore, of course, ate two of the flowers at the first possible opportunity, and promptly vomited them back up. Dana considered yelling at him, but he was already asleep on the windowsill, so it hardly seemed worth the effort, and she just cleaned up the mess instead.

After which, she mopped the building's entryway with the sweetest-smelling, and most environmentally sound, disinfectant commercially available, and then got a squeegee and some glass cleanser to work on the front door, which was forever smeared with fingerprints, and had to be washed at least three times a week. But it was a mild, springy day, and it was nice to be outside.

"Hey!" a deep voice behind her said. "Hold it right there, miss!"

Did all cops enjoy playing cops and robbers, or was Ray the only one? "Hi," Dana said, and nodded at his thin little rookie partner, who was leaning up against the side of their double-parked patrol car, eating something or other from a Taco Bell bag. "Hi, Spider."

Spider—who had to have a real name, although she had never heard it—looked up, wiping his mouth with a handful of napkins. "Yup," he said, and went back to eating.

A very young man, of very few words.

"Want some lunch?" Ray asked cheerfully.

Dana nodded, dropping her squeegee into the bucket of cleaning solution, and sat down next to him on the front steps while he rooted around inside his own bag, handing her a wrapped taco and taking an overstuffed burrito for himself.

"Had my buddy in the PDU pull the file," he said conversationally. "On that drive-by your kid thinks is some big arson conspiracy."

Dana stopped in thc act of taking a bite of her taco. "And?"

Ray shrugged. "If the kid lived in Harrison and went through the fire and all, sounds like it's just wishful thinking on his part."

"You're sure?" Dana asked.

Ray shrugged again. "Seems pretty definite, yeah. It was just little jerks shooting another little jerk over stupid little vials."

So what else was new. Dana sighed, lowering her taco. "As dumb and random as that?"

Ray nodded, gulping down half of what looked like a truly terrible cup of coffee. "Talked to one of the guys who caught the case. Said it was the same goddamn thing as usual, nothing to make them think otherwise. I mean, *nothing."*

New York, New York, a wonderful town. Guns, and drugs, and more guns and drugs. Dana looked down at her taco with much less interest. "Do they know who did it?"

"You know how many of those we get a month?" Ray asked, squirting hot sauce onto his burrito between bites. "A *night?* If we cleared *half* of 'em, it'd be a miracle." He crushed the empty wrapper, and reached for his second burrito. "What's the kid think? That it's some white-man cover-up?"

In a nutshell. Dana nodded.

"Well, don't know what to tell you," Ray said. "Everything *our* guys got said crackhead, drive-by, took him out pointblank with a TEC-9."

TEC-9. "That's, um, some type of gun?" Dana asked, aware that she sounded pretty stupid. Or, at least, naive.

Ray nodded. "Ugly, macho drug dealer gun."

She was going to have to take his word for it. "So—the kind of gun a pro would use?"

"*I* wouldn't," Ray said. "Too much noise, too much spray. What it is, is the kind of gun some fake tough guy who can't aim for shit uses."

Which would seem to support the theory that it was little jerks shooting another little jerk. "What about the fire?" she asked.

Ray shrugged, drinking down the last of his coffee. "Damned

if I know. It was *suspicious,* but it might also have been bad luck, since it was so windy that night and all. I don't know, I guess they're going to try and go after the owner on code violations. Like I said, haven't even heard any *rumors* going around. But, obviously, the fire department gets extra-freaked when they lose some of their guys."

Travis wasn't going to be happy, but it was the answer she had been hoping to hear. Frankly, she didn't want a person who would burn down a building full of sleeping families to exist.

Ray finished his burrito, and tossed the crumpled wrapper into the empty bag. "I got this real good buddy down at the DA's office, and he checked it out, too. Said there just wasn't much there. So—I guess maybe you want to consider the source."

A kid with an overactive imagination. Dana nodded. "Well, thank you for checking it out. I owe you one."

Ray grinned at her. "Serve and protect, babe."

The radio in the patrol car crackled, and Ray was on his feet before Spider even responded to it.

"We're out of here, Ray," he called, getting behind the wheel.

Ray nodded, handing her the Taco Bell bag. "Better go be a big, bad cop."

"Be a big, bad, *careful* cop," Dana said.

"Absolutely," he said, then winked and pointed at the top left corner of the door. "Missed a spot."

So she had.

Five

She believed it, but now she had to convince Travis. She went up to the school, getting there right before dismissal, and was gratified to see that he was sitting in his social studies class, and even seemed to be halfway paying attention.

Once the bell rang, they all slouched out of the room, with their knapsacks, baseball caps, and bulky jackets. Enrique stopped short when he saw her.

"I don't have tutoring today," he said accusingly. "I *seen* you already this week."

Dana nodded. "I know. I'm just here to talk to someone."

Enrique looked relieved, and continued on his slouching way.

They all seemed even rowdier and noisier than usual in the stairwell—probably because it was Friday—and she selected an out-of-the-way section of wall to wait.

Travis, who was tormenting Jamal, one of the smaller boys, by holding his Walkman up just out of reach, finally noticed her, and lowered his arm, Jamal grabbing his Walkman back and swearing at him as he checked it for damage.

"I'll be up in the gym," Dana said quietly.

Travis glanced around to make sure no one else had heard, then nodded.

She waited up there for about ten minutes, sitting in a dented folding chair, until he finally showed up, a basketball under one arm, looking quite at home in her army jacket.

"What took you so long?" she asked.

He shrugged. "Had to tell them I forgot something. So, you know, no one'd see me hanging with you."

Which didn't sound like a compliment. "Where are your books?" she asked. "Do you have homework over the weekend?"

He shrugged, but then let his gym bag fall, and she heard the distinctive thud of hidden-away books as it hit the floor. Good.

"They didn't come up with anything," she said. "My friend really checked around, too."

Travis frowned, and gave the basketball a hard bounce. "So, that's it?"

Pretty much. "Well, maybe if you went over to the precinct house in person," Dana said, "and—"

Travis shook his head. "No way."

"Then, yeah, that's pretty much it," Dana said.

"Okay," Travis said, and took a shot, the ball smashing off the backboard. "You can just make like I never talked to you. Doesn't matter, anyway."

Dana picked up the ball, shot, and missed. "Don't you feel better knowing that it was an accident? I mean, that doesn't make it any less tragic, but at least no one *meant* for it to happen. And maybe they'll prosecute whoever the owner was for letting things get run-down."

Travis didn't answer, dribbling to his left, and then pulling up to shoot.

"*I'd* feel better," Dana said. Ineffectually.

Travis glanced over before shooting again. "You still here, lady?"

She boxed him out, grabbing the rebound and keeping the ball.

"Come on, lady," he said. "Give it back."

She ignored that, holding on tightly. "If something *did* happen, there's a big piece missing here. Like if the guy you knew didn't do anything, how did he know about it?"

Travis shrugged. "He turned 'em down."

Maybe. But, some local junkie being involved in a major arson conspiracy still didn't play too well.

"*Knew* nobody'd believe me," Travis said.

She frowned. "Just think about it, Travis. Why would anyone want to burn down a building full of families and old people? Crimes are supposed to have motives."

"*Gen*trify," Travis said, snatched the ball away, and shot. Missed.

Unbridled cynicism, or a remarkably clear-eyed view of reality? Hmmm. Like they always said, follow the money. "Who owns the building?" she asked.

He shrugged. "Like *I* know, lady."

There was food for thought here. Possibly even a multicourse meal. "I know they're tearing what's left of it down," she said, "but are they going to rebuild, or put something else up instead?"

"I look like a mind reader?" he asked.

She thought well with athletic implements in her hands, so she helped herself to the next rebound, and dribbled out towards the foul line.

He scowled at her, hands on his hips. "Bring it back already, lady. It's not yours."

She kept dribbling. "If you want it back, *take* it back."

He promptly came out to guard her.

"Just take it easy," she said, since he looked a little too aggressive for her tastes. "I have a bad knee."

He stole the ball, throwing a fast shot up, and she was very free with her elbows while trying to get the rebound.

"You just fouled me 'bout *eighty* times," he said grumpily.

And felt nothing resembling guilt about it. "If I play too tough for you, I can let up," she said.

He drove for the basket—right through her—and she hit the floor a lot harder than she would have liked.

"You all right?" Travis asked, after making the shot.

Only maybe. She nodded, getting up slowly.

He looked worried. "Don't go telling me to play tough, if you don't want me to."

A mistake she wouldn't make twice. And it might also be worth it to remember that she was practically old enough to be his mother.

Of course, he could try remembering that, too.

He still looked worried. "I wasn't thinking you'd get up *hurt.*"

Neither was she. "I know. I'm fine." She took the ball and shot, keeping most of her weight on her right leg. "You sure you don't have any idea what they're going to build there?"

Travis caught the ball as it fell through the net, and passed it back to her. "I told you—we're on a stupid list."

She dribbled. "Does that mean you get to move back in?"

He shook his head. "My mother says rich people, probably."

Probably. It had been a terrible building on what was otherwise a very upscale block, and various local community groups had been inclined to protest its presence. Vociferously.

Certainly sounded like a motive to *her.*

Maybe even a couple of motives. Liberal as the West Side might be.

"You know, it's not my mother's fault," Travis said, very defensive. "We're just *poor.*"

She nodded.

"And it's not like my dad ran off, either," he said. "He *died.*"

Okay, she had assumed, at minimum, a divorce. "I'm sorry, Travis," she said. "I didn't know that."

He nodded, not looking at her.

"You must miss him a lot," she said.

He nodded.

She was going to have to remind herself to stop making assumptions about people.

"So, uh," he changed the subject, "you going to find out who owns it, maybe? If, you know, that's why they did it?"

A pretty big if. "Yeah, sure, I'll look into it," she said. "Go to City Hall, or the library, or wherever." Check out the local NIMBY types, too.

"What do I do?" Travis asked. "Go to the library, too?"

Dana shook her head. "No." Wait a minute. "I mean, *yes,* go to the library, but only academically. You keep up your end of the bargain and go to school." She paused. "Speaking of which. How was it?"

He flicked up a little jump shot. "Okay. I mean, you know."

In this case, she didn't know. "Everyone happy to see you?" she asked. Stunned, more likely.

"I guess," Travis said, and shot. "Boy, though, that math teacher guy is *really* stupid."

Dana lunged for the rebound without success, feeling the inside of her knee do the muscular equivalent of yelping. "What do you mean?"

Travis faked left, swept past her, and scored. "Like, today? On the board?" He dribbled back out. "He had, like, the problem right—you know, all the steps—but he added *way* wrong. Like, I had to tell him. How to do it right and all."

She would have enjoyed being in the room for that.

"What?" Travis asked, seeing her expression. "He was *way* wrong. And it'd make us, you know, learn it wrong."

Dana nodded, swiping at the ball, and missing. "Good of you to call it to his attention."

"Way, *way* wrong," Travis said.

Maybe she had created a monster here. He would become Super-Student, and be twice as impossible to be around as he had been before. She wrestled the ball out of his arms, slammed a solid elbow into him when he tried to grab it back, and banked one in off the backboard.

"Hey!" Travis rubbed his chest where she'd hit him. "That's not fair! I'm not banging *you* around anymore."

Had someone passed a law that she had to play fair? She shrugged, and shot again.

"Yo, Travis, that your new girlfriend?" someone yelled from the door. Amory, one of the other guys at the school, standing with Jamal and Desmond, who were also laughing.

Travis looked mortified, and shoved his hands into his pockets, abruptly turning away from her.

Dana picked up the ball, which he had dropped, and dribbled it a little. "I'm showing him some tricks."

"Don't think so," Desmond said. "I seen you *play.*"

"What do you want?" Dana asked. "I'm coming off knee surgery."

Desmond laughed raucously. "So, like, *used* to be, you were good?"

"Yeah," Dana said. "Before your time."

The boys—with the exception of Travis, who was pretending not to know her—seemed to find this pretty funny, and pretty unlikely.

Her knee actually *had* been surgically repaired—reconstructed, in fact—and at the moment, it hurt like hell. So, perhaps it was time to make an adroit, if limping, exit. Besides, there were four of them now, so they could have a game if they wanted.

She looked at Travis. "I'll see you later."

"No way," he said, and grabbed the ball away from her.

It was definitely a sign that she was getting old if teenagers were now too cool to be seen with her.

Not a terribly encouraging sign.

She had, briefly, belonged to a neighborhood political coalition on the Upper West Side—until remembering that being in rooms where Robert's Rules of Order were stridently enforced made her nervous—and knew the vice president well enough to ask him to meet her at one of the many coffee bars on Broadway. This particular one had shiny metal fixtures, tall, uncomfortable wooden stools, Billie Holiday on the sound system, and lots of very skinny people trying to look tortured while ostentatiously scribbling in battered journals and sighing a lot.

When she got there, Sid Rosenbaum was already sitting at one of the marble tables, peering through thick, black-framed glasses at *The Village Voice,* wearing a stretched-out maroon crewneck, baggy corduroys, and low-top white Converse All-Stars. Hard to believe he was independently wealthy.

"Hi," she said. "Sorry I'm late."

He looked up, his hair even more sparse and grey—and unruly—than it had been the last time she saw him. "Coming back into the fold?"

No. "I'm a terrible activist," she said. "I get too embarrassed." Most notably when she was forced to hold hand-lettered signs and, God forbid, chant slogans in unison.

Sid shrugged. "You could work the phones. Or maybe help on the newsletter."

The truth was that she just wasn't a joiner. Or, she sometimes uneasily suspected, anything resembling a good team player. "Well—let me look at my schedule," she said, and gestured towards the front counter. "You want anything while I'm up?"

He shook his head. "Try the caramel coffee, it's great."

Which she did, ordering an extra-large and carrying the cup back to the table. Once she sat down, Sid closed his paper and set it to one side.

"This isn't about the coalition?" he asked, squinting at her.

Since she wasn't, as Lieutenant Saperstein had so very stiffly pointed out, asking in any official capacity, she was going to have to come up with some sort of truthful, if elliptical, cover story. Outright lying had never appealed to her much. "I'm involved in—an inquiry," Dana said, and tasted her coffee. "Hey, this *is* good." A hint of butterscotch, without actually being sweet. It also, as coffee always did, made her desperately want a cigarette.

Sid nodded. "Best on the West Side."

Since he lived right around the corner, there was probably some proximal prejudice there. Certainly, the Chinese restaurant *she* always recommended was the one that just happened to be the closest to her apartment building. Sometimes, boldly, she might venture to the Empire Szechuan three blocks farther—but not often.

A cigarette would be *great* right about now—even if she had to go outside to smoke it, since New York had enacted a bunch of stupid, restrictive laws—and the guy at the table next to them had an almost full pack sticking temptingly out of the top pocket of his faded jeans jacket.

"Poets," Sid said, misinterpreting her gaze. "The place is lousy with poets."

Dana nodded, and resolutely looked away from the cigarettes.

"What sort of inquiry?" Sid asked. "That sounds so official."

Good. "It's not, really," Dana said. "But there's a lot of talk going on about the Harrison fire, and since I know you're pretty plugged into things, I thought you might have heard something."

Sid shrugged agreeably. "Like what?"

Okay. She might as well be direct. "Could neighborhood people have set the fire?"

He looked confused. "You mean, drug dealers?"

Dana shook her head. "I mean some activist group worried about crime and property values and all."

Sid stared at her, his eyes very wide behind his smudged glasses. "Are you talking about the coalition?"

"Not *your* coalition," Dana said quickly. "I just thought you might have heard if some—fringe—types were involved. I mean, word would get out, right?"

"Oh, come on," he said. "Around here, people's idea of anarchy is hogging the mike at community board meetings."

True enough. In fact, she had a hard time picturing any of the activists she knew venturing into the Harrison Hotel accompanied by a large *group* on a bright sunny afternoon—forget sneaking in alone in the dark of night, to execute a nefarious arson plot.

"You know, crime has gone down," Sid said, thoughtfully. "Not that they have any numbers yet—" He stopped, looking liberally guilty. "Don't get me wrong, it's awful that it happened—but having that place shut down has made a big difference in the neighborhood."

Was this just conversation, or did he know something? He was such a gentle, benign-looking guy—but, on the other hand, everyone she knew was pretty damn fed up with crime, and the general deterioration of the West Side, and it was possible that—

"Did you walk by there?" he asked.

Okay, he'd lost her on that one. "What do you mean?" she asked. "To see the damage?"

Sid shrugged. "I mean, ever."

"Well, sure," Dana said, uncertainly. "All the time."

"Did you avoid it, if you could?" he asked. "Go a different way, walk on the other side of the street, that sort of thing?"

Well—" Dana hesitated. *Yes,* as a matter of fact. There had always been drug dealers around, and people throwing stuff out the windows, and—she was starting to make a pretty good argument for torching the place herself. “Actually, my friend Karen got mugged up there one time, when she was going to the post office,” she said. “Some kids with a knife.”

Sid nodded. “My *son* got robbed on that block last spring.”

Which probably could have happened on any block in Manhattan—but, still. Karen had lost over thirty dollars—and gained ten stitches. And, ever since, she was nervous about walking around at night and talked a lot about going back to Dayton.

“What’s going to happen to the property now?” she asked. “Are they just going to put the same thing right back up, or—?”

Sid shrugged. “No, it looks like it’ll be some kind of yuppie high-rise.” He grinned a little. “And we’ll end up shouting ourselves hoarse at a bunch of meetings, fighting over the air rights.”

No doubt. Dana grinned, too. “So, the city isn’t going to take it over?”

He shook his head. “I heard Mitchell Brandon.”

A developer who made regular acquisitions—and headlines. “Isn’t that sort of quick?” she asked. “It’s only been a few weeks.”

Sid shrugged again, finishing off his coffee. “The guy’s a shark. Always has been.”

Well, yeah. Brandon was the kind of public figure who, on any given day, was equally likely to be on the front page of the tabloids *and* on *Nightline.* Quick with a quote, looked good in a suit, and always seemed to be a step ahead of the rest of Wall Street. Since finance and real estate frankly bored the hell out of her, she’d never given him much thought, but—it might be time to start.

“I don’t know,” she said, aloud. “Shouldn’t they put up subsidized housing or something there?”

He frowned at her. “You don’t think we already have more than our share around here?”

Well, okay, the concept of “oversaturation” did come to mind. She nodded, conceding the point. Every so often, she would read an article that would actually show a map of all the social service agencies in the neighborhood, and it was always *twice* as many as any other part of town. The West Side’s punishment for being tolerant.

“It was terrible,” Sid said, “especially about the poor firefighters, but—well, I don't know about *you,* but if I woke up one morning, and all the SROs, and methadone clinics, and shelters and so forth were suddenly gone from here, and over in Queens or someplace, I have to say that it wouldn't ruin my day."

The entire community would probably unite in a massive, raucous celebration. "So," Dana said, leaning back in her chair, "what, we're all becoming Republicans?"

Sid shook his head. "Not at all. I've lived here my whole life, and this neighborhood has always *wanted* to help people, but—" He paused, and then shook his head. "I'll tell you what, Dana, I don't think I've been at a dinner party in the last five years where people didn't have this exact same conversation."

The same held true for just about every gathering—brunch, lunch, drinks, whatever—she had been in lately, too. She nodded, looking out at the street where she could see a particularly—these things being relative—deranged and filthy soul shouting something or other psychotic while attempting to cross Broadway through very heavy traffic.

"Why'd you join the coalition in the first place?" Sid asked. "To help, right? Try and turn things around?"

Dana nodded. That was exactly why. Part of the proverbial solution, rather than problem.

"And, like most of us, got discouraged," he said. "Decided to direct your energies elsewhere."

Yeah. And here she was, sitting across from a man who'd been battling urban blight for the past quarter century. A sixties remnant, like the ponchoed denizens of Harvard Square. "Why do you stick with it?" she asked. "Don't you get frustrated?"

He shrugged. "Sure. But I *live* here, and—I'm not ready to just go inside, flip the deadbolts, and leave it at that, know what I mean?"

A sentiment they shared. "Yeah," she said, and drank what was left of her coffee. "I do."

Six

She was going to go to the library the next day and read up on the fire, but, naturally, one of the building's washing machines overflowed and it took her almost as long to mop up the resulting three inches of soapy water as it did to wait for the repairman to show up from Long Island City or wherever it was that the company was located.

Once the machine was fixed, and she had tied up an exceedingly large stack of newspapers and magazines for recycling, she took Bert out for a walk. Normally, in the late afternoon, they would go over to Riverside Park, but she found herself wandering up West End Avenue towards the side street where the burned shell of the Harrison Hotel was. After all this time it was unlikely, but she would have sworn that she could still smell the sodden stench of smoke that had hung over the neighborhood for at least a week after the fire.

Only part of the charred building was still standing, and the rest of it was boarded up. The lower floors actually didn't look too bad, but apparently there had been so much structural and water damage that the place had had to be condemned. By now, probably, street people and crack addicts had found some way in and would be squatting there until the first swing of the wrecking ball.

When there were certain kinds of tragedies, random New Yorkers usually left the area nearby strewn with anonymous bouquets, and there were still quite a few, mostly badly wilted, on the steps below the heavily padlocked front doors. It seemed sad, and pointless—and she felt like maybe she should go around the corner to the nearest Korean grocer and pick up a bunch herself.

"Not much to look at, that dog," a very gravelly voice behind her said.

She turned and saw an elderly, heavyset African-American man sitting in a sagging lawn chair on the slushy sidewalk, sipping something inside a small brown paper bag. "But *such* a nice personality," she said.

The man laughed, and sipped. "He do anything useful, that dog?"

Dana promptly sat Bert down and got him to shake hands with her. Then she looked up, seeing that her audience was unimpressed. "He's a fine cook," she said, "also."

The man laughed, and sipped.

Well, maybe not *fine*—but, *decent.* She straightened up, gesturing towards the burnt-out shell. "Terrible thing," she said.

The man nodded, rocking back in his chair a little.

"Did you see it?" she asked.

The man nodded, and indicated the faded red brownstone behind him. "Lived here, going on thirty years now."

Dana nodded, too, taking Bert's left paw as he offered it again. "What do you think happened?"

The man shrugged, and sipped. "Burned down, I'd say."

Right. The wind was starting to pick up, blowing in from the river, and she shivered. "Aren't you cold?" she asked, since he was only wearing a windbreaker and an old blue watchcap.

The man shrugged. "Like to take some air in the evening."

Okay. She looked across the street. "Is it true? What I heard?"

"Well, missy, that'd depend on what you heard, now wouldn't it," the man said.

She grinned wryly. For some reason, crusty old men always liked to give her grief. Always had. "You're having a little fun with me, aren't you, sir."

The man grinned back, showing a set of very nice dentures. "Gus."

"You're having a little fun with me, aren't you, Gus," she said.

Gus nodded, jovially.

"By the way, it's Dana," she said.

He thought about that. "They call you Danny?"

God forbid. She shook her head. *"Never."*

He nodded, and sipped from his paper bag. "So what'd you hear, Dana?"

Should she tell the truth, or make a suggestion provocative enough to get a strong, unedited reaction out of him? In this situation, provocation seemed to be the better course of action. "That people who lived there set it," she said.

"Why would they go and do that?" he asked.

Good question. Maybe it *had* just been a tragic accident, and she was letting her better judgment be swayed by an understandably distraught kid. Dana frowned. "Could it have been drug dealers, maybe? Some kind of revenge thing?"

"All I know, missy," Gus said, "is my wife heard the sirens, and she said, 'get up, Gus,' and I said, 'go back to sleep, old girl,' and she said, 'get up, and I got up, and it looked like the whole block was going to go." He shook his head. "Those firemen are heroes, I'll tell you. The wind was coming up hard from the river, even worse'n it is now, and it made that fire *dance."* He shuddered. "Never saw anything like it, and I surely hope I never do again."

She nodded, staring up at the charred skeleton of the upper floors. Of people's lives.

"Little *babies,* they brung out," Gus said. "Poor little babies. It was like to 've made me sick."

Dana nodded. Bert was getting restless, sitting and standing and sitting again, and she reached down to pat him a few times.

"He wants to be walking, seems like," Gus said.

Yeah. "Did you see anyone around?" she asked, very casually. "Anyone out of the ordinary? Not just that night, I mean any time before, too."

He cocked his head to one side. "Curious little thing, hunh?"

She nodded, attempting to appear ingenuous.

He sipped from his bag. "Your mother never told you what up and happened to that cat?"

Actually, yes. "I wanted to know the cat's name," Dana said, "and what it looked like, and how old it was."

Gus laughed. "I bet you did now." He squinted inside his paper bag. "I *do* believe I need another Snapple," he said, and fumbled through the larger brown paper bag crumpled near his feet, coming up with a kiwi-flavored one.

And she and Bert both needed some dinner. "Well, I'll leave you to it, sir," she said. "It was nice meeting you."

He nodded, popping open the bottle.

She hadn't accomplished much, but what the hell, she liked talking to strangers.

"There was a white man," he said after her.

Dana stopped. "A what?"

"Mean to say, you never seen one, missy?" He pointed up the block at an intense-looking, bespectacled blond man striding along, gripping his briefcase. "There. That's a white man. Right there."

Okay, okay, okay. "I guess I meant *when* was there a white man," she said.

Gus swigged some Snapple. "Now I *told* the po-lice, being as that's my lawful duty, but they said it was probably the welfare." He shrugged. "So I decided I would just set, and mind my own business."

As she should no doubt be doing. "So why'd he get your attention?" Dana asked.

Gus shrugged. "Why are *you* so all-fired curious?"

In all honesty, she wasn't even comfortable with small, innocuous fibs, but—well. "I don't know," she said. "Maybe it's just our having this conversation."

Gus shrugged agreeably, although she had a feeling that he didn't quite buy that.

"What made him stick out?" she asked. "He can't have been the only white person who went in there."

"Groups," he said. "They go in groups. Even the po-lice, they didn't never go in alone. And when the welfare did come, or the Housing Authority, or what-have-you, you *know* they'd be nervous. Talking loud, and maybe having a look around."

She was appalled to have the phrase "whistling through a graveyard" jump into her mind. But it had, after all, been a really bad building. It would be foolish to pretend otherwise.

"But *this* fella," Gus said, "he went right in, calm as you please. Saw him maybe two, three times."

It would be good if she had a notebook, and could write this down, but that would probably have been too obvious, anyway. "What did he look like?" Dana asked. "I mean, maybe he was with the management company, or—"

"Groups," Gus said. "They always went in groups."

The man had probably been on legitimate business, but—Dana frowned, mentally running over any one of a number of plausible explanations. "Did he come during the day, or after hours?"

Gus rocked back, narrowing his eyes at her.

"I'm *inquisitive,*" Dana said. "I'm just—one of those people, you know?"

Gus drank down some of his kiwi Snapple. "Daytime," he said finally. "As I'm recalling it. And—here's the thing. Seemed like he was a workman, one time, had a suit and some kind of folders, maybe, the other times."

Okay, that *was* suspicious. If someone had hired a professional arsonist, he—or, hell, *she*—would need to check the place out. "You sure it was the same guy?" she asked.

Gus looked deeply offended.

"Dumb question," she said. "Sorry."

He looked very slightly mollified. "Suppose now you want to know what he looked like."

Yep. She grinned at him.

He shook his head. "Maybe you should go and *join* the po-lice, missy." He stood up with a grunt of effort, then neatly folded his lawn chair and picked up the brown paper bag, bottles clinking. "I'd best get in for supper now."

And she was supposed to meet Peggy later for a movie, so she should get moving, too. "Thank you for talking to me, sir," she said. "Sorry about all the questions."

"Don't you worry," he said, starting up his brownstone steps, using the railing like a cane. "It was right entertaining."

Well—she'd gotten worse reviews.

He paused halfway up. " 'Bout forty, I'd say, mustache—dark, those glasses look like they don't have frames. Short hair, still had most of it. Walked sure of himself, like maybe he was in the service a ways back. Not much you'd notice, outside of that."

"Tall? Short?" she asked. "Fat? Thin?"

He laughed, unlocking his front door. "You beat all, missy. You really do," he said, and went inside.

She watched him go, feeling more than a little embarrassed, but also kind of pleased with herself.

Maybe she'd spent too much time matching television crime dramas—but, so far, this investigating stuff was really starting to grow on her.

She was late—only five minutes—to meet Peggy, who had already bought tickets and was checking her watch between glances at some bound galleys.

"Sorry," Dana said, slipping into the ticket holders' line next to her.

Peggy shrugged. "I give people seven minutes before I get mad."

Well—it was important to have standards.

Peggy put a slim silver bookmark in her bound galleys and then tucked the book under her arm. "Why are you limping?"

Dana automatically touched her knee. "Played basketball without my brace."

Peggy frowned at her. "That was intelligent."

Extremely. Dana reached into her pocket for some money. "What do I owe you?"

Peggy waved that aside. "Buy me a Diet Coke or something."

When one friend was obscenely, fabulously wealthy—and the other one wasn't—problems sometimes arose. Dana held the money out towards her.

"Oh, for God's sakes," Peggy said, and took it.

Sometimes, it seemed as though the bulk of their friendship was an epic battle of wills.

"I just think you should take better care of yourself," Peggy said, "okay? You only have one knee."

Dana looked down instantly. "Oh, hell—what happened to the other one?"

"Funny," Peggy said.

Well, she'd thought so. Dana pointed up at the marquee. "You think we're going to like it?"

"The *last* thing we saw was excessively mediocre," Peggy said.

That was true of most of the movies they saw. Dana nodded, and looked around at the rest of the people waiting. Standing on line was an inevitable part of living in New York, but that didn't mean that she had ever gotten used to it. So, to amuse herself, she decided to stand exactly the way Peggy was, right down to the incline of the head and the impatiently tapping foot.

"Don't," Peggy said. "I hate it when you do that."

"Occupational hazard," Dana said. Or, anyway, former occupation. To amuse herself further, she decided to stand like the firefighter instead. Arms folded, feet spread wide, aggressively self-contained.

"Who's that?" Peggy asked.

"I met this firefighter," Dana said.

Peggy nodded.

"When she gave orders, she dropped her voice," Dana demonstrated, "like this."

Peggy shrugged. "I do, too. Especially when there are a lot of men in the meeting." Then, she paused. "She?"

"Yeah," Dana said. "I don't know, I guess there are probably a bunch of them."

Peggy shrugged again. "I guess so. You didn't have a fire in your building or anything, did you?"

If she explained why she had been at the firehouse, Peggy would probably laugh at her. Make cracks about playing detective, and that sort of thing.

Valid cracks.

"I just kind of ran into her," Dana said—and must have sounded pretty uncertain, because Peggy looked at her sharply.

"What are you doing with yourself these days?" she asked, sounding a little too casual.

"Working," Dana said. "What do you think?"

"You can't be a super for the rest of your life," Peggy said mildly.

This could deteriorate into the kind of conversation she had had too many times with her parents over the last few months. Dana moved her jaw. "It's honest work."

Peggy just looked at her.

"I pay my bills, I don't have any debts, I can afford to go to a movie or a ball game now and again," Dana said. "So, what's the problem?"

"You're wasting a lot of education and God-given talent," Peggy said.

Well—education, at any rate. Dana shrugged. "My prerogative."

Peggy nodded, and they didn't look at each other. As the line started moving, they moved with it.

"I'm a little testy on this subject," Dana said finally.

Peggy nodded. "Hey, I'd bring you in tomorrow as a senior editor."

Which made her *a lot* testy. "I didn't ask," Dana said.

"No," Peggy agreed, "but you'd be great. All you'd have to do is work more regular hours, and—well—dress better."

The two main reasons she had spent her entire adult life avoiding nine-to-five jobs. Dana grinned at her. "I don't like rules." Authority. Convention. Structure.

Peggy nodded, her expression tight. "Don't want me for a boss, you mean."

That, too. Even though that was actually how they had met, when, while temping at a publishing house a few years before, Dana had been, briefly, assigned to a certain tyrannical, if gifted, young editor. "I don't want *anyone* to be my boss," she said.

"I know." Peggy shook her head. "But lately, you just seem—"

Lost, was the word she wanted. "Well, I really haven't been the same since that blender incident," Dana said sadly. Nothing like a non sequitur to lighten the atmosphere.

"It's been very courageous, though," Peggy said, without missing a beat, "the way you've come back from it."

They exchanged grins, Peggy gave her a little shove, and they moved up in line.

The movie was, in fact, terribly mediocre, and they decided that a halfway decent meal might be a good antidote. Chinese was usually their inevitable choice, but they decided to be bold and opt for Thai, instead. Dana, for one, was quite partial to satés.

"Do you cross the street?" she asked suddenly, while they were drinking their Singhas. "When you see a gang of hulking boys?"

"Christ, yes," Peggy said.

Hmmm. "Does it matter if they're black or white?" Dana asked.

Peggy shrugged. "It matters that they're *hulking.*"

Well, okay. That made sense.

"Besides," Peggy said. "It's gender, not race—you know that." She paused. "Although I would also cross the street if I saw a gang of hulking girls. I mean, can't be too careful, right?" She paused again. "Point being?"

"I don't know," Dana said. "I guess I've been thinking a lot lately."

The waiter appeared with their chicken saté appetizer, and she instantly helped herself. Peggy, who had a pretty healthy appetite of her own, was maybe half a second behind her.

"Is there such a thing as rich enough?" Dana asked.

Peggy's smile didn't get anywhere near her eyes. "Not according to my father."

Because that was the real problem. In the proverbial crime triumvirate, means and opportunity could probably be pretty easily established. *Motive,* on the other hand, was more complicated. Why would an incredibly successful multimillionaire, if not billionaire, want to be bothered with burning down a crummy SRO hotel in a neighborhood that was nice, but hardly blue-chip?

Now, Peggy frowned at her. "Going to be your usual forthright self?"

Dana looked up. "When am I not forthright?"

"Want a list?" Peggy said, and took another wooden skewer of chicken.

Well, for Christ's sake. "I'm always forthright," Dana said stiffly.

Peggy eased the wooden skewer out of the chicken—as opposed to Dana's strategy of simply eating around it. "I think you're confusing erudition with elucidation."

Dana thought about that. "Is English your first language?" she asked, after a pause.

Peggy grinned, and concentrated on her saté.

Nevertheless. "I consider myself *very* candid," Dana said.

Peggy lifted an eyebrow. "Hit a nerve, hunh?"

Not a chance. She was just a little—reserved. On the other hand, it might be a good idea to run the whole thing by someone who would give her an honest opinion. Find out if she was responding with rational moral outrage and civic concern—or was entirely, pathetically delusional.

"Promise you won't laugh?" she asked.

"No," Peggy said, "but tell me anyway."

Why not. Dana brought her up to date, managing to keep things pretty well in order, and when she finished, Peggy looked dubious, but not even the slightest bit amused.

"What does it have to do with you?" she asked.

"I don't know," Dana said defensively. "But there's no law against my poking around."

Peggy shrugged. "Actually, there probably *is*."

Probably. Their entrees had arrived and Dana spooned some rice, beef with hot basil sauce, and chicken masaman curry onto her plate. "No harm, no foul," she said.

Peggy frowned. "I despise sports metaphors."

Which was precisely why she had selected one. Dana winked at her.

"I'll tell you one thing," Peggy said. "No one's ever made a fortune without bending a few rules here and there."

It would be tactless, if tempting, to ask about the Woodruff millions. So Dana just glanced at her tentatively.

"Prohibition," Peggy said. "Land speculation, taking advantage of cheap labor—*I* don't know. It was all a long time ago."

And not really any of her business. "So," Dana looked around for the waiter to order another beer, "what do you know about Mitchell Brandon?"

"Not much," Peggy said, nodding when Dana indicated her glass and Dana held up two fingers instead of just one. "I think I've been introduced to him a couple of times at stupid benefits or whatever."

Peggy had always hated going to benefits; Sam, ever eager to be acknowledged publicly as a literary figure, had loved them. "What was he like?" Dana asked.

"Charming. Cocky. Ruthless." Peggy shrugged. "Pretty much what you'd expect."

"Thank you," Dana said, as the waiter arrived with their beers, and then she looked back at Peggy. "The kind of guy who'd do anything to get a piece of property he wanted?"

Peggy started to answer, then hesitated. "His wife's very active in fundraising for the homeless."

Oh, swell. "It'll be an incredibly ironic scene in the TV movie," Dana said.

Peggy winced. "Christ, don't even *think* like that."

"I could play the lead," Dana said cheerfully. "It'd be excellent."

"You'd better be kidding," Peggy said.

Yes. She was kidding. "Okay, but do you think he might have been involved?" Dana asked.

Peggy shook her head. "I can't exactly picture the man creeping around a tenement in the middle of the night lighting matches."

Neither could she. Dana sat back, folding her arms. "Can you picture him telling some underling, 'I don't want to hear about your problems, just get it done, I don't care how'?"

Now Peggy looked worried. "Very easily," she said.

Seven

Unfortunately, beyond newspaper accounts about the actual fire and its aftermath—most notably, the funerals for the two firefighters—the Mid-Manhattan branch of the New York Public Library was surprisingly lacking in information about arson in general. She knew so little about the subject that she had hoped she could find a few books and get a broad, if facile, grounding in the basics. Learn the jargon, at any rate. Besides, she'd spent her whole life rushing off to the library whenever she wanted to find things out, so why should her little sojourn as an uncertain investigator be any different?

There were, naturally, plenty of articles about Mitch Brandon—far too many to go through in one afternoon—but most of them were either puff pieces, or dull little stories about various real estate acquisitions. There were also a couple of biographies, including a blatantly self-serving "As Told To" book, but the truth was, that she didn't particularly want to know the guy's life story. At least, not in *depth.* Over the years, he'd been involved in a certain amount of litigation, but nothing, so far, that really leaped out at her. The general tenor of the feature articles—complete with pictures of the Great Man, out and about the city, with his lovely wife, Madeline—was that the guy was a son of a bitch, but people liked him, regardless. Admired his nerve.

The stories about the fire itself were somewhat more illuminating, if extremely depressing. Late at night, the temperature in the single digits, extremely high winds that had blown already dangerous flames completely out of control. Various technical problems, including a ladder truck that had crashed into a taxi on the way over, and a couple of frozen hydrants. Two firefighters killed, and one critically burned when one of the upper floors collapsed during a secondary search. Eighteen other firefighters treated at various city hospitals, three of whom were also admitted. Almost as many tenants carted off to emergency rooms with smoke inhalation, burns, frostbite, and/or various fractures and sprains. And, horribly, seven tenants—five children, a grandmother, and a male neighbor who had tried to rescue people before the fire department arrived—had been killed.

Nine people dead. Possibly—probably?—murdered.

A department spokesman described the fire as "suspicious," primarily due to the "heavy volume of flames, upon the arrival of the first-due engine," which, if she had her numbers right, was Lieutenant Saperstein's company. There had been several dramatic rescues. Other articles indicated that the investigation was continuing, although the area of origin seemed to be concentrated near a space heater that had been used to dry clothes, which would point to accidental causes. On the other hand, the sprinkler system hadn't been hooked up properly, smoke alarms had been missing or broken, and "numerous other code violations had been discovered." In article after article, the official word seemed to be "inconclusive."

She would have looked up the stories about the guy Travis knew who had been killed in the supposed drug-related drive-by—but things like that rarely made the papers anymore. Old news.

On that happy note, she went home.

Operating under the assumption that her life was still as normal as it had ever been, that night, she decided to remember to do the things that she always did. So she called her mother to chat aimlessly, had dinner with her friends Fred and Marsha—and their highly energetic toddler, then called her sister Elizabeth and tried to figure out a good time to go down to Baltimore to visit. Their sister Janet lived in Providence, because she was still going to RISD. She watched some *Nick at Nite* and *David Letterman,* and finished one of the new hardcovers on Peggy's spring list. With, of course, time in between to be amused, and enchanted, by just about every single thing her pets did.

All of which was very pleasant, and in no way related to crime, or violence, or other unsavory acts.

The next day, she had her regular tutoring up at Second Chance, and although she didn't see Travis when she got there, she figured he was just in one of the other rooms.

"You seen Travis Williams today?" she asked Shawn, as he was about to leave after their session.

Shawn shook his head. "He's skipping."

Oh, great. She slapped the reading workbook shut and headed downstairs to the main room where the teachers would be.

School was about to let out, and Gary, the pudgy math teacher, was erasing his portable blackboard while the students noisily gathered up their backpacks and jackets and Walkmans.

"Was Travis here today?" Dana asked him.

Gary made a face. "Not likely."

So much for their deal. Dana gritted her teeth. "I thought he was starting to do better."

Gary shrugged. "It never lasts. You'll get *old* putting too much energy into a kid like that."

Hmmm. Looked like she was going to get old. "Could he be sick?" she asked.

Gary just looked at her.

Well, damned if she wasn't going to track him down then. She saw Amory—Travis's closest friend, as far as she knew—over by the door and moved quickly to intercept him.

"You going to see Travis this afternoon?" she asked.

He shook her hand off his arm. "What's it to you?"

Translation—a churlish yes. Dana frowned at him. "Where?"

"I'm not telling you," he said.

Don't trust anyone over—around—whatever—thirty. Christ. "Where?" she asked, less patiently.

Amory glanced toward Gary and Laura, the social studies teacher, who were now organizing the glum little group that had to stay for detention. "You gonna get him in trouble?"

Yes. "Talk to me," she said. "I'm starting to feel short-tempered."

Amory let out a sullen breath. "Said we'd meet him in the park."

Good enough. She had figured out, early on, that no matter how rough and tough these kids looked, they tended to back down pretty fast. "Let's go," Dana said.

Two of the other guys, Desmond and Kyle, were waiting for Amory outside—and not thrilled about having her accompany them. Desmond was tall and pretty sure of himself, while Kyle was a twerpy little kid who fooled around a lot. To allow them to retain their dignity, Dana wandered along a few steps behind as they grumbled, and scuffed their sneakers, and slipped every so often on stray patches of ice. Winter was back, with a vengeance.

Travis was waiting for them on the stone wall above Riverside Park, bundled up in her army jacket. When he saw them—and her—he scowled at his friends.

Amory raised his hands defensively. "Sorry, man. She went and took an attitude."

Now, Travis scowled at her. "What do you want, lady?"

"A few minutes of your very precious time," Dana said, and popped the worn basketball out from underneath his arm. "Here." She passed it to Desmond. "He'll catch up with you later, guys."

"Hey, Trav, we'll stay, man," Kyle said, happily. "Pro*tect* you."

Desmond laughed, too. "This lady's scary. She up and threw the ball *hard.*"

A man jogging by glanced over, paused, kept running, and then came back. "Hey!" he said. "Leave her alone!"

They all, including Dana, looked at him with a certain amount of confusion.

"You need help, miss?" the man asked, managing to seem earnest, afraid, and self-righteous—simultaneously.

Travis and his friends looked at her now, unblinking.

"Yeah," Dana said. "Can you teach me a good pump fake?"

Travis and his friends were amused.

"Should I get a cop?" the man asked.

Travis and his friends were less amused. Deleteriously so.

"Everything's fine," Dana said. "Thank you."

"I can get a cop," the man insisted.

Yet another reminder of exactly how the road to hell was paved. "I'm *fine,"* Dana said. "Thank you."

The man didn't seem too sure, but he started running again, a little faster than seemed necessary.

Amory broke the very stilted silence. "You gotta thank him?"

Dana sighed. There was undoubtedly a severe headache in her immediate future. "I don't know," she said. "The more I know, the less I know—know what I mean?"

They all frowned.

"I-I just—" Kyle scrubbed away imaginary tears with his fist. "Why *can't* we all get along? You *know?"*

Dana laughed. She didn't know Kyle all that well, but she liked him. A real chipper kid.

"It ain't fair," Kyle said, gulping back mock sobs. "It ain't *right."*

Dana grinned. "Take a walk, guys. Your friend and I have some business."

They looked at Travis and then ambled away, Kyle still mumbling and sobbing and generally carrying on about what a hard, hard world it was, and why couldn't he just be *part* of it, like everyone *else?*

"I thought we had a deal," Dana said quietly.

Travis slouched back against the stone wall, his hands shoved in his pockets.

Christ. One step forward, five steps back. "What did you do all day?" Dana asked. "Hang out at some dumb arcade?"

"Not *all* day," Travis said.

And that was supposed to make it okay? Dana looked at him for a minute, then made up her mind. "Come on."

Travis stayed where he was. "What?"

"You're going to come with me, get your homework assignments, and apologize for blowing off school," she said.

"Yeah, *right,*" Travis said.

She had absolutely no power or authority over these kids, but they rarely caught on to that and called her bluff. "Let's go," she said, crossing the street without looking back. "I'll give you an update on the way."

He sighed, and looked terribly put-upon—but followed her. To maintain what little edge she had, she decided to let him be the one to initiate any further conversation. He kept up the silence for a block and a half, then sighed again.

"So," he said, "what you find out?"

Hearsay. Conjecture. Fanciful notions. "Did you notice anyone unfamiliar around the building?" she asked. "In the few weeks before the fire?"

He looked at her like she was an idiot. "You're kidding, right? There was like, you know, *traffic.*"

Under the category of general lawlessness, she presumed. Among other things, Harrison had been well known as a drug haven. "People in suits," she said. "That sort of thing."

He gave that some thought. "What, you mean, white people?"

Be nice if she didn't. "I mean, anyone out of the ordinary," Dana said.

He shrugged. "I don't know. Sometimes they'd come and inspect, or whatever. Like, you know, social services and stuff."

Okay. Now she was going to lead him, but she was going to lead him *wrong.* "But always alone," Dana said, "right?"

"Oh, yeah, right, lady," he said, and shook his head at her apparently infinite capacity for stupidity. *"Always."*

"So—" Dana pretended to mull that over—"not alone?"

"The damn *cops'd* come in with way a lot of backup," Travis said. "Forget, you know, whoever else."

Nicely corroborating Gus's input. "You ever see a white man alone in there?" Dana asked. "About forty, dark hair, mustache, confident, nicely dressed?"

Travis stopped to stare at her. "Whoa. You like, solved it already?"

Not even close. "Think about it, okay?" Dana said. "Let me know."

They were in front of Second Chance now, and Travis hung back, but she motioned him, forcefully, inside. Gary and Laura were still sitting at the front of the main room, overseeing the detention group and giving a little extra help, too.

"I'm gonna look stupid," Travis said sulkily. "In *front* of everyone."

It was nice that he went through life without ever complaining. "Just apologize," Dana said. "And don't make me spoonfeed it to you, either."

Travis nodded and went across the room, making it clear that he was dragging himself every inch of the way.

"What about your homework?" she asked when he came back.

He rolled his eyes, but went across the room again, returning with a folded sheet of notebook paper.

Well, at least it wasn't like pulling teeth.

He waved the sheet at her, then jammed it into his pocket. "We done now, lady?"

Almost. "I need five minutes," she said.

"Come on, lady," he said. "School's *over.*"

She ignored that and went out to the stairwell, sitting down on the top step. Making a point of not sitting next to her, Travis selected a step halfway down the flight, sprawling across it.

"Your friend who was killed in the drive-by," she started.

"He wasn't my friend," Travis said. "He was a guy I knew, that's all."

Whatever. "Why would they have approached him in the first place?" she asked. "Would he have seemed particularly reliable, or was he involved in enough other crimes, so he'd know what he was doing?"

Travis frowned. "I don't know. I mean, he was just a guy. Couldn't, you know, get a job or anything, so he was all the time hanging out."

"He was also a crackhead, though," Dana said, "right?" According to the police report, at any rate.

Travis shook his head. "He'd be drinking his brews, was all. I mean, you know, on account of, there wasn't much to do."

"What I'm asking," she said, "is if you were the landlord, or whomever, wanting to burn down the building, would he have been your first choice? I mean, what you want is someone who's going to do the job, not get caught, and *never* tell the police anything if he—" she frowned; statistical probability aside, she might as well be open to the possibilities— "or she—ended up getting arrested. Would that guy have been the most likely prospect?"

Travis shook his head.

Be nice if he could elaborate. "So," Dana said, trying not to grit her teeth, "there were other criminal types around who might also have been approached, successfully or otherwise?"

He nodded.

Maybe she should just go back and talk to Gus. He was obviously a man who kept his eyes open, and he would know who the major players were on the block. "Where did you go when you wanted to buy your stupid gun?" she asked.

Travis shrugged. "Just this junkie guy, on 107th. He has, you know, hiding places all over, if you want to buy stuff."

What a nice thought—and a reminder to avoid straying east of Broadway, whenever possible. Including, of course, Bloomingdale's—where she always got anxiety attacks. Dana moved her hand across her forehead, suddenly feeling very tired of this entire ugly mess. "Would *he* have been a likely prospect?"

"No way," Travis said. "Pipehead like that would never show up on time."

She kept expecting him to make some sort of jump from A to B here; he kept missing his cues. "I know there were a lot of drugs running through Harrison," she said, "and—"

Travis scowled at her. "Why? On account of how many black people lived there?"

Christ. "Because—as you and I both know—it was a terrible building," Dana said, *"okay?"*

Travis didn't answer, folding his arms across his chest.

Having to make her way, blindly, through all these verbal minefields was getting tedious. She took a deep breath, and tried again. "Was whatever criminality that was going on around there run by one lousy little gang of thugs, or were there competing factions?"

Travis shrugged, kicking one foot against the railing.

Was this intentional obtuseness? "Well," Dana said, "maybe one of them would talk to me and have something interesting to say about what happened that night."

Travis sat up much straighter, looking alarmed. "You can't go and talk to them!"

Having to deal with someone rude and uncooperative would hardly be a novelty. "Why not?" she asked.

"Because you can't," he said. "They're bad."

Laughing was probably the wrong reaction, but it was the one she had.

"No, see, lady, they're really *bad,*" Travis said. "Not TV bad, but *real* bad. Like—psycho, you know what I'm saying? I'm talking about guys'll eat a Big Mac with one hand, and nine you with the other."

Which was, she was pretty sure, slang for shooting her. Not an ideal scenario. Dana frowned. "So, you don't think there's someone out there who would talk to me for five minutes? It's not like I'm a cop, and could get them in trouble."

"No," Travis agreed. "All you can do is get *you* in trouble. And me, probably, too, for asking."

Okay. Not such a great idea, after all. "All right, no problem. I'll think of something else," Dana said, and pushed her ski jacket sleeve up high enough to check her watch. "Go find Amory and everyone, and I'll talk to you later."

He started to leave, then hesitated. "It's not like I'm scared or anything, I just—"

"I don't want to spend time with dangerous people, either," Dana said. "So, don't worry about it. I mean, ideally, we're going to turn on the news one of these nights and see that the arson squad has arrested a bunch of people, and that we can just forget about it, right?"

Travis nodded, but still hung back from the door.

"What?" Dana asked.

"You, uh," he lowered his voice, not that anyone appeared to be listening—or even nearby, "still going to look for more clues and all?"

With zest, and ineptitude. "Can't hurt," she said.

Eight

Since she was right in the neighborhood, she decided to stop by and plague the fire department again for a few minutes. If a certain lieutenant was on duty, it would be likely to be quite diverting—and she might even find out something or other that she didn't know.

When she got down to the stationhouse, though, she gave serious consideration to losing her nerve and just going home. Last time, she hadn't exactly been welcomed with open arms. On the other hand, extreme shyness and the investigatory process were almost certainly incompatible. So she took a deep breath and went inside, nearly falling over a firefighter who was using a small hose to clean some soot-covered tools, the water swirling into a metal drain in the floor. He glanced up at her with a combination of flirtatiousness and distrust.

"Lieutenant Saperstein around?" she asked.

He jerked his head to the left, and she walked around the side of the nearest shiny engine, seeing the Lieutenant standing with a balding man who redefined the word "strapping," both of them studying a bunch of gauges and dials and things on the truck with tremendous intensity, and jotting down notes.

"Oh, no," Lieutenant Saperstein said, lowering her pen when she saw her. "Not again."

"I came to play," Dana said, indicating a chessboard, which

was set up and ready to go over by the far wall.

There was a brief silence.

"Well, then," Lieutenant Saperstein said, looked at her watch, and sprang effortlessly over the battered sawhorse and toolbox that were blocking her path. "Let's do it."

Since she'd probably tear up her knee again if she jumped, too, Dana walked *around* the sawhorse to get to the small table.

Seeing what was happening, several firefighters in the midst of various maintenance chores gathered behind the table to watch. Dana was pretty rusty, and she'd never exactly been Kasparov, so it made her nervous to have an audience, but—what the hell. Lieutenant Saperstein indicated for her to take white, so she brought one of her bishop pawns out, slapping it down definitively.

"Look out," the balding firefighter said. "She's a flanker."

Lieutenant Saperstein examined her move for a second or two. "It's interesting. It's—aggressive. It's—*doomed.*" She grinned, and smacked her own bishop pawn against the board.

Well, okay. No KP to KP-4 here. She would just have to be cautious, and start developing her knights. "Did some homework," Dana said as she moved. "At my local library, no less."

Oddly, instead of countering, Lieutenant Saperstein brought out a knight's pawn. "Oh, really?"

Could she talk and play at the same time? Maybe. But if she had gum in her mouth right now, she would definitely have had to spit it out. Dana decided to go with her second knight. "Yeah. Only, the main branch had pretty much nothing about arson."

"John Jay," Lieutenant Saperstein said, and moved her bishop one space.

Only one? Hell, Dana would have gone two. Regretted it, maybe, but gone for it. She took her Queen's knight out further, just to see what would happen. "What do you mean?"

"John Jay *College,*" Lieutenant Saperstein said impatiently, moving a knight of her own. "You know, where those of us who are blue-collar go?"

John Jay was a criminal justice school in the City University system, and an NYPD stomping ground, but, okay, it must do fire science, too. However—somehow—Lieutenant Saperstein did not strike her as epitomizing the average blue-collar worker. Dana held her hand over her king pawn, then wavered, careful not to touch it and commit herself. Her opponent was likely to be a stickler about such matters. "You were the first-due engine company?"

Lieutenant Saperstein frowned at her. "I thought you came to play."

Right. Dana shut up and moved her pawn.

A firefighter came over with a cellular phone. "Mickey, for you, Lieu."

Lieutenant Saperstein smiled and took it. "Hey, pal," she said into the receiver. "Everything okay?" She listened briefly. "*Right* now? I'm moving my knight. What about you?" She listened again, and smiled again. "Well, that sounds good. Give her some fresh water, too."

Dana caught herself eavesdropping, and concentrated on the board, instead. She liked to get her queen out early—walk on the wild side—but maybe that would be a little *too* devil-may-care. So she went with a bishop, trying to remember all the stuff she had once known about controlling files and diagonals and such.

"No, wear the Goosebumps ones. They're in your second drawer, on the top," Lieutenant Saperstein was saying, making a swift move apparently without even checking the board first. "Okay. Just this once. Tell your father I said it was fine, just make sure you—Mickey?" She smiled and shook her head, lowering the phone to her shoulder.

"Your son?" Dana asked.

Lieutenant Saperstein nodded, and then put the telephone back to her ear. "Hi," she said—to her husband, presumably. "Sure. He'll fall asleep in the middle of it, anyway." She looked at her watch. "I hope so. It's been pretty quiet."

Dana surveyed the board, trying to figure out what the hell her opponent had in mind, since she was probably one of those people who could effortlessly see about ten moves ahead. Dana's limit was more like three or four. At best.

"Castle, for Christ's sake," a broad-shouldered firefighter with red hair said. *"Castle."*

Nor was she capable, in any way, of responding to gruff orders. Dana eased out a knight's pawn.

The red-haired firefighter shook his head in disgust. "Ah, Christ, you've had it," he said, and walked away.

The balding firefighter nodded. "Stick a fork in her—she's done."

Which must be true, since most of the rest of their audience was also drifting away now. But, as nearly as she could tell, they were just crepe-hangers.

Unless she was missing something.

Hmmm.

Lieutenant Saperstein moved again without looking, in the middle of some long explanation on the phone about where a container of frozen stew was, and how long it should be defrosted in the microwave.

Well, hell. If she wasn't going to pay attention, Dana would just attack. She moved her queen's pawn to free up her other bishop—and threaten one of the black pawns, while she was at it.

"I told you—right by the broccoli, Jake, you can't miss it," Lieutenant Saperstein was saying, sounding a little exasperated as she placed one of her knights next to Dana's king, catching her queen and rook in a very clever fork, the knight protected by a bishop so that she couldn't take it without putting herself in check.

God damn it—she should have castled. And one of the guys had even used the word *"fork,"* to drop her a gentle hint. Well, damn it all, anyway. What a stupid game. Dana looked across the table at Lieutenant Saperstein, who winked at her without pausing in her telephone conversation.

Damn it, damn it, damn it. Dana gritted her teeth, moved her queen to safety, and watched her rook be swept off the board, unanswered, by a lowly knight.

"Yeah, I'll call if it's going to be any later," Lieutenant Saperstein said, and hung up. She grinned at Dana. "No one ever sees that one coming—I don't know why."

So she was a hotshot, so what? *She,* personally, was a bad sport. Dana stared at the board, trying to see every possible threat before doing any attacking of her own. Then, she decided on her bishop, so that, next time around, however much too late it was, she could castle with her remaining rook. "Has there been a fire cause determination yet?" she asked, her hand poised to move.

Lieutenant Saperstein shook her head. "Boy, we sure are lucky," she said to the lone beefy firefighter who was still watching the game. "Here we are, in the poor old fire department, with *no idea* where to turn, and—thank God!—a civilian shows up, out of nowhere, to *help us out.*"

The firefighter nodded, but also looked at Dana with some sympathy. "Later," he said and went over to join a couple of the others.

Instead of answering, Dana moved her bishop.

"I mean, we're just *so lucky,*" Lieutenant Saperstein went on, with a noticeable lack of good humor in her eyes. "Only yesterday, I was saying to my captain, 'Captain,' I was saying—"

"Are you always this sarcastic?" Dana asked.

Lieutenant Saperstein thought about that. "No," she said, and then the good humor came back—along with some well-defined laugh lines at the corners of her eyes. "You seem to bring it out in me."

Seemed to bring it out in pretty damn near everyone. "I'd think you'd welcome a little civilian interest," Dana said stiffly. "I'm not trying to invade your territory—I just want to know what happened. There's something bad going on and, either it's being covered up, or maybe—"

"Check," Lieutenant Saperstein said.

What? Dana looked down. Oh, hell. And she couldn't castle her way out of it, either. She could stave off the inevitable for another couple of moves, but—she might as well just resign. Quit. Go home.

Break down and call her damn agent, see if he could send her up for something.

"You aren't going to play it out?" Lieutenant Saperstein asked.

Dana shrugged, and zipped her jacket. "What's the point?"

"Well—" Lieutenant Saperstein looked a little nonplussed. "I mean—"

"It's a dead end," Dana said, and tipped her king over on its side. "Believe me, you've made that *abundantly* clear." She stood up. "Thank you for the game. You're an excellent player."

Lieutenant Saperstein stood up, too. "Look, I wasn't trying to— " She stopped. "Okay. I *was* trying to— " She stopped again. "Why don't you sit back down for a minute."

Dana stayed where she was. "Why? You want to arm-wrestle now?"

Lieutenant Saperstein sighed. "I've been busting your chops. I recognize that, okay?"

Busting her chops. "I also think you've been hanging around too many men for too long," Dana said.

Lieutenant Saperstein nodded, and looked around the apparatus floor. "You don't know the half of it."

No, probably not. Their worlds were pretty far apart.

"I don't even know your name," Lieutenant Saperstein said.

Good point. Dana put out her hand. "Dana Coakley."

"Well, *that* explains a lot," Lieutenant Saperstein said.

Was that pejorative? "What do you mean?" Dana asked.

Lieutenant Saperstein grinned. "I used to know some Coakleys."

"Yeah," Dana said, "so?"

"They were incredibly stubborn and argumentative," Lieutenant Saperstein said. "Stood out, even in *my* neighborhood."

Yep. "And proud *of* it," Dana said. "What's your family name?"

"McCormick," Lieutenant Saperstein said, and shook her hand very briefly. "Molly McCormick."

Well, now, as it happened, she had gone to high school with a Brenda McCormick.

"Okay," Lieutenant Saperstein said, obviously reading her mind. "What do you know about McCormicks?"

Dana grinned at her. "They have incredibly high opinions of themselves."

Lieutenant Saperstein laughed. "Look. I can promise you that there's no cover-up, but— " She studied her thoughtfully. "Do you like four-year-olds?"

Dana shrugged. "Sure. I mean—yeah. Very much."

"Okay." Lieutenant Saperstein took a business card out of her shirt pocket and quickly scrawled something across the back. "Because when I'm off-duty, I really don't do much of anything without Mickey." She handed the card across the table. "Give me a call, and maybe we can have a talk."

Dana looked at the card, which said, *"Fire Department—City of New York"* across the top, complete with the department logo, and then *"LT. Molly Saperstein,"* with a station and a fax number at the bottom. "Okay." She tucked it into her jacket. "Thank you."

Lieutenant Saperstein nodded. "I hope you like burritos."

The antecedent of *that* remark was easy to guess. "Does Mickey like burritos?" Dana asked.

"Loves them," Lieutenant Saperstein said.

Right.

"Hey, Lieu?" one of the firefighters called from the house-watch office.

"On my way," Lieutenant Saperstein said, and headed over. Then she stopped, and looked at the chess set. "You know, you do a good job of opening up the board, but then you don't seem to know what the hell to do with yourself."

Dana had to grin sheepishly. "Story of my life," she said.

Detecting was all well and good, but it was wreaking havoc on her social life. She did, after taking care of various building chores, go back to the midtown branch of the library the next day to read up a little more on Mitch Brandon and his various financial exploits. He had spent the early part of his career as something of a slumlord, *that* much was clear. He had assumed ownership of rent-controlled buildings and—induced—longtime tenants to leave, financially, for sure, and possibly by using other, less savory methods. He bought tax-delinquent buildings, and threw up overpriced high-rises. When the city sat down to the bargaining table with him, they generally lost.

He had just enough money and power to consider himself somewhat above the law on occasion, but—as many a power broker had been known to brag—he had never been indicted.

Yet.

The next afternoon, she went down to John Jay, over on 59th and Tenth Avenue, pleasantly requested a visitor's pass at the main desk, and devoted a couple of hours to discovering that arson was an extremely complex subject that would, no doubt, require years of study, experience, and on-site observation. She Xeroxed a few articles—mainly so she would be able to master some of the basic concepts and terminology, but decided that she was pretty much out of her depth, and ought to leave such matters to professionals. Who were also, it was worth remembering, getting *paid* to do this sort of thing.

When she got home, there was a message on her machine from her friend Valerie asking if she wanted to go down to Theatre Row to a reading of a new play one of their mutual friends had written. Valerie was something of a flake, who spent a lot of time doing aerobics and getting her hair dyed new, interesting, and improbable colors, but she was a hell of a good actress—and deceptively intellectual. She was also one of those rare women who could wander about blithely in bright red cowboy boots, and still retain her credibility. Dana had done three shows with her over the years, and enjoyed every minute they had ever spent on stage together. Valerie was an artistic loose cannon—but never dull.

The reading ended pretty early, and since they hadn't liked the play much, they decided to make their excuses and head back uptown, instead of going out to dinner with everyone and having to prevaricate. Since Dana had used Bert needing a walk as her reason for having to hustle away, Valerie was amenable to their stopping by her building and taking him out. Especially since they both liked the playwright and in no way wanted to hurt her feelings.

"I still don't understand it," Valerie said, as they got off the Broadway local. "A female playwright, and she only wrote *one* woman's part."

"And the walk-on," Dana pointed out.

"Oh, please," Valerie said, waving that aside. "No wonder none of us can ever get any work."

True enough.

"It's *cold,"* Valerie said, as they came out onto the street. This, despite her being bundled up in a heavy coat and two thick sweaters over her turtleneck. Of course, she only weighed about a pound and a half—which might account for it.

Dana shrugged. "Berets are impractical for retaining heat."

Valerie looked worried and put her hand to her head. "Really?"

No. Dana grinned at her.

As they turned the corner and walked toward her building, Valerie suddenly stopped short.

Dana also stopped, uncertainly. "What?"

"Maybe we should wait before we go down there," Valerie said. "That kid looks like trouble."

Dana followed her gaze and saw Travis, pacing back and forth with his hands jammed into his pockets, visibly agitated. She sighed. "Good call."

Valerie's arm instantly disappeared inside her voluminous black leather bag.

"It's okay," Dana said. "I know him."

Valerie looked relieved and withdrew her arm.

"Exactly what weapon do you *have* in there?" Dana asked.

Valerie shrugged. "Hair spray. Legal *and* lethal."

Well, okay. Although if those were the only criteria, she, personally, would select Easy-Off Oven Cleaner.

Travis saw them then, and came hurrying over. "Where you been, lady?"

It was just possibly none of his business. Dana moved her jaw. "Off enjoying one of the many magical adventures that makes up my life."

A witticism that seemed to make no impression on him whatsoever, although Valerie laughed.

"He'll *talk* to you," Travis said urgently.

Was she in the mood for this right now? No. The idea of making some dinner was much more enticing. "Who?" Dana asked.

"You *told* me to find the worst guy who was, you know, a criminal in our building and all," Travis said, "and I did. So, come *on* already."

Okay, presumably this guy was the person who'd run the drug trade—or whatever else was going on—at Harrison. Dana shrugged. "Okay. Maybe I can meet him tomorrow afternoon, or—" No, she had a dentist appointment. "Friday, maybe, or—"

"You have to do it now," Travis said. "The guy says he'll talk, you gotta give him his props."

When she'd first started at Second Chance, it had taken her a while to figure out that "props" meant proper respect. "That's fine, but, as you can see—" Dana indicated Valerie—"I have plans with my friend right now. Tell him I'll do it another time, okay?"

"No problem," Travis said grimly. "I'll just be like, you know, *dead*—but, hey, no problem."

So some creep drug dealer she had never met was telling her to jump, and she was supposed to ask how high? Christ, how tiresome was *this?*

"So, don't worry about it, lady," he said. "If, like, some bystanders get hit, maybe it'll be on the news and you'll know what happened to me."

The string section was certainly out in full force tonight. "What about my props?" Dana asked. "I mean, isn't that a factor?"

Travis muttered something under his breath, and one of the only words she could distinguish was "stupid."

"I'm sorry," Valerie said, smiling nervously, "but what are you talking about?"

A very good question. Dana sighed. "He wants me to go meet with this damn drug dealer. This is Travis, by the way. Travis, this is Valerie."

"Oh. Nice to meet you." Valerie looked very interested. "This is for that school, right? Are you going to scare someone straight?"

Not bloody likely.

"I'll come, too," Valerie said. "Help you confront him."

Travis looked horrified. "If there's two of you, he'll think you're cops."

Despite their looking considerably *more* like Actresses in Winter Garb, what with chicly oversized shirts, large dangly earrings, and basic black footgear that could also be used to wait on table. Dana, however, considered herself far too retiring ever to don a beret.

"This is weird," Valerie said to no one in particular. "This is like television."

Like *bad* television. Dana frowned at Travis. "I thought we agreed that neither of us wanted to be around dangerous people. Remember that?"

"But you were right," Travis said. "Mojo says there *was* a white guy, made him an offer."

Mojo? Jesus. On the other hand, when it came to witnesses, maybe she couldn't be choosy. She glanced at Valerie before looking back at Travis. "How long will it take?"

Travis made a face. "What, you think he wants to spend *time* with you, lady? No way." He leaned over to look at her watch. " 'Fact, he's probably gone by now."

Dana weighed a few mental options. "Where is he?"

"Over on Amsterdam," Travis said.

So she could probably go, and be back, in about half an hour. "Okay," Dana said. "But Valerie gets to come, too, if she wants. I'm not going to be rude to her."

They both looked at Valerie, who must have, to some degree, lost interest in the conversation, because she was busy doing a small pirouette on the sidewalk.

Valerie stopped, in mid-spin. "What?"

This was not a woman anyone would *ever* suspect as being a cop. "Want to come?" Dana asked. "It won't take long."

"Cool," Valerie said, and twirled the rest of the way around.

Except—she should be honest here. "It, um, it might—" she *hoped* not—"be dangerous."

Valerie grinned, and patted her bulky pocketbook. "Lead on," she said.

Nine

The meeting place, it developed, was a seedy, almost deserted fast-food chicken restaurant on Amsterdam. Dana had actually been walking by it for years, without ever once thinking to go inside.

After doing so, her original assessment remained unchanged.

Travis looked at her accusingly. "He's *gone."*

So, it was her fault the guy was capricious? Dana shrugged. "We'll do it another time then, I guess." And—she was in no hurry.

"I know where he hangs," Travis said. "I'll go tell him you're here now."

"Well, wait," Dana said, "maybe—"

He was already halfway out the door.

The restaurant was empty except for a bored girl behind the counter reading the Spanish language version of *Cosmopolitan,* two aproned men—possibly a father and son—lounging by the grill and deep fryer, and an older Latino man dozing at a grimy table by the window, thick beard stubble white on his face, with the remains of his dinner piled on a plastic tray.

"This is all very confusing," Valerie said, sounding as though she were determined to be a good sport, but was starting to lose heart.

Explaining the whole story would probably only make it more

so. "I've kind of been playing detective," Dana said.

"Cool," Valerie said, ever unflappable, and then took off her beret. "When this Mojo guy gets here, you want to improv a good-cop, bad-cop thing?"

Upon which, Travis would probably pass out on the spot. Dana shook her head. "Let's play it by ear. I'm still sort of learning how to do this."

Valerie shrugged, and sat down at one of the less sticky tables. "Okay. Cool."

She absolutely treasured Peggy's incisiveness and just generally awe-inspiring mental agility—but it was very relaxing to be around someone as agreeably nonchalant as Valerie.

Someone who wouldn't point out that what they were currently doing fell into the category of sheer insanity.

On the other hand, if she were in a foxhole, she would want no one in the entire world sitting next to her more than Peggy Woodruff. In, with luck, a very bad mood.

"When they come," Valerie said, "use some of the stuff you did in *Extremities.* You were really scary in that."

To the degree that she'd unnerved herself—and been very relieved that it was only a four-week run. "That one spooked me a little," Dana said quietly. "It felt like—psychosis—every night."

"Plus matinees," Valerie pointed out.

Right.

"Dana, it was only acting," Valerie said.

Yeah. At least, she *hoped* so. But, sometimes, in mid-performance, the lines would seem to blur a little. "You know, I stopped playing sports for the same reason," Dana said aloud. "After high school. I just—I wanted to *win* too much." Had, frankly, not liked the person who would emerge at such moments.

Valerie shook her head. "You'll never see me quitting because I'm too good."

"It doesn't have anything to do with being good," Dana said. "It's more about *wanting* to be good."

"Weird," Valerie said, and drank some Diet Coke. "I mean, I thought you quit because you were sick of auditions, and head shots, and all the other garbage."

That, too. "I just—" Dana hesitated. "Maybe I made a mistake, maybe—"

"If you're asking me, *yes,*" Valerie said, "but you have to figure out what *you* want."

"I want a baby," Dana said without thinking.

Valerie laughed. "Sounds cool to me."

The glass door of the restaurant opened and Travis came in. Alone.

"So, where is he?" Dana asked.

"Has to make *you* wait some, now," Travis said.

Swell.

They sat there, under too bright overhead lights, for about fifteen minutes, Travis jittery, Valerie rather wide-eyed, and Dana increasingly annoyed and impatient. Valerie got up at one point and bought a large order of french fries and chicken, which then sat on the table, uneaten.

Finally, Dana stood up. "Forget it—I have a lot more interesting things to do than sit around here all night."

Upon which, of course, the door banged open and three black guys—no, *kids,* actually—came swaggering in. Baseball caps, big thick jackets, Timberland boots. So what else was new. Mojo, even though he was smaller than the other two, was easy to pick out, mostly because of the way he carried himself, but the dark glasses and brand-new shearling coat were pretty good clues, too.

The three workers all looked nervous, and one of the men eyed the phone on the wall, while the other man's hands went below the counter and stayed there, presumably getting ready to grab some kind of weapon—a baseball bat or metal pipe, Dana hoped, and *not* a shotgun. The young woman just stayed right where she was, behind the register, tightly squeezing her magazine. The older man by the window didn't even wake up.

Well, *someone* was going to have to break the tension.

"Hi, how are you," Dana said. "Thanks for taking the time to talk to me."

Which got no response whatsoever.

"Why don't we all sit down," she said, and selected the chair next to Valerie's, while Travis lowered himself into a seat at the next table, watching the taller backup guy the whole time.

After a minute, Mojo nodded once and sat across from her, the other two arranging themselves behind him. The tall kid was scowling back at Travis, while the other, massively built—oh, hell, *fat*—guy stared at her with such relentless, silent hatred that it was hard not to be unnerved.

Or, anyway, hard not to show it.

Nobody spoke.

"So," Dana said. "I guess Travis told you what's going on."

"Travis wanna be a white boy," the tall kid said, his voice slow and ugly. "Ever'body know *that.*"

Travis shook his head. "Fuck you, man."

"Yeah, you *get* in my face," the tall kid said. "You just *see* what happens."

Little boys, overwhelmed by their own testosterone.

"Shut up, Blade," Mojo said without turning.

Blade. Christ. Dana held out the plastic tray. "Drumstick? Anyone?"

No response.

Then Valerie shrugged, picked up a wing, and took a small bite.

"Good choice," Dana said, and looked at Mojo. "Anyway. I gather you were approached by someone?"

No response.

This was, obviously, an exercise in futility. She looked at Valerie, who shrugged again.

"Maybe he just isn't ready to come off-book yet," Valerie said.

Dana grinned. When in doubt, fall back on actor humor.

They all sat there, in complete silence. The—heavy-set—kid was still glaring, ceaselessly, at her, and it was beginning to get on her nerves.

"Do you have some sort of problem?" she asked.

"*You* my problem," the kid said.

Okay. Fine. Call her impatient, but she'd had *just* about enough of this. Time to move on. She finished off her Diet Coke and stood up. "Thanks for all your help," she said to Mojo. "You'll sleep better tonight, knowing that you did the right thing." She zipped up her ski jacket and motioned for Valerie to follow her.

"Don't, lady," Travis said, sounding quietly urgent. "He's got his Glock."

Oh, swell. Dana paused only long enough to frown at him. "Is it pointing at me?"

Travis sighed. Deeply.

Yet another nuance missed by the dumb adult, apparently. "What a relief," she said, and looked over at the two backup kids. "Do you have *your* Glocks, also?"

Blade gave her a grim smile; the fat kid just glowered.

"What about you, Street?" she asked Valerie. "Did you come fully equipped with your Glock tonight?"

Valerie nodded, indicating her pocketbook.

"Well, good," Dana said, and patted her waistband lightly before sitting back down. "We all have our Glocks."

For the first time, Mojo cracked a smile, and she saw that he had a couple of gold caps on his front teeth. "I show you mine, if you show me yours," he said.

"There's an idea," Dana said, and pulled a few dollars from her pocket, handing them to Travis. "Do me a favor, sport, and go buy me a pack of cigarettes, will you? Marlboro Lights, hard pack."

She would have expected him to argue, but after an uneasy glance at Mojo and his buddies, he took the money and left. Dana waited until the door had closed behind him before leaning forward across the table.

"Look," she said in a low voice. "Here's the deal. Regardless of how our conversation works out, Travis is off-limits, okay?"

"The fuck's that mean?" Mojo asked. "I do what I want."

"It means, leave him alone," Dana said. "He's just a nice kid, trying to make it through the day."

"What you think *we* are?" Mojo asked.

Sociopaths. "I think that isn't the issue," Dana said. "I'm just laying some ground rules here."

Mojo scowled at her. "I could fuck you up, baby. *Any* time."

No doubt. Dana looked at him with as little interest as possible.

He jerked his head in Valerie's direction. "I could fuck *her* up."

To Valerie's immense credit, she didn't react either—although her eyes looked pretty big. Probably hadn't had too many dinner meetings like this back in Minnesota.

Think dangerous. "Mojo, my friend," Dana said, pleasantly ferocious—kind of a new challenge, since she had generally gotten girl-next-door parts, "this is not a game I'm really enjoying playing. I find it *dull.*"

He stared her down a little; she stared back, and then she saw another flash of gold.

"You tough, baby," Mojo said.

Dana shrugged. "Well, you know, I have my props to consider."

Mojo grinned again, and took off his sunglasses, setting them on the table.

"So, talk," she said.

"I was just mindin' my own sweet business, *doing* business," Mojo said, "you know what I'm saying?"

If he had grown up in the suburbs, he'd probably be a freshman in college, on his way to a real business career.

"The Man comes by, and he wants to talk," Mojo said.

Dana frowned. "Would you mind clearing up this 'man' business for me? Do you mean *one* man, the cops, authority in general, white people—what?"

"Take your pick," he said.

This was eluding her.

Travis came back in and dropped her cigarettes and a pack of matches on the table rather ungraciously.

"Thank you," Dana said and pushed them over to Valerie—who never smoked offstage, but promptly lit one anyway. She returned her attention to Mojo. "You were saying?"

Mojo also helped himself to a cigarette, which he smoked somewhat ineptly, reminding her—again—that he was a kid. A posturing, probably homicidal, kid, but a kid nonetheless. "The man *was* The Man," he said.

Oh, whoa, wait a minute. Dana reached reflexively for a cigarette of her own.

"You quit," Valerie said.

Was it her imagination—or did the entire world seem to be

monitoring every single aspect of her daily existence? Dana struck the match against her jeans zipper—old bar trick, requiring *considerable* practice; always guaranteed to annoy and offend—and lit up. "Are you saying that the guy was a cop?"

Mojo shrugged. "Seemed like."

Too vague. "Did he show you?" Dana asked. "A badge or anything?"

Mojo looked insulted. "You think I don't know Five-O, baby?"

It still seemed pretty unlikely. If it were true, it would be horrifying—and also cut off a number of her most logical options. The only place she'd be able to air her conspiracy theories would be the Civilian Complaint Review Board.

Who probably wouldn't buy it, either.

"The man want to do business, and the man got a wad," Mojo held his thumb and forefinger apart to show her the thickness of the roll of bills, "to spend, and he don't want *much,* you know what I'm saying? Open him a couple of doors, and like that."

Making him an accessory before the fact. "So you helped him," Dana said.

Mojo shrugged. "I show him *my* wad, and he move on."

Just like that? "How come?" Dana asked.

"You got a lot of people living there," Mojo said. "Old people, little ones. That shit was *cold,* you know what I'm saying? *Mad* cold."

Nice to know he drew the line somewhere. Dana started to light another cigarette, then remembered the one she still had. "So, you knew what was going to happen—and you didn't warn anyone?"

"Five-O tells me I don't know nothing, I don't go tellin' no different," Mojo said.

Christ, could the man have been an actual cop? A *former* cop? Someone gone rogue, on a misguided quest to clean up the neighborhood? Or just, as Gus had observed, someone who'd spent time in the service and seemed, as a result, very sure of himself? "Dark hair?" she asked. "About forty, well dressed?"

Mojo shrugged. "If you say so, baby."

Dana let out a short burst of smoke. "I'm not saying, I'm *asking.*"

Mojo cocked his head, the gold caps appearing again. "You mean, *axing* me?"

A locution she had always found unfailingly annoying. But, it was nice to know that the kid had a sense of humor. "Whichever you prefer," she said.

"Well, since you *ax* nicely," Mojo said.

She hadn't planned ever to like a drug dealer.

"I tell you one thing," Mojo said, "he got ice eyes."

About which, considering the company he kept, Mojo should know. She hadn't even seen the fat kid *blink* yet. "Was he wearing glasses?" Dana asked.

Mojo shook his head.

So, either Gus had seen a different man—or this had been a different disguise. "Mustache?" she asked.

Mojo nodded. "Short, not like those big ol' ones Five-O usually wear, lessen they got *ambition,* you know what I'm saying?"

Unfortunately. "Management," Dana said.

Instead of answering, Mojo leaned over to Blade. "She look like she don't know nothin', but then—she do okay."

Sounded like a yes. Dana knocked her ashes into her empty Diet Coke cup. "If you're right, and he's a cop, do you think he's from this precinct?"

Mojo shook his head. "Not 'less he's hidin' himself. 'Round here, I *know* Five-O. 'Specially the bossmen, you know what I'm saying?"

Well, yeah. Drug dealers tended to spend a lot of time in interrogation rooms, didn't they. "Would you be willing to talk to the fire marshals about this?" she asked, already knowing the answer.

Mojo just looked at her.

Well—it would have been irrational *not* to ask.

"And you best not, baby," he said, "or I'll fuck you up."

Yeah, yeah, yeah. As threats went, that one was more effective the first time around. Her cigarette had pretty much burned down, and slowly, Dana stubbed it out. "Okay, but you could be in danger. They already took someone else out. A guy people called Horse-man." A nickname she'd automatically assumed came from heroin, but Travis had sighed, looked pained, and told her that it came from Colt .45 beer, and didn't she know *anything?*

Mojo looked amused, and glanced over at Travis. "Shit, is *that* what you think?"

Travis shrugged, and didn't meet anyone's eyes.

"He got *took out,"* Mojo said, "but it weren't the Man, it was business, you know what I'm saying?"

Oh, Christ. Was he confessing to murder right in front of her? Dana sat up straight. "*Your* business?"

Now, Mojo looked annoyed. "Wasn't my errand boy. Some fools, down Schomberg way."

A building plaza, on 110th. She was relieved that it wasn't him—and appalled that they were having such a matter-of-fact conversation about someone's violent death.

"No way," Travis said. "He told me people were after him, on account of the fire."

"Shee-it," Blade said, stretching the word out. "That dumb motha thought *pigeons* was after him."

Little boys, shooting other little boys, over stupid little vials. Dana looked at Mojo. "Is it okay if I tell the police, anonymously, that that *particular* senseless murder was committed by some people who hang out near the Schomberg?"

Mojo's nod was so magnanimously majestic that, Glock or no Glock, she felt like smacking him.

"Do you have a name?" she asked. "Or a description?"

Mojo yawned and started examining his—rather long—fingernails.

Yeah, she felt a lot like smacking him. "All of which," she said, "I'm assuming, doesn't change the fact that you were approached by someone who was planning to burn Harrison down."

"Oh, she quick," Mojo said to his minions. "She just so *quick."* He held his fist up at her. "You *go,* girl."

It had been hard as hell to stop smoking, but she lit another, remembering, easily, why she had always enjoyed it so much.

"That it?" Mojo asked.

Dana nodded, and he and his self-anointed soldiers got up noisily, the kid with the baby fat still glaring at her. All three of them looked incredibly young, and cocky—and not long for this earth.

"I see *you* later," Blade said to Travis.

Dana shot a look at Mojo, who digested it, then shrugged a few times.

"Yo, don't go fucking with the brother," he said to Blade, who scowled, but subsided.

Good. He was a kid of his word. She watched as he made something of a production of putting on his sunglasses and adjusting the set of his Georgetown cap. "Is this really what you want, Mojo?" she asked. "I mean, do you have fun?"

"Twenty-four, seven," he said.

Twenty-four hours a day, seven days a week—and she doubted it.

He looked at her with almost no expression. "Tell you what. You come get in my rack, baby, and I *show* you fun."

Which was probably supposed to be intimidating, but just made her sad. She sighed. "There's more to life, Mojo."

"That's 'cause you ain't been with *me,"* he said.

Trying to help a kid like Travis, who—sort of, maybe, sometimes, kind of—actually *wanted* help, was hard enough. These three were long past any of that. From someone like her, anyway.

"It was very nice meeting all of you," Valerie said, somewhat unconvincingly.

Mojo showed her his gold caps; the other two had no reaction at all.

"What's your real name?" Dana asked, as they started to leave.

Mojo stopped, and peered over his sunglasses at her. "Why for you want to know?"

"So if I run into you on the street someday, I can say hello properly," she said.

He grinned. "William," he said, straightened his sunglasses, and then he and the others left the restaurant as swiftly and ominously as they had arrived.

For a minute, it was very quiet.

"Hey, youse!" the older of the two countermen yelled. "I don't want no trouble in here!"

How very helpful—after the fact.

He came out with an ancient baseball bat, waving it menacingly. "I'm talking to youse!"

Valerie went up to the counter with a very gracious smile. "May I have another Diet Coke, please? A medium?"

The workers all stared at her, but she kept smiling, and finally, the younger man started drawing it, while the girl rang up the sale and Valerie chatted with her in her amazingly idiomatic and fluent Spanish.

Travis dragged himself up, looking very tired, and sat down where Mojo had been.

"That helped," Dana said. "Gives me a little more to go on."

Travis nodded dully, rubbing his hand across his eyes.

"They won't be bothering you," she said. "William promised."

He nodded, and looked tired.

Dana checked her watch. "You should probably head home, it's getting late."

He nodded, but didn't move.

Okay. Maybe he needed a little time to come down, too. It had been a pretty tense half hour there.

"That guy, Blade?" he said. "We got history."

She'd noticed.

"When I was little, and we were living in Douglass Houses?" he said. "Me, and Blade—except he was just, you know, Gregory, then—and his brother Marty, and this other guy, Shakur? They were like, my best buddies. We were just little kids, but we were tight, you know?"

Which explained a lot about their barbed interplay. "What happened?" she asked.

Travis shrugged unhappily. "I don't know. *Stuff.*"

Bad stuff. Dana moved her jaw. "What about his brother and Shakur?"

"Marty's, you know, um, upstate," Travis said, glancing at her to make sure she knew what he meant, "and Shakur's still like, rehabbing." He paused. "I heard he's like, a quad now." So, one of his three childhood friends was in jail, one was a quadriplegic—presumably from a shooting, and the third one was a—still walking and talking—drug thug. All things considered, Travis was one hell of a success story.

"Well." He pushed himself to his feet with obvious effort. "I gotta go."

"You going to be all right?" Dana asked.

Travis shrugged. "It's not *that* late, lady."

"I don't mean just tonight," she said.

He sighed. "I don't know, lady," he said, and looked miserable. "I really don't know."

Ten

Valerie must have been waiting, discreetly, up front, because she didn't come back to the table until after Travis had slouched glumly off. She sat down, wrapping both hands around her soda cup.

"That was all *totally* weird," she said.

Dana nodded, lighting—against her better judgment—yet another cigarette.

"I think we should call him William What-a-Waste," Valerie said.

Again, Dana was in complete agreement. "I'm sorry to have gotten you involved in all of that, but—well, it didn't seem like something that was going to wait until tomorrow."

Valerie shrugged. "It was very interesting. I mean, I never get to talk to criminals."

One woman's perspective.

"If we were the types," Valerie said, "I bet we could write a really colorful feature article about it."

Dana laughed, instantly picturing the dramatic spread *New York Magazine* would run, complete with a gritty picture of the two of them standing in front of a graffiti-covered building on a trash-strewn block, looking hopelessly out of place. Although Valerie did, in fact, live in a terminally seedy part of the East Village.

"So, you're going to be a private investigator now?" Valerie asked.

Dana blinked. "A what?"

"You know, a PI," Valerie said. "That's what you're doing, right?"

"Well—" Dana frowned. Sort of. If toddling aimlessly through the land of Make-Believe counted. "Not *officially.*"

Valerie gulped down some Diet Coke. "Why not?"

"Well—" She hadn't, actually, given the idea any serious consideration. "I don't know. I just can't."

"Why not?" Valerie asked. "You're an adult, you can do whatever you want."

"Yeah, but—" Dana stopped, trying to imagine the conversation during which she shyly confessed her new career ambition to her loved ones. "I mean, I went to Brown."

"Oh," Valerie said, nodding. "So it'd be okay for someone who went to a *state* school, but not for you Ivy League chicks."

Open mouth, deeply insert foot. "I didn't mean it that way," Dana said quickly. "I just—"

Valerie shrugged again. "You'd be good. When you were talking to them, you were really natural."

Yeah, right. "Come on," Dana said. "I was really acting."

Valerie grinned at her. "You're good at acting, remember?"

Were she to do such a thing, her parents would definitely regret the day, lo those many years ago, when they had given her *The Hardy Boys Detective Handbook* for Christmas. "I think you have to be a former cop," she said uncertainly. "Or—a burly ex-con trying to go straight."

"I think you watch too much television," Valerie said.

An offense to which she would be forced to plead guilty. "Yeah, but think about what detectives actually do," Dana said. "They go into bad neighborhoods, and get threatened a lot, and—"

"What have *we* been sitting here doing?" Valerie asked.

A good point.

"I just figured that's what you were planning," Valerie said. "I mean, you have to have a career, right?"

Somehow, she couldn't quite see herself sitting in her low-rent one-woman office, pouring Jack Daniel's into her day-old coffee and adopting a grim, possibly even embittered, loner persona. "I don't know," she said aloud. "Maybe I should just be thinking about—law school, or something."

"Well," Valerie said, "you *did* go to Brown."

Okay. Apparently, she wasn't going to live that one down any time soon.

"Were you summa?" Valerie asked.

Dana shook her head. "Just magna."

"Oh," Valerie said, and drained what was left of her soda. "I was summa."

As far as she was concerned, a few too damn many of her friends had also been Phi Beta Kappa.

Not that she was—oh, say—competitive.

"What did you get on your SATs?" Valerie asked.

Dana ignored her, staring at the pack of cigarettes.

"How about we go up to the West End, finish those off, and get ripped?" Valerie suggested.

Not the sort of thing she liked to do regularly—but, what the hell. It had been a stressful evening, so far. "Sounds good," Dana said.

Since they knew a couple of actors who worked at the West End—which was true of many of the bars and restaurants around town—they ended up closing the place. Although she had spent a good deal of her late teens and early twenties drinking too much, alcohol was pretty much a part of her past these days, and when she woke up cotton-mouthed and nauseated the next morning, she remembered why. Fortunately, even when out of practice, she had always had the tolerance of the average rugby team and so, had rarely managed to relax enough to do too many things that she regretted. Mostly, she just got—witty. Very witty. *Too* goddamn witty. And, occasionally, loud.

A jerk yuppie who lived on the fourth floor had told her to let herself into his apartment and perform a few small fix-it tasks he could easily have done himself and then, further infuriating her, he left an envelope marked *"Superintendent"* on the kitchen table.

When she opened it, she found two limp dollar bills inside.

Fortunately, she was too mature to turn around and break his new goddamn dimmer switch, or sabotage the pulsating shower head she'd installed.

Maybe a career change *was* in order.

After going to the dentist and then taking Bert for a chilly walk in the park, she called the number Lieutenant Saperstein had given her, and talked to her very nice, if rather muddled, husband. The upshot of the conversation was that her call would, without a doubt, maybe tomorrow, or the next day, or—well, *soon*—be returned.

Since it would be nice to have a feeling of accomplishment, she decided to mop the halls, foyer, and elevator two days early. She, personally, thought that life seemed much more pleasant when the building smelled clean and fresh.

Although she hadn't noticed much correlative effect on her most recent Christmas tips.

Once she was finished, she decided that the most appropriate reward would be to allow herself to lounge in front of cooking shows for at least an hour. Jacques Pepin and Marcia Adams were her favorites—but she wasn't picky. As far as she was concerned, the entire concept of the Food Network was a thing of great beauty.

Halfway through the third consecutive show, she called Peggy's office.

"It's before five," Peggy said, sounding very grouchy when she finally came on the line.

When she had once looked up the word "curmudgeon" in the dictionary, the primary definition had, in fact, said, "see Margaret Woodruff." "I've been watching cooking shows," Dana said.

"Oh." Peggy paused. "What time should I come over?"

That was more like it. "As soon as you get out of whatever stupid meeting you're making your literary slaves go to next," Dana said.

"Are you going to make a roux?" Peggy asked. "I really enjoy it when you make a roux."

Damn the caloric consequences. "Count on it," Dana said, and hung up.

First, though, she pounded some boneless chicken breasts—more because she felt like pounding than because she had a sudden need for paillards—and set them to marinate in her own version of jerk sauce. It came out differently every time, but she usually liked it, anyway. She started with dry sherry, peanut oil, soy sauce, and a couple of dashes of rum and hot sauce, before adding brown sugar, cumin, cayenne, allspice, ginger, cinnamon, black pepper, lots of onions and garlic—and, as was generally her policy, whatever else she came across that struck her fancy.

One of her flaws as a cook was her occasional tendency to be rather too bold. Her sister Elizabeth, who was a woman of precision, would always ask her, uneasily, "Aren't you going to measure *anything?*" Upon receiving an answer to the contrary, Elizabeth would either leave the room—or turn her chair in the other direction so she wouldn't have to watch. Her other sister, Janet, who lived on Lean Cuisine and boxes of macaroni and cheese, would make comments about how gross it all looked, and that their mother would be *sick,* for a *month,* or maybe even *longer,* were she to witness Dana's cavalier culinary ways—but she still always managed to put away several helpings.

She really missed her sisters, actually. Wished they lived closer.

When Peggy showed up at about seven, bearing chardonnay, Bass Ale, and Diet Coke, Dana was in the middle of making a very small batch of peach chutney. Bert and the cats had, as ever, gathered nearby to watch her on the very likely offchance that she might toss snacks their way.

"Should they really be on the table like that?" Peggy asked, mildly.

As far as Dana was concerned, it was a victory that neither cat had yet ventured onto the *counter,* so she just shrugged.

Peggy dumped her beverage bag and an overstuffed leather satchel on the table next to Theodore, who was unruffled by this. She opened the satchel and took out three new hardcovers. "Want some review copies?"

Always. "Thanks," Dana said, handing her a corkscrew and a wineglass.

"You don't want any?" Peggy asked.

Dana shook her head, opening both a beer and a Diet Coke. Caffeine and alcohol were, to her way of thinking, a lovely, two-fisted combination. She glanced over her shoulder. "You as tired as you look?"

Peggy sighed and draped her coat over one of the four chairs, Edith promptly ambling over to investigate it, her tail twitching. "Much more so." She sat down and got to work opening the chardonnay. "What are we having?"

"Looks like a Caribbean influence tonight," Dana said.

Peggy nodded. "You going to do the achiote business?"

In Latin cooking, red achiote seeds were heated in oil, which was then strained and stirred into rice to give it a bright yellow color. "I thought I'd save some calories and use turmeric," Dana said.

Peggy shrugged and poured herself some wine. "Don't let me get in your way."

Since she wasn't the sort of cook who took kindly to interference. Dana glanced at the clock, lowered the gas under her chutney, and put the chicken—complete with its marinade—in the oven. It was too early to start the rice, so she started peeling carrots and slicing them diagonally.

"He's been calling me, the last few days," Peggy said.

Sam. Dana stopped slicing. "And?"

"I don't know," Peggy said, and slugged down some wine. "Mostly, I've been screening, but—" She stopped.

"But you feel awful, and lonely, and tempted as hell to get back together," Dana said.

Peggy flushed a little. "Something like that, yeah."

She would sauté her carrots in a little butter and honey, with dill and white pepper—but, not yet. She picked up her beer and Diet Coke and sat across from Peggy, moving Theodore to one side.

Peggy looked even more embarrassed. "He says that 'straying' made him realize that I'm the only woman he wants."

"Ouch," Dana said.

"Yeah." Peggy sighed. "My parents keep asking how he is, and I keep saying, just fine."

Double ouch. It had taken the Woodruffs a long time to accept the fact that their beloved, well-bred daughter was living in sin with an often indigent artist, but once they had, they had embraced Sam fully, inviting him to any and all family occasions, eager for him to take her hand in marriage. But, despite their many hints, it had been Peggy's sister Rachel—somewhat ironically, since she was a lesbian—who had produced the first grandchild. In fact, Rachel was already pregnant with her second, both sired by her partner's brother.

"I can pull it off until Easter," Peggy said, "but then they're going to notice."

Yeah. The empty place at their massive dining-room table in the duplex on 71st Street was going to be pretty obvious. Especially since Sam rarely stopped talking.

"Well, anyway," Peggy said, and drank some more wine.

"For what it's worth," Dana said, "I often feel pretty alone myself these days." Months. Whatever.

Peggy frowned at her. "So, what, I should just shut up and put in my time?"

Dana leaned back in her chair far enough to turn on the heat under her rice pan. "I was making an observation, that's all."

"Okay," Peggy said. "You're right. You've been having a run of bad luck, too."

Dana nodded. A *long* run.

"Is it okay if I kvetch a *little* bit, though?" Peggy asked.

"Sure," Dana said. "Just don't start me off."

Peggy reached for the wine bottle to refill her glass, hesitated, and then went over to the refrigerator, taking out a Diet Coke. "You haven't met anyone interesting lately?"

Dana had to grin. She had actually been meeting a hell of a lot of interesting people lately. "No one I want to *date,"* she said.

Peggy sipped some of the Diet Coke, made a face, set it aside, and poured herself some more wine. "Well—when we least expect it, right?"

If one were operating under the presumption that there was a God, yeah. There was some steam escaping from the pan and

Dana got up to add the rice. "You get a bunch of invitations to society stuff that you turn down, right?"

"Believe me, Dana, there is no one at those things you want to meet," Peggy said. "The Smugness Quotient alone is enough to send you screaming out of the room."

Dana put the cover back on and turned the heat down. "I need a situation where I can get access to Mitchell Brandon."

Peggy lowered her glass. "You haven't given up on that yet?"

Dana shook her head, opening the oven to check on the chicken.

"What are you going to do?" Peggy asked. "Just walk up and accuse him?"

Probably. "Well, I might err slightly on the side of subtlety," Dana said.

Peggy kept frowning. "Are you familiar with the words 'slander' and 'libel'?"

Oh, please. "Are you familiar with the phrase 'cocktail party conversation'?" Dana asked.

"I don't think you'll be able to get near him," Peggy said, "and even if you did, what then?"

Dana shrugged, setting her chutney pan on a wooden cutting board to cool. "I don't know. Play it by ear, I guess."

Peggy leaned back, folding her arms across her chest. "Okay. Fine. But what if you're right about all of this? He could be dangerous."

In the middle of a room full of Upper East Side matrons? Not likely. "Oh, come on," Dana said. "I mean, I've seen him on *Charlie Rose.*"

Peggy looked more worried than convinced.

"Okay." Dana sat down. "I'm not really going to walk up to the guy. I just want to see him in action. As more than a magazine story."

"Look, it's your life, you're free to do something stupid, if you want," Peggy said, "but I don't have to *help* you."

Dana slumped her shoulders and made herself look very, very sad.

"Well, I don't," Peggy said, defensively.

Dana nodded, pulled in a shuddering breath, and brushed a napkin across her eyes. Blinked out a couple of tears. *Actor* tears.

Peggy shook her head—ignoring her wonderfully spontaneous performance. "Even if it's some charity where his wife is on the board, that doesn't mean he'll show up."

Dana nodded. Sadly. Sniffled a little.

"And I am definitely not coming along," Peggy said.

"Well, no," Dana agreed, and dropped her napkin. How tiresome not to have an appreciative audience. "You'd cramp my style. I'm going to be on the prowl for WASPs."

"And welcome to them," Peggy said without enthusiasm, then looked at her for a minute. "This is a *very* bad idea."

Dana grinned, and got up to start sautéing her carrots.

"You're looking for trouble," Peggy said.

Absolutely.

Eleven

It took Peggy a few days, but she came up with a ritzy gallery opening, the proceeds of which were going to benefit children's cancer research. The lovely, and ever blond, Madeline Brandon was co-chairing the event and, therefore, highly likely to attend. It seemed more than within the realm of possibility that her husband might, also. In the meantime, Peggy was, well before the fact, absolving herself of all responsibility for any repercussions from what she still thought was an egregiously ill-conceived plan on Dana's part. Since Dana thought it was a pretty *good* plan, all things considered, she just smiled, and thanked her, and left it at that.

She did, however, need a date for this occasion and since her neighbor Craig was always a good sport, he enthusiastically volunteered. The opening was going to be on Friday and he duly promised to clear his social schedule and wear one of his funkiest ties.

Molly Saperstein called her back and, sounding uncomfortable, suggested that they meet for lunch on Wednesday and that, since getting Mickey ready generally made her late, they meet at her apartment in the Village. Dana agreed and wrote down the address, aware that she was a little nervous about the prospect of their hanging out, too. Forcing a nonexistent friendship.

Wanting to tie up loose ends, she passed the word along to Ray that, in fact, she had it on good authority that, instead of a wide-reaching arson conspiracy, little boys *had,* indeed, shot another little boy over stupid little vials, and that they hung out somewhere near the Schomberg. She hadn't even had to call him since he'd seen her walking up 105th Street when he and his partner were cruising the neighborhood, and pulled over to say hello.

"Do I want to know *how* you know this?" he asked, leaning up against his patrol car as Spider silently and suspiciously scanned the street in both directions, his eyes hidden by very dark sunglasses.

"No," Dana said. "I don't think you do."

Ray nodded, grinned wryly, and slapped his notebook shut. "You still owe me a beer."

"Yep," she said, and gave them a wave as they pulled away.

There was a small follow-up article in the *Daily News*—a publication that was one of her secret pleasures, although she also plowed through the *Times* every day, regardless—about the fire, but the only information it really gave was that the investigation was ongoing, and that the firefighter who had been gravely wounded was still recovering at the Burn Center at New York Hospital–Cornell Medical Center.

She decided to go back to the library and look at the coverage that papers *other* than the *Times* had given the fire, see what else she might pick up. The main difference, she quickly and unsurprisingly discovered, was that the other city newspapers tended to take a more dramatic, human-interest-oriented approach, complete with lively action verbs and lots of atmosphere.

She was, however, startled to read that a Lieutenant Mary Saperstein, "who was later treated and released at an area hospital for unspecified injuries," was expected to be nominated for a department medal for heroism, after rescuing five civilians, as well as a probationary firefighter, under "extremely hazardous conditions." The article went on to explain that Lieutenant Saperstein courageously entered the burning building and initiated search and rescue operations, without the protection of a hoseline, since the frozen hydrant had caused a delay in getting water on the fire. An official spokesperson was quoted as saying that the lieutenant "had performed to the very highest standards of the department, risking her own life in order to save others."

Dana was, somehow, kind of pleased that "despite repeated attempts" by the reporter, Lieutenant Saperstein had remained, then and later, unavailable for comment. A Captain Brian McCormick, brother of Lieutenant Saperstein and the commander of a ladder company in Bed-Sty, contributed only a terse "She's a good firefighter." Period.

The only other new coverage she came across was a short, defensive interview given by the man who owned the management company that had run the building, a Gary Kiser, who insisted that he had been very concerned about the safety of his tenants and made regular, timely repairs, but that his efforts had been negated by persistent vandalism and the general carelessness of the troubled population the building served. A Eulalie Evans, who had been trying to form a tenants' association, countered this, insisting that constant complaints about broken windows, uncollected garbage, and various plumbing and heating problems had gone unheeded—and the City Housing Authority confirmed her version of the story, stating that violations had been reported on a number of occasions.

She finished up the last of the articles at the library on Wednesday morning, and then had to hurry and jump on an express train downtown, so she wouldn't be late for her burrito lunch. The Sapersteins lived on West 10th Street, and although in that neighborhood, Dana had expected a walk-up in a brownstone, the address turned out to be a smallish doorman building off Sixth Avenue. Either firefighters got paid more than she thought—or Molly's husband, Jake, had a pretty lucrative profession. Or, possibly, both.

When the doorman sent her up, a tall, lanky man with glasses and dark, greying curly hair opened the door. He was wearing a rumpled Oxford shirt with thin cranberry pinstripes, black flannel slacks, well-broken-in loafers—and just looked like an altogether comfortable guy to be around.

"Hi, you must be Dana," he said, putting his hand out. "I'm Jake. Come on in." He closed the door behind her. "She'll be out as soon as she gets Mickey suited up. Want some coffee or anything?"

Always. "Oh, no, thank you," Dana said. "I'm fine."

She looked around at the living room which was, like most New York apartments, very cluttered, but in a nice way. Sturdy old wooden furniture, book-crowded shelves, an Oriental rug that had seen better days, lots of toys—mostly plastic trucks and Lincoln logs—on the floor. The television was tuned to CNN, although the volume was very low, and the coffee table was covered with newspapers and magazines. One corner of the room was taken up by a wooden table with a beautiful built-in chessboard, complete with polished wooden pieces—some tipped over. She could see into the kitchen over an eating counter, and it appeared that the Supersteins owned just about every culinary gadget ever invented. There were also—Dana felt herself instantly lapse into covetousness—copper pans with shiny bottoms hanging on the wall and some Calphalon, for good measure.

"You must be pretty serious cooks," she said.

Jake shook his head. "Don't look at me. When it comes to that, Molly's the star."

Well, now that she thought about it, there were a hell of a lot more cookbooks by, and about, firefighters than would seem to be indicated. Certainly, she'd never read a *stockbrokers'* cookbook, or one by, say, claims adjusters.

"You—work at home?" she asked, hoping that she wasn't venturing into tactless territory. It certainly didn't *look* as though they were living on one salary.

Jake nodded. "Computer systems consulting, mostly, although I do some programming and data retrieval, too."

Granted, her knowledge of computing didn't extend much further than the average ATM machine, but that sounded intentionally vague. "So, you're a sort of like a professional hacker?" Dana said.

"No," he said quickly, glancing in the direction where his wife must be. "Nothing like that."

Or something *exactly* like that. She couldn't help grinning at him.

"That is, nothing illegal," he said, and coughed self-consciously. "I just do some troubleshooting, now and then. Nothing too interesting."

For her purposes, it might be very interesting. "So, wait." Dana looked down the hallway, able to hear a small boy laughing, but not seeing anyone yet. "Can you look people up? Pull their financial records and so forth?"

Jake stuck his hands awkwardly in his pockets. "You sure you don't want any coffee?"

Right. She grinned again, and shook her head.

A small fluffy grey and white kitten came bounding down the hall, with Mickey following almost immediately behind. He looked to be about four years old, with his father's curly hair, and a bright-eyed, puckish face that probably owed a lot to his mother's side of the family. He stopped short, giving her a big smile.

"Are you Mommy's friend?" he asked.

His mother had, by now, appeared behind him, her expression almost as uncomfortable as her voice had sounded on the telephone when she'd set up this lunch.

"Well—more like Mommy's albatross," Dana said. "Are you Mickey?"

Mickey nodded, smiled, and went after his kitten, who had jumped up on the chessboard, knocking over two more pieces.

"I, uh, guess you've met Jake," Lieutenant Saperstein said, looking like an actual civilian in an oversized Brandeis sweatshirt and jeans. She carried herself differently, too, at home—her walk not quite girlish, but the swagger was definitely gone.

Dana nodded. "We were chatting about law and order."

"One of your favorite subjects," Lieutenant Saperstein said, uneasily.

Dana shrugged. "Well, except for fine literature, art, and music."

Lieutenant Saperstein smiled. Uneasily.

"Try to look less eager, Lieutenant," Dana said. "You'll make me nervous."

Lieutenant Saperstein smiled again, but still seemed reluctant as she put on a heavy navy blue pea coat and stuck a pair of red gloves in the pockets.

Mickey pulled on her arm. "Can I wear my fire coat?"

"*May* you wear your fire coat," Lieutenant Saperstein said automatically. "Sure." Then, as he ran off down the hall, she crossed to the chess table, lifting down the kitten.

"She's very cute," Dana said.

Lieutenant Saperstein nodded, patting the kitten before setting her on the floor and picking up the scattered chess pieces. "Do you know anything about animals?"

And how. Dana nodded.

Lieutenant Saperstein carefully put each piece back in its correct spot. "Is there any way to train her not to get up here?"

Presumably, she wanted an honest answer. "No," Dana said. "Not really."

Lieutenant Saperstein frowned. "Speaking sharply won't be enough?"

If cats could giggle, the kitten would probably be doing so. Instead, she was purring and rubbing against Dana's legs, with the occasional swat at her right shoelace. "You could maybe try spreading some fresh orange peels around," Dana said. "Supposedly, they don't like the smell." Which had, of course, never stopped *her* cats from doing whatever the hell they felt like doing at any given moment.

Lieutenant Saperstein looked at her husband, who shrugged.

"I'll try it while you're gone," he said.

Mickey came running out with a small turnout coat—black with yellow reflective stripes—and it took a few minutes to get him into the coat, a knitted hat, and some mittens, as well as give him a chance to kiss his kitten, and his father, good-bye—both of which, he did more than once.

Finally, they were out in the hall, waiting for the elevator.

"I brought this," Lieutenant Saperstein said, indicating her Channel 13 tote bag, "to make you feel more at ease."

Christ. "Give it a rest, Lieutenant," Dana said. "I'm a *building superintendent,* okay? Not exactly silver-spoon stuff."

Lieutenant Saperstein frowned. "I thought you were an actress."

"Leave of absence," Dana said briefly.

"Oh." Lieutenant Saperstein thought about that. "Are you a decent super?"

Dana shrugged. "I know when to call a plumber, and when to do it myself."

"I wish you'd move in here, then," Lieutenant Saperstein said. "Our guy is terrible."

Okay, good. Sounded like a suspension of hostilities.

"I just—I don't *lunch,*" Lieutenant Saperstein said, "okay?"

Dana shrugged. "But you eat lunch, don't you?"

"We're getting burritos!" Mickey said happily.

"That's right," Lieutenant Saperstein said, resting her hand gently on his head.

He smiled up at her, and leaned against her hip—and Dana thought about how utterly *swell* it would be to have children.

Yesterday, if possible.

"Do you like burritos?" Mickey asked her.

Well— "I like enchiladas," Dana said.

Mickey looked up at his mother doubtfully.

"It's okay," Lieutenant Saperstein said. "Enchiladas are good, too."

Mickey nodded, but still looked skeptical.

When the elevator doors opened, there was an elderly woman already inside—a slightly downtown version of a dowager—and she and Lieutenant Saperstein exchanged nods.

"We're going to have lunch!" Mickey told her.

The rest of them all smiled, although, with typical New York elevator protocol, an instant, intimate conversation did not ensue.

It was cold out—winter seemed to be in no hurry to leave—and when they got to the street, Dana pulled her zipper up a little higher.

"Do you ski?" Lieutenant Saperstein asked.

The row of clattering lift tickets would seem to make the answer self-evident—but, Dana nodded. "Do you?"

Lieutenant Saperstein shook her head. "Too dangerous."

Dana laughed. This, from a woman who ran into burning buildings for a living.

"What?" Lieutenant Saperstein asked, looking uncomfortable again.

"We have different definitions of danger," Dana said.

"Oh." Lieutenant Saperstein relaxed. "Right. I see what you mean."

"Zordon!" Mickey was saying into his mittened wrist. "Come in, Zordon!"

"Come in *please,"* his mother said.

"Come in please, Zordon," Mickey said without missing a beat. Then, he stopped short. "It's morphin time!" he shouted, and started doing inept karate kicks down the block.

"Not too far," his mother warned.

Mickey smiled back at her, and confined his clumsy kicks to a smaller area.

The kid was, without question, a knockout. "I really like him," Dana said.

Lieutenant Saperstein's grin was almost identical to her son's. "He has his moments."

Such unconvincing modesty.

By the time they were seated in the restaurant and the waiter had appeared with warm tortilla chips and salsa, Mickey had told her, at length, about the Power Rangers, the Fire Museum, and, of course, his kitten, who was named Amy. With him there, they couldn't talk about anything arson-related—which was probably for the best, because they both ended up relaxing, and sharing various bits of their backgrounds.

"So," Dana said, when the conversation inevitably turned to Jake. "How'd you meet him?"

Lieutenant Saperstein—Molly; yeah, it was Molly now—leaned over to cut some of Mickey's guacamole-covered chicken. "The New School."

Highly unlikely, since almost everyone she knew had taken a class or two down there at some point, hoping for just that outcome. "Seriously," Dana said.

Molly shrugged. "Seriously."

Wow. If she hadn't been impressed by the Lieutenant before, she was now. "Hunh," Dana said, and then gave in to the temptation to ask the obvious question. "Which class?"

Molly laughed. "The film class. You know, the one they do at the Town Hall now."

Richard Brown. "I already *took* that class," Dana said—with more outrage than she'd intended.

Molly laughed again. "Come on. You seem like the type who always has a boyfriend."

Yeah, right. Dana gritted her teeth. "I'm the type about whom people *say* that, before they go off and date someone else. Or—even better—I'm like a sister, and they feel like they can tell me *anything,* and they don't want to lose that."

Molly dipped her napkin into her water glass and wiped Mickey's face. "So I guess you're just going to have to be patient."

What fun. Maybe her best bet was to try and find a congenial convent.

Molly ruffled Mickey's hair. "How you coming, buddy? Getting full?"

Mickey nodded, although he had made such a mess on his plate that it was hard to tell how much he had actually eaten. "Can we go to the park?"

Molly glanced at Dana, then nodded. "For a little while, sure."

Mickey looked at Dana, too. "Mommy likes to play in the park," he said.

Judging from the way they interacted, she couldn't quite see Molly bouncing around on a teeter-totter, while Mickey sat on a wooden bench, flipping intensely through a magazine. "Don't you like to play in the park?" Dana asked.

Mickey shook his head. "I like to watch. And then, with the money, we get ice cream."

Dana looked at Molly. "You hustle chess games in the park?"

"I wouldn't call it hustling," Molly said, sounding maybe too insistent. "They all know me now." She rubbed Mickey's shoulder. "Let's go to the park where *you* play, okay, Mick?"

Mickey seemed equally enthusiastic about that idea and in the end, they went to a small playground, that was more crowded than Dana would have guessed on such a cold day. There were a few overprotective mothers on the sidelines, although primarily, the children seemed to have been accompanied by nannies.

Mickey immediately found a little girl he knew and they started taking turns on the slide, while Molly watched in apparent repose, but looking very alert.

"You know, I can't tell you anything without breaching department confidentiality," she said.

Since she might have expected as much, Dana shrugged. "Okay."

"But, since I have a feeling people are talking to you who aren't talking to our guys, my plan," Molly said, "was to pump you for everything you've got."

Dana glanced over. "The plan changed?"

Molly nodded, watching as Mickey climbed up the ladder to the slide and came swooping down.

So probing questions on her part were probably out, too.

"I can't even figure out why you care so much," Molly said.

The answer to that one was elusive even to the participant. "I don't know, either," Dana said. "But, increasingly, I do."

They watched as Mickey and his friend moved on, laughing, to a seesaw.

"It's like I woke up one day, and—" Dana stopped. "I envy your clarity."

Molly looked confused. "My what?"

"When you go to work, you always know that what you're doing is right," Dana said. "That it *means* something."

Molly shrugged. "There are plenty of jobs like that."

Maybe. Dana let out her breath. "My friend Peggy says that art matters, in and of itself, but—" Which was likely to lead into "What is Art?" pretentiousness, a topic she was usually able to avoid, unless fueled by alcohol. "For a long time, I haven't been sure of what I'm been doing, or why, and—I want to be."

"So, be a cop," Molly said. "Or an EMT, or there's social work, and teaching, and—all kinds of things."

No doubt. Hell, maybe the police academy was the answer. If

she could handle the rules, and the rotating shifts, and the ever present militaristic hierarchy. And, Christ, *guns.* "Were you scared?" she asked. "When you went in to rescue all those people?"

"It's my job," Molly said shortly.

Dana suspected that there was a lot more to it, so she waited.

"Overconfidence breeds complacency," Molly said.

Which sounded so much like a direct quote from some department manual that it seemed pointless to respond.

"One of the little girls *died,*" Molly said. "Maybe you didn't read that far?"

No. The article hadn't specified that part. "It wasn't your fault," Dana said, cautiously.

Molly didn't answer right away, and the silence seemed very heavy. "People do funny things in fires," she said, after a while. "You have to search under beds, in closets—" She sighed. "A little child might even climb inside a toy chest, or a drawer, or something."

Dana nodded, although the reality of that was really too horrible to imagine.

"She was curled up in the bathtub," Molly said. "I had trouble finding her."

Jesus.

"I put my mask over her face," Molly said, "just in case, but—" She looked out at the jungle gym, and raised her voice. "Mickey! Be careful, okay?"

He waved at her and swung himself upright, looking, in his turnout coat, like an agile, energetic, and *fearless* miniature firefighter.

"What about the probationary firefighter?" Dana asked, more because she was curious, than because it was any of her damn business.

Molly shrugged that off. "He was doing fine, he got turned around, that's all. I just went back and pointed him in the right direction."

It seemed likely that she was glossing over the details of the "went back" part. For that matter, what was a rookie firefighter doing running around in the most dangerous part of the fire, anyway? "Was he where he was supposed to be?" Dana asked.

Molly looked at her thoughtfully. "No one in your family was ever on the job?"

"Too stubborn and argumentative," Dana said.

"Right," Molly said, but still looked serious. "You seem to have a pretty good instinct for this stuff."

Dana shrugged. "Beginner's luck."

"Maybe," Molly said, and then winced as Mickey started swinging incautiously around again.

Despite the cold, it was a nice afternoon, with enough sun to make it seem unseasonable.

"I really love Jake," Molly said.

Which was maybe a non sequitur, but Dana nodded.

"Only I'm afraid—" Molly hesitated, obviously embarrassed, then went on anyway. "I think I'm probably replaceable. In the scheme of things."

Judging from the way his eyes had followed her around the apartment—probably *not.*

"But I can't *bear* the idea of orphaning my son," Molly said.

So she had been scared that night. Still was, somewhere deep inside, from the sound of it. Maybe even every single time that alarm went off.

Now, Molly looked right at her. "People *have* told you some things that can help us, haven't they?"

Tough call, but— "Yeah," Dana said. "I think they have."

Twelve

They didn't talk about it anymore because Mickey chose that moment to fall down, bang his elbow, cry briefly, and then cheer back up. Molly decided that he was starting to look cold, and so they headed back to the apartment, pausing only to buy him a hot chocolate to go at a deli, Dana jumping at the chance to pick up a large coffee for herself, although she drew the line at the pack of cigarettes she was *really* craving.

"You, um, heading right home?" Molly asked when they got to her building.

Dana shrugged. "I'm pretty flexible." Certainly, the Strand, her favorite bookstore in the city, was beckoning, only a few blocks away.

Molly nodded, taking a sip of Mickey's cocoa without meeting her eyes.

"It's easier for me to say yes or no if I know what you're asking," Dana said.

"Well, I was going to go up to the Burn Center, and I thought—" Molly paused. "The truth is, I don't much like going by myself."

Oh. "The firefighter who got so badly hurt?" Dana asked hesitantly.

Molly nodded.

She was going to feel very out of place, but if she was being asked, it must be important. "Okay," she said. "Sure."

Once Mickey was upstairs, and settled down with a snack and a game of checkers with his father, they walked over to Union Square to get a train uptown, after Molly stopped at the Wiz to buy a couple of jazz CDs, explaining that Jim—the injured firefighter—liked music. Left unsaid, was the implication that he wasn't well enough yet to read—or even use his hands.

When they got to the hospital, Dana was surprised to see so many off-duty firefighters, all these weeks later, standing around the waiting room. The talk she'd always heard about "the brotherhood" was also, apparently, backed up by action.

The mood of the room—at least as far as some of the men were concerned—changed abruptly when they came in, indicating that the brotherhood wasn't all that friendly towards their *sisters.* A couple of the men actually turned in the opposite direction, while others just looked grim. The rest exchanged silent nods with Molly, who paused to get a medical update from one of them before going in to visit Jim.

They had agreed on the way over that Dana wouldn't go in, and so she went over to lean against an open space of wall. A firefighter in his mid-twenties, with light brown hair and the predictable bushy mustache, glared at her.

"You another one of the fire dykes?" he asked.

"Cool it," the older man next to him said in a low voice.

The kid firefighter shrugged, folding incredibly muscular arms across his chest. "I'm just asking."

"Yeah, well, look at her," the other man said. "This one *might* weigh in at one-oh-five."

One hundred and twelve, actually—but body weight was the *one* category of life where she didn't mind being underestimated.

On the other hand. She frowned at the younger man. "How long have you been in the department?"

"None of your business," he said.

Two or three years, she was guessing. "She's got at least a decade on you, maybe more," Dana said. "I think she's earned her place."

"They don't belong on the job," the guy said. "Didn't then, don't now."

Personally, she would never have the patience—forget the drive—to work in an atmosphere where that way of thinking prevailed. Dana was tempted to tell him to go find the probationary firefighter whose life Molly had saved and ask him how *he* felt about having women in the department, but she pushed away from the wall, instead. It wasn't worth the aggravation.

There was a soda machine down the hall, and she decided to kill some time by buying a Coke, waiting in line behind a girl who was about thirteen years old and seemed to be having some trouble getting the machine to work.

"Lose your money?" Dana asked.

The girl nodded, her expression so unhappy and scared—well beyond the ordinary annoyance of balky vending machines—that it was pretty likely that she was related to the burned firefighter.

"What kind do you want?" Dana asked.

The girl pointed to the orange soda and Dana hit the button a couple of times, thumped the side of the machine even harder than might be necessary, then gave up and dropped some more change in, upon which a can of orange soda came banging out.

"There you go," Dana said.

The girl hung back, shaking her head. "I don't have any more money."

Dana handed her the can and got a Coke for herself. "It's on me."

"Thank you," the girl said, shyly, and took a sip. "Are you here to see my father?"

Her father. Hell. "I came with my friend Molly," Dana said.

"Lieutenant Saperstein?" the girl asked.

Dana nodded.

"She's really nice," the girl said. "She comes a lot."

Despite having to walk the gauntlet of the brotherhood's disapproval. "I'm really sorry about what happened to your father," Dana said. "He's a very brave man."

The girl nodded, tears in her eyes.

"I'm sure he's getting better every day," Dana said, although, in fact, she had no idea.

The girl shrugged unhappily and drank her soda.

Molly came down the hall, her expression hard to read, although it brightened when she saw the girl. "Hi, Theresa."

"Do you think he's better?" the girl asked, obviously wanting confirmation.

"I do," Molly said. "Much better. How are *you* holding up?"

The girl ducked her head. "Fine, thank you."

"Well, remember, call me if you need anything." Molly saw one of the firefighters beckoning towards them. "Here, go see what your uncle wants, and I'll talk to you later."

Theresa nodded, her shoulders slumped as she walked down the hallway.

"Is her father better?" Dan asked.

"No," Molly said, and then let out her breath. "Why don't we get out of here?"

Which they did, making their way through the group of somber—and still predominantly uncommunicative—firefighters.

"Do they think you did something wrong that night?" Dana asked, not that it was any of her business, once they were in the elevator.

Molly glanced over. "What? Oh, probably. But mainly that's just the same old garbage about us being on the job in the first place."

All these years later? "You must get tired of it," Dana said.

Molly nodded, very grim. "My whole career, I've been tired of it."

The elevator stopped to let a few people on, who got off on the next floor.

"I wonder if they'd come like that, for me," Molly said. "Stand the vigil. Some of them might, out of respect for my brothers, and my father, but—on the whole, I think I'd be on my own."

"I'd come," Dana said.

Molly laughed. "You probably *would.*" Then, she looked over. "Thanks."

Dana just shrugged self-consciously. Molly must have felt a little embarrassed too, because neither of them spoke until they were outside, standing on the corner.

"Thank you for coming with me," Molly said, sounding quite formal. "My brothers are usually working different shifts, and—well, even if we could get someone to watch Mickey, I really hate to put Jake through it, he—" She stopped, letting out her breath. "He doesn't much like thinking about the Burn Center."

No. Logically, a working firefighter's loved ones wouldn't.

"Well," Molly said, and glanced at her watch.

Yeah. "My dog's waiting for a walk," Dana said.

They both nodded, and then stood there for another minute.

"A man who gave the impression of being a police officer was flashing a lot of money around, trying to recruit some help before the fire," Dana said.

Molly looked extremely alert. "A *cop?*"

"No proof," Dana said. "It was apparently just the impression he gave. But, when it comes to that, I think my sources are pretty sharp."

Molly nodded.

"And he was seen more than once," Dana said.

Molly nodded again, then let out her breath. "The autopsy was inconclusive."

Since nine people had died, it was hard to be sure exactly which autopsy she meant.

"The elderly woman who lived in the fire apartment," Molly elaborated. "She was found in bed, with an extremely high blood-alcohol level, which was, we're told, habitual."

There was a thread here somewhere, but Dana couldn't quite find it. "So—the fire *could* have been a careless accident? Like, maybe she knocked over the space heater or dropped a load of laundry on top of it or something before she went into her room and passed out?"

"Individually, certain things that happened that night could have been a coincidence," Molly said, clearly selecting each word, "but put together, it's reasonable to assume they were intentional."

The woman really was a born press agent. "Are you saying that she was murdered before the fire started?" Dana asked.

"There, um, wasn't much left to evaluate, frankly," Molly said. "But they didn't rule out the possibility. And it seems pretty definite that she wasn't involved, since she was in there, and none of her valuables had been removed."

Dana frowned, not sure what that meant.

"If someone has pets, for example," Molly said, "and they conveniently aren't there the night the place burns—well, that's something of a red flag. And if *I'm* suspicious, I always look around to see if there's a television. Even the poorest people you could imagine will pretty much always own a television."

Well, okay. That made sense. "But the space heater was the cause," Dana said.

Molly shook her head. "The space heater was the *point of origin.* The heavy fireload in the nearby area is what raises questions. Although, if you've ever been in buildings like that, the sheer *squalor* can be—" She stopped, shuddering. "Well, let's just say it's possible that the place could have been overflowing with trash, and clothes, and boxes, and God only knows what else."

"So, this wasn't someone dumping gas on the floor and lighting a match," Dana said.

Molly shook her head. "Not by a long shot. In fact, that would have been much better, since it would have obviously been an amateur, getting back at an ex-girlfriend, or the landlord, or something."

The rush-hour traffic was noisy around them, and it was either really weird to be having this conversation here—or else, maybe, it was exactly the right place. Appropriately chaotic and anonymous.

"The landlord," Dana said—although she was really asking. A Gary Kiser, as she recalled.

Molly shrugged. "Maybe. It's the usual place to start."

"The *developer,"* Dana said.

Molly didn't answer right away. "Is that a theory, or do you know something?" she asked finally.

Gut instinct probably didn't count for much—certainly not

when it came to rules of evidence. "The former," Dana said.

"Someone like that can be guilty and still seem clean," Molly said.

True enough—the man had never been indicted.

Yet.

"You know something, though, don't you?" Molly said.

Not until Friday. "I—" Dana hesitated, not sure how much she should admit about this— "have an unexpected avenue of approach."

Molly frowned again. "Look, I really can't recommend—"

"You can't forbid," Dana said, "can you?" Could she? No. This was *America.*

Molly looked uneasy. "I could put the red caps on you."

The New York City fire marshals, she had gleaned from her reading, were called "red caps," because they traditionally—of all inventive things—wore red baseball caps. "You could," Dana agreed. Of course, the tenor of their afternoon together thus far indicated that she wouldn't.

"I don't like it," Molly said.

"What if the guy who seemed like a cop was a fire marshal or something?" Dana asked. "Maybe they were just responding to an air of authority, without being able to pin down the exact profession."

"Not a chance," Molly said without hesitating. "No one in the department would ever do that. They would *never* endanger the other members."

Dana couldn't really remember ever reading about a case like that in New York, but firefighters had certainly committed arson in other jurisdictions, over the years. And with the amount of money likely to be involved in all of this—well, many stranger things had happened.

"I mean, if that's your approach," Molly said, "you might as well start looking into the Kennedy assassination, know what I mean?"

Okay. Point taken. "Are arrests imminent?" Dana asked. "Justice about to be served?"

Molly looked annoyed. "And what? You're just going to come

swooping in like Mighty Mouse, and save the day?"

"Well—more like Underdog," Dana said.

Molly didn't smile.

Christ. "If we have to keep having this conversation," Dana said, "it's going to be a serious impediment to our friendship."

Molly frowned.

"For the record," Dana said.

Molly kept frowning. "What if you screw up our chances of getting a conviction?"

Did she look stupid? Besides, the last she'd heard, there hadn't even been a cause determination yet. Dana shrugged. "How likely is *that,* as the days and weeks pass?"

Molly didn't answer right away. "Just don't get hurt," she said quietly.

Since she was operating in pretty much complete obscurity, that was not on her current list of worries. "No problem," Dana said.

Molly did not look convinced. "You might be in over your head."

Probably. Dana shrugged.

"I also want you to keep me up-to-date every step of the way," Molly said. "So I can pass whatever information you have along."

Hmmm. That sounded kind of like—a *rule.* An order, even. "Will I get a better name than Deep Throat?" Dana asked.

Molly smiled. "I'll work on it," she said.

The gallery opening started at seven o'clock on Friday night, but she and Craig got there about half an hour late. It crossed her mind on their way downtown that her societally-skilled quarry might well have made a brief appearance and already headed off into the windy night, but she decided that this was a matter entirely beyond her control and she might as well just enjoy herself. See what happened.

They took the No. 1 train down to 59th Street and then walked over to 57th Street, to the extremely jazzy gallery where the benefit was being held.

"What do you think," Craig said, flinging one end of his white silk scarf over his shoulder. "Dashing, or fey?"

Well— "Somewhere in between," Dana said.

"Exactly the look I was going for," Craig said, and then glanced over. "I think *you're* leaving too much to the imagination."

She had opted for a plain black sweater dress—that she had kind of thought fell in graceful curves—and pearls, hoping to appear tastefully, conservatively chic. As a concession to the Art World, her earrings were brightly colored, and street-fair funky. "That was the plan," she said.

Craig shrugged. "You're in great shape, you should advertise."

Dana Coakley, Slut on a Rampage. An image she couldn't quite picture, somehow. On the rare occasions that she would get cast against type and end up tottering around the stage in miniskirts and spike heels—and sometimes, worst of all, nothing but undergarments—she had found the situation intermittently exhilarating, but also so embarrassing that she had to act *extra* hard to keep from losing her concentration.

When they got inside, their coats were whisked away by a young, expertly made-up blond woman, and an equally overly attractive blond man bearing a tray provided them with glasses of champagne.

"Not bad," Craig said, looking around the crowded main room. Most of the guests were in evening wear, although the artists and their hangers-on were easy to pick out because they were wearing things like string ties and high-top sneakers, and had much wackier haircuts. The female art types were displaying little touches like the occasional pair of combat boots or dresses cinched in at the waist by belts with huge metal buckles, but enough of them were of indeterminate gender to make such assessments difficult.

"Remind me why we're here again," Craig said, tasting his champagne and nodding approvingly.

She had decided against sharing her investigatory delusions with anyone else. "Because Peggy had invitations she didn't want, there are free drinks, and I thought it would be fun," Dana said. All of which was true, actually.

Craig shrugged. "Okay. Maybe I'll meet some nice, talented, tormented painter and fall madly in love."

"You and me both," Dana said.

"Oh, yeah," he said, and grinned at her. "You bohemian thing, you."

Was she ever going to live down having dated a banker, relatively short term as it had been? And hell, Tim had been a very decent guy, always bringing little treats for her pets when he came to pick her up and that sort of thing.

The gallery was on two spacious levels, with open staircases leading up to the second floor on both sides of the wide main room. There was a—quite good—jazz combo set up in one corner of the room and a long bar in the other corner. Several smaller rooms opened off the main area and she could see that they were mobbed, too. Some people were looking at the various paintings and sculptures, but the rest seemed to be more interested in the social aspects of the scene.

With the exception of a celebrity here and there, she saw absolutely no one that she knew. The rich and famous appeared to be having a very nice time mingling, and she got the distinct impression that favors were being traded, and million-dollar offers made and rejected, all around them. Without a doubt, she was surrounded by more dry chuckles, deep-voiced pronouncements, and confident contraltos than she had ever heard before.

"I'm suddenly reminded that I'm a kid from Boise," Craig said.

Dana laughed. She was feeling very much like a girl from suburban Massachusetts, herself. "Let's check out the art."

Craig finished the rest of his champagne and put his empty glass on the tray of a passing waiter. "Good plan."

The art was, for the most part, not very interesting. Mammoth canvases with random splashes of incompatible colors and such.

Craig polished off his second glass of champagne. "How much longer do we have to make this scene?"

She had yet to catch a glimpse of Mitchell Brandon—or his, as she was perpetually described, lovely wife Madeline. "Can you humor me for another half hour?" she asked.

He sighed. "Next time, we do something *I* like."

Which, in his case, almost certainly meant the Cloisters. Or maybe the Botanical Gardens. "Fair enough," Dana said.

They ended up by the bar on the second floor, talking to a black-haired bartender with an interestingly craggy face and a bouncy cocktail waitress, both of whom were, naturally, struggling actors. The bartender, whose name was Stefan, seemed to be quite taken with Craig—and vice versa.

"It's been really slow out there," Stefan said, and looked at Craig. "Have you been getting sent up for anything lately?"

Craig shook his head. "Just voice-overs."

"I'm so tired of temping," the waitress, Kari, said, "I can't stand it."

Dana nodded. She had hated temping—and telemarketing, and catering, and just about every other job like that she had ever had. Waiting on table had been, by far, the least arduous.

"Ah, don't talk to her," Craig said. "She was getting *work,* and she quit, anyway."

Stefan and Kari both looked—as members of the acting community generally did upon hearing that piece of information—appalled.

"Seemed like a good idea at the time," Dana said, and drank some of her seltzer. Craig hadn't switched over yet, but she had decided that complete clarity of mind was a definite priority tonight.

Kari shook her head, picking up a fresh tray of champagne. "At this stage, I'd be happy with a callback," she said, and plunged back into the crowd.

It turned out that Stefan was from Bozeman, Montana, originally, and he and Craig started swapping stories about growing up in that part of the country while Dana looked around at the murmuring crowd. There were so many greying, distinguished men that it was hard to tell them apart. But then, she heard a voice she recognized from television and looked more carefully until she saw a tall, fiftyish man in black tie, who, judging from the hearty laughs of the clearly successful—and complacent—men standing around him, was as charismatic a raconteur as his media reputation had always suggested.

Mitchell Brandon. In the undeniably handsome flesh.

Thirteen

She either hadn't expected him to be quite so attractive in person—or hadn't expected herself to be so intimidated by that. On the other hand, she'd lived in New York long enough not to be impressed by the rich and famous anymore. Much.

But, Christ, he was, without a doubt, caddishly handsome. She had always had a thing for men who looked like intellectual jocks, and—from here, anyway—Mitchell Brandon seemed to be the personification of grey-haired virility.

And, she should keep in mind, possibly the lead conspirator in a mass murder.

He just didn't *look* the part.

Craig seemed to be quite happily occupied by Stefan, and so she wandered a few steps away, trying to figure out how to make her approach. On the whole, they did not look like a group of men who enjoyed making small talk with women—especially much younger women.

Okay. Okay. If she could recall her Men 101 textbook, there had been an entire chapter entitled, "Make *Him* Come to *You.*" And, since she'd played her first lead part back in tenth grade, she'd thought of herself as being able to act a little, so if she couldn't, for a few minutes here, however far away it was from her actual personality, do some femme fatale stuff—well, she would have to be very ashamed of herself.

Then again, she was kind of out of practice.

But, since the guy didn't seem to be in any hurry to go anywhere, there was nothing wrong with warming up first. Work out the kinks on a self-satisfied WASP her own age, maybe.

Although she'd always hated the concept of wasting her best stuff during the rehearsal period. Being a batting-practice hero.

If she were more self-aware, she might think that she was—stalling—a little, here. And they looked like their conversation was winding down, so this was her perfect, and possibly only, opportunity.

Besides, not that she wanted to fall into actor-speak, but if she thought too much, she would, as they said, read too cerebral. So, okay. She took a deep breath and drifted a few feet closer to the group, not stopping until she found a spot where she would be standing quite alone—and be very noticeable.

She shifted her weight to one hip—adorably? stiffly?—God damn it, stop *thinking,* Dana, one of her acting coaches had always yelled—let her hand shake uncertainly, and then reached into her black evening bag, pretending to look for cigarettes.

Whereupon, she frowned at her lack of success—yes, it was fun to play games!—started fumbling through her bag again, sighed in frustration, and looked around for assistance.

To her great amusement, Mitchell Brandon came over, smoothly pulling a sterling silver cigarette case from the left inside pocket of his dinner jacket.

Dana did her best to blush prettily. "Was it that obvious?"

"I noticed," he said—and, damn it, up close, his *voice* was sexy as hell, too.

"I suppose I have to step outside to smoke it," she said—not without pique, most of it genuine. Laws could be tedious.

He nodded. "I imagine so."

"Well, I'll just tuck it away for a bit, then." She took a cigarette, nodded her thanks, and then turned to listen to the jazz combo. They were playing "Tuxedo Junction," which was, as it happened, a favorite of hers. Anyway, this guy was likely to be *captivated* by any show of indifference on her part.

Indeed, he was smiling as he tucked away the cigarette case.

"Have I seen you before?" he asked.

Oh, Christ, with her luck, he and his wife probably subscribed to the Manhattan Theatre Club or something. And with extraordinarily bad timing, a woman who Dana was pretty sure she recognized as Mrs. Brandon, was talking to some people maybe thirty feet away. Dana shook her head, and listened to the band.

"I don't think I have," he said. "I always remember a—" he looked her over without even pretending that it was anything *other* than a sexual assessment—"face."

"Do you now," Dana said. With a *staggering* lack of interest.

He smiled again, and watched her listen to the music—and she made a point of letting her hips move very gently to the beat.

"Attend a lot of these?" he asked, gesturing around the crowded room with one hand.

"I love functions," Dana said, and nodded toward the band. "I love this *song.*"

His smile changed, distinctly, into a grin.

"If they play 'Skylark' next, I'll just be beside myself," she said.

"And what would happen then?" he asked.

This femme fatale stuff was, she had to admit it, pretty amusing. "Well," she said, and paused an extra half-beat, "luckily, there are no barnyard animals in here to frighten away."

Now he laughed outright, and then extended his hand. "Mitch Brandon."

Dana nodded, and shook it. "Delighted," she said, just a little bit vaguely.

"I don't believe I got your name," he said.

"Really?" Dana said, and extricated her hand from his with some difficulty. "How uncharacteristically coy of me."

He laughed again, and glanced around. "Are you—with anyone?"

"How do you mean?"

He grinned at her.

Jesus. So much for subtlety. She looked down at his left hand, and then away. "Nice ring."

"Oh, I don't give that much thought," he said.

"Really," she said, and looked in the direction of the woman she was pretty sure was Madeline Brandon.

"I didn't mean that quite the way it sounded," he said.

"Oh." She shrugged. Yeah, *right.* "My mistake."

He moved barely perceptibly closer. "Or, perhaps, exactly the way it sounded."

"Imagine that," Dana said.

He looked her over some more. "I know *my* imagination's going wild."

"How—" she let her gaze travel blatantly downward "—uplifting—for you."

He laughed again. "Who are you? How come I haven't met you before?"

"Oh, I don't know," Dana said. "Probably because old money, and new money, don't really mix." She glanced in his wife's general direction. "But I guess you already know that."

He frowned slightly.

On that note. "Well," she said, and gave him a small, enigmatic smile. "You'll excuse me."

"I hope we see each other again," he said.

He could count on it. "Well, I *do* consider myself Destiny's handmaiden," she said.

He was, momentarily, flummoxed by that, and she moved past him.

"Nothing more attractive than a man with rapier reflexes," she remarked.

"Always happy to provide a woman with pleasure," he said without hesitating.

Okay. Not bad. She grinned and started to walk away, but then paused. "Oh. Congratulations. I think what you're doing is wonderful. Rebuilding for those people whose apartments were burned."

"I don't know what you're talking about," he said, sounding terribly urbane.

The hell he didn't. She let her hands go onto her hips. "The Harrison Hotel? Formerly on New York's fabled Upper West Side? They tell me you're rebuilding the victims' homes."

"They're mistaken," he said, his eyes suddenly very cold.
"So, wait. What happens to the victims?" she asked.
"I believe they've all been relocated," he said smoothly.
She believed that he was—in fact—*mistaken.* "Oh," she said. "How nice. I must have misunderstood. Let me withdraw the congratulations, in that case."
His jaw tightened a little. "I'm not sure why it would interest you, anyway."
Dana shrugged. "Just a concerned citizen."
"Well, I enjoy getting input from the little people," he said.
They looked at each other, both still cordial, but significantly less so.
"I don't think I got your name," he said, unsmiling.
And he wasn't going to. "I don't think so, either," she said, and started to leave.
His hand fastened around her arm to stop her, his grip extremely painful in the second or two before—probably only because they were in public—he let go. "If I may be so bold," he said, "who—exactly—the fuck are you?"
Fuck. Interesting. "What's the matter, Mitch?" she asked, very pleasantly. "You seem rattled."
They looked at each other, Dana aware that the charge of sexual tension in the air had changed to mutual, carefully masked, menace.
"Well. Maybe I'll see you again," she said, and walked away without looking back.
Despite the crowd, her back felt very exposed, and she was relieved when she got to the bar and could lean casually against the polished wood. She felt herself trembling and hoped, for her own self-respect, that it didn't show.
Stefan was occupied by fixing drinks for some people, and so Craig drifted down the bar to stand next to her.
"Were you just talking to Mitchell Brandon?" he asked.
Dana nodded, glancing out at the people milling around, unable to locate him now.
"Wow," Craig said. "What was he like?"

Exactly as Peggy had described him—charming, cocky, and ruthless. "About the way you'd expect," she said.

"Wow." Craig shook his head. "Neat."

Dana had to grin. Talking about Boise must have made him regress into Country Mouse phraseology.

Craig looked down at Stefan, who was busily mixing and pouring. "Pretty cute, isn't he?"

"He's really—neat," Dana said.

"All right, all right, all right," he said, flushing. "It's just a word."

"It's a *keen* word," Dana said.

He flushed more. "Look. You want a drink?"

So much so that it was alarming. "Sure," she said. "How about a gin and tonic?"

He nodded and moved down the bar to ask Stefan, who nodded and started making it.

As she waited, someone came over—preceded by the scent of expensive perfume—next to her, and Dana was somewhere between startled and horrified to see that it was Madeline Brandon. She was slim, and blond, and had probably had a face-lift or two—but the woman, without question, looked smashing in her long red velvet dress.

"Scotch and soda, heavy on the soda," she said to Stefan, her voice reeking of finishing-school polish.

Stefan nodded, putting Dana's glass in front of her. She nodded her thanks, and waited to see if Mrs. Brandon's coming over had been a simple coincidence.

"It's certainly a lovely party," Mrs. Brandon said.

To her? Well, yeah—there was no one else around, since Craig was pretty fixated on Stefan. Dana nodded. "You must be pleased by the turnout."

"Oh, yes," Mrs. Brandon agreed. "Quite."

The smile wasn't even close to her eyes, so Dana was guessing that this encounter was not, in fact, just a coincidence.

"That's a very becoming dress," Mrs. Brandon said. "May I ask who designed it?"

If dulcet tones could kill—she would be lying on the floor in a writhing heap at this very moment. "I bought it off-the-rack," Dana said. "In a fit of whimsy."

"I see," Mrs. Brandon said without even a glimmer of amusement. "Perhaps I'll try that myself, sometime."

A writhing, *moaning* heap. "Marvelous way to kill an afternoon," Dana said.

"Yes. I'm sure it must be," Mrs. Brandon said, and studied her. "I can't seem to place you, dear, although I'm sure we've met."

Just as Dana was about to say, "I'm sure we have," Craig laughed.

"It'll make *anyone,"* he said in a deep commercial voice—hell, by now, he was probably drunk— "feel like a king."

Served her right for not briefing him before they got here. "I think we've probably just seen each other at occasions like this," Dana said, infusing the statement with great confidence.

"No doubt," Mrs. Brandon said, and smiled with gracious disdain. "Enjoy your evening, dear."

"You, too," Dana said, and watched her walk away.

Craig shook his head, holding a martini. "Jesus. What is it with you and those people?"

Nothing good. Dana picked up her gin and tonic. "You got me," she said.

They left shortly thereafter—although Craig made plans to go to the Film Forum with Stefan on Sunday before they did—and once they were out on the street, Dana was so tired that she could have fallen asleep right there on 57th Street.

"Well, *I* had fun," Craig said.

That made one of them. But Dana nodded, wishing that she weren't still feeling so unnerved. Maybe she should have come up with a better strategy, like leaving it to the authorities, and not—well, it was too late now. The proverbial ball had been set in motion.

"If I didn't know better," Craig remarked, "I would swear you had an agenda in there."

Yep. She grinned at him. "Just seeing how the other half lives."

He made a face. "I'll pass, thanks." Then he put his arm around her. "Come on, I'll buy you a hamburger."

Yes. With a nice cup of diner coffee in a plain white mug. Nothing even remotely fancy. "Sounds great," she said.

Peggy called bright and early—way *too* early—the next morning to find out how the opening had gone, and Dana wasn't sure how to answer, since she was still trying to figure it out herself. Also, to wake up.

"I don't think he was very taken with me," she said finally.

"And?" Peggy asked, sounding impatient.

"And I don't know," Dana said. "Craig and I left, and got something to eat. Thanks for letting me use your invitations."

"That's it?" Peggy said.

Dana yawned. What the hell time was it, anyway? She looked at her clock. Eight-thirty. Christ. "I just wanted to see for myself if he's the kind of man who could destroy other people."

"I'm surprised you didn't come right out and ask him," Peggy said.

Well, as a matter of fact— "For all intents and purposes, I did," Dana said.

Peggy sighed audibly. "Terrific. Heard from his lawyers yet?"

"I haven't even *walked the dog* yet," Dana said, hearing a sharp little note in her voice.

"Oh." Peggy paused. "I thought you'd be up. When should I call back?"

"In several *hours,*" Dana said. Testily.

"Enjoy your slothfulness," Peggy said, and hung up.

Over the next few days, Dana didn't get much deducing done—or, really, anything else—because the super from one of the other buildings her landlord owned in the neighborhood was recovering from a bout of diverticulitis, and she had promised to pick up his duties for the next week or two, since he would certainly do the same for her. However, the extra workload was enough to make her have trouble remembering to do normally rudimentary things like—eat.

She was standing at her kitchen counter on Wednesday afternoon—because if she sat down, she would doze off within seconds—eating a granola bar and flipping through the *Times* Food Section before she had to go do some more painting in a vacant apartment, when the phone rang.

"Dana! Honey!" a hearty voice said at the other end of the line. "How are you?"

Her agent. Former agent. Whatever.

"Hi, Terence," she said, taking a Coke out of the refrigerator. "What's up?"

"Just checking in," he said. "Have you come to your senses yet?"

Would he still be calling her like this when she was eighty? Dana laughed. "No. Sorry."

"There's still interest out there," he said. "I get calls from producers, and what am I supposed to tell them? It's your biological clock? You're in rehab? You're simply *wacko?*" He paused. "Anyway. When are we having lunch?"

She had always gotten a kick out of her agent. "Whenever you want," she said.

"*That's* what I like to hear, I—oh, hang on." He put her on hold, and then came back. "I've got to take this one, okay, sweetie? Just give Nancy a call and let her know when you're free so she can put it in my book, okay? Thanks. *Great* to talk to you, hon, can't *wait* to see you."

Before she could say good-bye, the phone had already clicked in her ear. She hung up, shaking her head. On a day like this, when she was exhausted, and dizzy from paint fumes, her muscles so stiff and achy that the concept of lifting her arms over her head seemed beyond her capacity—the thought of jumping back on the auditioning treadmill seemed less horrific.

On the plus side, doing so much hard physical labor meant that dieting no longer had to be a major facet of her life. Not only did she not have to worry about having to be as thin as actresses who were living on seltzer and hot-air popcorn, and spending all their spare time working out, but she was burning lots of calories and could eat pretty heartily, anyway.

However, they called it *work* for a reason.

The next day, she finished up pretty early, and after doing her bi-monthly building smoke alarm check, with the help of a candle, a stepladder, a pocket of fresh batteries, and her pass keys—something she had done regularly even *before* she met a firefighter, and thought about such matters—she decided that she would take some time to pursue her investigative grail.

The notes she had taken at the library indicated that the name of the Harrison Hotel's management company was the Kiser Realty Corporation, and since it was listed in the Manhattan Yellow Pages, she didn't have a whole lot of trouble finding the place.

The building was on a side street off lower Broadway and she looked around a little before going inside. The block was decent, and the entryway was fairly clean, but she got the distinct impression—from the battered, mismatched label-maker tape next to each buzzer, the slight stench of urine, and the lack of security—that Mr. Kiser was a lot closer to insolvency than he was to successful.

There was lots of static on the intercom, but she was buzzed in, regardless—another sign of a small operation. Naturally, she hadn't really formed a plan yet, but she had purchased one of those long tan reporter's notebooks on her way downtown and was wearing her London Fog raincoat—so, maybe he would jump to conclusions.

Unless, of course, he suspected her of playing dress-up.

A little worried that she was maybe being too obvious about the Girl Reporter thing, she tucked the notebook deeper into her pocket and took the pencil out from above her ear and put that away, too.

Time to get away from Method and just worry about not bumping into the furniture.

The office was small, with a receptionist sitting at a wooden desk up front, a couple of other desks—unoccupied—behind her, and a glass-doored office beyond them. The receptionist, who looked about forty, with curly brown hair and reading glasses, was typing into an older-model computer, but she stopped and took her glasses off.

"Yes?" she asked.

"Hi," Dana said, and gave her an exceedingly unthreatening smile. "Is Mr. Kiser in?"

The receptionist looked at her watch, and shook her head. "Was he expecting you?" she asked, with an accent that Dana was pretty sure was Queens, as opposed to Brooklyn.

"I was just hoping I might catch him," Dana said. In both senses of the word. "Is he in?"

The receptionist checked her watch—a white Swatch—again. "No, but he should be back soon. If you'd care to—"

"That'd be nice," Dana said. "Thanks." She motioned toward the framed school pictures—not wildly flattering, but also not without charm—on her desk. "Are those your children? They're cute."

The receptionist looked pleased, nodded, but then pulled over her appointment book.

It was going to be hard to answer questions about the nature of her business. "How old are they?" Dana asked.

"Oh." The receptionist lowered her pen slightly. "Well, Paul is nine and Jessica is almost eleven."

"It must be hard," Dana said, "bringing them up in the city. I mean, I guess if it were me, I'd try to get them into parochial school, and hope for the best, but—"

The receptionist put down her pen completely. "Do you know what parochial schools *cost* these days?"

From there, it was easy to jump into an animated conversation, and soon, they were drinking mediocre coffee, and Dana was hearing rather more than she felt comfortable knowing about the receptionist's—Sonya's—ex-husband Rick and, Gawd forgive her, what a complete waste of the earth's oxygen he was, and how she would just as soon *quit* this lousy job, but then again, it wasn't really that bad, and at least she *had* a job, right? Dana was able to get in very few words edgewise, but she contributed the occasional nod or head shake, and that seemed to be sufficient.

Before she was able to find out exactly what it was that made the job so lousy, and what Mr. Kiser was like, the office door banged open and a short, bald man came in, carrying an overstuffed leather briefcase. He was wearing a three-piece, ill-fitting tan suit, and had one of those perpetually perspiring faces that always made Dana think of Richard Nixon and that traitorous upper lip.

Sonya straightened up, pretending that she had not been participating in anything resembling a gabfest. "Here are your messages," she said, handing him several pink slips of paper. "Bill went up to 19th Street, and he said he'd check in as soon as he figured out what was going on."

Mr. Kiser grunted, as opposed to saying thank you, and flipped through the papers.

"Oh, and this is—" Sonya stopped, and looked at her blankly— "uh—"

Out of a surfeit of caution, she hadn't actually introduced herself. Dana put down her coffee and stood up. "Hello, Mr. Kiser. May I speak with you, sir?"

He looked her over, and apparently wasn't impressed. "I'm very busy, miss," he said. "What do you want?"

"Ten minutes," Dana said quickly. "That's all."

He didn't seem overjoyed, but he motioned for her to follow him back to his office.

"You should really have gone through my girl and made an appointment," he said, scanning some papers on his desk. "This isn't a very good time."

His girl. "It won't take long, sir." Dana pulled out her notebook, since, as ever, she would be more comfortable if she had props. In both senses, of course. She had made a few notes on the train about various bits of information she had gathered so far, and she flipped the notebook open. "Frankly, some allegations have been made, and before we go to press, I thought you might want to address them."

For the first time, he really looked at her. "What allegations?" he asked, tensing.

The fact that he seemed alarmed, rather than interested, seemed to indicate some co-conspirator status. "Well, the fire, sir," Dana said, very calm. "We thought you should have a chance to deny or refute some things we've uncovered."

He stared at her, one hand gripping the edge of his desk. "I don't have to talk to you," he said.

"No, sir, you don't," she agreed. "That's the beauty of it. I just thought you might *want* to."

Both of his hands tightened into fists, and he leaned forward with his weight on them. "Get out of here, bitch. I don't want to talk to you, or anyone like you. I've got nothing to say. And you can just tell that to whoever sent you here."

Now, if people were going to go and swear at her on a regular basis, she would have to rethink this detecting stuff. She didn't mind conversational profanity—had been known to use quite a bit of it herself—but having people direct these remarks, insultingly, *at* her, fell into another category entirely.

She took her time standing up, closing the notebook, and shoving it back into her pocket. "See you on the front page, sir," she said.

He moved out from behind his desk, blocking her way. "Who are you? You can't threaten me."

Why not? She shrugged. "It's only a threat if I'm telling the truth, sir." And it was for a good cause. Besides, if he was as guilty as he was acting, she *would* be seeing him on the front pages one day soon.

They looked at each other, and she had the distinct impression that, as opposed to Mitch Brandon's menace, what she was seeing here was fear.

"I'm not out to hang you, sir," she said. "We just want to hear your side."

He glared at her. "Well, you can go through my attorney."

She reached for her notebook and pen. "May I have his or her name and number?"

"Just get out of here, bitch," he said. "Before I *throw* you out."

Hmmm. Bitch, again. She looked at Sonya, whose eyes were very big behind her glasses. "If I didn't know better," she said, "I might think he was hiding something."

Which would suffice for an exit line, and she left.

Fourteen

Just for fun, since it was close to the end of business hours, she decided to hang around across the street and see what happened when he came out and realized that she was still there. She had, as always, stuck a paperback in her pocket to read on the subway—or while standing on one of the innumerable lines she would find herself in on a daily basis. In New York, even something as pedestrian as going to the post office could be as drawn out as an afternoon at the DMV, and she had learned never to leave her apartment without some form of portable entertainment. Paperbacks were perfect because they didn't take up much space, and it wouldn't decimate her day if she lost one in a taxi or something—as opposed to a hardcover, which would cause a certain amount of despair.

So, she found a mailbox to slouch against—a street lamp would be too cliched, and a doorway would be likely to have been used as a urinal in the not too distant past—and picked up where she'd left off in her book.

At ten after five, Sonya came outside, buttoning up a black wool coat. She saw Dana, looked annoyed, and crossed the street.

"How come you didn't tell me you're a reporter?" she asked accusingly.

Because she wasn't. Dana shrugged, put in the Knicks ticket

stub that she was using to keep her place, and stuck the book under her arm. "You didn't ask."

"Well, thanks a lot," Sonya said. "He was up there screaming at me, because I didn't screen you well enough."

Which had certainly not been her intention. "I'm sorry," Dana said. "I didn't mean to get you in trouble."

"Well, you did." Sonya glanced up at the building as though he might be staring down at them, and then hunched her shoulders. "It's not that it's such a great job, but I can't afford to lose it, okay?"

No, she had absolutely no right to play around with someone else's livelihood. Dana sighed. "I'm really sorry. I didn't think."

"Well, *think* next time," Sonya said.

Dana nodded, guiltily. Getting innocent bystanders in trouble hadn't been part of the plan.

"Besides, do I look like someone who'd work for a murderer?" Sonya asked, her hands on her hips. "Or, did you and your uptown accent just assume I'm too stupid to know, one way or the other?"

Hell, she hadn't considered that at all. Then, Dana frowned. "I don't sound uptown. I'm not even *from* New York." If anything, she had a generic East Coast accent, characterized more by rapidity of speech than anything else.

"You're definitely not boroughs," Sonya said, sounding unfriendly.

If ever there was a goddamn class-conscious town, this was it. Dana sighed again. "I figured, if he burned the place down, he was probably keeping it to himself."

"Well, then, you've never even spent an hour as a secretary, have you," Sonya said. "I *know* what's going on in that office." Then she looked at her watch, and headed briskly down the street.

Dana caught up with her in a few jogging steps.

"I don't have anything more to say to you," Sonya said, very stiff. "I have to get home so my sitter can leave."

Dana held her hands up, making it clear that she wasn't holding her notebook. "Look. This is off the record."

Sonya looked extremely irritated. "I have to go."

Dana nodded. "I know. I just—is there any chance he had something to do with it?"

"First of all, they're not even sure it was arson," Sonya said, "and anyway, the poor man's barely keeping his head above water. You really think he's going to risk jail?"

Financial trouble made him *more* likely to have torched the building, not less.

"He didn't even have decent insurance," Sonya said. "And he was trying to bring it up to code, but no matter what improvements he put in, they just kept trashing the place."

They. Which was likely to be followed by a "people like that" generalization.

"Why don't you go after that creep Brandon and *his* people?" Sonya asked. "They strong-arm everyone in town, and no one ever touches them."

Okay, now they were getting somewhere. "The man's a multimillionaire," Dana said. "Why would he bother taking such a big risk?"

"Because he *can,*" Sonya said. "Where've you been? That's how people like that operate."

A different context for the "people like that" than she'd expected, but what the hey. "Had he been trying to acquire the building?" Dana asked. "Before the fire?"

Sonya hesitated, then looked at her watch again and walked more swiftly.

"That's all I want to know," Dana said, keeping pace. For now, anyway. "Was he trying to buy your boss out?"

Sonya avoided her eyes. "I don't know."

In other words—yes. "Come on," Dana said. "I don't want to have to keep digging, and making you all uncomfortable. If you can give me something to go on, I can move the focus wherever it belongs."

Sonya hesitated some more, then looked around the packed sidewalk uneasily.

It would be humane, but too frustrating, to back off now. "You can bail your boss out here," Dana said. "Just point me in the right direction."

Sonya shook her head firmly. "Leave me alone. I don't know anything."

Except that it was clear that she knew all too well. "Okay. Just give me a name," Dana said, to keep the pressure on. *"Anything."*

They were at the subway entrance now, and Sonya stood poised at the top of the steps, obviously afraid that Dana was going to follow her down—and maybe all the way to Queens.

Which, at this rate, she just *might.*

"I don't know any names, but—" Sonya stopped.

Dana nodded, and moved slightly closer, on the—it turned out, accurate—assumption that it would make her nervous.

"Look, in this business, it's all consortiums, and dummy corporations, and—you don't know who owns what," Sonya said. "But—" She stopped again.

Dana felt like a complete bully, but she moved another step closer, anyway.

"All I know, is that since the fire, Gary's been scared to death," Sonya said quickly. "Okay? And he didn't do it, so that isn't it."

Indicating that he had either gotten threats, or just had some very strong suspicions. Dana nodded. "And you figure Brandon is behind it."

Sonya clutched her pocketbook with both arms. "I don't know. And—I don't *want* to know. Okay?"

Okay. Time to stop tormenting this nice, hardworking woman, who wanted nothing more than to pay her bills and put food on the table. "Thank you," Dana said, and backed off *literally,* as well as figuratively. "I'm sorry to have kept you. I promise I won't bother you again."

"Good, because I won't talk to you again," Sonya said, and hurried down the steps without looking back.

Dana let her go, feeling very guilty. Browbeating had not been on her list of things to do today.

No matter how helpful it had been.

The odds were against his being even remotely cooperative, but she decided to walk back around the corner, wait for Mr. Kiser to come out, and see if she could intercept him.

Tempting as it would be just to call it a day, and go home and get something to eat.

It was too dark to read without getting a headache, so she alternated between leaning against various objects and peering at her watch. With the sun down, the temperature had also dropped and her raincoat wasn't much protection against the cold. To break the monotony, and try to warm up, she paced back and forth for a while before going back to leaning.

After about an hour, she gave up. Bert was going to need his walk soon, and there was so little chance that Kiser would actually tell her anything that she was probably wasting her time. Besides, it was really cold.

While she was standing on the subway platform, reading again and waiting endlessly for an uptown R train, she suddenly got a funny feeling and lowered her book. In the city, people were *often* watching other people, either out of boredom, or psychosis—or both, but it almost seemed as though—Christ, maybe she spent too much time reading books. Watching crime dramas.

She glanced at the people standing nearby, none of whom appeared to be out of the ordinary. Mostly business people, some students, the odd artistic type here and there. The train was taking forever to come, and everyone looked put out, but no one seemed to be paying even the slightest bit of attention to her.

On the downtown side, maybe? One man *did* look away a little too quickly, but—well, hell, sometimes men looked at women, and vice versa, and were embarrassed when they got caught. Paranoia was sometimes a healthy urban choice, but that didn't mean that someone was *after* her. And even if someone was, it was probably just a run-of-the-mill pickpocket. All she was doing here was giving herself the creeps.

Just to be safe, she wandered down the platform—staying, of course, well away from the edge—towards the token clerk's booth. It was the most populated and well-lit spot, and—it couldn't hurt.

She kept looking around, but still, no one seemed any more suspicious than her fellow New Yorkers *usually* did. Which was, granted, sometimes pretty suspicious, but—she was overusing her imagination, that's all. The fact that she made a practice of trusting her instincts didn't mean that they were always—or even *often*—right. She liked to tell herself that Irishness made her extremely extrasensorily acute, but that was probably just Celtic hubris.

It was a tremendous relief to see the train coming, and she made a point of jumping onto the most crowded car. For a second, she had a nightmarish tabloid-driven flash of the tightly packed car making it *easier* for some anonymous stranger to stab her discreetly, and then slip away in the confusion, but then she decided that she ought to re-grasp reality, open her book, and think of other things.

Although she was tired, she took the precaution of switching to the No. 6 train at 14th Street—not exactly the most direct route to the West Side—and then getting off at Grand Central to disappear in the late-rush-hour mob for a while. It was probably a waste of time, but she justified the detour by picking up the lone *Boston Globe* at one of the newsstands. Midtown was the only place she could ever find it, and this way, she could at least have some fun reading about what the Red Sox were doing at spring training.

Once she figured she had lost her almost certainly imaginary stalker, she dodged her way down to the Times Square Shuttle to take her normal route home. At some level, she felt like a complete fool, but she went ahead and got off a stop early, and walked circuitously to her building, by way of Sloan's, Blockbuster Video, and a Love's drugstore. Considering how tense she felt at the moment—antacids had been among her purchases at the drugstore—maybe she wasn't cut out for all of this.

And she still felt terrible about bullying a perfectly nice woman from Queens.

When she brought Bert out for his walk, she stuck to a route that took her past secure doorman buildings and the ever-busy Broadway—and noticed absolutely nothing unusual, beyond the fact that it was colder than ever. There had been a lot of snow this winter, which she hated, because it meant that she had to get up at the crack of dawn to shovel the building steps, the walkway, and the entire stretch of sidewalk out front. Then she had to sprinkle rock salt—which made her environmentally uncomfortable; or cat litter—which made a muddy mess—all over the place, and monitor the situation every few hours. The landlord, Mr. Abrams, worried constantly about the dire possibility of litigation, should some passing citizen take a stumble on his property. This was probably both wise, and responsible, of him, but it sure as hell made *her* life more difficult.

A couple of wet, slushy inches did fall during the night, but by the time she got outside, it was already melting. She shoveled the heavy mess away, and put out only a little bit of salt, as a precaution. Then, since she was still covering for Mr. Morales, the sick super at 320, she went down and cleared the slush away from his building, too.

It was a day full of niggling tasks that kept going wrong. Pipe fittings she couldn't loosen, a floodlight bulb that broke when she slipped off the ladder, the head of her hammer snapping right off when she struggled with an embedded nail.

All in all, not one for the record books.

Her mother called after dinner, and while Dana was feeling pretty cranky, she attempted not to sound that way—although her mother heard it, and so she allowed as how she had maybe had a long day, and then they spoke of other things, primarily the various types of good and bad luck their relatives were having, her parents included on this list. In both categories.

"So what are you thinking careerwise, lately?" her mother asked, after about twenty minutes.

Speed of lightning, roar of thunder, fighting all who rob and plunder. But since she wasn't sure about the whole thing herself yet, it would be foolish to share the idea at this point. "I think I'm getting tired of spending all my time taking out other people's trash," Dana said. And tonight, what with Mr. Morales, she would have double duty again.

"Well, I'm not surprised," her mother said, although she was obviously trying not to sound judgmental.

They had this conversation about every third phone call these days—but that was no reason not to have it again. "What do you think I should be doing?" Dana asked.

"Something like Second Chance," her mother said without hesitating.

Maybe teaching *was* where she was going to end up, but—Dana shook her head. "You know how much they *don't* pay? I'd end up out in Hoboken with two roommates."

"There are worse things," her mother said, although her voice lacked conviction.

Not much worse.

"Besides," her mother said, "if you're not going to be acting, you're not tied to New York anymore."

There were days when she would leave at the drop of even the smallest hat—and days when doing so seemed like a mistake she would never stop regretting. "I guess so," she said. "But I was thinking more along the lines of maybe going to law school, or—something." Maybe at Easter, she could broach the notion that it wasn't so much law school, as law *enforcement.* Of the self-employed variety. They would all be alarmed, but, probably, privately intrigued.

"Well, it's an idea," her mother said.

Dana laughed, since her parents had always made it pretty clear that they weren't fond of lawyers. At all. "Beats getting offered tampon commercials."

Her mother laughed, too. "You have a point, there."

When they hung up, her mother gave her the usual "be careful" warning, to which Dana responded reassuringly, feeling a small, but not insurmountable, conscience tweak. After all, she was *trying* to be careful.

The trash had to be taken out as late as possible since otherwise, homeless people tore the bags open, looking for bottles and cans to return for the deposit, and the garbage that got strewn everywhere was the responsibility of the building, not the sanitation department.

Which, in all likelihood, had something to do with certain uncharitable thoughts she would find herself having about denizens of the street, every time she was forced to clean up after them.

Bert very much wanted to come along with her, but worrying about his dashing into the street at any moment made her tense, and tying his leash to the iron gate that blocked access to the basement made *him* tense.

"Stay," she said, and pulled on an old sweatshirt, her Patriots cap, and some thick work gloves. Despite the cold, doing the trash was such hard work that wearing anything heavier would have her out of breath and perspiring in about three minutes.

The temperature had dropped, and an icy, slippery sleet was falling. She did her building first, complaining a lot—and swearing a *little*—under her breath, then walked the couple of blocks to Mr. Morales's building. She passed a bundled-up dog walker or two, but otherwise, the streets were pretty quiet.

The gate leading to his basement was on Riverside, and she shivered in the wind and sleet as she tried to unlock the old metal padlock that served as security. It was frozen, or else her hands were a little frozen, and she paused to let out one frustrated breath before trying again. This time, it worked, and she dropped her keys in her pocket and started to unlatch the gate.

"Dana Coakley?" a low voice said behind her.

She turned automatically, expecting Mr. Morales to have staggered up out of his sickbed, and had barely enough time to register that the man was a complete stranger before she saw the gun—an actual *gun*—in his hand, and pretty much went blank.

"Give me a reason," he said, his voice hard to understand through the scarf covering most of his face, a lowered hat shadowing the rest of it. All she could tell for sure was that he was *big.*

That she was in trouble.

There were headlights coming, and gun or no gun, she decided to jump in front of the car, in case the people might stop, and—they did stop, but it was a van, and the side door was open, and—oh, *Christ.*

It occurred to her, finally, to run, but she only made it a couple of steps before she slipped on the ice, and the man, along with at least one other, dragged her inside the van and slammed the door shut in about a second and a half.

"Go," someone said. "Go!"

"Not too fast," someone else said. "Just take it easy."

The van was lurching forward, skidding on the ice, and she made a panicked lunge for the door as more than one pair of hands slammed her down. There was thick plastic covering the floor, and—oh, Jesus, they were planning on having something to *clean up,* they—she tried for the door again, and this time, some of the hands were fists before they got her pinned, and something cold and heavy dug in just below her eye.

"Don't *move,*" the man from the street said through his teeth, pressing the gun even harder against her face.

Her mind, her heart, and her breath were all racing at once, but she didn't move, waiting for whatever unspeakable nightmare was going to happen next.

For whatever was left of her life.

Fifteen

For a very long minute, nobody else in the back of the van moved or spoke—maybe trying to scare her even more—and she realized that in addition to trembling horribly, she was crying, too. One of the men holding her down laughed, so he must also have noticed.

"I-I think you're making a mistake," she said, her voice sounding so scared that some tiny, rational part of her brain was deeply ashamed.

The same man laughed, while the others—there seemed to be two more, not counting the driver—just looked down at her, their ski masks looming out of the dark. There was a strange loud sound in her ears and she realized that it was her own breathing—and that they could hear it, too. Knew how scared she was. So she gulped a couple of times, trying to stop.

"I—look," she said, weakly. "I only have a little bit of money, I—" Dana. The man had called her Dana. Dana *Coakley.* This wasn't random sadistic monsters, this was *deliberate.* Premeditated. This was—Christ, who was it? "I don't know what you want, but—"

"I want you to shut up," the man with the gun said.

She shut up, every muscle in her body so tense that it made the trembling even worse.

He looked down at her, only his eyes visible through the mask, then abruptly yanked the gun away from her face. "All right," he said to the other two, and moved to sit on some sort of crate near the front, his body bulky enough to block what little street light was coming in through the windshield.

Were they maybe going to let her go now? Figured she was scared enough? She eased herself up onto one elbow, and then, when no one stopped her, up a little higher, ready to dive for freedom at the slightest opportunity.

One of the men—the one who had laughed—had moved behind her, and she glanced back at him, and then at the other one, who was very slowly pulling on a pair of surgical gloves. She sat up all the way, so many terrifying possibilities running through her mind that even thinking them was paralyzing.

"She's pretty small," the man holding the gun said, without much interest. "Try not to kill her by accident."

As the man with the gloves moved toward her, silent and featureless behind the mask, the other guy grabbed her upper arms, twisting them behind her back. She tried to pull free, but he just laughed, and tightened his grip.

The gloved man drew his hand back, and she wasn't sure if she actually said, "Please, don't"—or just thought it. But, either way, he hit her, and it hurt so much that she was almost more surprised than anything else. Actually, no, *not* almost—but, somewhere inside her head, still surprised, as she tried to avoid the next blow, her upper body bouncing off the chest of the guy behind her.

It was—businesslike. Methodical. Dispassionate. She wanted to fight back—her legs were free, and she could probably kick him instead of just struggling pointlessly, but if she *hurt* him—made him angry—he would hit her even *harder,* and—she heard a snap—her nose breaking?—and groaned, feeling blood, and tears, and pain, so dizzy and scared that all she could do was pray for them to stop, and that she wouldn't be dead by then.

The man with the gun was saying something about "working the cage," so the punches were slamming into her ribs now, and each time, she would hear little weak groans and gasps bubble out. The man holding her was clearly enjoying all of this, and kept muttering such graphic, mostly sexual, threats into her ear that, suddenly overwhelmed by fury, she drove her elbow back into him as hard as she could, managing to twist free and lunge blindly to where she thought the door might be. For a second, her hands scraped across the metal handle, but she couldn't make it work, and they were swearing and dragging her away.

She was remotely aware of more pain—it seemed as though they were both hitting her now, but then, the guy with the gun must have told them to stop, because she was just lying on the sticky plastic, so dazed and hurt that she wasn't even sure if she was conscious or not.

A hand knotted in the front of her sweatshirt, pulling her up, and the one with the gun seemed to be talking at her, but she couldn't focus on what he was saying. Then, he did something to a couple of her fingers that was so painful that she heard a sort of yelping scream come out, and woke up enough to pay attention.

"Next time, it's a rape murder," he said. "Hear me?"

Jesus—*next* time?

"Come on, man," the big guy who'd been holding her said, laughing again. "We got her here, let's do her now."

"Shut up," the man with the gun said, and turned to the driver. "Slow down a little."

Dana wanted to ask exactly what it was that she had *done,* why they were so mad, but she couldn't seem to get her mouth—or her mind—to work right, and besides, they would probably start hitting her again.

The man with the gun slid the van door open, then shook her to make sure she was listening. "Anyone asks, you got mugged," he said. "The police can't help you, *no one* can help you. Got it? You talk, and you're *dead."*

Then they were shoving her out, and she landed half in and half out of an icy puddle, hearing a distinct crunch inside her shoulder as she slammed against the cement. The van pulled away, and more wet snow and ice splashed onto her.

She was too hurt and afraid to move, so she stayed right where she was, letting the filthy slush seep into her clothes. She *wanted* to pass out, but couldn't quite seem to do it, and soon, she was so cold from the puddle that she used her legs to push herself out of the gutter and up onto the sidewalk, groaning all the way.

Throwing up seemed like another good idea, but she couldn't manage that, either, so she just lay there, shivering. She realized, then, that they might come back, and that she had to get away from here before they did. Get away *now.*

Okay. Okay. She'd start by turning over. She pushed, tentatively, against the cold gritty sidewalk with her left hand, but trying to move her shoulder was so excruciating that she gasped and slumped back down again.

Oh, Christ. She was in trouble here. Wherever the hell here *was.* What if they'd taken her miles? What if—all right, all right. More crying and panicking weren't going to help much. She took a deep breath—which *hurt*—and tried again, using her legs and good arm to do the work, allowing herself to make any whimpering sounds she needed to make to get through the agony of jarring her shoulder. Once she was lying on her back, she rested for a minute, trying to breathe—shallowly—her way through the aftershocks of pain, looking up at a lone orange-tinted street light through the eye that would still open partway.

There were headlights coming, and—pain or no pain—she dragged herself around the side of the nearest building to hide, praying that they wouldn't see her. The car passed—an ordinary car, not a van—without even pausing, and she relaxed a little, finding enough courage to look around and see where she was.

The street was dimly lit and deserted, and she seemed to be next to an auto body shop. It was closed up for the night, with several cars parked crookedly on the embankment behind her, one car illegally on the sidewalk. Across the street, she could see a cast-iron fence and trees, so it must be some kind of park. Nothing looked familiar, and she hunched against the brick wall of the garage, shivering, not sure what to do. It *really* hurt to breathe, and she pressed her good arm against her side, hunching lower.

Except they still might come back. Hurt her more. It took a couple of tries, but using the brick wall for support, she managed to stand up—and was so dizzy that she almost collapsed. She waited the dizziness out, then straightened up all the way, her right arm hanging uselessly. Christ, she'd gotten hurt before, but—this was something new. Something much more serious.

She still wasn't sure where she was, but it was so isolated that it had to be somewhere near the river, and she took a few lurching steps toward what might be Eleventh Avenue. The sidewalk was treacherously rutted with haphazard, grimy piles of snow, and she fell once, feeling her jeans tear at the knees. It hurt, but everything else hurt, too, so she didn't bother groaning and just staggered up again.

More headlights passed, and didn't pause, and it occurred to her, dully, that seeing a huddled figure stumbling along a New York City street wasn't exactly uncommon. In fact, as she got closer to the corner, she could see a small homeless encampment running along the side of the park. There were thick piles of clothes and blankets that almost certainly concealed people, with a dark, scuttling shape here and there behind the fence, and the ubiquitous sound of bagged cans and bottles being moved.

There was a locked chain-link fence closing off a delivery-truck-filled parking lot, and she used it for support, each step seeming to take more effort than the last, keeping a bleary focus on just making it to the corner.

It *was* Eleventh Avenue, and she stayed in the shadows, shivering, trying to figure out what to do next. To make her brain work. Everything seemed to be closed, except for a gas station down the street, but she didn't want strangers to see her like this—or to call the police—so she staggered off the other way, past the park. But, even in this weather, there seemed to be some prostitutes and furtive men—who were presumably drug dealers, pimps, or both—lurking near the cast-iron fence, and they might come after her, so she veered into the street, a car beeping its horn and swerving past her.

Okay. Okay. It would be stupid to get run over. She couldn't see very well, but there didn't seem to be much traffic—was it late?—and as soon as there was a break in the headlights, she doggedly made her way across. There were a few more bundles of rags and cardboard boxes against the buildings that were probably really human beings, but no one bothered her, and she just kept going.

Her first instinct was to try and walk home, except that she still wasn't completely sure where she was, and—it would also be stupid. Pay phone. She needed a pay-phone.

There was one on the next corner, but when she lifted the receiver, there—naturally—was no dial tone. She was so cold and afraid that she wanted to burst into tears, but she forced herself to keep going until she found another one across the street.

Money. Reaching awkwardly across her body with her good hand, she forced it into her wet front pocket, pulling out some change. Her fingers were so numb that she dropped most of it, and she stared, stupidly, at the icy sidewalk, exhausted by the thought of having to try and pick the money up. She felt around in her pocket some more, retrieved another quarter, and shoved it into the slot, dialing clumsily.

She was afraid that the machine might pick up, but Peggy answered right away, sounding half-asleep.

It was such a relief to hear a familiar voice that she had to gulp back more tears.

"Hello?" Peggy said again, then let out her breath. "Goddamn it, Sam—"

"It's me," Dana said, except that her voice would barely come out because she couldn't really move her jaw. "I mean, I'm sorry, I—"

"What do you want?" Peggy asked impatiently. "Do you know what time it is?"

No. "I—" She *really* wanted to cry. "I'm sorry to call so late, I—"

"What's wrong?" Peggy asked, her voice switching from irritation to alarm. "You sound really weird."

"I'm sorry, I, uh—" The sidewalk seemed unsteady under her feet and she sagged against the telephone. "I-I need help."

"Where are you?" Peggy said. *Demanded.*

Oh, Christ. Dana looked around, hanging on to the phone so

she wouldn't fall. "I don't know. Somewhere in the Fifties, I think."

On the other end of the line, she could hear Peggy suck her breath in, but her voice was very calm when she spoke. "I'm going to need a little more than that, okay, Dana?"

Dana looked in the direction of the nearest street sign, but couldn't seem to get the eye that was still working to focus. Christ, where was she? "There's a park," she said slowly. From this angle, it looked more familiar and she frowned, trying to remember why. "I think I see people playing softball there."

"They're playing softball right *now?*" Peggy said.

Well—no. Christ, it was freezing out. "In the summer," Dana said. "When I go by in a cab. It's on Eleventh."

There was a brief silence on the other end. "Okay. Somewhere in the Fifties, on Eleventh," Peggy said. "Look, don't move, all right? I'm on my—"

"Wait a minute," Dana said, and dropped the receiver, hearing Peggy yelling for her not to hang up. She made her way over to the street sign, squinted at the blur until it made sense, and then lurched back to the telephone. "Fifty-third. South—um—East corner."

Peggy let out her breath, obviously relieved to hear her voice again. "Okay. Fifty-third and Eleventh. You want me to call the police, or—"

"No police!" Dana said—almost shouted.

"Okay, okay," Peggy said, her voice extraordinarily calm. "Take it easy, all right? Is there someplace warm you can wait until I get there?"

Not likely. "I'll be fine," Dana said, noticing for the first time that her teeth were chattering as much as her swollen jaw would allow. "Don't worry."

"On my way," Peggy said, and hung up.

She wasn't sure where to wait, but then she saw a small, crooked stoop in front of an old abandoned building and went to sit down on it. The sleet was falling again, harder than before, and she ducked as low as she could, using her good shoulder to try and shield herself.

At this point, she was more tired than anything else, and it was hard to stay awake. She let herself doze, jerking awake every time a car went by, but none of them stopped. Also, luckily, none of them were vans.

It seemed like a long time before she heard a car door, and saw Peggy jumping out of a taxi, holding an extra coat and looking around frantically.

"Over here," Dana said, although it came out as more of a groan.

"Oh, Jesus," Peggy said, and hurried over, bundling her into the coat. "Are you all right? What happened?"

Was she going to lie to her best friend? Who had gotten up in the middle of the night, out of a sound sleep, no questions asked? Dana swallowed, and reached for the stair railing to try and pull herself up.

"I got mugged," she said.

She didn't want to go to the hospital—for one thing, New York emergency rooms were a horror show; for another, she hadn't even *started* on her very high deductible yet for this year—but Peggy made it clear that she wasn't going to argue about it, so Dana just slumped into the back seat of the cab and struggled not to doze off again.

Then, they were in a chaotic emergency room, where Peggy filled out forms and got testier and testier, the longer they had to wait. Dana tried to pay attention, but mostly just slept, wrapped up in the warm, probably too expensive, now blood-stained, wool coat. Someone in scrubs came out to check her over at one point, and there was a lot of talk about it being a busy night, and could she hang on a little longer, and they would get to her as soon as they could.

Finally, she was taken down for X-rays—a lot of X-rays—and then, into a curtained treatment room, with Peggy barreling on in right after her.

"Excuse me," one of the nurses said, trying to block her way. "You'll have to wait—"

"Come on now, you just let me through," Peggy said sharply. "I'm her sister."

The nurse nodded. "That's fine, but—"

"I'm *staying,"* Peggy said, looking even more threatening than she sounded.

"All right," the nurse said, and backed off. "Fine. Whatever."

More than one doctor came in, studying the various X-rays, talking about things like possible splenic trauma and lung contusions, and could they do a closed reduction of the AC joint, and where was an orthopod when they needed one? They also used words like "cracked" and "fractured," the meanings of which were perfectly clear.

For the most part, they acted as though she and Peggy weren't even in the room, but when they asked what had happened, she said again that she had been mugged, and everybody made a lot of remarks about how dangerous New York was, and how they all had every intention of moving at the first possible opportunity, and that it was just *criminal* that people couldn't walk around on the streets anymore—in the middle of which, there was another loud flurry of activity outside the curtains, and for a few minutes, her treatment room cleared out.

"Jesus," Peggy said. "This is a nightmare."

Dana looked up with an effort, groggy from whatever painkillers it was that they had given her. "I told you I didn't want to come."

"Yeah, I know," Peggy said, and reached over to touch her good arm lightly. "Hang on. It won't be too much longer."

The *hell* it wouldn't.

Sixteen

After the interns and residents finally finished patching and stitching and splinting her up, the attending wanted to admit her for the next day or two—more for observation than anything else, although at least she didn't have a concussion. Dana was going to argue, but after one look at Peggy's expression, she meekly agreed and was wheeled upstairs.

Other than a few quick calls to make sure that her pets would be okay, and one significantly longer call to her boss, Dana spent most of the next thirty-six hours in a painkiller-induced daze. Mr. Abrams had been very cranky when she told him she wasn't going to be able to work for—well, a while, anyway—and he made cross remarks about his supers dropping like flies, until she pointed out that she had been accosted—and suffered several broken bones—while *on his property*—upon which he became suddenly sympathetic, telling her to take some time off, rest up, and let him know if he could do anything, anything at all.

She *really* wanted to call her family and let them know what was going on, but what would she say? Her parents, and at least one, if not both, of her sisters, would immediately depart for New York—and they would be even more upset when they saw how she looked. If they discovered how, and *why,* she had gotten hurt, all hell was going to break loose—and she wanted to avoid that, if possible. Since the hospital was only going to keep her for a couple of nights, her family might not ever—if she was lucky—even find out that this had happened.

Frankly, *she* couldn't handle thinking about the whole thing—let alone discuss it with anyone else. Since they were helping out with her pets, Craig and a couple of other people from her building came to visit, with bright bouquets, but other than that, Peggy was the only person who even knew that she was in the hospital—and Dana wanted to keep it that way.

The day that the hospital released her, Peggy left work early—purely of her own volition—and came to pick her up. Dana signed insurance forms, made depressingly complicated payment arrangements, accepted brand-new prescription slips, listened to detailed medical advice, and just generally nodded politely whenever it seemed to be appropriate.

A very nice, round-faced orderly wheeled her outside, and helped her inside the cab Peggy had already hailed.

"Do you feel as awful as you look?" Peggy asked, once they were on their way uptown.

Instead of answering, Dana tried to smile—which pulled at her stitches.

Peggy nodded. "I figured."

For the most part, they rode in silence, with Dana huddling into Peggy's too-large coat that she still had from the night of the attack, feeling as though she was going to be shivering for the rest of her life. In the hospital, the floor nurses kept bringing her more blankets, but she still could never *quite* get warm.

With a lot of concentration, she managed to lift her head enough to look over at Peggy, who was sitting very straight, looking uncharacteristically nervous and unsure of herself. Also, tired.

"I, uh—" No matter what the doctors said, her jaw sure *felt* dislocated—"I'm sorry," Dana said. "I think I ruined your coat."

Peggy looked confused. "What? Oh. Don't worry about it."

They both could use a little humor right about now. "You, uh, have a good dry cleaner?" Dana asked.

Peggy smiled for a second, then looked worried again.

Humor maybe wasn't what she wanted to convey here, anyway. "I meant, *thank you,*" Dana said, and was acutely embarrassed to feel tears come spilling out. "Really. I don't know how I'll ever—"

Peggy cut her off, looking pretty embarrassed herself. "Forget it," she said.

Not likely. Not *ever.* Dana swallowed a couple of times, and tried to stop crying, without much success.

"Think of it this way," Peggy said. "If it had been the other way around, you would have been much more polite to the doctors."

Probably. Smiling hurt almost more than anything else, so Dana didn't bother—but at least she thought of doing it.

Even with Peggy helping her, she almost fell trying to get out the cab when it stopped in front of her building. The steps were slippery, too.

Steps for which she was responsible.

"Salt," she said weakly. "I have to get salt."

"I don't, um—to eat?" Peggy asked.

Dana shook her head, which made her so dizzy that she lurched to one side, knocking both of them off-balance. "The steps," she said, and almost burst into tears again.

"Come on," Peggy said, gently. "You'll feel better once we're upstairs."

To Dana's relief, they didn't run into any tenants on the way. Even polite expressions of concern would probably send her off the deep end right about now.

When Peggy unlocked her door, the animals seemed fine, if unusually eager to see her, and after clumsily patting each of them, Dana found her way to a chair. Bert, in particular, was beside himself, and kept trying to jump on her—banging her separated shoulder repeatedly.

"Does he need a walk?" Peggy asked, trying, cautiously, to haul him away.

Did he? What an exhausting thought. "I have no idea," Dana said, and struggled to stand up. "Probably, yeah."

Peggy shook her head. "Don't worry, I'll take him."

Except, of course, Peggy wasn't exactly an animal person—and had also already done more than her share. "No, it's okay," Dana said. "I can—"

Peggy frowned at her. "I'll *do* it, okay?"

Too tired to protest, Dana sank back down, watching Peggy snap on his leash. "You, um, have to bring plastic baggies," she said. "To clean up after."

"I know," Peggy said defensively. "I've seen you do it."

And almost certainly been disgusted.

The thought of crying some more was tempting, but she just sat and waited, only staggering up to her feet when she realized that the cats needed to be fed and probably to have their water dish filled.

She was trying, ineffectually, to do so, when Peggy came back in and relieved her of the job, even remembering—to her surprise—to give Bert a Milkbone before ushering Dana into the bathroom to get cleaned up and ready for bed.

Changing into a fresh Lanz nightgown was a very painful process, but Dana managed to do it—and avoid even the slightest glance at the mirror. When she came out, Peggy was waiting with a glass of water and two of the pain pills. Dana took them without any discussion, still barely able to open her jaw enough to get them into her mouth, and then was also cooperative about getting into bed with several quilts on top of her.

"I'm okay now," she said, hearing her voice shake. "Thank you for everything. You should go back to work."

"I think they can struggle along without me for the afternoon," Peggy said wryly.

Well, yeah. In fact, in all probability, most of Peggy's staff was delighted by this turn of events.

"Listen, I have to ask you something," Peggy said, before turning out the light.

Dana opened her eyes.

Peggy looked at her with great intensity. "You *were* telling that rape advocate the truth, right?"

The rape advocate had been one of the many people who had come through her treatment room back in the ER. Dana nodded.

"Okay. But, I—" Peggy frowned, and then stopped, apparently thinking better of proceeding. "Okay. Do you need anything else?"

To *sleep.* Dana shook her head, and closed her eyes again.

She had thought that she would feel better after a few hours of sleep—but she had thought wrong. In fact, the pain was even worse, and getting out of bed seemed utterly insurmountable. Finally, though, she eased her way to a sitting—and groaning—position, so stiff that she might as well be in a body cast. Walking the ten feet to the living room seemed beyond her capacity, but—after what felt like about an hour and a half—she made it, to find Peggy sitting at the kitchen table, taking extensive notes on a legal pad, as she talked on the phone and drank tea.

"Considering that I am, for once, *delegating* here, it seems little enough—" She saw Dana, and paused. "All right, look. Just take care of it, and I'll call you back." She hung up the phone, looking concerned now, instead of piqued. "What's going on? Why are you up?"

"I've got an audition later," Dana said. "I don't want to be late."

Which Peggy didn't seem to find amusing.

"Well," Dana said, and tried to sit down across from her. Jesus. If being elderly felt like this, she was already dreading it.

"Are you hungry," Peggy said, "or—?"

Dana shook her head just enough to convey a no. Edith jumped up onto her lap, which hurt so much that she almost swatted her, before remembering that that would be a terrible thing to do.

"Do you feel as bad as you look?" Peggy asked.

Yes. Like death would be a step *up.* Dana nodded, already regretting this ambitious foray out of bed. The bottle of pain pills was in the middle of the table and she tipped one out, taking it with the glass of water Peggy handed her.

"One of the cats threw up, before," Peggy said. "It might be sick."

Theodore, probably. "It's okay," Dana said. Christ, if this was what an *un*broken jaw felt like, she wouldn't be able to handle a broken one. "They do that a lot."

Peggy was clearly appalled, but she just nodded.

Christ. Had she *ever* been this exhausted? Felt so lousy?

"I wrote the messages down, but you've got about fifteen hang-ups on your answering machine," Peggy said.

That many? Dana lifted her head about half an inch. "Telemarketers, maybe?" Then she realized that if she had been answering the phone, at least some of the calls would probably have been *threats.* "Weird," she said, not having enough energy to elaborate.

"I thought so, yeah," Peggy agreed.

It was very quiet, except for the radiator clanking, and her embarrassingly labored breaths.

"Of course, the call I *answered,* where a man growled something obscene about hoping that I'd gotten the point was even stranger," Peggy said.

Off the top of her head, that one was going to be hard to explain. "Well," Dana avoided her eyes, "that *is* strange."

It was quiet again, although Peggy's obvious, if silent, fury seemed deafening.

Using her good arm for support, Dana pushed herself to her feet. "You know, maybe I will have something to eat, after all."

"It was an odd neighborhood for you to be wandering around in, late at night," Peggy said, watching her open the refrigerator.

Couldn't this conversation *wait?* Dana took out a Coke and awkwardly opened it. "The Ensemble Studio Theater's down near there," she said, after a minute.

"Oh." Peggy nodded. "Good show?"

They both knew that she was lying, so this was a stupid charade.

"You're very lucky, though," Peggy said, and pushed some wrinkled bills toward her. "I found these when I was unpacking the clothes you were wearing." She paused. "*Most* people who get mugged don't come home with any money."

No. They didn't, did they. And, of course, insofar as an explanation was concerned, her mind was a complete blank.

"Go figure," Dana said, finally.

"They must have missed that pocket," Peggy said.

Yes. What luck.

"Although," Peggy looked at her steadily, "considering what close friends we're supposed to be, the truth might be another, perfectly valid, option."

Right. But she was too tired to get into it—and would rather not give the whole situation a lot of thought, anyway.

Christ, she was tired.

"Well?" Peggy asked, looking tense.

"I don't know," Dana said.

Peggy frowned, and glanced over at the triple-locked front door. "Well, who did this to you?"

Good question. In fact, *very* good question. Especially since they hadn't come close to identifying themselves, and right now, she didn't really feel up to pondering the possibilities. "I have no idea," she said—the enormity of which was really quite terrifying.

Peggy didn't seem to like that answer much, but it did have the advantage of being true.

The conversation wasn't even close to being over, but Bert was bouncing around and making it clear he needed another walk, so Peggy got up to take him, grimly stuffing several Baggies into her coat pocket.

When she got back, Peggy went straight to the sink and made something of a production of washing her hands, rubbing the lather well up her forearms. Then, she turned on the gas beneath the kettle on the stove.

"Going to sterilize yourself with boiling water now?" Dana asked, trying to bend over enough to unhook Bert's leash.

"I'm sorry," Peggy said, and unsnapped his leash herself. "It's gross, okay?"

Mostly, she didn't give it any thought, but yes, sometimes, it was gross.

Peggy took down two mugs, and set up the filter and coffee in Dana's drip coffeemaker. Then she sat down to wait for the water to boil, making very pointed eye contact.

"I'm really not sure what's going on, and I don't want to get you involved," Dana said.

Peggy scowled at her. "Wake up—I'm *already* involved."

Unfortunately, yeah.

"Look, I think we'd better call the police," Peggy said. "The longer we wait—"

Dana sighed. "I don't even know who it was. Hell, I don't even really know *why* it was. But I *do* know that when they started making threats about rape-murders and all, if I told anyone—they weren't kidding."

Peggy sighed. "Well, I think that's why we need the police, isn't it?"

Dana shook her head as vehemently as she could, which wasn't very, but still probably got her point across. Even if the police believed her, what were they going to do—move in? Follow her around twenty-four hours a day?

"Okay," Peggy said, sounding as though she might be grinding her teeth. "Fine." The kettle started whistling, and she got up to turn off the heat, banging around more than was necessary as she made the coffee.

Dana let out her breath—which hurt. "I'm sorry, okay? I just—this one's new for me, and—I kind of just want to do exactly what they said, and pretend none of it ever happened."

"What if we hired a private investigator or something?" Peggy suggested. "Or, I don't know, some security, or a bodyguard."

"Sounds economical," Dana said.

Peggy shook her head impatiently. "Let's not worry about *that* aspect of it, okay? I mean, Jesus Christ, there are some lunatics out there who apparently want to—"

Kill her. Yeah. Dana sagged far enough forward to rest her head on her good arm. "So, I'll go away for a few days," she said. And what, hope they *forgot?* "Or—I mean, if I have to, I'll move."

Peggy looked surprised. "Really? I mean, obviously, *yes,* that would be the most intelligent alternative, but—really? *Move?"*

Would she? Just up, and pack her stuff, leave all her friends, and this stupid violent city, and go to God knows where to do God only knows what?

"I don't know," Dana said quietly. "I wish I did."

They looked at each other, and then Peggy sighed, and went back to making coffee.

Dana spent the next few days alternating between sleeping heavily, and having terrible, complicated nightmares, which were either pharmaceutically induced, posttraumatic—or some combination of the two. She told anyone who stopped by or called—including Mr. Abrams, who appeared at one point with a large bunch of flowers, his face going pale when he saw her—that she had been mugged.

Except, of course, she didn't tell her family anything. Since they talked regularly—to, and probably too often, *about* one another—they had all called at some point in the last day or two, and all been extremely suspicious about the way she sounded. Dreading the possibility of one of them sensing serious trouble, with some weird Irish intuition thing, Dana allowed as how she had God-awful flu—and felt just plain stinking *lousy.*

This last part requiring no acting ability whatsoever.

She was going to have to tell them the truth if she did something drastic like—relocate, or join a Franciscan order—but until then, explaining that she had been stalked and beaten by ruthless killers and was, even now, in moments of brief lucidity, more terrified than she would have guessed humanly possible, wasn't exactly going to be happy, or restful, news.

Peggy happened to be there when she was going through the "oh, I'll be fine, just taking it easy, drinking lots of fluids" song and dance with her sister Elizabeth, and when she hung up, Peggy looked at her with absolutely no expression.

Dana sighed. "Don't think so loud."

"Loud*ly,"* Peggy said.

Yeah, fine, whatever. "They already worry about me living in New York," Dana said. "What am I supposed to do, tell them *fiends* are after me, I'm so hurt I can't even *breathe,* my life is a complete disaster—and, oh, hey, how about those Celtics?"

Peggy shrugged, but rather judgmentally.

"If I hadn't had to call you that night, I would have lied to you, too," Dana said, without taking the time to think, first.

"What a comforting thought," Peggy said, and went back to the manuscript she had been reading.

Prolonging the discussion was not likely to improve it, so Dana poured herself a glass of juice to take back to bed, an operation that was far more strenuous than would normally be the case. When she'd told Elizabeth she was drinking lots of fluids, she had actually been telling the truth, because she still couldn't chew, or even really move her jaw enough to do more than shove a straw between her teeth on the side of her mouth that didn't have stitches. Craig had been stopping by regularly with odd, thick health shakes—or, more enjoyably, milkshakes from McDonald's—and she could manage things like thin soup, if she let it cool enough first, but in addition to feeling drugged and in pain, she was increasingly so damn *hungry* that it was sometimes hard to think of anything else.

Even the notion of being raped and murdered for no readily apparent reason.

The hang-ups, at least, had stopped, and she could only hope that they had decided that she had been duly scared off, and was no longer worth their time and attention. Christ knows she had no intention of pursuing any of it any further. If the police and fire departments wanted to see justice served, that would be swell and all, but she, for one, was *out* of it.

She also hated every second of having to impose on people this way and, even though the idea was unpleasant, she was going to have to go out in public someday.

Someday *soon.*

She took a trial run that very night, wrapping up in a heavy jacket and scarf, with a Red Sox cap pulled down low so passers-by wouldn't notice the bruised, swollen shape that had once been her face, and then walking Bert very cautiously to the corner and back. She had told her neighbor Maryanne that she was—gun-shy—since the mugging, and Maryanne, very sweetly, waited for her just inside the foyer, and was encouraging and enthusiastic upon her safe return.

Her morning walk—all the way around the block this time,

fighting a wild panic attack with almost every single step—was equally uneventful, but at this rate, it was going to be *weeks* before she even made it as far as Barnes & Noble—forget anywhere off the West Side. And, since it would be nice to resume some tiny semblance of a normal, if recuperatory, life, she was going to have to take some kind of positive action.

Obviously, they must have been following her, or staking her out, or something, before she'd been attacked, so the first thing to do was figure out if they were still around. Valerie was one of the many people she had avoided calling, and telling about the supposed mugging—she hadn't even returned Valerie's two "what's up, haven't heard from you" calls on her answering machine—but this wasn't something she could do alone, and out of everyone she knew, Valerie was the *least* likely to ask uneasy, or accusatory, questions.

So she called her, and after exchanging appropriate pleasantries and finding out exactly what it was—celery sticks—that Valerie was crunching so loudly, Dana took as deep a breath as she could manage.

"Uh, I was wondering," she said. "If I wanted you to do me a kind of strange favor, would you promise not to ask me why?"

"Sure," Valerie said, and crunched. "What's up?"

The key, would be making sure that this would, in no way, endanger—or even overly involve—her. Dana took her time answering, still trying to figure out a decent plan. "I need to go out, and—I'd tell you what route I was going to take, and all—and have you see if anyone's following me."

"Whoa," Valerie said. "More detective stuff?"

Self-preservation stuff, actually. Dana nodded. "Pretty much, yeah."

"Cool," Valerie said, crunched some more, and then audibly swallowed. "When do we start?"

Seventeen

In the end, the plan was pretty simple. Dana would leave her apartment at two o'clock, and head up Broadway to the post office. Then she would come back on Amsterdam, before cutting over to Broadway again and making stops at a predesignated Korean grocer, a card shop, and a bodega. Then, in case they were more worried about her going somewhere than just wandering around the neighborhood, she would go down into the subway, emerging a short time later from the other entrance.

Throughout which, Valerie would be someplace nearby, lurking about entirely unnoticed.

Dana *hoped.*

Just after two, she left her building, avoiding the temptation to look around and see exactly where Valerie was. She had said that she was going to wear a disguise, which would, with luck, be nondescript. For her part, Dana had warned her that she'd had a little accident recently—what, walked into a mantelpiece?—and not to be surprised to see her looking a little battle-scarred.

Although her own first glance in the mirror had been a shock.

She took her time running her manufactured errands, trying to make them seem casual and inconsequential, and wishing that she didn't feel as though there was a large red target painted on her back. Broadway was usually pretty busy, and if someone wanted to take a quick shot at her and run away, the person wouldn't have much trouble disappearing into the crowd.

The whole excursion was very stressful, and also damned tiring, and after leaving the subway station, Dana was so worn out that the thought of walking the rest of the way home seemed beyond her capacity.

Naturally, a homeless person came lurching over from a nearby doorway, and started begging her for change, shaking one of the predictable blue and white cardboard coffee cups.

"Can I have a quarter, miss?" the woman asked, in a sort of slurred, imperious whine.

Not that she was drifting ever closer to Republicanism, but Dana was so instantly and irrationally furious that she felt her good hand clenching and had to concentrate on looking straight ahead. Christ, you'd think they would give her an injury dispensation.

"Come on, miss," the woman said, looming closer. "Buy me a sam'wich, miss."

Normally, of course, she would have just quickened her pace and the person would have veered over to bother someone else, but at the moment, she wasn't moving well enough to outdistance anyone.

"Come *on,* miss," the woman said, more insinuatingly aggressive now, giving her good arm a light push. "Buy me a sam'wich."

Dana *absolutely hated* it when strangers touched her in New York, and she was going to whirl around and snarl something unpleasant—if not, in fact, obscene—until she realized that it was Valerie, wearing an uncannily accurate homeless outfit, right down to the odd smear of dirt here and there.

If you were going to ask an actress to put on a disguise, it was always smart to ask a very *talented* actress.

"So, do I get that quarter or not?" Valerie asked, and shook her cup.

Dana grinned, although not too widely, in case anyone was watching them. "That's good," she said, looking her over. "That's very good." Jesus, the walk, the voice, the cup, the bulky layers—all of it was right on the money.

"Yeah, I thought it was okay," Valerie agreed happily, then

shook her head. "Boy, I'm glad I'm not *really* homeless, though. When did you turn into such a damn New Yorker?"

Well, yeah. Somewhere along the line, hostility and humanity had traded places, hadn't they.

To her detriment.

Valerie looked down into her cup, which had quite a lot of change and a few bills inside. "Come on. I'll buy *you* a sandwich."

Dana hesitated. "Did you see anyone, or—?"

"No, you're cool," Valerie said. "I got to your block way early and there wasn't anyone around then, either. Well, I mean, UPS and people like that, but no one stayed any longer than they had to."

Dana nodded. Okay. One worry down. "Um, look," she said. "I'm sorry I was rude, I—"

Valerie waved that aside. "*Everyone's* sick of the homeless, okay? I don't mean it's good, but it isn't what you'd call unusual."

No. Compassion fatigue, they called it. Sort of like—collateral damage, and necessary losses.

"So, come on," Valerie said. "Let's go eat."

She was so ravenous all the time—still—that it was a hard offer to turn down. Not that she could chew, but she could probably get some soup or something. Scrambled eggs, maybe. However, in the interests of caution, she hung back. "Just in case, I don't want anyone to see you with me."

"First of all, there's no one there," Valerie said, "and second, they would never recognize me again."

Well, no. This filthy, ragged apparition in no way resembled the actual Valerie, so it was probably safe.

They went to the nearest diner, and although the waitress obviously didn't want to seat them, Valerie started waving her bills around and going into imperious character again.

"If you'll notice," Dana said to the waitress, aware that with her current, odd Spirit of '76 look, she probably seemed pretty disreputable, too, "she actually smells quite nice."

Valerie nodded. "Bijan. And *loaded* with moola, to boot."

The waitress didn't like it, but led them to a small table well away from anyone else. Valerie sat down first, dumping the contents of her cup on her place mat to count the money.

"Did people actually give all of that to you?" Dana asked, easing herself down.

"Yup," Valerie said, and grinned. "Bless their little liberal hearts."

Hmmm. Dana frowned. "Maybe we should just put it in a poor box, or—"

"Are you kidding?" Valerie asked. "I *earned* this—believe me."

Which didn't make it any less weird. "I'll spring for this, anyway," Dana said. "I mean, you did me a big favor."

"And what," Valerie said, "you're Guilt Queen now, so we'll have to give all of this to the first homeless person we see when we leave?"

Dana nodded. "Can we? I'll pay you back."

Valerie swept the money back into her cup and set it upright. "No sweat. I had a fun time."

A fun time. Dana liked expressions like "a fun time." She unzipped her jacket—the guy in 5E had zipped her into it when she ran into him on her way downstairs—and slipped it off her bad arm and onto the back of the chair.

Valerie looked much more serious. "I know you warned me, but I'm still not sure I would have recognized you without the Red Sox cap."

Dana shrugged her good shoulder. "It looks worse than it is."

Valerie just looked worried. "Was it that Mojo and his creepy friends?"

It would have been better if it *had* been. Amoral teenagers were somehow less terrifying than cognizant, educated-sounding adults. "No," Dana said. "Don't worry, it was no big deal."

Now, Valerie looked hurt. "When did it happen? I mean, how come you didn't *call* me? I could have been bringing you groceries and all."

Another friend whose feelings she was managing to hurt. Dana nodded, taking out a pack of cigarettes—yes, she had backslid entirely—and lighting one. "I know. I've just been—kind of numb, I guess." Then she squinted at one of the smears on Valerie's face. "That's not makeup, is it."

"Potting soil," Valerie said.

Well, yeah, now that she looked more closely, she could see little bits of vermiculite here and there.

"So, talk to me," Valerie said. "I mean, are you in trouble, or—"

The Question of the Week. Dana shook her head. "I think that whoever they were, they just wanted to make sure that they'd scared me off."

"Well"—Valerie looked worried again—"did they?"

Dana nodded, and exhaled some smoke. "Damn straight," she said.

The soup du jour was mediocre split pea, but she enjoyed it, anyway. It was pretty pathetic that her jaw couldn't handle the Saltines that came with it, but at least she got the soup down.

Valerie wanted to come home with her and, as she put it, *minister* to her, but then she admitted that she was early person at the restaurant where she worked and should probably go shower away her potting soil so she wouldn't be late for her shift.

On the whole, Dana was relieved, because she really needed some time alone. Total hibernation had a definite appeal right now. The phone kept ringing, but she screened all of the calls, only picking up when she heard Peggy. All week long, their conversations had been stiff and uneasy, and this one, unfortunately, was no exception, with Dana insisting that she was fine, no problem, they could talk again tomorrow, and Peggy answering with terse sures, and whatever-you-says.

Hanging up, she felt a certain amount of dread—a few years earlier, she'd had a terrible, apparently permanent, falling out with her closest friend from college, for no good reason, and there was something distinctly familiar about the way she and Peggy were currently speaking to each other. Or, more accurately, speaking *at* each other.

Either way, she just took another painkiller—even though it was too soon—made sure that the door was triple-locked, and climbed into bed with the lights out. The cats were quick to join her, and she slept endlessly, waking up only to take Bert for a long-overdue walk, and then going right back to bed.

A pattern she repeated the next day, except *this* time, she didn't pick up the phone at all, and when the doorbell rang—Craig, probably—she didn't answer that, either. Sleeping was easy; sleeping was *safe.* In fact, if it hadn't been for Bert, she probably wouldn't have gotten out of bed at all.

When she was awake, she would stare at the ceiling, or her bookcases, still trying to get her mind around the fact that some complete strangers had been punching her. Repeatedly. Jesus. *Punching* her. She and her sisters had been known to kick or push each other when they were little, but, on the whole, the most violent things they had ever done involved slamming doors, and/or bursting into tears. They had never physically hurt one another. Made cruel, cutting, even eviserative, remarks—sure; but never caused *injuries.* Violence in her family had always been exclusively verbal.

She had never had a boyfriend who would have done such a thing, or, as far as she knew, even *known* anyone who had. She had never been mugged, manhandled—or even pummeled in junior high. Christ, the only times she could ever remember being struck in her entire life had all happened on the basketball court when she tried to get rebounds away from taller people and ran into elbows, instead. Big deal.

And now, here she was, locked up and terrified inside her apartment, because she'd, what, made overly pointed cocktail party conversation at a gallery opening? Chatted pleasantly with a slumlord's secretary? Christ. It didn't make any sense at all. Plus, she had been very careful not to tell anyone her name, so there was no way that they could have found her. After all, New York was pretty damn big. Without knowing who she was, there was no way they could have—except, wait a minute, she *had* told someone her name. Told *one* person. Period.

And then, suddenly, masked men had appeared who knew her name, and knew exactly where to find her. Funny coincidence, that. Now that she was thinking about it, clearly, for the first time, even though they had worn masks, she was sure of two things—they had been white, and they had been very large, physically confident men.

Just like the vast majority of—firefighters.

God*damn* it, anyway.

When she dialed the fire station, and asked for Lieutenant Saperstein, it took a few minutes before she came on the line, sounding very efficient.

"This is Dana Coakley," Dana said.

Molly's voice relaxed. "Oh, hi. How are you?"

Wondering, at the moment, if she'd been set up. "I'm all right," Dana said, shortly. "Um, look. Do you think we could talk for a few minutes? Away from the firehouse?"

"Well, why don't you just stop by," Molly said. "I just came on and I don't get relieved until tomorrow."

"Could I meet you then?" Dana asked. "It won't take long."

Molly sounded a little uncertain about the whole thing, but they agreed to meet at the Firemen's Monument on 100th and Riverside, after her tour was over.

"I might be running late. I mean, you never know—" Molly laughed nervously "—there might be a fire."

"No problem," Dana said. "I'll wait."

The next morning, she got to the memorial just after nine and sat on one of the cold marble benches overlooking Riverside Drive, the park, and the West Side Highway below. It was very windy, and she realized that she hadn't dressed warmly enough.

Too late now.

She did, at least, have a pack of cigarettes, and promptly began making a dent in it. Breathing smoke didn't hurt any more than *regular* breathing with broken ribs, and curtailing vices wasn't currently at the top of her list of things to do, anyway. Right now, shivering and feeling sorry for herself were both taking precedence.

"To the Heroic Dead of the Fire Department," the monument read. It was purely coincidental, of course, that it was a convenient place in the neighborhood for them to meet; Dana had actually walked Bert right past the statues and fountain on nu-

merous occasions, without giving them much thought. On a warm day, the benches were very comfortable, and there were almost always people sitting on them, but the monument itself was more of a backdrop than a shrine. A landmark people in the neighborhood knew, probably without being able to describe it beyond, "you know, at 100th, where that fountain thing is."

She was about to give up and head home to get under her quilts when she saw Molly coming down 100th Street in her pea coat, limping badly and looking very tired, with a white gauze bandage covering most of her left ear. As she came down the stone steps, she noticed Dana and stopped, startled.

"What happened to you?" she asked.

Good question. Dana shrugged. "What happened to *you?*"

"Bad fall," Molly said without elaborating, and sat down at the other end of the bench, favoring her hip. Even though her hair was wet, as though she had just showered, she still reeked of smoke. "What's your story?"

"I was beaten and terrorized by thugs," Dana said, making her voice equally stiff and offhand.

Molly frowned at her. "Seriously?"

Well, *yeah,* seriously. "Oh, wait, you're right," Dana said. "I slipped in the shower, reaching for my Prell."

Molly frowned again, digesting that. Then she rubbed her temples with one hand, looking even more tired.

"They knew my name," Dana said, "and you're the only one I told."

Molly looked up sharply. "Wait a minute—you think *I* had something to do with this?"

Dana nodded. "I think it was firefighters. Who else could it have been?"

Molly stared at her. "Firefighters? Why the hell would firefighters want to beat you up?"

Why, indeed. "All I know," Dana said, "is a bunch of big, athletic white men dragged me into a van, punched me around, said they'd kill me if I didn't stop what I was doing, and you're the only one who could have put them on to me."

"Shit," Molly said, shook her head, and got up to leave.

"Is that a yes?" Dana asked.

Molly turned. "You think I would have people come after you? Do that to you? To *anyone?"*

No. Not really. "Maybe it's some kind of cover-up you don't know about," Dana said. "Or—"

Molly shook her head impatiently. "Covering up what? I did the initial size-up, so if anyone screwed up that night, it was *me.* If you think they would have covered that up—they would have loved publicizing it, believe me. Hell, they'd *celebrate* if they could find a way to prove I couldn't measure up."

Maybe.

"Besides, it's not their style," Molly said. "I've been on the receiving end of a lot of—" She stopped. "Some of the guys might be capable of having a few, and then pushing you around a little, but their thinking we're physically incapable is the whole point. So roughing you up would be—they would never do anything that blatant."

Food for thought. Not that she was convinced. Dana lit another cigarette.

"Did they have New York accents?" Molly asked.

Had they? Dana tried to think back. The one who had been enjoying himself so much, maybe. The one in charge had sounded—not quite refined, but definitely educated. From out of town.

"You may have noticed," Molly said, grimly, "we tend to have real heavy New York accents. You know, the blue-collar thing."

Now that she thought about it, that was true. The accents, that is. "*You* don't really," Dana said. "Maybe just a few words here and there."

"I'm from Woodside, I'm not ashamed of it," Molly said, and then just shook her head, obviously not interested in pursuing the subject any further.

"I just can't figure out how they—" Out of nowhere, Dana pictured Craig leaning up against the bar at the art opening, saying, "It'll make *anyone* feel like a king"—and then, a few days later,

Terence had called, telling her about some mythical producer who'd been asking about her. Terence never would have given out her address or anything, but if someone purportedly in the business had wanted to know about "the girl in the Royal Coffee commercials," potentially with an eye to hiring her, he certainly would have said who she was. Tried to get her an audition.

"What?" Molly asked.

"It wasn't you," Dana said. "I just figured it out." Christ, she was so stupid. "I know who it was."

Molly shrugged. "And?"

And she should have followed her original instincts. Dana stood up. "I'm sorry I dragged you out like this. It wasn't—since it happened, I've been having trouble thinking clearly, and I'm treating people very badly. I'm sorry. I won't bother you again."

"So, now what?" Molly asked, without smiling. "Back to being Underdog?"

Not a chance. Dana shook her head. "I'm going to stay the hell out of it from now on. Enough with the Amateur Hour already."

"You must have been doing something right," Molly said. "Or else, why would they bother coming after you?"

She'd been embarrassing herself, is what she had been doing. Dana felt for another cigarette and tucked her head out of the wind, so she could light it in the shelter of her sling. "I bluffed the right person, that's all. I don't know a goddamn thing."

Molly sighed. "If it makes you feel better," she said, "neither do we."

So evil was going to triumph over good. *Swell.*

"How bad are the injuries?" Molly asked, watching the way she moved.

Dana shrugged, not looking at her. "I've had worse." Which was a complete and total lie. "Does your ear hurt?"

Molly automatically lifted her hand toward the gauze, then lowered it. "Not much. It's just gotten a lot more sensitive to heat over the years."

To being burned. And it almost certainly hurt like hell. Dana nodded, taking a final rib-stabbing drag on her cigarette before putting it out—she was, after all, standing next to a fire protection professional—and tossing the butt in the nearest trash can.

"How bad are the injuries?" Molly asked, again, and tapped her own forehead significantly.

Very possibly permanent. "Fine," Dana said. "No sweat."

Eighteen

There didn't seem to be much else to say, and they ended up walking—at a very slow pace—east on 100th Street, separating at Broadway so Molly could go get on the subway and Dana could stop at the drugstore to refill her painkillers before going home and, as planned, easing her way into her bed, under her quilts, and staring at nothing.

Another exciting and productive day.

Since she had familial tendencies in that direction, she was well aware of the signs of depression—and that she was developing most of them. She had trouble falling asleep—and even more trouble getting up, her thinking seemed muddled—at best, and she was finding syndicated reruns of shows like *Beverly Hills 90210* deeply moving. Hell, even *Melrose Place* seemed heartrending lately.

If she hadn't recently misplaced her sense of humor, all of this might have led her to believe that she hadn't been cut out for a risky, death-defying, ever-adventurous investigatory lifestyle *anyway.*

She had resumed most of her super duties—of which, many more could be done one-handed than she would have guessed—but other than that, she pretty much stayed holed up in her apartment, only going out for necessities like cigarettes, a visit to an internist the hospital had recommended to have her stitches removed, and a couple of trips to her dentist, whose prognosis about the current state of her jaw and the possible dental and temporomandibular implications was extremely pessimistic.

Her face was healing pretty well, and once she was allowed to take the splint off her nose, she was relieved to see that it didn't look as bad as it could have. It didn't look *great,* but it wasn't horrible, either. She still had dark shadows of bruises here and there, especially under her eyes, but to the unsuspecting stranger, she would probably look more tired than anything else.

Wanting to return to some semblance of a normal life, she went back up to Second Chance on her regular volunteer day. To her amazement, after looking worried when he saw her sling, Travis bought her explanation about being in a bad taxi crash—a new story, for variety's sake—on the 86th Street Transverse, and when he asked her if she had found out anything else about the fire, she told him, pleasantly, that she was stumped, and they would just have to hope that the authorities came up with something. He accepted this with surprising alacrity, too, proceeding to tell her, with much more interest, that the school was letting him play on the basketball team again, since his attendance had improved, and he was wondering if she might, you know, if she wasn't like, busy or anything, want to maybe come to one of his games sometime. She, of course, told him that she would be delighted.

When she was walking home, she saw several police cars parked in front of an SRO on Broadway, although the cops were all standing around, looking bored enough to indicate that whatever the excitement—probably a drug bust or a fight—had been, it was now over. It occurred to her that if Ray was there, he might ask her some questions she didn't feel like answering, but before she could go the other way, he had already seen her, and detached himself from Spider and some other officers waiting by the building entrance.

"Haven't seen you around," he said, looking her over with cop eyes, instead of ordinary friendly ones. "What's up?"

"Not much." Dana motioned toward the SRO. "What happened here?"

"False alarm," he said. " 'Man with a gun' run."

Oh. Terrific. She resisted the immediate urge to cross the street.

"So," he said, pointedly. "What's *up?*"

Dana shrugged, avoiding those expressionless eyes. She didn't see Ray in full cop mode too often, and it was a little unnerving. "You know me—clumsiness rules my life."

"Oh, yeah?" He didn't smile. "Looks more like someone jacked you up pretty good."

Dana just shrugged.

"Maybe I should get my sergeant over here," he said, "see what he thinks?"

This conversation was living up to all of her worst expectations.

He kept looking at her. "Seems to me, you still owe me a beer. Let's make it tonight."

"I can't," she said. "Maybe next week, or—"

He shook his head. "Tonight. I'll see you at the Abbey, seven-thirty, eight o'clock."

If she argued, or caused any sort of scene, his sergeant *would* come hustling over. "Fine," she said. "See you then."

When she got to the bar that night, she saw Ray in a back booth along the wall, facing the door, sitting with a dark-haired guy about their age, who was wearing a conservative dark suit—Brooks Brothers, from the look of it—and a skinny red tie. He was probably one of the precinct detectives, who just happened to be sartorially sedate. In fact, he looked downright preppy. The kind of guy who had gone to school with at least one Kennedy.

If she had to do this at all, she would infinitely prefer to speak to Ray alone. Going through official channels was precisely what she had been warned *not* to do.

She thought about leaving, but Ray was already on his way over.

" 'Bout time," he said, checking his watch.

"Why did you want to meet here?" Dana asked. The Abbey tended to be more of a neighborhood and Columbia hangout than a cop bar. "I thought you liked the Dive."

Ray shrugged. "It gets too noisy there. Come on."

She stayed by the door. "Who's the suit?"

"My buddy Kevin," Ray said. "He's with the D.A.'s office."

Nifty. Someone from the precinct detective squad might have been preferable. Less on-the-record. But she kept herself to a frown, instead of saying something impolite, and followed him over to the booth.

The dark-haired guy stood up, and she was surprised by how big he was. Football-big. She was also surprised by how quickly he took in her sling and stuck out his left hand instead of his right.

"You must be Dana," he said. Fairly deep voice. *Strong* hand. "I'm Kevin Gallagher."

She nodded and shook his hand without commenting, then hung her ski jacket up on the wooden hook above the booth before carefully sitting down next to Ray.

One of the waitresses came right over, and since Ray and his friend were both ordering another round of beers, Dana decided to ignore the fact that she was still on painkillers and order one for herself.

None of them spoke much until the waitress had returned with the beers, taking away the empty mugs already on the table.

Dana decided to break the silence. "So. Do we have an agenda here, or is this just good, hearty fun?"

"A little of both," Ray said.

She wasn't particularly in the mood for *either.*

"You know, you look familiar," Kevin said. "Did you go to Bowdoin?"

An attempt to establish commonality, to make her more forthcoming? Dana shook her head. "No. Did you?"

"No," he said. "But I knew a lot of people there."

Ray laughed. "She's the one who did all those commercials. Remember I told you?"

"Oh," Kevin said, then nodded. "Right. Okay."

Upon which, this already not wildly successful conversation died again. She didn't want to be here in the first place, so *she* certainly wasn't going to rescue it.

"Ray's been bringing me up to speed about some of the things he thinks you may have been doing recently," Kevin said, after a long pause.

Dana elected to misunderstand him. "My last show was an Off-

Off of *Extremities* down in the Village. Since then, it's been pretty slow."

Kevin looked at Ray, who shrugged, trying to pay attention both to the conversation, and to the Knicks game playing on one of the televisions over the bar.

"What did you do to your arm?" Kevin asked.

Looked like he was opting for subtlety. Dana drank some of her beer. "I separated my shoulder."

He nodded. "Pretty painful. How did that happen?"

Might as well try another new tale of woe. "Wiped out on a mogul," Dana said.

Kevin nodded. "Bang up some ribs at the same time?"

Jesus, he could tell that? Maybe because she was still walking almost as quickly as oil-based paint dried. "Yes," Dana said. "It was quite a nasty spill."

"Must have been," he agreed.

Christ, this was tedious. He seemed like a real stiff, too. What kind of guy hung out in a bar with his suit jacket on, and his tie perfectly knotted? Hard to put him together with rowdy, amiable Ray—who, she could see, was still sneaking glances at the Knicks game.

She tapped his arm to get his attention. "Is it okay if I go now?"

Ray looked away from the television. "Take it easy. Finish your beer."

Somehow, that sounded more like an order than a suggestion. If both of her arms had been working, she definitely would have folded them.

"I don't know why this has to be so difficult," Kevin said. "Ray was under the impression that you might be in trouble, and could use some help."

Dana nodded. "In which case, my first instinct would be to convene, publicly, with law enforcement officials? Try again, Counselor."

Kevin looked at Ray, who shrugged apologetically.

"She's not usually like this, Kev. Swear to God," he said.

Kevin moved his jaw, then nodded and refocused on her.

"Okay. Look. You've obviously been threatened in some way. So, why don't you tell us about it?"

She looked at Ray. "Would you describe this as custodial questioning?"

He grinned. "This is me, having some beers with a couple friends."

Her cue to drink more beer, while expressing irritation with every visible fiber of her being.

"Watch a lot of *Court TV?*" Kevin asked, looking pretty damned irritated in his own right.

"Sure do," Dana said. She was going to light a cigarette, but this guy was probably one of those personally offended types. Which was another reason to dislike him. "I do a great little riff on fruit of the poisoned tree, if you'd like to hear it."

"Absolutely," Kevin said. "I love listening to legal novitiates mangle things."

Any second now, one of them was going to swing a bar stool. On the other hand, the phrase "legal novitiates" had a certain beauty. Maybe he was really smart. Of course, he could also just be really *Catholic.* "What does the word 'supercilious' mean to you?" she asked.

Ray held up his hands in a time-out sign. "Come on, kids. Let's play nice."

They had been leaning forward, and now they both leaned back.

"You want the real story, fine," Dana said. "You can have it."

Kevin reached into the overfilled briefcase on the bench next to him, taking out a yellow legal pad and a navy blue felt-tip marker.

"Those are environmentally unsound," Dana said. Jesus, she really was being a bitch on wheels here. What the hell was her problem? "You should only use the white ones."

"I use whatever the city can give me," he said.

Should she antagonize him further by making a crack about petty pilfering at the workplace, or would he belt her one? It was easy to tell that, for all his civility, there was a serious temper lurking in there somewhere.

With luck, considering recent events, not a violent one.

"Think I want another beer," Ray said quietly, and motioned for the waitress to bring over a fresh round.

Dana reached over to push the legal pad aside. "Don't bother taking notes, because nothing I say is going to leave this table."

Kevin yanked the pad back. "We can't promise that, we both have obligations to the system."

Officers of the goddamned court. "Well, *I'm* a maverick," Dana said, "concerned solely about serving justice, in a complicated and uncaring world."

"Wait a minute." Kevin uncapped his felt-tip pen with his teeth. "Say that again, slowly, so I can get every single word."

So she'd felt compelled to make her *own* remark of great beauty, so what. "Put it this way. If you come after me officially, I'll deny we ever even met," she said.

Kevin shrugged, and gestured around them. "Then I'll subpoena the whole place, and they can all testify otherwise."

"Then *I'll* make insane, spurious allegations about UFOs and J. Edgar Hoover, and make sure to blow whatever credibility I had right out of the water," she said.

He looked—no, scowled—at her, then stuffed the legal pad inside his briefcase. The waitress carried over three more beers, and after she had gone, Kevin leaned over towards Ray.

"Careful," he said. "That woman *may have been* a spy. She could be working for *anyone.*"

He wasn't supercilious, so much as smug. "All right." Dana—painkillers be damned—drank more of her beer than was probably wise. "I went up to Mitchell Brandon at a party, accused him of being behind the Harrison fire, and a few days later, several men attacked me and said that next time they'd kill me."

"And," Kevin said.

Dana took another couple of gulps of beer. "And that's it. Now, I'm no longer interested in the whole thing, to the degree that if I saw an article in the *Times,* I'd burn the paper and throw the ashes away."

"Couldn't you just burn that one page?" Ray asked, and winked at her.

Dana smiled a little. "No, because I am *so* disinterested. I mean, the arson squad never wanted my help before—they certainly don't need it now."

Kevin's hand moved, casually, toward his briefcase. "We could start by prosecuting them for assaulting you. We might be able to turn one of them, get more information that way."

"They didn't identify themselves, they had masks, and it was dark," Dana said.

He frowned. "But you're sure Brandon sent them."

"I'm in a complete tailspin," Dana said. "I'm not sure what *day* it is."

Ray glanced away from the game. "Tuesday."

Every party needed a court jester. "There won't be any obvious evidence," Dana said, mainly to Kevin, "but I think if you all look for a previous pattern of behavior, involving earlier property acquisitions, within the appropriate statute of limitations, something's likely to turn up."

"Is that how they do it on *NYPD Blue*?" Kevin asked.

Did he know that he looked like a football player? Much too big, and *dumb*-looking to boot. Dana leaned forward, resting her weight on her good arm. "Evidence that is illegally procured by an officer of the court, and/or anything that develops from said evidence, is inadmissible, because of due process." A mighty nice definition of fruit of the poisoned tree, if she did say so herself.

Kevin's eyes narrowed. "It's not so much an issue of procurement, as the illegal conduct."

A nuance.

"Could we use that evidence or information if we confirm it by entirely independent means?" he asked.

Dana finished what was left in her glass. "If you can *prove* it, pal—feel free."

For the first time all night, he grinned, and while it was something of a frat-boy smile, that didn't make it unappealing. "Ray, I think we should buy this woman another drink."

"Sounds good," Ray said, and motioned for the waitress again.

They were watching the game, and starting in on a fourth round, when Ray suddenly sat up straight.

"Tasha's going to be pissed," he said. "I'd better call her."

Dana had a little trouble getting out of the booth to let him past—in addition to injuries, she would have to make this her last beer tonight—and sitting back down took concentration, too.

With Ray gone, it seemed very quiet.

"I'm not supercilious," Kevin said. "Self-righteous, maybe, or judgmental—but, not supercilious."

Well, okay. That one had apparently bugged him. She couldn't think of a response, so she settled for an amiable shrug, then looked fuzzily up at the basketball game.

"I'm very sorry those men hurt you," he said.

He sounded sincere, even. She shrugged again, embarrassed.

"It wasn't representative," he said, the last word coming out a little slurred. They'd been in here at least a couple of rounds longer than she had. "I mean, I hope you have a more compassionate man in your life who was able to—I don't know—make you feel better. About us, I mean."

He had just done a pretty good job of it himself. "Thank you," she said. "That's very nice of you."

He shrugged, and looked down inside his mug, his expression distinctly remote now. Or—disappointed. Sulky. *Some*thing.

"What?" she asked.

He shook his head, then looked over his shoulder in the direction Ray had gone. "Look, I'll be right back. I have to hit the men's room."

Since when was "thank you" considered an offensive remark? But she just shrugged, and watched the Knicks.

Ray was the first one to come back, taking his jacket down from the coat rack.

"Tasha's not so happy with you?" Dana said.

He nodded wryly. "She hates it when I go out drinking after work. I was going to tell her it wasn't just with the guys this time, but—" He raised his hands, demonstrating the sort of overreaction that would have gotten. "*Bad* idea."

Dana checked to make sure that Kevin wasn't on his way back to the table yet. "Is he always so angry?"

Ray shrugged his jacket on. "Pretty much. The poor guy brings his job home." He glanced at his watch. "You want me to walk you back?"

Not when he already had an argument waiting for him. "No, I'm fine," she said. "Thank you, anyway."

"It's not out of my way," he said—although it almost certainly was.

Then, Kevin appeared behind him. "Don't worry about it. I can walk her."

Ray looked relieved. "Thanks—I really gotta get moving." He paused to aim a finger at her. "You remember anything, or *anything* else happens, you tell me right away, okay?"

Maybe. "I don't think anything else is going to happen," Dana said, and shook her head as he reached for his wallet. "I owed you a couple of drinks, remember?"

"Okay. Now I owe you," he said, and headed for the door.

Left alone, Dana looked at Kevin uncomfortably. "I'm really fine walking by myself, I mean—"

"Well, I'm going to do it anyway," he said, picking up his mug to drain what was left in it.

What little energy she had had been sapped by the combination of painkillers and alcohol. "Fine," she said, and caught the waitress's eye so they could get the check.

They paid the bill with the least possible amount of conversation, and although he held the door for her as they left, his body language was so rigid and unfriendly that she really would have preferred trekking down Broadway on her own. It wasn't *that* late.

"Do you live in the neighborhood?" she asked, just to be polite.

He nodded. "Down on 84th."

For lack of a better idea, she nodded, too.

"You're right nearby?" he asked.

"Just down here a few blocks, off West End," she said.

Now it was his turn to nod, and they walked down Broadway in silence. It was pretty windy, and he turned his coat collar up, then looked down at her critically.

"It's cold," he said. "You should zip your jacket."

One-handed? She would have just said that she was fine, but

he was annoying her too much to let him off that easily. "I can't, with the sling," she said. "I have to have people do it for me."

He stopped short. "I'm sorry. I should have realized that."

She felt about four years old, having to have this near-stranger zip her up, but she *was* cold. It took him a couple of tries to get the zipper to catch—either because he was worried about hurting her arm, or because he was uneasy about touching her in what seemed, in this context, to be a fairly personal way. At minimum, it was paternal.

"Thank you," she said.

He nodded, avoiding her eyes, and stepped away.

"I'm sorry about the supercilious crack," she said. "My personality has taken a turn for the worse lately."

He shrugged. "It didn't bother me."

Yeah, right.

Walking along, not looking at each other, it felt like the end of an adversarial date. The kind where the guy had enough manners to make sure you got home in one piece, but didn't bother even pretending that he was going to call again. Not that she wanted him to call her.

Since this wasn't a date.

Since he was a stranger, and an angry one at that. It was just as well that she would never have to meet him again.

A relief.

"Why *do* you know so much about the law?" he asked.

She grinned at him. "So I watch *Court TV,* so shoot me."

He nodded. "I figured."

Okay, not smug—*patronizing.* "I read me a book once, too," she said, "and I got like, totally good retention."

He smiled, but still barely looked at her.

"There's also, of course, my time in prison," she said.

He smiled again, and looked away.

Okay. Fine. What a sparkling personality he had. "I'm right down this block," she said, pointing. "I think I can make it from here."

He shook his head, walking her all the way to the front door of her building.

"Do you want to call up, and have whomever come down and meet you?" he asked, very formally.

"My dog is smart," she said, "but not *that* smart."

He looked surprised. "I was under the impression that you were living with someone."

What? "You were under the wrong impression," she said, and took out her keys. "Thank you for walking me."

He started to say something, then just nodded and stepped back. "Right. Well. I'll wait until I see you're on the elevator."

In lieu of what? Coming upstairs and carefully searching and securing the apartment for her? She grinned, and unlocked the front door.

"You should stop throwing accusations around at parties, maybe," he said.

Good plan. She nodded. "Thanks." Time for a little cop-show legalese. "I'll take that under advisement."

"Do that," he said.

She nodded, realized that she was lingering as though this *were* a date—which it wasn't—and she was expecting him to ask her out, or beg for her phone number—neither of which, he was going to do. She was just—letting alcohol slow her reactions. Her better instincts.

"Well." She opened the door all the way. "Thanks again."

He nodded. "Good night. Take care of yourself."

"You, too," she said.

They looked at each other, looked away, and then she, resolutely, went inside. Because it hadn't been a date at all.

Not even remotely.

Nineteen

She was sure she had been more buzzed than drunk, but the next morning, she unquestionably felt hungover. Sluggish. Out of sorts.

So, as had become far too easy, she slept too late, and then went to bed too early. She also let the answering machine pick up all of her calls—none of which she returned. Her dysphoria was such that she couldn't even *act* her way out of it.

The following day was very much the same, and she was lying on the couch in the late afternoon, smoking and watching *Court TV*—which, somehow, was only intensifying her sense of gloom—when her intercom buzzed. Probably the UPS guy. Not that she was expecting anything, but as the super, she ended up taking in everyone else's packages. In fact, considering how much time they spent together, one day, she would probably end up *marrying* the UPS guy.

Instead, it was Molly Saperstein. Which was strange, but what the hell. She considered putting out her cigarette, but it didn't seem worth the trouble of walking all the way back over to the ashtray, so she didn't bother. As was always the case when the intercom rang, Bert was jumping around and barking, while the cats waited in habitual perches to see who it was, edgy and alert.

Molly came down the hall, wearing her uniform under her pea coat, carrying a well-stuffed gym bag and a square Tupperware container, with a thick manila envelope under her arm. Although they had never met, Bert was overjoyed to see her. Molly's expression had been fairly somber, but she smiled and shifted the gym bag to her other hand so she could pat him.

"Cute dog," she said.

Dana certainly wasn't going to disagree.

Molly handed her the Tupperware container. "I told Mickey you weren't feeling too well, and he thought we should make these for you."

Mickey was a very nice kid. Dana peered through the plastic, seeing what she presumed were brownies. "Thank you. I appreciate it."

Molly nodded, then hesitated. "It's none of my business, but—are you on a bender?"

Incapacitating physical injuries and personal hygiene were difficult to integrate successfully. Dana frowned at her. "You ever washed your hair one-handed, bent over a too-tall sink?"

Molly shook her head.

All right, then. But that didn't mean she couldn't try to retrieve some good manners. "My apartment looks like Calcutta," she said, "but do you want to come in, or—?"

Molly shook her head again. "I'm on my way to the firehouse. I just—you didn't hear?"

Hear what? Dana shrugged.

Molly's expression was somewhere between control and utter blankness. "Jim Petruzzi died a few hours ago. It's all over the local news, if you turn it on."

The firefighter who had been in the Burn Center all these weeks. "I'm sorry," Dana said, picturing his daughter standing helplessly by the soda machine in the hospital corridor that day. "I mean—I really am."

Molly nodded. "We came on the job at the same time, and—" She stopped. "Well, let's just say that he was one of the good guys. Often one of the few."

Dana knew that she should have a response, but she couldn't think of one. "What happens now?"

Molly shrugged, with no expression at all. "I put on my dress uniform and go to yet another funeral."

One fire, ten funerals. No arrests.

"Well," Molly said, abruptly. "I'd better get going. It wasn't our company, so they're not going to take us out of service, but—it's going to be a tough tour for everyone."

No doubt. Especially when that alarm went off, and they all had to jump onto the truck, trying to forget little things like—grief, and—mortality. "I'm sorry," Dana said, for lack of a more helpful remark.

"I'm sorry for his *family,"* Molly said.

Yeah. Notions of heroism and the ultimate sacrifice probably weren't going to be very comforting to them any time soon. Dana let out her breath. "The, um, fire marshals will be sure to come up with something now, right?"

"Haven't so far," Molly said, "but I hope so." She glanced at her watch. "Well. I just thought I'd stop by." She started down the hall, then paused, taking the envelope out from underneath her arm. "Oh. Jake sent you this."

Jake had? Dana started to reach for the thick envelope, then withdrew. "What is it?"

"I don't know," Molly said, without meeting her eyes. "I didn't ask."

Downloaded information of some sort. Hacker stuff. "I don't want it," Dana said. "I mean, give it to the red caps."

Now, Molly looked at her. "They can get all of this *legally."*

Financial records. Paper trails, probably. "But—" The thought of even having information like that in her apartment made her panicky. "I don't want it. I don't want it anywhere near me."

Molly sighed. "Look. I'm not saying for you to take any chances, but you were finding things out, Dana. Whatever the hell you were doing, you were doing right."

And had almost gotten killed, as a result. Dana stayed where she was.

"Please just take a look," Molly said. "Maybe a fresh eye would help. Then, you can just be a confidential informant, or—it doesn't have to be dangerous. I don't want it to be dangerous. But whoever these people are—" She shook her head. "I don't care *how* they're stopped, I just want them off the street."

A lovely sentiment, but Dana, for one, wanted no damn part of it.

Molly checked her watch, then sighed again. "I really have to go. But you're probably right, you shouldn't be involved. Just forget I said anything."

Dana nodded, relieved to be off the hook, but also feeling unexpectedly guilty.

"It was stupid of me," Molly said. "But Jake was digging into databases, and—" She let out her breath. "The truth is, I guess I was rooting for you. You know? It was all so driven, and—" She looked sheepish. "When I was little, Underdog was my favorite show."

They were close enough in age to share a certain cartoon history. "My mother used to pin this red towel to my pajamas, so I could have a cape when I was being Mighty Mouse," Dana said.

Molly smiled for a second, nodded, and then headed down the hall.

"Leave the envelope," Dana said after her.

Molly stopped. "You sure?"

No. "Can't hurt to look," Dana said.

She *hoped.*

If she was supposed to follow the money, there was a colossal amount to follow. Seven figures, eight figures, *nine* figures. Numbers that would have intimidated her even in a Monopoly game.

Annual reports, SEC and UCC stuff, voter registration and DMV records, real estate transactions, property tax assessments, even some personal telephone and credit card bills. So much information that she wasn't quite sure how to organize it, or what exactly she should be trying to find. Besides, if there was some obvious smoking gun, the authorities would, presumably, long since have come across it.

The only thing she could say with total certainty was that the guy was very, very rich.

When her intercom buzzed again, some time later, she wasn't going to answer it, but finally she did, feeling irrationally nervous when she heard Peggy's voice. Then, maybe just to make *sure* they would have some kind of argument, she lit up a cigarette—an immature tactic, at best—before going over to open the door.

Peggy was, as ever, dressed smashingly in one of her endless supply of chic business suits, with a bulging satchel in one hand and a bag smelling distinctly of Chinese food in the other. She stopped a few feet from the door, and they looked at each other.

Peggy broke the silence. "You don't return your calls these days."

Not promptly, at any rate. "Well, you know how it is," Dana said. "Having a complete breakdown just takes up so much *time.*"

Peggy nodded. "I've heard that."

Dana nodded, too, slouching against the door jamb, and they looked at each other again.

Did she want to endanger this friendship any further than she already had—or was it time to throw herself upon the mercy of the court? "I think I owe you an apology. I, um, haven't handled this very well," Dana said, "and—thoughtlessness would appear to be a large component of that."

"Yeah, I've noticed," Peggy agreed.

Okay, the court was going to take a hard line on this. Dana looked down at the floor, feeling very guilty.

"On the other hand," Peggy said, "I don't get *nearly* enough opportunities to behave selflessly, and this has been sort of a treat."

Well—America was a melting pot, full of people who had different perspectives.

"You have, of course, sent an effusive recommendation to the Canonization Committee," Peggy said.

Dana relaxed a little. Maybe they were going to be able to ride through this one, after all. "Yep. It went out yesterday."

"Good," Peggy said. "Now, here's the deal. I'm going to help you, whether you like it or not."

An extremely tempting offer. "It's too dangerous," Dana said. "I really can't let you— "

Peggy looked quite outraged. "What am I, your *sidekick? I* don't think so. Now," she gestured with the takeout bag, "let's eat this before it gets cold."

Dana was going to argue, but then she just nodded and opened the door all the way. "Come on in," she said.

They ate amidst the computer print-outs, which Peggy surveyed, while asking various specific and financially incomprehensible questions.

"Didn't you ever take an economics course?" she asked, finally.

Dana shook her head, pouring each of them some more coffee. "Too boring."

Peggy frowned over the papers for a few minutes, then pushed them aside. "Are you sure Brandon's the one?"

At the moment, she was kind of, all too literally, betting her life on it. "Put it this way," Dana said. "I'm sure he bears the ultimate responsibility."

"Well, this is all very ugly," Peggy said.

Dana nodded, lighting her third after-dinner cigarette.

"Made no less ugly," Peggy said, frowning harder, "by the fact that you have reverted to an old, and unhealthy, habit."

Dana chose to ignore that, tossing Bert a piece of leftover Paradise chicken from her plate.

"Regardless," Peggy said, apparently deciding to overlook that. She looked at the pile of computer printouts, then sat back, folding her arms. "Now. In an attempt to repair the tattered shreds of your life—I suggest we nail this bastard."

If you were going to have a sidekick, it was good to have a supremely confident one. "Fine with me," Dana said.

Which did not, of course, mean that either of them could come up with a particularly inspired, or even plausible, way of doing so.

After Peggy had left—no doubt, with her thinking cap *very* tightly in place—Dana watched the late news, flipping among the local affiliates to see what kind of coverage they were giving the third firefighter's death. It was uniformly grave, and laudatory—and almost every station finished with a solemn "the investigation is still ongoing" and flashed a phone number for viewers to call with anonymous crime-stopper tips.

She really hoped that those phones were going to ring off the hook.

The weather forecast was for heavy, wet snow, the spring storm predicted to hit the city after midnight, with the requisite travelers' advisories and such given. The various weather people were extremely jocular, making little secret of the fact that they found inclemency *fun*.

Since she would be out there doggedly shoveling the wet mess with one arm, Dana found the notion exhausting. Sometimes, when it snowed, she would go out every couple of hours to clear it away, since an inch or two at a time was more manageable than waiting until the storm was over, but tonight, she was too tired. Maybe, if the gods smiled on her, the snow would swiftly turn to rain and be washed away by the time she woke up.

In the morning, the first thing she did was to check the fire escape—and then felt sick to her stomach when she saw at least six or eight inches piled up out there. Bert would be happy, because he loved snow, but it was a pretty lousy start to *her* weekend.

She bundled up, awkwardly, and was taking two precautionary painkillers when she heard a distinctive clinking. She couldn't see the front of the building from her apartment, but the sound of shovels was unmistakable, and she felt a surge of so much affection for her landlord that she wanted to sit down and write him a thank-you note before whoever he had sent over had even finished.

She went downstairs, with Bert in tow, to see who it was, and offer them coffee or something. In all probability, it would be Mr. Morales and his fourteen-year-old son, Luis, or maybe the two Greek brothers Mr. Abrams sometimes hired for big jobs like painting the halls and making roof repairs.

She could see, when the elevator opened, that it was two men, neither of whom looked at all—she stopped, realizing that one of them was Kevin Gallagher.

Shoveling her walk? At—Christ—it was barely eight o'clock on a Saturday morning. And—he didn't even know her.

It would have been less surprising to see *Peggy* out there, doing manual labor.

She stepped outside tentatively, not even feeling the shock of the wind-chill factor. "Uh, hi," she said.

Kevin looked up from his shovel, his cheeks red either from the exertion or the cold. "Hi," he said, and went right back to work.

The other guy, who was endearingly goofy-looking, with light brown hair that was simultaneously floppy and thinning, grinned at her. "Hi. I'm Peter."

Sure, why not. Dana grinned back. "Hi, Peter. This is Bert."

"I see," Peter said, and leaned on his shovel, with a very disapproving expression. "And do you live with Bert?"

Dana felt her grin widen. Did that mean that Kevin had been talking about her? "Yes."

"Oh, my," Peter said. "And do you share sleeping quarters with *Bert?*"

She had no idea who he was, but she liked him. "Yeah, but we have separate beds." She glanced at Kevin, who was stubbornly shoveling away without looking at either of them. "Do you and *Kevin* share sleeping quarters?"

Peter nodded sadly. "Yes. But we sleep head to foot, so it's okay."

"Shut up, Peter," Kevin said through his teeth, without pausing in his shoveling.

"And if you'll notice," Peter said, "he has very *big* feet."

Dana automatically checked his feet—battered leather hiking boots—and saw that they were, indeed, big. Huge, even.

"They're in proportion," Kevin said stiffly. "I can't help being tall."

Dana laughed, but then had such an overpowering and instinctive erotic thought on the subject of proportion that she flushed and looked away, pretending to adjust the mitten she'd pulled onto her injured hand.

"I suppose now you're going to *walk* this *Bert?"* Peter asked.

Peter was a kick. "Um, look," she said. "This is very nice of you guys, but you really don't have to—"

"I think you should take him around the block," Kevin said, his voice perhaps a shade too authoritarian for her tastes. "He seems frantic."

Hardly a rare state of affairs in Bert's life. "Would it be all right if I walked him two blocks, Counselor?" Dana asked. "Or, or maybe I could go a block and a half, then turn around a few times, head in a different direction, and *then*—"

Kevin set his jaw. "I wasn't telling you how to walk your dog," he said, much too reasonably. Humoring her. "I was just suggesting—"

Dana grinned at Peter. "What do you think? Does this seems like a chemistry experiment gone wildly awry, or what?"

"Just go already," Peter said, "so we'll have some time to talk about you behind your back."

She really hoped—and doubted—that he was kidding. "Right." She looked down at Bert, who had jumped the gun, and was urinating on a pile of freshly cleared snow. "Okay. Good idea."

Suddenly so self-conscious that she knew she was blushing again, she started to walk past them, but then Kevin leaned his shovel against the side of the building and stepped in front of her.

"What?" she asked, apprehensive in spite of herself.

He frowned, zipped her jacket up, then stepped away. "It's very cold out here," he said, quite gruffly, and picked up his shovel again.

If he didn't watch it, she was in danger of becoming deeply smitten. "Could you fix my scarf, too?" she asked. "Tie it in a small, attractive bow?"

He started to put the shovel down, paused, blinked a few times, and resumed digging.

Dana looked at Peter. "Should he *really* waste so much time being whimsical?"

Peter shook his head, amused. "Once you get around the corner, your ears are going to burn."

Which was probably why she was putting it off. "Well," she said, shrugged her good shoulder as though such trivial matters could never disturb her, and set off, hoping that she wouldn't slip and fall and make a further fool of herself.

She walked Bert three blocks, mainly because she was dreading going back, and when she did, Kevin and Peter exchanged glances and kept digging away.

Had they been discussing her womanly attributes—or her more castrating ones?

Perhaps she would rather not know.

"I, uh—" Her voice came out a little squeaky, and she cleared her throat before going on. "I'll just take him upstairs, and then I'll come back down and help."

"We're almost done," Kevin said.

Well, yeah, they'd finished the steps and entryway, and were now working on the sidewalk.

"Then, maybe—" she had a feeling that neither of them had given her a rave review "—I could bring you down some coffee, or—that is, you could come *up,* if you wanted, or, uh—"

Peter nodded. "Sounds good. I think a homemade, three-course breakfast would be—"

Kevin glared at him.

"Then again," Peter said. "I have places to go, and things to do today."

Okay. The critic whose opinion mattered the most here must have given her an abysmal notice. "I—" Instead of being squeaky, her voice shook slightly this time, and she looked at Kevin. "You probably have plans, too."

He shrugged. "I'm going to have to spend a few hours at the office, because I'm OT starting next week."

"Overtime?" she guessed, feeling stupid.

"On trial," he said.

Now, she felt *very* stupid. Besides, if he wasn't interested, what was he doing shoveling her walk—unasked—in the first place? "Well, okay," she said, and twisted Bert's leash more tightly around her hand. Jesus. What an incompetent heterosexual she was. "I"—she might as well turn this into a *spectacular* failure—"was going to offer to buy you breakfast, to thank you, but—"

"I have some time," Kevin said.

How very grudging. "Fine," Dana said. "Don't worry, I'll eat really fast."

Peter laughed, then shook his head. "Good one, Kev. Way to go."

And how.

Peter leaned toward her. "Don't take it personally," he said in a very loud whisper. "He's Dating-Challenged."

That made two of them. "Okay." She looked at Kevin. "If I take Bert up, will you still be here when I get back?"

Unexpectedly, he grinned at her. "Only one way to find out," he said.

Twenty

When she returned, Peter was gone, but Kevin was leaning against the side of the building, looking very tense.

"It's only breakfast," Dana said, but then couldn't resist pausing, artfully. No point in letting all of those years of theatrical training go to waste. "We can wait a day or two, before you meet my parents."

Was it her imagination, or had his eyes widened? Clear blue eyes, as it happened. Nice eyes. All she had to do now, was make some sort of biological-clock crack, and he would start running towards 84th Street as fast as his very tall legs could carry him.

"I'm kidding," she said, in case he wasn't sure.

"I knew that," he said defensively.

Maybe.

They looked at each other, and then away.

"We, uh, we could go over to one of the diners on Broadway," she said, "or—?"

He shrugged. "Sure."

"Okay, then," she said, and started down her terribly well-shoveled walk.

They didn't speak much—or even, really, at all—on the way. She slipped once, crossing 99th Street, and he put his hand on her back to steady her, and then took it away. She knew she should make some sort of joke about her general poise and aplomb—but she couldn't think of one.

In fact, at the moment, she was drawing a blank on a number of the most basic autobiographical details of her life.

Going into the diner, he held the door for her, and she had a feeling he was also going to unzip her coat, but she beat him to it. She did, however, let him hang it up for her. After which, he hung up his own jacket and sat down, pushing up his sweatshirt sleeves. A dark green Dartmouth sweatshirt, that had seen better days.

"Order anything you like under a dollar fifty," Dana said.

He smiled briefly and glanced at his menu.

"Coffee?" the waitress asked.

They both nodded, and the waitress went off. She returned, filled their cups, stood there long enough to determine that they weren't ready to order yet, and went off again.

"Well," Dana said, to break the silence. "Are we having fun yet?"

Kevin smiled, and looked at his menu again.

At least this wasn't—strained.

"What's your case next week?" she asked.

"Double homicide," he said. "A fairly unpleasant one, too."

To her way of thinking, double homicides were *always* unpleasant.

"Do you think you'll win?" she asked.

He shrugged, and set his menu aside. "The evidence is pretty solid, but most of my witnesses stink. The jury's going to hate them."

Okay. "Do juries like *you?"* she asked, out of genuine curiosity.

He took his time answering. "I guess they think I'm pretty uptight, but they like the moral outrage."

Okay. Fair enough. She grinned, and looked down at her menu.

Once they had ordered, the food came pretty quickly—which was good, because the conversation was labored, at best. She couldn't help feeling shy about eating in front of him—she had gotten an omelet, since that was easy to chew—and he didn't seem to be making much headway on his pancakes, either. Every so often, they would meet eyes, or make desultory remarks about Life in the Big City, or some such—but, on the whole, this wasn't exactly the most wildly successful social encounter she had ever had.

She was able to establish that he was from Chicago, and had grown up in a family of cops, and was the first Gallagher to choose the legal side of law enforcement. It wasn't clear *why*. He also still wasn't really eating.

"Are they terrible?" she asked, indicating his plate.

He looked surprised. "Oh. No. No, no, they're fine," he said, and took a bite.

Which didn't change the fact that he seemed to be having trouble swallowing. More so than leaden pancakes would seem to indicate.

He started to take another bite, then put his fork down and sipped some coffee, instead.

"What?" she asked.

He flushed slightly. "I, uh—frankly, I need a Prilosec."

Well, yeah, he *seemed* like the kind of guy who would have an ulcer.

"It's not you," he said quickly. "It's just—sometimes I get a little—"

"Nervous?" she guessed.

He was obviously embarrassed, but he nodded, then glanced at her for a second and fished around inside his jacket until he came up with a roll of antacids. He chewed a couple, blinking, and put the roll away.

It was none of her business, but—"I thought you weren't supposed to drink caffeine, or alcohol, when you have an ulcer," she said. Both of which, she had certainly seen him do. The waitress had already refilled his cup *twice*.

"Well," he said, then frowned, and drank some more.

Was it her imagination, or was it just possible that Kevin Gallagher might not always be the easiest person to be around? If she had any sense, little red warning flags would be springing up all over her brain. Rough seas; trouble ahead.

What flags? She didn't see any flags.

"Why is it that you smell so heavily of cigarettes, but never actually seem to light up?" he asked.

A man so terribly afflicted by moral outrage would certainly vociferously disapprove of smokers. And, not that she was making excuses, but—"I had quit for almost eleven months," she said. Ten months, two weeks, and three days, had she—oh, say—been keeping *track.* "But—I know it'll sound crazy—I seem to be on edge, lately."

He nodded, and she was relieved that it appeared to be sympathetic, rather than pejorative.

Anyway. She took a bite of her ever-colder omelet.

"Why did they break your fingers?" he asked.

Well, *that* was direct. Although, in light of the other injuries, she had actually given her fingers very little thought. Besides—she was left-handed. She looked down at the two—somewhat grimy, unfortunately—splints sticking out of her cast. "I, uh—" She might as well risk a direct answer; what did she have to lose? "I was kind of passing out, and they wanted me to pay more attention to what they were saying."

He nodded. "Did you?"

Well—*yeah.* "Seemed like a good choice," she said.

He nodded again. In other company, she might have expected a gasp—or, at least, a widening of the eyes, but an ADA who routinely handled multiple homicides was probably hard to shock. Maybe even hard to *interest.* He probably had to be cold and contained to handle his job, but—Christ.

"Well, anyway," she said, and put some grape jelly on her toast.

"This has to be pretty far out of your normal life experience," he said.

What—being out on a date? Oh, yeah, nice guy.

"Why doesn't it seem to have rocked you more?" he asked.

Okay, now she was lost. She ate some toast. "I don't know what you mean."

He shrugged. "You were brutally assaulted and threatened, and you act like you lost a quarter in the dryer."

"Oh—more like fifty cents," she said.

He didn't smile.

Yes—humorlessness was always enchanting. She was well out of *this* one.

"If you'll forgive my saying so, you seem like a woman who goes out of her way to make life difficult for herself," he said.

Somehow, she didn't recall asking for his opinion. "Well, I think you're probably the expert when it comes to that, Kevin," she said, and tilted her wrist just enough to catch a quick glimpse of her watch. "Although you probably *see* yourself as an expert on *everything."*

His eyes narrowed, but he also seemed to be considering smiling. Rejecting the idea, but still considering it.

"I think it would take us only about three weeks to tear each other apart, Dana," he said. "What do you think?"

"More like three *days,"* she said, and checked her watch again. Not that she had any place she had to be—but he didn't know that.

"Am I keeping you?" he asked.

Against her better judgment, she shook her head. "I was just trying to get on your nerves."

He nodded.

"Did it work?" she asked.

He nodded again, but this time, the smile was in his eyes, too. She smiled back, and then, they both looked away.

The waitress appeared with a fresh coffee pot, and neither of them argued when she refilled their cups—or took away their barely touched plates.

Kevin was stirring sugar into his coffee, adding it half a packet at a time, tasting it until he was satisfied. A process that seemed considerably more complicated than it needed to be. He saw her watching, looked uncomfortable, and took what appeared to be a rebellious swig from the cup.

Okay, fine. Whatever.

They sat in reasonably congenial silence for a couple of minutes.

"I wasn't brave," she said—to her own surprise.

He looked up, focusing on her to a degree that was maybe unnerving.

Too late to quit now. "You, uh, you have this image of yourself," she said, "you know? I mean, you go for years, figuring out *exactly* how you would react, under various circumstances, and then—" She stopped. Was she really going to admit something like this to a near-stranger? Better that, than a close friend, maybe. Less humiliating.

He was waiting for her to go on, although she might have preferred stern, critical questions. Emphasis on the critical.

"I was very disappointed in myself," she said.

He nodded.

Well, okay. He was certainly accepting the notion of her timidity without much disagreement, wasn't he. She decided that she had confided far more than had been indicated, and concentrated on her coffee, instead.

"How did you think you'd react?" he asked.

Heroically. Like an action movie, sort of. "Witticisms," she said. "Savoir faire. Sang-froid."

He grinned. "You thought you'd become French suddenly, too?"

Which didn't strike her funny, somehow.

"I'm kidding," he said.

She nodded, not looking at him.

"How many were there?" he asked.

She let out her breath. Should she really have brought all of this up? "Four, if you count the guy driving."

"Yeah, the driver counts," he said. "How many guns?"

Was he trying to hammer in the cowardice thing? "I only saw one," she said quietly.

He shrugged. "Only takes one."

Especially when it was pressed directly against your face.

"So, what did you do that was so terrible?" he asked.

"I don't know," she said. "Cried, trembled a lot, didn't fight back—that sort of thing."

He shrugged again. "Sounds like a rational response, to me."

Maybe. "I just sat there cooperatively, and let them do it," she said.

"Maybe you followed your instincts, and that's why you're still alive right now," he said.

Yeah, right. Dana shook her head. "Maybe I was such a pathetic, craven little thing that they figured they didn't have to *bother* killing me. I was already so spooked—Christ, before they even started—that all they had to—well." Not one of her finer moments.

It was so quiet at the table that she was even more humiliated.

"Trying to destroy your self-respect was probably their *intent,"* he said.

If so—they'd done well.

"If you're not already, you might want to talk to someone," he said.

She frowned. Wasn't that what they were doing right now?

"Someone professional," he elaborated. "A PTSD specialist, preferably." He reached for his wallet. "Actually, I probably have some names of people we use downtown, if you'd—"

"No," she said. "I mean, thank you—but, I'm really not—"

"Just a suggestion," he said.

She nodded, checking her watch for real, this time. He glanced at his own wrist, and frowned.

"You, uh, probably have to go do case prep," she said, "right?"

He nodded. "Actually, yeah, but—" He stopped. "Look. Do you want to press charges?"

Press charges against masked men she could in no way identify, who would still probably have her killed? She shook her head, catching the waitress's eye and indicating that they needed the check.

"Don't rip yourself up for doing whatever you had to do, Dana," he said. "You're still alive—so you must have guessed right."

She was still alive because they'd realized that she was nothing more than an annoyance—and a very *small* one, at that.

When the check came, he reached for it, but she managed to get her hand there first and then pay it without too much argument. She let him help her into her jacket—he was starting to get very deft at zipping her in—and then, he held the door for her.

They were going in different directions, so they stood on the corner for a minute, not quite making eye contact.

"Um, thank you very much for shoveling," she said. "It was really a big help."

He shrugged, his hands deep in his pockets. "No problem. Happy to do it."

They both nodded, and then stood around some more.

"Well," she said. "Okay, then."

He nodded. "Yeah."

What now? Should she make an inane "good luck on your trial" remark, and then he could tell her to take care of herself, and they could nod again, and—

"Well," he said, and shifted his weight.

Without giving the idea any analysis, she took a step closer to him, but then realized that, with her current lack of mobility, she wasn't going to be able to lean up high enough.

"Would you mind bending down slightly?" she asked.

He looked uneasy, but crouched a little. She only had enough nerve to kiss him on the cheek, so that's what she did, and then she stepped back.

"Thank you," she said.

He nodded, flushing slightly, then reached out to touch her arm for a second. "Look, um, maybe sometime, we could—I don't know—maybe—"

"Yeah," she said. "I think I'd like that."

It had been a pretty grueling morning, and when she got home, she went straight to bed, without even bringing along a book. The cats were thrilled by this turn of events.

The phone rang around lunchtime, and after giving the matter some thought, Dana decided to answer it.

"Listen, I've been thinking," Peggy said.

Well, why should today be different from any other day?

"Unh-hunh," Dana said, trying to decide if the spot she saw

on the ceiling was a deposit of New York soot, or just a shadow. "Was it terribly exhilarating?"

Peggy made an impatient sound. "No, come on, pay attention to me."

Yes, ma'am. "Okay," Dana said. "What?"

"If you *really* wanted to find out what was going on with me, professionally, what would you do?" Peggy asked.

Oh, good. An answer that was child's play. Dana laughed. "Talk to one of your many disgruntled employees, what else?"

"Exactly," Peggy said.

Dana wasn't quite sure where to go from there, but they decided to meet at the Science, Industry, and Business branch of the New York Public Library, where Peggy assured her all of the information they needed would be stored. The SIBL—as it was known—branch was in the old Altman's Building, and unlike much of the library system, it was something of a technological marvel, with lots of computers available for use to the general public, all of them hooked up to extensive databases.

Which Dana somehow found more intimidating than wonderful.

The unexpected snowstorm seemed to have put the city in a pretty bad mood, especially because of the deep, slushy puddles that lay in wait next to every single curb. The journey from the subway to the library was considerably more treacherous than usual.

When she got there, Peggy was already waiting. She seemed to know exactly where to go, so Dana just followed her.

"What are we looking for?" she asked.

"*Standard and Poor's,*" Peggy said. "And maybe *Moody's* or *D&B's.* Check the SEC filings. That sort of thing."

None of which really meant anything to her. "Couldn't I just get a job tempting for the company, maybe?" Dana asked. "I could probably find out stuff that way."

Peggy shook her head. "You want people who had *power.* So, we check his upper management, try to find someone who left in the last year or so, and hope it was under bad circumstances. Then, they'll be happy to trash him."

How come Peggy was better at this than she was? But Dana just shrugged and trailed after her.

"I still have all that stuff from Jake Saperstein," she said. "And a lot of it was financial."

Peggy nodded. "We'll go over it again, later."

Well—okay. Whatever. They had to wait for a while before they were assigned to a computer work-station, but Peggy spent the time flipping confidently through various business directories and there turned out to have been a surprising amount of turnover in Brandon's corporation. Names that were listed one year, and gone the next.

"Here," Peggy said, writing down the names of the former executives on a file card and handing it to her. "I'll find out where they're working now, so we'll know who's still in town, while you do a newspaper search, see what pops up."

As opposed to joining the computer age, Dana had always preferred browsing through the stacks, or ambling around and chatting people up—but this was undeniably more efficient and more user-friendly than she would have anticipated. Two of her names showed up as obituaries, and others had simply retired. The rest of the people had just "moved on" for various reasons, some of them presumably less amicable than others.

"Well?" Peggy asked, standing behind her, with a stack of file cards.

"I don't know," Dana said, scrolling hesitantly to the first page of the Business Section once she had found the proper daily edition. Microfilm machines were really more her speed. "Most of them still seem to be in the city."

Peggy leaned over to skim her notes. "What did you get on Wilcox?"

Well, it was written right there in plain, only somewhat sloppy, English. Dana pointed halfway down the page. "Bear-Stearns. But I don't know if his leaving ended up being a lateral move, or a promotion."

Peggy frowned, squinted at her handwriting, then checked her own notes. "Lateral. So, in his case, it might just have been mediocrity. What about Zimmer? He's the closest to our age, so I think he's our best bet."

Dana tapped his name on her legal pad, then returned her attention to the screen.

"Okay," Peggy said, nodding as she read. "That's good—I have contacts over there. *Who's Who* says he went to Haverford, but we still might know people in common."

Peggy seemed to be about ten minutes ahead of her here. Maybe even twenty. It was annoying. "Okay." Dana carefully copied down the basic facts about one of the other departed executives, who was now the CEO of some Chicago company. "Now that we know where he works, what exactly is it that I'm going to do with this guy?"

"Lunch," Peggy said. "What else?"

Twenty-one

It took her a few days to get through to Horace Zimmer—using both Peggy's contacts, and a guy she had known at Brown who went off to Wharton, and was now a hotshot Wall Street mogul—and the only time Zimmer would agree to meet her was for a short breakfast meeting after his Tuesday squash game. She didn't like the peremptory note in his voice, but he was in mergers and acquisitions, so he might be very helpful. For her part, she told him that it was simply a routine inquiry, and he needn't be concerned. She was purposely vague about *why* she was conducting this inquiry.

The sling looked stupid with her dress-for-success outfit, but she was still supposed to keep her shoulder immobilized, so she wouldn't impede the healing process. If he didn't like it—tough.

Horace Zimmer turned out to be exactly what she had expected—self-satisfied, abrupt, arrogant. His suit was, of course, expensive, grey, and well-cut, and his silk tie was exquisite, if bland. He had a reddish face, and his hair was slicked back from his post-squash—which he probably thought of as *combat,* as opposed to mere exercise—shower.

"Who did you say you were with?" he asked, frowning over the business card—discreet name and phone number, only; made on her friend Fred's computer—she had given him, and then checking his overly ostentatious Rolex.

Hadn't they taught grammar at Haverford and Wharton? "I'd prefer to keep my own counsel on that, Horace," she said, evenly. "I'm sure you understand."

Nothing in his expression suggested that such was the case.

"Your involvement in this matter will, of course, be kept entirely confidential," she said.

He glanced down at her card again. "You SEC?"

She left a nice little pause before answering. Playing all these different roles really was a gas. What was she drawing on here, *Other People's Money?* Or just the concept of nameless three-letter government agencies? "Again," she said, "I'd rather not elaborate on that, but—well, it would be fair to say that a wide interrogatory net is being cast here."

He frowned.

Yeah, this was pretty entertaining. "A net which, I might add, in no way focuses on you," she said. "It involves a previous employer. But we would very much welcome any assistance you were able to offer."

"What's in it for me?" he asked.

What a winsome fellow. She shrugged, and took a sip from her goblet of orange juice. "Is Mitchell Brandon on your list of favorite people?"

"Is he on yours?" Horace asked.

Dana shook her head pleasantly.

"Then we have something in common," he said.

She'd thought they might, yeah.

"Did he finally trip himself up?" Horace asked.

Dana smiled. Pleasantly.

"We all play fast and loose," Horace said, "but he's a whole new dimension."

"Is that why you left the corporation?" she asked.

He frowned again. "I thought this wasn't about me."

She shrugged in the most benign way imaginable. "And I stand by that."

"Yeah, well, I don't want to get involved," he said, "okay?"

There was a shocker. Dana nodded, tapping her fork very lightly against the tablecloth. Flipping a quarter up and down, ominously, repeatedly, would have been all the more amusing—but perhaps just a bit *too* much so.

"He's a slumlord with a good tailor," Horace said. "What else do you need to know?"

Dana nodded, tapping.

"I wasn't exactly his right-hand man," Horace said. "But—there was a lot of trickle-down around there. It was a way of doing business."

Dana nodded, and tapped oh so lightly.

Horace coughed, and then shifted around in his seat. Amazing that something so simple could make him this jittery.

"Social triage," he said. Blurted, really.

She stopped tapping. "What?"

"That's what they called it," he said. "Big joke around the office. Force out the welfare queens and the old ladies with thirty years of rent control, bring in the yuppies, and there you have it. Social triage."

Jesus. As phrases went, that one was pretty chilling. "Is that, of necessity, illegal?" she asked.

He shook his head. "Usually, all you have to do is offer a few thousand in balloon payments, and they're stupid enough to take them. I mean, come on. It's not like they *know* any better."

He was a prince, a veritable prince. "But, not always," she said.

He checked his watch. "You tell me. Listen, are we about to wrap up here?"

Okay. What the hell. Especially if he was going to sit around and try to be furtive. Besides, she wasn't enjoying his company much. "The Harrison Hotel," she said.

"Probably," he said, sounding as though he didn't care much one way or the other. "Up there, if it's west of Broadway—he wants it."

"And whatever Mitchell wants, Mitchell gets?" she asked.

"Well—" He stopped, then frowned, and reached for his briefcase. "That's all I have to say."

"Who would he have had do it?" she asked.

He shrugged and stood up. "Hired help, I don't know. Plenty of people out there'll do anything for money."

Specificity would be nice here. She gave him her best gimlet-eyed stare. "It would be nice for us not to have to have a follow-up visit, Horace."

"You people can make your case on your own," he said. "I don't know a thing." He indicated his place setting. "Tell the government thanks for breakfast."

She would have to tell Visa, actually. But she nodded, trying not to communicate the degree of irritation she felt.

He must have sensed it, though, because he looked a little nervous again. "Look, I'm not—remember that gas explosion off Central Park West?" he asked. "The place had to be razed?"

Not personally, fortunately, but— "About three or four years ago?" she asked.

He nodded, pulling on his Burberry coat.

Now that she thought about it, that lot currently had—a modern luxury co-op building on it. Of all things. "Okay. Are we going to be able to find a smoking gun?" she asked.

"Doubt it," he said tersely, and walked out of the restaurant.

Although she hated eating alone in public, breakfast had been so expensive that she decided to stay and finish her coffee. Besides, she needed some privacy to figure out what she was going to do next. And—hey—the coffee was *good.*

She had a feeling that their conversation should have been more productive, if she'd known how to steer it right. Detective stuff seemed, very much, to be an acquired skill. Which she had yet, fully, to acquire.

She took up the table long enough to feel compelled to tip extra heavily, and her waiter was significantly more friendly on the way out than he had been on her way in.

After she got back uptown, she had to try the firehouse three times before she caught the engine company in quarters.

"I have some advice for the red caps," Dana said, after she and Molly had exchanged the requisite hellos and how-are-you's.

"Maybe they want to look into that gas explosion on Eighty-ninth Street. Back a few years ago?"

"Yeah, I remember," Molly said. "But—you didn't take any chances, right? I really don't want you to—"

In the background, the alarm sounded loudly.

"Christ, what a morning," Molly said, and hung up.

Having duly reported her information, Dana went down to the basement to spend some time on the never-ending chore of sorting recycleables. This was what she was supposed to do, right? Find out various fun facts, alert the authorities, and then resume her normal life. Going beyond the bare minimum would be—shortsighted. Ill-advised. Downright idiotic.

On the other hand, if she didn't make some kind of direct moves herself, she was going to have to spend the rest of her life looking over her shoulder, haunted by the specters of incipient rape—gang rape—and murder. It might be better just to know, one way or the other, instead of walking around flinching all the time.

It might also be nice to find out if she were even *capable* of intestinal fortitude.

To start feeling comfortable looking in the mirror again.

This was going to be an imprudent strategy—but, what the hell.

Her first step was to check the telephone book and get the exact address of Brandon's downtown corporate headquarters. Then she packed a grey sweater dress, a pair of decent shoes, some sunglasses, a clipboard, a carefully addressed business-size manila envelope containing little more than her phone number, an easily folded canvas briefcase, a hairbrush, and some masking tape into an old army knapsack.

After that, she put on a sweatpants/worn pullover/backwards baseball cap combo that would suffice to suggest that she was just a run-of-the-mill messenger. She also, in the interests of efficacy, temporarily discarded her sling.

Considering that *months* generally passed without her going anywhere near Wall Street—below SoHo, for that matter—it was deeply bizarre that she was going to go down there twice in the same day.

The main floor of Brandon's building had an impressively intimidating security desk. She considered turning around and walking right out, but then chewed hard on her gum—she hated gum—and walked over.

"Got a delivery for—" she made a point of checking the address on the envelope "—Mitchell Brandon?"

The broader of the two beefy guys put his hand out. "We can take it here."

Dana shook her head. "I'm s'posed to, you know, get him to sign for it."

The two guards exchanged glances.

"Good luck," the one with the crew cut said.

"Who's it from?" the other, very blond, one asked.

Dana shrugged, and looked at her manufactured return address. "I don't know. Some law firm."

The guards looked at each other again, and then the one with the crew cut scribbled out a pass, and motioned for her to sign in.

"Take it to the receptionist area on the forty-ninth floor," he said. "They'll sign off on it for you."

"Whatever, Jack," Dana said, snapped her gum, scrawled a fake name on the sign-in sheet, and headed towards the bank of elevators the particularly Aryan one indicated.

She rode up with three dark-suited business types—two male, one female—all of whom made a point of *not* standing near the lowly messenger. Just for fun, she decided to make eye contact with the woman.

"So. Have you had your colors done?" she asked.

The woman frowned, but beyond that, didn't acknowledge her.

"I'm a Winter," Dana told the two men—who also ignored her.

She pitied Republicans; she honestly did.

By the time the elevator reached the forty-ninth floor, she was alone. The doors opened, and she stepped into a reception area that could only be described as beautifully appointed. Lush, even.

The carpet, however, was thick enough to turn the strongest of ankles.

She was trying so hard not to stumble that, of course, she did, and everyone in the waiting area looked up from their copies of *Forbes* and the *Wall Street Journal.*

Her dignity was probably shot, but she managed to recover her balance and give the terribly elegant young receptionist—a supermodel type, if ever there had been one—a sheepish grin.

"Hi," she said, and motioned towards the tasteful bouquet of lilies arranged on the desk. "Nice flowers. Got a delivery for Mitchell Brandon?"

The receptionist nodded, extending her very slim and pale hand for the envelope. "Do you need me sign to sign for it?"

Which was her cue to nod, and leave gracefully—but she found herself shaking her head. Looking for trouble. "Oh, no. He has to sign for it himself."

The receptionist smiled with exceptional impersonality. "That won't be possible. If you'll just—"

Dana shook her head very sadly. "*He* has to sign it. Himself. If he doesn't, I get fired."

Now the receptionist frowned at her. "Miss, I'm afraid you—"

"In *ink,*" Dana said. "Right here, right now. And—it would be better if we could bring in a notary public, too."

"What company are you from?" the receptionist asked. "We certainly do not do business this way."

If it weren't for the getting-killed part, this detective stuff would really be the best job in the world. Talk about endless opportunities for incorrigibility and amusement. At the moment, she felt nothing if not puckish. "Come on, do you want me to lose my job?" Dana asked. "Just humor me, give him a buzz. You can tell him it's—one of the little people."

Even the people in the waiting area who considered themselves to be above such petty matters all seemed to be watching now.

The receptionist glared at her, but when she spoke, her voice was almost as modulated as ever. "Miss, I'm going to have to insist that—"

"*He* has to sign for it," Dana said. "Him. The Big Cheese. Nobody else."

The receptionist must have pressed some kind of alarm button, because a thick wooden door slid silently open and a burly, if distinguished, fortyish man in a dark suit came out, flanked by two younger, and even burlier, associates.

"Miss, I'm going to have to ask you to—" he started—and then stared, apparently recognizing her at almost the exact same instant she recognized him. Or, at any rate, his *voice.*

And, as it just so happened, the *last* time she'd seen him, he'd been pointing at a gun at her inside a speeding van.

She turned to the receptionist. "Never mind. I've unexpectedly achieved total clarity here." She dropped the envelope on the desk. "Make sure he gets this." Then, she pressed for the elevator and gave the man a slight smile. "Good to see you again. My regards to the others." She glanced at his two associates. "Then again, maybe you *are* the others."

"Miss Coakley," the man said, equally brusque, "I think maybe you'd better come along with—"

The elevator doors opened, and she jumped on, pressing for the first floor, and then the "Close" button. It was to her benefit that they weren't going to want to cause a scene in front of all the people in the waiting room. They would definitely come down after her—and also make sure she was stopped before she could get out of the building—but, she had come prepared.

She pressed the "Stop" button—which set off an alarm—and took the masking tape out of her knapsack. She ripped off a piece and then jumped up to cover the lens of the security camera with it. For good measure, she added a second piece.

Then, swiftly, trying to ignore her shoulder's inability to work right, she yanked off her messenger's outfit and pulled on the grey dress and nice shoes. Superman might be able to change fast—but he had nothing on *actors.* She turned off the "Stop" button, then pressed a whole row of floors farther down. Might as well keep them hopping.

As the elevator began descending again, she stuffed her knapsack and its contents into the canvas briefcase, zipped it shut, brushed her hair, took out her gum, and put on her sunglasses and some lip gloss.

She let the door open and close a few times, and then got off briskly on the forty-first floor. She stopped to frown at the receptionist there, making a point of seeming quite put out.

"This isn't forty?" she asked.

"Forty-one," the receptionist answered, barely looking up.

"Well," Dana said—with perfect Peggy Affront—and then pressed for another elevator.

After a very long minute or two, during which she could feel her heart thumping uncontrollably, a different one opened and she got on. A businessmen with a leather briefcase was already inside—and had pressed the "Lobby" button. She nodded at the man, and stepped to the side of the elevator for the ride down.

Aplomb. What was needed here, was aplomb. There was a security camera filming her, and she was an efficient young businesswoman now. There were going to be people waiting for her on the main floor, and if she didn't step off with utter confidence, and stride directly to the exit, they were going to see through her in about half a second.

Another well-dressed man got in on the thirty-eighth floor, and on the thirty-fifth floor, a third man—this one gripping a walkie-talkie, instead of a briefcase—joined them.

Security.

She *wanted* to gasp, and duck, and go into a total screaming panic, but with a concerted effort, she kept herself from even blinking.

At first, the security guard seemed to dismiss her, but then he paused and scrutinized her more carefully.

She lowered her sunglasses about a quarter of an inch. "I beg your pardon," she said, snippily.

"Oh." He coughed. "Excuse me, miss, I—"

"That's *Ma'am* to you, chum," she said, and pushed her sunglasses back up.

When they got to the lobby, she felt sick to her stomach, but she stepped off quite smartly. There were at least ten security guards waiting near the elevator she *should* have gotten off, but while a couple of them looked at her suspiciously, the guard who had ridden down with her shook his head, and they returned their attention to the other elevators.

She desperately wanted to run, but she forced herself to stop and check her watch first. Then she walked with a controlled, if crisp, pace, keeping her eyes on the main exit every step of the way.

A man on his way in held the door for her and she nodded her thanks, and then went outside. Glancing back over her shoulder would have been tempting—but imbecilic. She walked steadily, calmly, heading for the subway, wishing that her back felt less like a target.

The train took forever to come, and she spent every second worrying that a scowling slew of guards was going to show up and drag her away. She gripped her canvas briefcase handle, feeling herself trembling. Her bronchial tubes were probably constricted, too, because she couldn't seem to get her breath.

Not that she was—cowardly—or anything. Not a chance.

Finally, an uptown express train pulled in and she got on. The doors closed, and she sat down, heavily, in a free seat.

What she had just done had been undeniably foolish—but, at least she'd pulled it off.

Once she got home, she had chain-smoked her way through almost half a pack before the phone rang. Of course, it could be anyone, but she doubted it.

She swallowed, stubbed out her latest cigarette, and picked up the receiver. "Hello?"

"I'm assuming this is the right number," a familiar—and, yes, charismatic—male voice said.

Oh, boy. Mr. Brandon, his own very self. "You're assuming correctly," she said.

"Okay." He paused. "You wanted my attention? You've *got* it."

Now what? She took a deep breath—and felt pain in her ribs. Pretty severe pain, actually. "I think we need to talk."

"Clearly," he said.

She should probably have thought this out, first, but— "If you're interested, I'll be in the Oak Bar at six-thirty."

He didn't answer right away. "I think that's rather public for what we have in mind, don't you?"

For what *he* had in mind, maybe. "You want to show up under some highway, or on an abandoned pier, fine," she said. "Knock yourself out, Mitch. But *I'll* be at the Oak Bar."

There was another long pause before he spoke. "Six-thirty, it is, then."

Outstanding. "Can't wait," she said, and hung up.

Twenty-two

Backup seemed to be indicated here. Peggy was, of course, in the middle of some interminable meeting, but Dana used the phrase "dire circumstances" and the secretary put her through.

"This had better be good," Peggy said, when she picked up.

Well, hmmm. "He called," Dana said.

Peggy remained silent.

Oh, for God's sake. "Not Kevin," Dana said. "Brandon. I'm meeting him at the Oak Bar at six-thirty."

"Are you *entirely* insane?" Peggy asked.

Quite possibly.

"This seems very foolhardy to me. I don't like it at all," Peggy said. "Why don't we stay on the former employees' route?"

Because it was boring. Dana lit another cigarette. "I'm just letting you know—so you can pursue my untimely demise, if you're so inclined."

Peggy sighed. "All right, already. We're trying to steal a writer from Holt. I'll call her agent, get him to meet me for a drink." Then, she sighed again. "Attempt not to do anything moronic until I get there."

Dana grinned. "Who, me?" she said, and hung up.

Her shoulder was throbbing and unresponsive, but she had no intention of giving Brandon the satisfaction of seeing that. She would just take another pain pill and tough it out for a few more hours.

It took some time deciding what to wear, since she was going for both professional, and provocative. Luckily, she had sent Victoria's Secret a goodly amount of money over the years, and had several "straight from the office to the gala" sorts of dresses, predominantly red or black. She decided to go with a black dress—and bright red lipstick.

She arrived ten minutes early, and when she told the maitre d' who she was meeting, he didn't seem to believe her, but she was seated in a large, exclusive booth, anyway.

The bar was quiet, and subdued, and predominantly male. One notable female presence, looking elegant in a saffron linen suit, was Peggy, sitting across from a tweedy man in the middle of the room. They seemed to be engaged in animated, only moderately argumentative, conversation, and Peggy didn't even look up when Dana went by.

She wanted a drink with every fiber of her being, but she took the precaution of ordering coffee, in order to preserve whatever acumen—probably limited—that she possessed.

It seemed to be a pretty safe bet that he would try to unnerve her by being late, so she had thought ahead and brought along a small, worn hardcover to read in a gracious and refined manner. Flaubert. Not her usual fare, but as a fictive choice, it had a certain, rarefied élan.

He showed up at quarter to seven, and even in a roomful of successful and wealthy people, his entrance attracted some attention. She knew that he had spotted her right away, but he took his time crossing the room, pausing at various tables to exchange remarks and handshakes.

When he finally deigned to come over to her booth, she read another page before lowering her book and placing a wispy gold-filigree bookmark between the pages.

"Well," he said, and she could tell he was amused in spite of himself. "It's a pleasure to see you again, Dana."

She responded with an aloof nod, setting her book to one side. "I, too, am elated, Mitch."

He grinned, and sat down across from her. "You're looking well."

Oh, please. Anything he could do, she could do better—chitchat included. "Yes, I just got back from Antigua," she said. "It was—as ever—divine."

Before he could try to top that, a waiter soundlessly appeared.

"Your usual, sir?" he asked, with what might have been a slight bow. Either way, the word "obsequious" came to mind.

Brandon nodded, and the waiter gracefully hustled away.

"Creme de menthe?" Dana asked. "Melon Ball?"

"Sloe gin fizz," Brandon said.

Okay. She was going to have to grin now, too.

The waiter reappeared, setting down Brandon's drink—some kind of single malt scotch—and smoothly refilling her coffee cup. He paused for a bare second, until he was sure they weren't going to order anything else, then left.

Brandon lifted her book to check the title, seemed to fight off another grin, and put it back down. "So," he said. "You're—a building superintendent, is that the story?"

Dana sipped her coffee.

"In the normal course of events, I generally find myself dealing with—brighter—people," he said.

She looked at him steadily. "You called me, remember?"

He leaned forward and touched the corner of her mouth, where the stitches had been—and a small scar now remained. She jerked her head away, and he withdrew, smiling.

Bastard. Probably smeared her lipstick, too.

"My understanding is that a—return engagement—may be arranged," he said.

She took out a small compact mirror, and fixed her lipstick. Then she sprinkled a few crystals of sugar into her coffee, and stirred it.

He grinned again. "You've got industrial size, don't you. I *like* that."

She tasted her coffee, then pushed the sugar bowl aside. "You called me."

"And *you* put on a smashing outfit and got here early," he said.

Touché. She shrugged. "This is what I wear around the apartment."

He smiled at her. "Then, I'd like to spend some time around your apartment."

Not in a trillion years. "Is that before, or after, the—return engagement?" she asked, and paused. "Or, perhaps, *during?"*

He laughed, and tasted his scotch for the first time. "Well, how about that. A woman who can play hardball, and remain attractive."

She sipped her coffee.

"Hall of Fame," he said.

Baseball was one area where she could easily hold her own. "First year of eligibility," she said. And there would have been unanimity, if the guy from the *Globe* hadn't subjected her to the same insult Ted Williams had once received.

He grinned again. Broadly. "I *like* you. I wish I didn't."

Well, yeah—it was going to make her so much harder to kill.

"I keep a suite upstairs," he said. "For—business purposes."

The man was a walking sexual sledgehammer. "How nice for you," she said, with tremendous uninterest.

The smile stayed, but there was something unquestionably savage in his eyes now. "I think it would be in your best interests," he said. "Perhaps even a precondition."

What an enticing spin that put on things. She met his gaze very calmly and directly.

"Let's be honest," he said. "You're a little girl in way over her head."

He was going to have to do better than that. "Well, now, am I mistaken, Mitch, or does that betray pedophilic impulses on your part?" she asked.

The already dark expression in his eyes intensified.

Should she quit while she was ahead, or make a bad situation worse? "I also can't help wondering," she said, "why, if I'm so inept, are *you* running scared?"

He moved his jaw, then drank some scotch. "Don't kid yourself, Dana. As far as I'm concerned, you're just an inconvenience.

It's easier to handle the situation civilly, but frankly, I don't care one way or the other."

Whoa. Sounded like—a threat.

"What's it going to take to make all of this go away?" he asked.

A lengthy prison sentence.

"Or, more precisely, to make *you* go away," he said.

She shrugged, noticing, in an abstracted sort of way, how badly her shoulder hurt. With luck, he couldn't tell.

"Under any other circumstances, you're exactly the sort of person I'd like to bring in," he said. "Nerve and initiative are more difficult to find than you might think."

Was it her imagination, or was he offering her a *job?* There was something over the edge of rationality about all of this. She sat back, resisting the urge to look over at Peggy for reassurance. No matter how crowded the bar was, sitting across from this man was really scary.

"What would you say to something in the mid-six figures?" he asked.

Actually, her first instinct would be to say *thank you.* She shrugged, keeping her face immobile. "Are we talking about a one-time-only payment, or is that per annum?"

The side of his mouth twitched a little. "It's negotiable."

She nodded, pretending to give the idea some serious consideration. "And exactly what would I be expected to do for my mid-six figures?"

"That's negotiable, too," he said—and winked at her.

Yeah. Pretty much what she'd figured. "Not interested," she said, and reached for her book.

His hand came out to stop her, fastening painfully around her wrist and, with admirable subtlety, twisting it in the wrong direction. "Don't be stupid," he said. "Your options are very limited here."

He was hurting her—a lot, as it happened—but she didn't want to make a scene by trying to yank free. From a distance, he probably just seemed to be flirting with her. He increased the pressure, and she had to suck in her breath.

"I'm disappointed, Dana," he said, watching her face. "I'd heard you were a crier."

And she knew damn well *where* he'd heard it. She turned, and looked around until she caught the waiter's eye. As he hurried over, Brandon abruptly released her wrist and picked up his drink.

"Could you please bring me a fresh cup?" she asked the waiter, indicating her coffee. "I'm afraid I've let this one get cold."

The waiter nodded, and whisked the offending cup away.

The look in Brandon's eyes was so murderous that, inside, she could feel herself shaking.

"Take the money and disappear," he said. "It's really your only choice."

Her only *safe* choice. She stood up, draping her purse strap over her bad shoulder. "Excuse me. I feel a sudden need to wash my hands."

Without waiting for his reaction, she went out to the Ladies Room off the main lobby, sinking down onto a well-cushioned chair as soon as she got inside. Actually, it was more of a Ladies Lounge, with an anteroom, and an attendant, and everything. What she needed right now, was the *resting* part. Hiding felt like a good idea, too.

The attendant seemed concerned, but she shook her head and closed her eyes, rubbing her wrist reflexively.

The door kept opening and she would look up eagerly, but each time, it was a woman she didn't know. Finally, after far too long for her tastes, Peggy came in, going directly over to the mirror to check her reflection.

"Took you long enough," Dana said grumpily.

"We were throwing numbers around." Peggy adjusted a few stray wisps of hair. "I couldn't just get up."

Dana stared at her. "You mean, you're actually making a *deal?"*

Peggy nodded, looking very pleased. "Yeah. We're talking about a two-book, with an option for a third." She shook her head. "Do you realize what a coup this would be? My God, every publishing house in town has been—" She stopped. "Well. How's your drink going?"

Dana just shook her head, slumping down into her very comfortable chair.

Peggy returned her attention to her reflection, making various tiny adjustments to her hair. "If you don't mind my saying so, you could be a little less obviously attracted to him."

"The feeling passed," Dana said, "believe me."

Peggy shrugged, repositioning a bobby pin. "I thought it was rather unseemly, that's all."

What a perfect time for a lecture on morality. Besides, for better or worse, in this area, her sins were generally almost entirely confined to Thought Crime. No doubt, to her detriment.

Peggy looked at her in the mirror. "For a minute there, I was afraid he was hurting you."

Dana nodded, automatically rubbing her wrist again.

Peggy looked worried. "You all right?"

"I'm peachy," Dana said. Keen. *Terrific.*

Peggy nodded, and resumed tinkering with her hair. "So. Where does it stand?"

"Pay me to back off, and/or kill me." Dana paused. "He also keeps propositioning me."

"Oh, he's *pond-phlegm,"* Peggy said.

Dana had to laugh.

"I'm serious," Peggy said.

Well, yeah. That's why she was laughing.

An elderly, very upper-crust, woman had just come out to wash her hands, and she appeared to be making a concerted effort not to listen to their conversation. She did, however, take her time at the sink.

"You know, Dana," Peggy said, thoughtfully. "Why don't we just push him in front of a bus?"

Now, the elderly woman stared at them.

"She's kidding," Dana said quickly. "She's overwrought."

"He's *swamp-swine,"* Peggy said, and then turned to the elderly woman. "I'm just getting started here. Be advised."

The elderly woman looked at them, looked at the attendant—who was also pretending not to listen—and swiftly finished washing her hands.

"Dross. Guano. *Ordure,"* Peggy said.

Dana shrugged, as the elderly woman lifted an eyebrow at her. "She reads a lot."

The elderly woman left, somewhere between amused and alarmed, and the attendant took a position as far away as possible from them.

"I'm serious," Peggy said. "We just shove him under the M104, and—" she snapped her fingers "—all of our problems are gone."

Dana laughed. Peggy probably wasn't serious, but sometimes it was hard to be sure. Then, she looked at her watch. "I'd better get back out there. He's going to wonder what's taking me so long."

"Let him think you were crying," Peggy said. "He'll probably think it's funny, so he won't be suspicious."

"Oh. Good idea." Dana closed her eyes for a couple of seconds, took a deep breath, and then let several tears fall. She grinned at Peggy, sniffed pathetically, and squeezed out a few more.

Peggy watched her for a minute, then shook her head. "I don't know, Dana. Sometimes, I can't help wondering if you *ever* express a genuine emotion."

She tried to use her powers for good—but, okay, even if she didn't take advantage of it much, she had always been able to cry on command. "It's a gift, Peggy," she said, a little offended. "My God, they love actors who don't have to use glycerin between takes."

Peggy shrugged. "I'm sorry. As far as I'm concerned, it smacks of insincerity."

It was *still* a gift. *Some* people just didn't appreciate artistry, when they saw it. She got up and blotted her eyes with a paper towel, removing almost all of the evidence, leaving just enough so that he would suspect the possibility of terrorized weeping on her part. What the hell. Then, she dropped a dollar in the attendant's wicker tip basket and turned to leave.

"Don't go anywhere with him," Peggy said from the mirror.

An unnecessary warning. "I wouldn't cross the *street* with him," Dana said, and opened the door to go.

When she walked back into the bar, there was a well-fed, white-haired man in a muted chalk-stripe suit standing by their booth, talking to Brandon. They both watched her walk over, and she was very glad that she wasn't close enough to be able to hear what they were saying.

Brandon stood up when she got to the booth—oh, yeah, the guy had great manners—and the other man stepped aside, although not enough so she would be able to avoid brushing against him.

Yes, there were times, just now and again, when she intensely disliked men. Instead of playing his little game, she stopped and put her hand out, instead.

"Hi, I'm Dana Coakley," she said. "And you're—?"

The man shook her hand, giving her an extra squeeze she didn't appreciate. "Phil Winthrop. Benton, Winthrop, and Knowles."

Okay. Whatever. "Of course," she said. "I knew your face was familiar. I'm relocating from the London office, so I'm a little out of touch." She gestured toward Brandon. "Mitch here, among others, has been very nice about presenting me with various options."

Mr. Winthrop frowned, but then apparently decided to take that at face value. "I see. What's your legal background, Miss Coakley?"

"Well, I'm admitted to the New York bar, of course," Dana said, "but"—oh, why not—"despite my innately litigious nature, I think bond trading is where I really feel most at home."

Brandon sat back down, his expression unreadable.

Mr. Winthrop reached into his inside jacket pocket and extracted a business card. "Regardless, maybe we should have a conversation sometime soon."

These people head-hunted right in *front* of each other? "Thank you," she said, and handed him one of the same discreet cards she'd given Horace Zimmer. "Certainly, I'm interested in exploring a number of different avenues."

Mr. Winthrop studied her card. "Unusual name, Coakley."

"Yes," she said. "Memorable, I like to think."

Mr. Winthrop nodded, nodded at Brandon, and went back over to his table.

Dana started to sit down, then stopped, looking dismayed. "Ut-oh," she said, and glanced after Mr. Winthrop. "If anything happens to me, he's going to be *yet another* loose end who can connect us, isn't he?"

Brandon glared at her.

"See, that's your problem, Mitch," she said, sitting down and taking a sip from her fresh cup of coffee. "We both know that I may not have a lot of proof—beyond, of course, the fact that an innocent man would never have overreacted like this—but you really have no idea what it is I *do* actually know—or who I've told about it. And, you know, I have a feeling there are loose ends *all over town."*

Was it her imagination, or was that a malevolent look he was giving her? Without question, it was *fierce.*

"Now, I'm trying to remember," she said, and let her eyebrows furrow. "Did I tell any reporters? It's so hard to keep track."

Brandon shook his head. "Nice try. You forget that I just watched you effortlessly lie to a reasonably intelligent man, who bought every word of it."

"Well." She made herself look modest. "Years of training."

At first, he just seemed angry, but then he paused. "How about a part? A *great* part."

What? Dana frowned, not sure where he was going with this.

"The female lead," he said. "Big budget, summer release, location shoot—whatever you want. All I have to do is make a few calls, and—it's yours."

The scary part was that he was the kind of person who probably *could* buy her a slot in Hollywood. Who could buy damn near anything he wanted, at any given moment. "The hero's girlfriend?" she asked. "Or an actual, three-dimensional, fully realized role?"

"Whatever it takes," he said.

Not that she was tempted, but—as offers went, it was a lot more seductive than a simple mid-six figures payoff.

"That *is* what you want, isn't it," he said. "More than anything?"

It had been during most of the waking moments of her entire life.

"Well?" he asked.

"We'll call you Hardy," Dana said to no one in particular. "Joe Hardy. You'll be twenty-two years old. They'll put a new wing on that baseball museum in Cooperstown—dedicated to you. The Hardy Shrine."

He must have gotten the reference, because he sat back, frowning again.

"Now, if you could guarantee that the Red Sox would win the World Series this year, *that* might be a different story," she said.

He didn't smile.

Fine. Either way, they had pretty much played out the string here. Besides, her only real intent had been to let him know that she was still in one piece—and wasn't going away anytime soon. She hadn't exactly expected him to burst into tears, and tell her everything. She started to gather up her purse, and her Flaubert, but then paused. "Oh. Just one question."

He gave her the same sort of look the sly, but guilty, culprits always gave Columbo.

"How do you go about hiring your security staff?" she asked.

His eyebrows came together in a frown. "What do you mean?"

"Well," she said, very pleasantly, "do you raid the staffs of places like—I don't know—Cineplex Odeon, or do you go after—oh, say, former cops, and retired military people?"

His face was so blank that she knew she'd made him nervous with that one.

"Because," Dana said, "it's just possible that a lot of witnesses *saw them around.*" Saw *one* noticeably militaristic man, anyway.

Brandon still didn't say anything, looking at her in a more speculative way than he had before.

"Just a thought," Dana said, and eased her coat on as gracefully as possible, trying to make it seem as though her right shoulder still worked normally. "See, the thing you have to remember, is that I'm really the least of your problems, Mitch. All I am is the wild-card civilian who's getting in the middle of things. At minimum, you should be getting a fall guy ready."

Brandon moved his jaw. "Sometimes, one's subordinates get overeager, and do things of their own volition, with the mistaken impression that they're acting under your directive."

Iran-contra, anyone? "Not bad," Dana said, standing up. "Give Dershowitz or someone a call, see if he buys it."

They looked at each other for a minute.

"Watch your back," she said. "All I am is the enemy you can see."

"Advice you could take yourself," he said.

Right.

He tilted his head, making it clear that he was mentally, graphically, undressing her. "That really *is* a smashing dress," he said. "Glad you wore it for me."

He *wished.* "Hope not to see you again, Mitch," she said, and walked out.

Twenty-three

Going home, she switched cabs three times. Obviously, they already knew where she lived, but—it seemed safer. She and Peggy had also agreed not to see each other, in person, for at least a day or two, because—well, it couldn't hurt. When it came to looking for trouble, there were *limits.*

The phone rang just before ten and, anticipating threats, she hesitated before answering. It was a very pleasant surprise to hear Kevin Gallagher on the other end.

"I hope this isn't too late to call," he said, formally.

"Early to bed, late to rise, that's me," Dana said.

"Oh." He cleared his throat. "Well—"

She cut him off. "But, of course, you know I'm kidding."

"Of course," he said.

Right. Dana decided to relent and change the subject. "How's your trial going?"

"Rogue witness today," he said. "I had to spent a lot of the afternoon rehabbing the mess he made this morning."

If the two of them stayed—or became—whatever they were, she was going to have to go down to Centre Street sometime and watch him in action. "Think you salvaged him?" she asked.

"At the expense of the jury's affection," he said wryly.

Ooops.

"So, I, uh—" He stopped. "That is, what did *you* do today?"

She knew she shouldn't laugh, but it was unavoidable.
"What?" he asked, sounding worried.
"Long day," she said. *Strange* day.
"What happened?" he asked.
Time to dust off her Fifth Amendment rights. Or else use her currently ever-so-shiny skills as a prevaricator. On the other hand, they had just met—should she really start lying to him this soon?
"Well," she said, "it was—" What? "It ended up being busier than I'd anticipated." And stressful, what with being repeatedly threatened and all. "It was—unusual."
"Nothing rogue on your part, I hope," he said.
Nothing *but.* "Well, the jury of my peers was greatly disturbed," she said, and left it at that.
"Okay," he said, after a pause, then coughed. "Look, I was wondering—if you're free on Saturday, maybe we could—I don't know—go to a movie or something?"
Yes! "Sounds good," she said.

The next day, she went back to the library, and read up on the building explosion on West 89th Street a few years earlier. Two deaths, several critical injuries, major structural damage, a leak in the gas line, thought to be accidental, a routine investigation proceeding. The property was ultimately sold to a group of mostly unidentified investors, and some eighteen months later, opened its doors as a luxury high-rise.
No surprises. No apparent smoking guns.
Early Thursday evening, she met Peggy up at the Second Chance gymnasium, so she could go to Travis's first basketball game. Peggy was less than thrilled by the idea, but doggedly showed up, with a thick manuscript box under her arm.
They sat about halfway up the bleachers, among a sparse, but very vocal, crowd. As the two teams—Second Chance was playing one of the other alternative schools—did their warm-up drills, Peggy put on her glasses, took out her manuscript, and got right to work with a blue pencil.
"I really don't like this, Dana," she said, without looking up. "It's much too loud for me."

Dana nodded. "I know, but I promised. It's a big deal for him."

Peggy surveyed the court for a few seconds. "Well—at least they're not terribly tall. Tall players bore me a great deal."

Dana grinned, and watched as the Second Chance players tried to turn simple layups into soaring Michael Jordan miracles, missing many more than they made. Gary, the math teacher who also served as a volunteer coach, kept blowing his whistle and trying to bring them back down to earth—in every sense—but he wasn't having much luck.

Travis caught sight of her, then—and looked so happy that she was immediately glad that they had come. He tossed the rebound he had just caught to Amory, and jogged over to see her.

"Yo, you came," he said, sounding genuinely pleased.

Dana shrugged. "We wouldn't have missed it."

"Not for the world," Peggy said, with deep irony, still reading away.

Travis cocked his head at that, but then pointed at two women sitting down in the first row. "That's my mother, and my aunt. You'll come say hi, after?"

"Absolutely," Dana said.

He nodded. "Told 'em, you know, that you would. If you like, came."

One of the things that continually amazed her about these kids was how *very* little it took to make them happy. She gestured down toward the court where Amory was going out of his way to ignore them. "Amory isn't going to say hello?"

Travis shook his head. "No way. Not in front of everyone like this."

Just for fun, Dana shouted, "Hi, Amory!" and waved enthusiastically at him. Wildly, even. Amory looked mortified, and turned away.

"Yo, that was mean," Travis said. "You're a mean lady."

Yep.

Travis indicated his brand-new red Second Chance uniform shirt with the number 32 on the back. "Not bad, hunh?"

"Well, I think you earned it," she said.

Travis looked pleased again. "So, like, I got a ninety in history, right? And my teacher just goes, she goes, whoa. *Whoa,* she said." He grinned at them, and then went back down to join his teammates.

"Probably has no idea what a living hell he's made of your life," Peggy said, reading.

No. Probably not.

Peggy looked over from her manuscript. "He's a nice kid. I would have tried to help him, too."

Dana nodded, and watched as the starting fives took the floor, and the volunteer referee got ready to throw the first jump ball.

Midway through the second quarter, she got an idea.

"Best defense is a good offense," she said.

Peggy frowned at her. "Please don't discuss sports with me, Dana."

Yeah, yeah, yeah. "I want to get into his house," Dana said. "Poke around a little, see if there's anything incriminating."

"Please don't discuss breaking the law with me, Dana," Peggy said, with the exact same inflection.

What a crummy sidekick. Dana shrugged. "It's better than waiting for them to come get me. It's the last thing he'd expect."

Peggy turned a page. "It's also, I feel compelled to point out, a criminal act."

"We'll think of something clever," Dana said. "Something legal." She'd have to go back to John Jay and read up on search and seizure, but she was pretty sure civilians were immune to its strictures. More so than the police, anyway. "It'll work out fine, don't worry."

Peggy just frowned at her.

"Hey, it was your idea to get *on* the ride," Dana said. "You can get off whenever you want."

Peggy looked annoyed—but didn't argue.

"We could bring them a delivery, maybe?" Dana said. After all, it had worked last time.

Peggy made a face. "What, put on little UPS uniforms? Get serious."

Okay. Hmmm. Dana tried to think of something else. "Maids?"

Peggy shook her head, scrawling an emphatic note next to one paragraph. "Oh, please. They most certainly already have a regular staff."

Yeah, probably. Dana slouched down to watch the turnover-dominated game. Then, suddenly, she sat up.

"Caterers!" she said.

"What do you mean?" Peggy asked, looking dubious.

"It's going to be great," Dana said, and then grinned at her. "Trust me."

The idea took some planning, but none of it was insurmountable. Craig and the bartender from the art gallery, Stefan, hadn't worked out as a couple, but had become pretty good friends, so getting in touch with Stefan was easy. It turned out that the Brandons hired the same caterers regularly—and even had an upcoming cocktail party scheduled. He seemed to feel that it would be easy enough to scrounge up a couple of extra uniforms, and then she and Peggy would be able to slip into the place, unnoticed, in the pre-party crush of activity. They might actually have to *work* the shift—but she had decided not to share that aspect of the situation with Peggy yet.

On Friday afternoon, right after she had gotten home from her first physical therapy session for her shoulder—having discovered that complete, unfettered and, most important, pain-free use of her arm was nowhere in her immediate future—the phone rang. When she heard an unfriendly Mitchell Brandon on the other end, her already lousy day went further downhill.

"Yeah? What do you want?" she asked stiffly, feeling her hand clench around the receiver. Her stomach started hurting, too. Instantly. As though *she* could use a Prilosec.

"I thought I'd pass along a rumor," he said.

She swallowed, looking around her apartment uneasily. The animals were acting perfectly normal—strewn about in positions of utter somnolence, in fact—but could there be someone hiding in here, ready to kill her at any given second, and this was the cruel way she was going to find out?

"Obviously, I don't know the details," he said, "but there's going to be at least one arrest sometime in the next week or so."

So he had taken her advice and found himself a goddamn fall guy. "And how much did *that* cost you?" she asked. The mid-six figures, at minimum, presumably.

There was an ominous pause before he answered, and she resisted the urge to gulp again.

"I have no idea what that means," he said smoothly. "But, with this situation now resolved, I want to make it clear that I don't expect to hear from you—or *of* you—ever again."

"Likewise," Dana said, and tried to hang up, but he beat her to it.

The notion of some fall guy looming in the New York's tabloids' future was intriguing—and frustrating. Presumably, he would be painted as a guy with a grudge, or some random lunatic, and everyone else would get off scot-free. Although he probably *was* crazy, since with ten murders, life without parole was the best deal this person could hope to get, and was any amount of money in the world worth *that?* Then again, maybe Brandon had just had his people set up some poor—in every way—entirely innocent person, who could be put in the wrong place at the wrong time. Or else, maybe—before she went any further, she'd better find out more information.

She tried Molly at home first, and then reached her at the firehouse. Since her shift was almost over, they agreed to meet at Starbucks for a very fast cup of coffee shortly thereafter. Dana, personally, was tired enough to need some caffeine right about now.

When Molly came in—with a small bandage above her right eyebrow—it was pretty clear that she was in the same boat, fatiguewise, and they went for Grandés, instead of just Talls.

"Are you all right?" Dana asked, indicating the gauze.

Molly looked very tired, but waved that aside. "Little steam burn. Nothing to it."

If she were Jake Saperstein, she would almost certainly spend her daily life with her stomach in a perpetual knot of anxiety and dread.

"Anyway," Molly said, and indicated their overly expensive coffees. "Is this social, or—?"

It would be nice if all of this stupid crime stuff would just go away, and this *could* be exclusively social. "Well, sure," Dana said, "but—" Why not get right to the point. "I kind of heard that they're about to make an arrest."

No one seemed to be paying even the remotest sort of attention to them—and Dana had damn well *checked,* more than once, from the moment she'd walked in the place—but Molly looked around anyway.

"Who told you that?" she asked quietly. "It's not exactly public information."

A very evil criminal told her. "Did it come from an anonymous tip?" Dana asked. "Or information the red caps developed on their own?"

Molly shrugged. "They haven't exactly been briefing me, Dana. But word's been going around that they're getting close. Which is good news for you, because you relax and go back to normal."

Except they weren't getting close.

"In fact," Molly said, cautiously, "you're going to have to back off now. The Department really *needs* this one."

"And that'll be it? Case closed? Regardless of whether he's guilty?" Dana asked.

Molly looked around some more, then sighed. "Look, just stay out of it, okay? If you get in the way and do anything that screws this up—"

Dana nodded, cutting her off. "So, it doesn't matter *who* gets arrested, as long as *someone* does?"

Molly frowned at her. "Hardly. But if this is all they can get, they'll certainly take it."

It would be tactless to remind her of the Waldbaum's fire, back in the late seventies, during which six firefighters had been tragically killed—and some poor innocent schmuck ended up serving over ten years in prison, for a fire that it later turned out wasn't even arson. "Whoever it is, is a fall guy," she said. "I know that for sure. They're throwing it in your lap, because they just want all of it to go away."

Molly shrugged. "At some level, don't you?"

Well, yeah, but—"At the expense of our system of justice?" Dana asked. "And little things like, I don't know, the sanctity of the Constitution?"

"Oh, give me a break with the law and order stuff," Molly said. "You're an *actress,* for Christ's sake."

Okay, okay. They were both tired today. She had to remember that they were both tired. And that steam burn might hurt as much as her shoulder currently did. Dana picked up a napkin and slowly crumpled it in her left hand, pressing it into the smallest ball possible.

"I didn't mean that quite the way it sounded," Molly said, more calmly. "I just—there comes a point at which you have to give up. Move on. Right?"

Yeah. And they were just about there. It was time for things like reason, and practicality, to prevail. Dana moved her jaw—and winced. "Can they tie in the gas explosion at Eighty-ninth Street I told you about?"

Molly shook her head. "Not from what I've heard. I mean, it's been a few years, and I guess the property's changed hands more than once, but they really aren't consulting me on a regular basis, you know?"

Okay. Dana thought about that. Thought about *everything.* "Do you think any of this arresting is going to come before Tuesday morning?"

From the way Molly's posture straightened, it was obvious that she didn't like the sound of that. "Why? What's so important about Tuesday?"

It was the day *after* the Brandons' cocktail party.

She and Peggy spent most of Sunday lingering over brunch at the Popover Café, and arguing about whether to make their catering debut. After, of course, thoroughly rehashing, dissecting, and overanalyzing her previous night's movie date with Kevin Gallagher. It had been very nice, if occasionally stilted, and he had kissed her good-bye in an encouragingly ungentlemanly way. They had also not discussed crime or criminals even *once.* No doubt to his relief, as much as hers.

"So," Peggy said, once they had returned to their original subject. "What makes you think you can just walk right into the man's apartment without being recognized?"

Yes. That would be a problem. Dana ate a bite of French toast, spread with whipped strawberry butter.

"On top of which," Peggy went on, "depending on who's invited, someone might recognize *me,* and wonder what the hell I'm doing passing canapés."

Dana ate more French toast. It had been prepared from thick homemade challah with what appeared to be swirls of cinnamon, and was only a little bit too eggy. "They'll just think you're slumming."

"I'm serious," Peggy said. "You're also forgetting that your mobility isn't exactly a hundred percent yet."

True. And there was always something very pathetic about waitresses trying to carry trays while wearing slings. Dana rolled her shoulder experimentally. It felt—weak. *Heavy.* "So, no problem. I'll just take it off."

"Yeah, great idea, way to take care of yourself." Peggy shook her head. "Look, do you really think this is worth the risk? I mean, as far as I'm concerned, it lacks inherent logic."

Of all terrible things to lack. "I don't have anything major in mind," Dana said. "Mainly, I just want to poke around a little, let him know someone was there, see what it scares him into doing."

"Having you *killed,* in all likelihood," Peggy said.

Well, okay—that would be bad. The French toast, however, was delicious. "Look," Dana ate another piece, "if you're not comfortable with this, I really don't mind doing it by myself."

Peggy sighed. "And he's just going to have all sorts of incriminating papers lying around for you to find? Come on. If there *is* anything like that—which I doubt—it's off somewhere in a safety deposit box, or, I don't know, buried in a file at some law firm he has on retainer."

That was possible, maybe even probable, but—"The guy's incredibly arrogant, and he doesn't strike me as being big on trust," Dana said. "If there *are* papers, I'll bet he has them at home, where he can keep them under his control."

"Maybe," Peggy said, and took a healthy swallow of her mimosa. "But I still don't like it."

Had crime fighting *ever* been advertised as a jubilant romp through freshly fallen snow? An idyllic day on a windswept beach? No. "I agree," Dana said. "It's a totally stupid idea, it'll probably have unspeakable repercussions, and why should you be in the middle of all that? So, don't worry about a thing. Play it safe. Stay home. I'll be fine."

"You about finished?" Peggy asked.

Actually, she could probably come up with *at least* five more minutes' worth of martyred remarks, but she nodded cooperatively. Sweetly, even.

"Let's be honest," Peggy said. "More than anything, what this has turned into is one of your goddamn Coakley grudges. If he hadn't been stupid enough to have those men hurt you, you would have given all of this up, long ago."

Probably. Her family did tend to hold grudges, long past the point of rationality.

"So if I'm going to risk *my* well-being, I really want a better rationale than that or, at least, a better plan," Peggy said. "We need something a little more sensible than your simply wandering in and hoping for the best."

Details, always with the details. Dana shrugged. "So you can wait outside, as backup, and if I don't show up at some designated time, you can—I don't know—call the police."

Peggy shook her head. "I don't think so. You clearly need a chaperone."

Oh, she did, did she. But, now that she thought about it, they *did* need backup. Armed, if possible. Her brunch had come with a little fruit cup, and she ate a small, slightly off-season cantaloupe square. Then, out of nowhere, she remembered Mojo. No—*William.* "What are the moral implications of hiring a drug dealer?" she asked.

Peggy looked skeptical. "For what—doing your tax returns?"

"For backup," Dana said. "He would have a gun, so—"

Peggy cut her off. "Absolutely not. We are *not,* in *any* way, going to involve ourselves with guns. Not a chance."

Philosophical consistency could be very inconvenient. "No, seriously," Dana said. "This is going to be dangerous, and I really don't want you to get hurt." For that matter, she didn't particularly want to get hurt herself. "Besides, if he's already a criminal, wouldn't having him do this be a *positive* thing, since it's for the greater good?" Presumably, anyway. "Or am I falling into an ends justify the means thing here?"

Peggy shook her head. "Are you listening to yourself, Dana? I mean, seriously."

Okay, but some kind of backup still seemed to be indicated. If they were, in fact, going to go through with this. "Wait a minute," Dana said. "I've got it."

"What?" Peggy asked, obviously dreading the answer.

Why hadn't she thought of it right away? It was such an easy—and logical—solution. "Valerie," Dana said.

Twenty-four

Valerie was not only happy to participate—she was *eager* to do so. She wanted to be in on every single moment of illegal activity, but they decided it would make more sense for her to work the shift, and then Dana and Peggy could just sort of magically appear, in their carefully wilted little uniforms, during the noisy commotion of the cleaning-up process, and join in with the others. With luck, by then, Valerie would have been able to scout around a bit and find a good place for them to hide until the Brandons had gone to bed, and then some illicit searching could take place.

After the caterers finally packed up and left, Valerie would hang around somewhere outside and wait for what one could only hope would be their swift and effortless escape. Valerie was more than agreeable to all of this—and cagey about the exact way she would blend into her surroundings outside and attract absolutely no attention whatsoever, although she did allow as how she had already *done* homelessness, and that a new tactic was in order, so she wouldn't get stale.

Peggy's only—predictable—response to this was a dismissive "Actors. *Christ.*"

The party was supposed to break up at about nine, and so Dana and Peggy decided to meet near the Brandons' building just after eight-thirty, and wait for the first little cluster of tray-bearing caterers to come downstairs to the small, private parking garage. Since she didn't know what time she'd would get home, Dana had arranged for Craig to take Bert for his late walk—after promising that she would watch *Double Indemnity* with him *again.*

The Brandons' building was on Park Avenue in the Seventies and, of course, extraordinarily exclusive. They stood on a side street near the garage entrance, in their black uniforms and white aprons, and Dana hoped they didn't look as conspicuous as she felt. They were also each carrying a small knapsack with more comfortable clothes to change into, and—with considerable uncertainty, feeling rather like she had seen too many "Get Smart" episodes—Dana had packed a few things that seemed like appropriate detecting supplies.

Or, okay, *spy stuff.* And makeshift spy stuff, at that.

Peggy paced back and forth across the same ten feet of sidewalk, her arms tightly folded across her chest as she stared out at Park Avenue. "This is awful, I can't believe this."

Nothing had even gone wrong yet. "What?" Dana asked, rubbing her forehead. She definitely should have taken a couple of Advil before coming over here.

"Look." Peggy gestured down Park Avenue. "I'm about to do something simultaneously lawless and ludicrous, and I can see my parents' building from here." She shook her head. "My God, if they had any idea."

Yes, the Woodruffs' response to this situation would, indeed, be a terrifying sight. Especially Peggy's ever conventional and judgmental father.

Come to think of it, her *own* parents wouldn't be all that excited to hear what she was planning on doing tonight. She also didn't want to imagine what—other than never asking her out again—Kevin Gallagher's reaction would be if he knew where she was right now. And where she was going to be in an hour or two. *Burdeau v. McDowell*—yes, she'd taken another trip to John Jay—she'd tell him. *Coolidge v. New Hampshire.* They were going to be *fine.*

Peggy gritted her teeth, and paced some more. "This is a bad idea. This is a very, very bad idea."

As pep talks went, that one wasn't terribly inspiring. But, hell, she was nervous, too—there was no use pretending otherwise. Maybe they should just wait for Valerie to come down, and all go out for a beer. Abandon the entire, ill-advised notion.

"What happens if we get caught?" Peggy asked.

Nothing good. Dana shrugged, felt a sharp pain—she had left the sling off tonight—and started some pacing of her own.

"Last chance to come to your senses," Peggy said.

It was tempting. It was sensible. It was *incredibly* tempting. Dana looked over at her, hoping to be talked out of this. "What do you think?"

Peggy stared down in the direction of her parents' building. "Hey, I never liked the idea in the first place."

Dana nodded, and tested her shoulder's range of motion—with the familiar discouraging results. If they ran into trouble, she wasn't going to be much help fighting their way out of it.

If she even had the damn guts to fight back. This time.

"However, I absolutely hate it that, on top of everything else, he persisted in propositioning you," Peggy said.

Where had that come from? Dana stopped pacing. "What do you mean?"

"It was utterly denigrating," Peggy said, her expression very angry, "and—well, it just bothers me."

Even though it seemed like the least of a long line of offenses. "Murder and arson are pretty bad, too," Dana said.

Peggy nodded. "They're *very* bad." Then she nodded again, looking unexpectedly sure of herself.

Inspired, even. "So—we're going to go in?" Dana asked, just to be sure. "Give this a try?"

"Damn right," Peggy said. "Let's *get* him."

Sounded good to her.

Stefan had told her that the caterers would probably pull their two vans into the building's parking garage, so that they could unload directly on and off the service elevator, and if they waited somewhere nearby, that's where they would be met.

Shortly after nine, a tall, actory guy in black pants, a bow tie, and a white shirt opened a side door by the garage and looked outside.

"You Stefan's friends?" he asked.

Dana and Peggy nodded.

"So, come on," he said, and held the door open wider. "Help us clean up."

They looked at each other, and then followed him inside.

"So, what's the deal here?" the guy asked, sounding only moderately curious, as they walked toward the service elevators.

They had planned a lame, little cover story, and she might as well try it out. "It's kind of a prank," Dana said. "Too long and complicated to really get into."

The guy shrugged. "Okay. Why not?"

As they waited for the elevator, a stocky, older man in a maroon, monogrammed uniform came striding over from a small security booth, scowling.

"What's going on here?" he demanded, looking at the guy. "Did I just see you let these people in?"

"Yeah," the guy said, without batting an eye—yeah, definitely an actor. "One of the girls went home sick, so they had us call in a couple subs to help with the clean-up."

The guard looked at Dana and Peggy, who both nodded.

"Hello," Peggy said.

"How ya doin'," Dana said—just for the fun of being slangily conversational.

The guard looked somewhat appeased. "It should have been cleared with me first."

Dana nodded. "Sorry. We came straight from another job."

"Lousy *tips,*" Peggy said, sounding sulky.

"*Totally* lousy," Dana agreed, and they nodded again, in unison.

Were they Frick and Frack—or were they Frick and Frack?

The guard gave that some thought, then returned to his little booth, where Dana could see a small black and white television tuned to a basketball game.

"You two must pull a lot of these pranks," the actory guy said admiringly.

Dana nodded. "Oh, yeah."

"Constantly," Peggy said.

After that, it was very easy. Almost too easy. The elevator came, and they rode up to the penthouse. Several caterers laden down with heavy trays were waiting in the carpeted private hallway when the elevator opened, and they either didn't notice—or didn't care—that one of their fellow workers had been joined by two total strangers, as they got on, and Dana and Peggy and the actory guy got off.

They went in through what must be the servants' entrance—of all things—and the guy pointed them in the direction of the kitchen before going off to help Stefan disassemble the bar and pack up the liquor.

From the sounds of cultured conversation drifting down the hall, there were a few guests still lingering, but the party had, otherwise, pretty well wound down. A maid was handing an unnaturally slim—and wrinkle-free—woman her fur coat in the foyer, while the man with her said something both snide and hearty, and Dana recognized Madeline Brandon saying good-bye to them.

"They aren't even aware that we exist," Peggy said quietly.

"Welcome to the service industry," Dana said. "It's a whole new world."

Peggy nodded, and adjusted her apron tentatively.

The kitchen was crowded with hot, tired workers, all of whom were bustling around with dull efficiency. Everyone was wearing identical black and white uniforms, and the women all had their hair securely and severely pinned back, so blending in was effortless.

Valerie was standing at the end of a gorgeous butcher-block table, loading a cardboard box with uneaten puff pastries.

Accustomed to moving through crowds of distracted waiters, Dana went over right away to join her, while Peggy followed her somewhat haltingly.

"Howdy," Dana said, and transferred several pastries into the box.

Valerie grinned at her. "You made it. Cool."

They watched as Peggy bumped into a woman lugging a crate

of glassware who swore, and shoved past her. Peggy did not seem to be amused by this.

"Has she ever had a normal job?" Valerie asked.

"She might have worked at a museum one summer," Dana said. "And she tutored French for a month, maybe, during college."

Valerie laughed, and went back to packing up puff pastries.

Peggy finally made it over to them, looking extremely surly.

"You were in her way," Dana said, just to start trouble.

Peggy didn't answer, slamming a few pastries into the box.

"Neatly," Dana said. *"Neatly."*

"Shut up, Dana," Peggy said, glaring at her. "You already owe me *big* for this."

Valerie grinned. "I was going to say, I wish I could stay in here with you guys, and do the searching part, but—no way. I'll be safer on the streets."

Dana grinned, too. They *were* being a little short-tempered, weren't they. Pre-thievery jitters, no doubt. "So we would like to truly finish, what was foolishly begun," she said. "For the story's not ended, and the play is never done, until we've all of us been burned a bit, and burnished, by—the sun."

"This plum is too ripe," Valerie responded.

All right—way to pick up an out-of-context line. *"Sorry,"* Dana said.

Valerie lifted a pastry to her mouth, then looked over at Peggy. "Please, don't watch me while I'm eating."

"I hate actors," Peggy said through her teeth. "I have *always* hated actors."

Not a wise remark to make, considering the personnel in this room. And, to make matters worse, she had missed her cue.

"May we be serious now?" Peggy asked.

Dana and Valerie both grinned at her.

"What do we need to know about the layout?" Peggy asked, all business.

How not fun.

Valerie gestured toward a swinging door behind them. "There's a hallway through there, with a spare bedroom on the right. We put our coats on the bed, so I don't know how big the closet is.

The live-in maid's room is on the left, and there's a bathroom, too. Then, if you're out in the front foyer, you'll see a big living room, and dining room and all, and if you keep going that way, there's a sort of library at the end. It looked like he might use it as an office."

Dana nodded, trying to picture all of that mentally.

"As far as I can tell, their bedrooms are down the other way," Valerie said. "We were told that whole area was off-limits."

"It's not a duplex?" Peggy asked.

Valerie shook her head. "No, but it's *huge.*"

A couple of caterers deposited some more platters of leftover hors d'oeuvres on the table, and Dana and Valerie began packing them away in a fresh box.

"Enjoyable as this hands-on work is," Peggy said, "I think we really ought to go take our places before one of them comes in here and recognizes you."

Dana nodded. They should make their move while all of the caterers were still busy hustling around without giving them a second look, too.

"Just so you know," Valerie said, "they have a dog. Some kind of little terrier thing, so it might be yappy."

Dana stuck a couple of pastries in her pocket, to use as potential treats. "Do you know its name?"

Valerie shook her head. "I heard Mrs. Brandon just sort of talking baby talk to it."

What a disgusting image. Dana looked at Peggy. "All right, you go first, and I'll be along in a couple of minutes."

Peggy nodded, edging her way through the catering traffic much more successfully this time, going through the swinging door without anyone seeming to notice. Presumably, most of them had made trips out to the bathroom over the last few hours.

"You really want me to wait until five to call the police?" Valerie asked.

"We'll probably be out much sooner," Dana said. "I just want to make *sure* they've gone to bed before we start looking around." She glanced over. "What about you? Are you going to be safe out there? You should go over to Lexington, and find a coffee shop or something."

Valerie nodded. "I probably will, for a while. But why don't we make it four, okay? In case he gets up at the crack of dawn to check on the stock market in Japan, or something."

It still needed to be late enough so that any building security would be likely to be dozing, or at least off-guard. "Four-thirty," Dana said.

Valerie nodded again. "Deal. Hold off until right before then, and I promise I'll make enough of a diversion outside, so no one'll notice you on their security cameras or anything."

That sounded pretty risky. "What are you going to do?" Dana asked, uneasily.

"It'll be in character," Valerie said. "It'll be *great.*"

Make that—extremely risky. But they didn't have time to argue about it, so Dana just nodded, took a deep breath, and headed for the swinging doors.

The hallway was exactly the way Valerie had described it, although she opened doors to both the bathroom and a large linen closet before she found the one to the bedroom. Except for the caterers' coats on the bed, it did appear to be unoccupied.

The closet was at the far end of the room and she knocked very gently before opening the door. The inside smelled musty enough to indicate that it was used for storage, and Peggy was sitting on the floor in one corner, already changed into black leggings, a navy blue hooded sweatshirt, and very clean white Tretorns.

"Is that what the well-dressed burglar is wearing these days?" Dana asked.

Peggy sighed. "Just get in here before someone sees you."

Dana closed the door, then felt her way past plastic garment bags to the opposite corner in the dark. The closet was fairly large, but it still felt cramped, and airless.

Not that she was having another attack of nerves. No, not at all.

She was suddenly very aware of her heart beating, and after sitting down among some stacked boxes, she took a few, quiet calming breaths. The closet was pitch black, except for the tiny bit of light that came in from the crack at the bottom of the door.

"Are you as scared as I am?" Peggy asked in a low voice.

"Much more so," Dana said.

They sat in complete silence—which was a challenge in and of itself—for a long time. The cleanup must have been completed, because they heard voices as people came in and out of the room, collecting their coats. Gradually, the voices faded away, and then, the light in the bedroom went off and they both jumped as the closet got even darker.

"What if a maid or a cook or someone *does* sleep in here?" Peggy whispered.

"Then we're in big trouble," Dana whispered back.

They sat silently for what seemed like an endless period of time—which turned out to be, according to Dana's watch, more like twenty minutes.

"I'm going to change now," she said softly.

"Really? Into what?" Peggy asked.

It wasn't the funniest joke in history, but they were both tense enough to laugh anyway. Quietly.

She took her time changing—her black hightops, black sweatpants, and a black turtleneck—trying to waste as many minutes as possible. She had a little black watchcap she had planned to wear, too, but Peggy would probably make fun of her, so she left it in her knapsack.

"Are we really going to wait until two?" Peggy asked.

Dana turned on her penlight to check her watch again. Christ, it wasn't even eleven yet. "You want to take chances?"

Peggy sighed. Heavily.

They kept sitting in the dark, Dana veering between tension and drowsiness every few minutes.

"Can I borrow your flashlight and read?" Peggy asked.

What kind of self-respecting criminal brought a book along? Dana blinked a few times, shaking herself fully awake. "I think we should save the batteries."

"Yeah, but I have an author lunch tomorrow," Peggy said. "I really wanted to do another readthrough."

Christ. "We're going to be in *prison* tomorrow, Peggy," Dana said, "remember?"

"Oh." Peggy sighed again. "Right."

They sat, and sat, and sat. Dana's bad knee got so stiff and achy that she had to straighten it out at one point—which Peggy must have interpreted as a kick, because she kicked back.

"I'm just stretching," Dana said, feeling childish—no, peevish; peevish was really the right word—enough to return the kick. Hard.

"*That* time you weren't," Peggy said.

Damn right.

They sat some more. Twelve-thirty. Twelve thirty-seven. Twelve forty-four. Twelve fifty-one.

"What happened to saving the stupid batteries?" Peggy asked.

Dana didn't bother answering, just snapping the penlight off, and they sat in noticeably fractious silence.

"No one ever told me that being a criminal was so dull," Peggy said finally.

It had come as a surprise to her, too.

At about one forty-five, they both cracked.

"I begin to think I would *prefer* prison," Peggy said.

Dana stretched out her bad knee again, massaging her quadriceps. "I begin to think this *is* prison."

Peggy stood up, bumped her head on the clothes rod, and growled an indecipherable obscenity.

"Ready to go risk life and limb?" Dana asked.

Peggy growled something more readily distinguishable, but equally obscene.

Charming. Nothing like stress to bring out one's finest characteristics. "You wearing gloves?" Dana asked, pulling on a latex pair she'd bought at Pathmark.

"Of course," Peggy said. "I'm not a *complete* amateur."

Maybe not, but they were both the next best thing. Dana checked to make sure her various accoutrements were handy, her knapsack comfortable on her back, and then—what the hell—put on her watchcap. Might as well go all the way with this. Duly costumed, she took a deep breath and slid the door open.

They stood without moving, *hearing* silence, and *seeing* darkness. Dana didn't want to risk turning her flashlight on, so she felt her way across the room until she found the bedroom door. Behind her, Peggy stumbled—not quietly—over something, and Dana wasn't sure if she wanted to slug her, or laugh hysterically.

Instead, once she was sure Peggy had picked herself up, she eased the bedroom door open a couple of inches and listened with all of the concentration she could manage, making a point of ignoring her heartbeat. Wheezy snoring from the maid's room, a hum that must be the refrigerator. No voices, televisions, music—or anything whatsoever to indicate that anyone was up.

"Well?" Peggy asked, barely audible.

No time, as they said, like the present. "Let's go," Dana said, and stepped out into the hall.

Twenty-five

There was a small light on above the sink, but other than that, the kitchen was empty, so they walked softly across the linoleum, pausing every few steps to listen again.

"Did you get the idea for your outfit from a *Charlie's Angels* episode?" Peggy whispered.

Yeah. So? Either that, or *The Hot Rock.* "You look very nice and monochromatic, too," Dana whispered back. Except for the damned Tretorns, which were so new they practically glowed in the dark.

"We're thieves," Peggy said. "We're creatures of the night."

Right.

They were making their cautious way past the foyer and towards the living room, when they heard a small scrabbling sound—and froze.

Claws. Dog claws.

Swell.

A scruffy-looking beige terrier came trotting down the hallway, whining a little—and almost certainly on the verge of loud barking.

Dana bent down, clicking her tongue in a friendly way, and then broke off a piece of one of the puff pastries in her knapsack.

"Good dog," she whispered. "Come here, boy."

The dog gobbled the pastry without hesitation, wagging his tail the whole time, and she fed him several more pieces, patting him throughout.

"You pat him, too," she said to Peggy. "So he knows you're his friend."

Peggy made a face, but tapped him once on top of the head. Dana gave her some pastry, and Peggy flinched when the dog took it from her hand, but then gave him another stiff pat.

"Okay?" she asked, wiping her hand on her leggings.

Well, it was going to have to be, wasn't it.

There was an antique lamp on in the foyer, but other than that, the apartment seemed to be dark. Peggy gestured down the wide hallway to the left, then folded her hands to mimic a sleeping motion, and Dana nodded.

So far, so good.

She tucked the dog under her arm—did that count as kidnapping?—and they crept down the hall in the other direction. The whole situation suddenly seemed very funny, and she took a couple of deep breaths, trying not to laugh. They were, for Christ's sakes, committing an actual criminal act. On *purpose.* She snuck a glance over at Peggy, then started slinking along the wall in an exaggerated pantomime of a cat burglar.

Or, in this case, small dog burglar.

"Cut it out," Peggy said, starting to smile.

Dana grinned, tried to look serious—and then stopped short so Peggy would crash into her. Peggy promptly punched her in the back and Dana laughed, which set Peggy off, too. If they got caught, the tabloids were going to call them "The Giggling Gangsters," or something otherwise impossible to live down.

"All right, all right, get serious," Peggy whispered.

Dana nodded, and slunk down the hall, singing—very softly, complete with the requisite hand gestures, using the dog as a live-action prop—"Little Rabbit Foo-Foo."

"Grow up," Peggy said. "And he hops through the forest, not down the avenue."

"In *your* neighborhood, maybe," Dana said, and went on—quietly—with the song, pretending to bop the dog on the head.

Looking exasperated, Peggy stopped and made a time-out gesture, and Dana nodded. They should fly straight now. Not let down the long line of self-respecting criminals who had come before them.

There was an ornate silver bowl on a nearby buffet and Peggy picked it up, putting it on her head. They both laughed, and then Peggy replaced the bowl. Dana set the dog down inside it, and they laughed again.

"I think we could make a jury like us," Peggy said thoughtfully. "Acquit us."

Dana nodded, lifting the dog out of the bowl, and he wagged his tail. Which made him a turncoat—or a co-conspirator?

Peggy, in the meantime, was squinting through the dim light at what appeared to be an original Monet on the wall.

"Is that what I think it is?" Dana asked.

Peggy nodded.

Wow. Pretty cool.

"I've always heard they have an incredible collection," Peggy said, moving down the hallway to examine the next painting, which was a landscape. Dutch, maybe.

They looked at each other, and then, without having to discuss the idea, veered into the living room to check out whatever paintings were displayed. They wandered around the room counterclockwise, with Dana pointing her penlight at each painting, which they would study, and then move on. One Seurat was especially beautiful, and they paused a little longer.

"I have to start going to more museums," Dana said. "Take advantage of where we live."

Peggy nodded, looking at the painting.

"Although I *did* get to the butter sculptures," Dana said.

Peggy glanced over. "Really? How were they?"

Hard to describe. "Very nice," Dana said. How vague. "Very intricate."

Peggy nodded, and they walked into the next room, the centerpiece of which was a gorgeous grand piano. Peggy reached out to touch the polished wood with a black-gloved hand, and Dana could practically *hear* her salivating.

"No," she said. "And don't take that glove off, either."

Peggy flushed and withdrew her hand. "I know, I know."

Nevertheless, it would be better to remove her from the temptation. "Come on," Dana said. "We don't have that much time anyway."

They found the room Valerie had described without much trouble, as the dog trotted happily along behind them, seeming very pleased not to be the only one in the apartment who was awake.

It seemed to be a combination of a library and den, and everything about it felt overpoweringly *male.* Brandon's lair, apparently. Leather-bound books, oak furniture, lots of glass-doored wooden cabinets, including—oh, nifty—a *gun* collection. There was also an elaborate and expensive computer setup on the hand-carved, antique desk.

"So. What exactly are we looking for?" Peggy asked.

Well— *"Clues,"* Dana said. Yeah.

Peggy sighed, and then pulled experimentally at a couple of the desk file drawers. "They're locked."

Dana grinned, slid some of her superintendent tools out of her knapsack, and went swiftly to work, holding the penlight in her mouth—the way she was certain real burglars habitually did. The dog curled up besides her, seeming very content.

"Wonderful," Peggy said. "We've now crossed the line into criminality."

They had crossed that line *hours* ago. Dana frowned at her. "I fix locks all the time—I'm not going to break anything."

Peggy frowned back, and folded her arms, sitting on the edge of the desk to watch. "I feel like James McCord."

Watergate humor. What a treat. Dana took out a tiny screwdriver, rethought her selection, and selected an even smaller one. "That's funny," she said. "You *look* more like Sturgis."

Peggy laughed, relaxing slightly. "Luckily, Dana, you're very bright. It's the reason I put up with you."

Hmmm. *The?* Dana stopped what she was doing. "There aren't any other reasons?"

"Nope," Peggy said. "Sorry." She slid over next to the computer and pushed the power switch. The screen lit up, and the printer started humming as it warmed up.

"Turn it off, that thing is really loud," Dana said.

"*Singing* is also loud," Peggy said, her fingers moving rapidly over the keyboard as she punched up the hard-drive directory.

Or—presumably that's what she was doing. Dana wasn't big on computers.

"IRS heaven," Peggy remarked, scrolling from page to page of whatever file she had pulled up.

Dana's screwdriver slipped, leaving a distinct scratch on the metal. Except—maybe that was okay. If he knew someone had been here, that might rattle him all the more.

Not that she wanted to cause any gratuitous damage.

"What we need here, is a team of federal prosecutors and MBAs," Peggy said, opening, exploring, and closing files with admirable speed.

"Anything interesting?" Dana asked.

Peggy cocked an eyebrow at her. "You mean like a memo that says 'Pay so-and-so to light fire, laugh all the way to the bank'?"

Well—yeah. That would be kind of ideal. Dana succeeded, finally, in unlocking the top desk drawer, and was pleased to see a small ring of keys inside, which almost certainly—yes!—fit the other drawers.

"You realize," Peggy said, "that you've given him so much forewarning that he's almost certainly deleted, or destroyed, anything incriminating."

Again with the details. Dana flipped, somewhat aimlessly, through various financial folders. "Even if you delete, isn't there still a shadow file there that you can retrieve, if you know what you're doing?"

"Sometimes," Peggy said. "But—it's highly technical, and even if he were stupid enough to keep evidence around, it would be buried somewhere we wouldn't be able to find it. Especially, given our time constraints."

Dana automatically looked up at the clock on the wall, seeing that it was past two-thirty. Already. "So—what? You want to leave? Cut our losses?"

Peggy sighed. "Dana, look at all these files. Look at all these disks. Aren't you getting a little sense of—I don't know—futility here?"

Such unswerving, relentless negativity. Dana decided to ignore her, relocking the first file drawer and moving on to the next.

"At least he's organized," Peggy said, flipping through a file of disks. "If we can just figure out how his mind works."

Tax stuff. This drawer seemed to be devoted to tax stuff. Charitable contributions, too. Lots of them. Hard as *that* was to believe. "Look for things like 'tax delinquent,' 'SRO,' and—Jesus, I don't know—'feasibility studies,' " Dana said. "Stuff like that."

Peggy nodded, glanced at the clock, and kept scanning disks.

Why wasn't there a file drawer helpfully marked "Real Estate Acquisitions"? Or, better yet, "*Illegal* Real Estate Acquisitions"? There didn't seem to be anything relevant in the desk, so she moved to the wall where wooden file drawers had been discreetly built in. A reasonable search of this place would take days, and they were limited to minutes.

The dog followed her over, and plopped down again. She patted him, and he banged his stringy little tail against the floor.

Mergers, overseas holdings, various incorporations, margins, stock options, bonds—Christ. She *should* have taken a damned economics course at some point. Then, out of nowhere, something clicked inside her head.

"I've got it," she said, feeling her heart start to beat faster.

"Leaving me to hope that it's not contagious, considering how much time we just spent together in a tiny closet," Peggy said, popping disks in and out of the disk drive.

"Eighty-ninth Street," Dana said.

Peggy stopped in mid-eject. "What?"

"He doesn't know I know about that," Dana said. "If there are still records, he didn't bother destroying them."

Peggy frowned, her hand still on the disk. "I thought your fire friend said nothing turned up on that."

Granted, but— "They didn't have access to his private files," Dana said.

Peggy paused—and then looked so alert that Dana knew *her* heart had started beating faster, too.

"It'll be under the street address, or the Caldwell Arms, or—" Dana tried to remember the current name of the building "—uh, I think it's, uh—oh, come on, we walk by it all the time."

Peggy nodded, closing her eyes to concentrate. "Park something."

Dana's guess would have been "West something," so the actual name must be mundane. Something like—she pictured the building's entrance—modern, glitzy, and sterile, with a large fountain— "Wainwright," she said. "Wainwright—Terrace, or Tower, or—something like that."

"Circle," Peggy said. "Wainwright Circle. It has that dumb driveway."

They looked at each other, at the clock—and then got back to work, scanning files, folders, and disks even more quickly.

"Did you bring any disks?" Peggy asked. "I don't have time to go through all of the West Side real estate, so I think I should just start copying them."

Yes. She had actually thought ahead, and gone over to the Wiz to buy a small box. Dana pulled three out of her knapsack and handed them across the wide desk.

"Good for you," Peggy said. "We'll make a fine criminal out of you yet."

Dana grinned, and moved down to the next file drawer. It was in the one after that, where she came across an overstuffed folder with a low-numbered West 89th Street address. The first few pages all listed a corporation she had never heard of, and various applications to build on the site, and construction bids, and counteroffers. And—Wainwright Circle. There it was. And in all these papers, there was *bound* to be something he wouldn't want the authorities to see.

"I think this is it," she said, and looked around the room until she located an expensive home copying machine on a table behind the desk. "Should I copy the pages, or just steal the whole thing?"

Peggy hesitated.

"By photocopying, we're already stealing his paper, so it's only a question of degree," Dana said, anticipating the ethical argument with which she was going to be presented.

Peggy looked uncomfortable, but then she nodded. "All right, all right, just do it."

Yeah. The clock was ticking. She turned on the machine, and began copying pages as quickly as she could. Unfortunately, with all of the staples and paperclips on the documents, she had to do most of them individually, instead of feeding them in.

Peggy turned off the computer, and put the disks back exactly the way they had been, sticking the duplicates she had made in her sweatshirt pocket. "Hurry up, okay?" she said. "We're already tempting fate by—oh, Christ."

Dana looked up from the copying machine. "What?"

Peggy pointed at the dog, who was trotting out of the room, his tail wagging, obviously on his way to greet someone.

"Damn," Dana said, and turned off the copier and her flashlight. Then she gathered the copies and the originals together, stuffing them back into the folder, as Peggy quickly moved to close the still-open file drawer.

A light had gone on down the hall, and they looked for a place to hide. Peggy indicated the couch, Dana nodded, and they scrambled behind it, trying to be as quiet as possible.

Now, a light came on in the den, and they heard someone walk into the room. Heavy footsteps. Male. There was the sound of a match striking—presumably, he was lighting a fire in the fireplace; had he come in here to burn heretofore undestroyed evidence?—and then they heard liquid pouring into a glass. To relax. He had come in here to relax.

They sat utterly still, and Dana found it hard not to hold her breath. Maybe he just couldn't sleep, and had come down here to get a book, or—no, he was taking something out of his desk. Next, they heard a sigh, and the sound of him sitting down in the big leather chair near the fireplace.

Oh, great. He was planning on *staying* for a while. She looked over at Peggy, who just shook her head, and then closed her eyes.

Okay, okay. They would just wait him out. No problem. They had plenty of time before Valerie was supposed to call the police, so there was no reason to panic. As long as neither of them sneezed—the very notion of which made her want to do so—or did anything else to alarm him, they would be fine. He probably just couldn't sleep. Once he had finished his drink, he would go back to bed. No reason to panic. None at all.

Peggy mouthed, "What do we do?" at her, and Dana mouthed, "Wait" back. Peggy pantomimed a deep sigh, and Dana nodded. Her thoughts, exactly.

Upon which, of course, she was possessed by devilment, and felt compelled to elbow Peggy and make a Little Rabbit Foo-Foo gesture at her. Peggy showed her a fist, and she grinned, repressing an urge to snicker. Loudly. Somehow—even at funerals—when *forced* to show decorum, she found it almost impossible. A further outgrowth of her general authority problem, no doubt.

The dog seemed to be restless, too—she could hear him lying down, getting up, and lying down again—and it had just crossed her mind that the dog was potentially a problem, when the dog *became* a problem by running around behind the couch and trying to climb into her lap.

Dana set him back on the floor, trying, silently, to shoo him away.

"What are you doing over there?" Brandon asked from his chair, his voice distracted. "You lose your ball?"

The dog must have recognized the word "ball," because he let out a little yap, and looked at Dana with great anticipation.

"Come on, Felix," Brandon said, "get out of there."

Felix?

She tried—without success—to make the dog leave, and then looked over at Peggy, who was just shaking her head.

Brandon got up, heading towards them, and they stiffened.

Done in by a tiny terrier. How ignominious.

"What are you doing back there?" he asked, sounding cross. "Bad dog."

Dana tried to think of a way out of this—should they leap up and knock the guy down? Run away? Just duck lower and hope for the best?—but she couldn't seem to get her mind *out* of the fear mode, and into cogency.

Peggy was biting her lip, and then her expression brightened. She mouthed, "Trust me," and before Dana could stop her, she was already standing up.

"Jesus Christ!" Brandon said, clearly very startled. "Who the hell are you?"

"I'm sorry, sir," Peggy said, sweetly shy and flustered. "I—oh, this is so embarrassing."

"Who are you? What the hell are you doing here?" he asked.

"Well, I-I—" Peggy stopped, and hung her head. "I'm one of the caterers. When I saw you tonight, you were so—I just—I know it was stupid, but when the others left, I *stayed,* I—I just couldn't help it. I'm sorry, I—" she looked unhappy "—What you must think of me."

Margaret Woodruff, acting *girlish.* It was disgusting, really. Nauseating.

"What exactly are you trying to say?" Brandon asked, sounding bemused now.

"Well," Peggy started to make her way out from behind the couch, "I—" she stepped over Dana "—excuse me."

Excuse me?

"Pup," Peggy said, only a couple of seconds too late, and then scooped the terrier up into her arms. "He's a very cute dog, sir, but—oh, my, right in my way." She walked out into the room. "Anyway, it was just sort of an impulse, staying behind, and I guess I was hoping you and I—oh, I don't know. But I'll certainly understand if you don't ask me back."

"At the very least, I should call your employers," Brandon said. "And I should *probably* call the police."

"I know, sir," Peggy answered. "What can I say? I'm ashamed."

Brandon laughed.

"Well," Peggy said, and sighed. "I guess I should just go now, and we'll forget this ever—"

"What's going on?" a taut female voice asked from the door.

Mrs. Brandon. Oh, this just got better and better.

"A most terrible misunderstanding," Peggy said, shyly. "A snafu, even. But I was just leaving."

In a moment here, Dana was going to have to intercede—but she had to get her nerve up, first.

There was a pause, and then Mrs. Brandon spoke. "Mitch, this had *better* be good."

"Hey, I've got nothing to do with it," he said. "This young woman is obviously very disturbed, and she—"

Mrs. Brandon cut him off. "Fine. Call the police. I want her out of here, and I want to press charges."

This must be where the desperate measures for desperate people thing kicked in. Dana quietly unzipped her knapsack and slid out the small tape recorder she'd brought along. She had bought it back when she was acting, and would always leave it in the last row, late in the rehearsal period, to make sure she was projecting to the back of the house. So she knew it picked up voices well.

She checked to make sure the volume was turned all the way up, then pressed "Record" and set the machine down on the floor, near the wall.

"I'm not really a prowler," Peggy was saying. "Technically speaking, I'm only a *lingerer.*"

There was no response from the Brandons, and Dana squinted at the tape to make sure it was turning, and everything was working all right. This was no time for technical difficulties.

"I've merely—tarried," Peggy said, with what might have been a panicky note in her voice. "Hardly seems worth involving the authorities."

"Hey!" Brandon said.

Before Dana had any time to wonder why he sounded so vehement, she saw the dog coming behind the couch again.

Served her right for currying his favor.

"Is there someone else back there?" Brandon asked. No, demanded.

Fuck. In fact, total, *unmitigated* fuck.

"No, of course not," Peggy answered. "Silly old Felix is just—"

Dana stood up.

"Oh, *fuck,"* Brandon said.

And how. Dana nodded, coming all the way out into the room. "I'm with you there, Mitch." She nodded at his wife, who was wearing a blue silk bathrobe and had her arms wrapped across her chest. "Hello, Mrs. Brandon. It's nice to see you again."

Peggy glared at her, looking almost as furious as Mrs. Brandon did. "I was *about* to talk my way out of this."

The hell she was. Dana shook her head, patting the dog absentmindedly as he crossed in front of her.

Brandon sat down, rubbing his temples. "I am getting *very* tired of you, Dana."

They were together on that one, too.

"Find whatever it was you were looking for?" he asked.

Dana shook her head.

"That's it. I'm pressing charges," Mrs. Brandon said, and went over to the desk, picking up the telephone.

Her husband moved even faster, crossing to one of the heavy wall cabinets. "Wait a minute, Madeline," he said. *"Don't."*

Mrs. Brandon scowled at him. "I will not. I'm calling the—"

Brandon turned around, holding something in his right hand.

A gun.

Naturally.

Twenty-six

It would be nice if he were going to point it at his wife—but, no, he was aiming it at them. She snuck a glance at Peggy, who seemed more perplexed than scared. Dana, personally, was veering in the exceedingly afraid direction.

"On the whole," Peggy said, breaking the silence, "I think that a body at rest really ought to *remain* at rest."

Dana grinned. That had "Freeze!" beat any day.

"Mitch," Mrs. Brandon said, her voice sounding measured, still holding the phone. "What are you doing? I think we ought to give this some thought."

Brandon did something to the gun that involved a loud snap, and Dana flinched almost as hard as Peggy did. "You go on to bed," he said. "I'll take care of everything."

Mrs. Brandon nodded, her expression darkening noticeably. "I've heard *that* before."

"So you were right," he said. "The rape murder was in order."

Jesus. Dana stared at this apparently well-bred, cultured woman, and then took an instinctive step back. "That was *your* idea?"

Mrs. Brandon looked at her without commenting, and then looked away.

"Well," Dana said. So much for sisterhood. "Let's hear it for the Ladies who Lunch."

Peggy nodded. "Probably picked it up at Miss Porter's."

"Foxcroft," Dana said. Maybe Madeira.

"Give me a girl at an impressionable age," Peggy said, "and she is mine for life."

Dana laughed. It was *much* easier to be brave, when your acerbic sidekick was along for the ride.

"Take a seat, girls," Brandon said stiffly. "Now."

Girls? Whoa.

"Now," Brandon said.

Peggy sat down on the couch, with her ever excellent posture, crossing her left leg neatly over her right. Dana—probably just to prove a damn point to herself—stayed right where she was.

"You'd be surprised by the amount of pleasure I would take in hurting you," Brandon said, so softly that it was scary.

No. She wouldn't be. But, temporarily accepting defeat, she sat down.

Mrs. Brandon released her breath. "Look, Mitch. Let's just call the police. Have them locked up."

Brandon shook his head, picking up the phone with one hand, pointing the gun with the other.

"The wild allegations of common thieves?" Mrs. Brandon said. "No one's going to believe them."

Her husband frowned at her. "Just go on to bed, Madeline, all right?"

Mrs. Brandon frowned back—and then sat down.

"What," Brandon said impatiently, "you want to lose everything? You want accusations spread over every tabloid in town?" He gestured toward two framed photographs on the mantelpiece, of a boy and a girl, dressed in prep school uniforms, in stiff school-picture poses. "You want *them* to find out about it?"

When Mrs. Brandon answered, her voice was very even. Chillingly so. "I don't want you to do something you don't think over very carefully."

"I don't see any other options," Brandon said. "I've let it go much too far, as it is."

Mrs. Brandon thought about that, and then slowly nodded. Brandon also nodded, and started dialing.

"If we make a run for it," Peggy said, barely moving her mouth, "one of us might make it."

"Might," Dana said.

Peggy looked frustrated, but didn't pursue the idea any further.

"There's a problem," Brandon was saying into the phone, not taking his eyes off them. "*Two* problems, to be precise."

His end of the conversation was so depressing, that Dana tried not to listen, but he seemed to be telling whoever was on the other end that the guy could do whatever he wanted, as long as the body wasn't found, but that the other one was going to require more finesse. Something that would look accidental—and unconnected.

The inference being that *she* was headed for the originally threatened brutal sex crime—and Peggy wasn't. This time, though, she was *damned* if she was going to go quietly. The second she sensed the inevitable, she would do something to make sure Brandon shot her. Fatally. If she was going to die anyway, she wasn't going to give him the satisfaction of getting to hear about the ugly details, later.

The strange part was, at the moment, she wasn't scared. She *was,* admittedly, on the verge of vomiting, but other than that, she was surprised by how clear-headed she felt. Resigned. Relaxed, almost.

Mrs. Brandon—whose face was utterly expressionless, except for her eyes, which had kind of a glittering thing going—was staring at Peggy, as though she were trying to place her. "Do we know each other?" she asked.

"We've met," Peggy said shortly.

The look in Mrs. Brandon's eyes sharpened. "When was that?"

Peggy shrugged, doing a remarkable job—to Dana's way of thinking—of feigning boredom and disdain. "On several occasions, as I recall."

Mrs. Brandon kept studying her, those eyes so icily calculating that Dana would have found it hard to meet them. "You're someone's daughter," she said finally. "But I can't remember whose."

Peggy looked right back at her, with such tremendous serenity that Dana was tempted to clap. "My father's Lawrence Woodruff, if that helps you."

Mrs. Brandon's eyes got bigger. "You're *Katharine* Woodruff's daughter?"

Peggy nodded pleasantly.

"Oh, Jesus," Mrs. Brandon said, and looked over at her husband, who seemed to be making another call. Making some more, violent plans.

"And will you be at St. Bart's," Peggy asked, "in a black linen suit, pausing to clasp her hand compassionately after the service?"

Mrs. Brandon didn't answer, her face hard to read.

"My parents being who they are," Peggy said to Dana, conversationally, "countless of New York's most socially prominent individuals will feel compelled to attend. No doubt, these lovely people will be among them."

Brandon had hung up the phone and was heading over to the leather chair across from them, the gun seeming quite comfortable in his hand.

"Mitch, this is a little more complicated than you may have realized," Mrs. Brandon said, and jerked her head in Peggy's direction. "She's Larry Woodruff's daughter."

Brandon seemed staggered by that for a second, but then he shrugged and sat down. "Well, last I heard, the fabulously rich commit suicide, too."

Peggy inclined her head in Dana's direction. "Sometimes, we get discontent."

It was hard to believe that someone so incredibly impossible could also be so goddamn lovable. Dana grinned at her. "What a dump."

"Oh, she's good," Peggy said. "She's very, very good. First, Frank Sturgis, and now—I'm speechless. Really."

Mrs. Brandon was still staring at her with squinty eyes. "Lesbian?" she asked.

Mistaking her for Rachel, of course.

Peggy turned to Dana, looking outraged. "Did she just call me a thespian?"

Oh, for Christ's sakes. "Lesbian," Dana said, grinning again. *"Lesbian."*

"Oh," Peggy said, and relaxed. "Well, that's all right, then. But—I *won't have* anyone calling me a thespian. I simply won't have it."

Was it her imagination, or had Brandon's eyes just glazed over a little?

"You," he said, pointing the gun at Peggy. "Get up."

Peggy hesitated, and Dana saw her hand clench nervously for a second.

"It's more difficult if we have to shoot you first, but hardly insurmountable," he said.

Peggy looked over at her, and catching a flash of fear in her eyes, Dana felt scared again, too.

Brandon motioned towards the bar with his gun. "Go over there and make some drinks. I want to get your blood-alcohol levels up."

Christ. Was there anything worse than forensically sophisticated criminals?

Peggy got up—could it be that she *wanted* a drink?—and went over to the bar. She surveyed the various bottles, and then rubbed her hands together. "Okay. I'm going to need some grenadine, and a blender, a lemon, and—"

Somehow, Brandon didn't seem to think that was funny.

"Then again, nothing wrong with straight Scotch," Peggy said, and selected a bottle. She looked at the label, frowned, and exchanged it for a more expensive brand. She carried it, and two glasses, back over to the couch, and poured them a couple of healthy drinks.

"L'chaim," she said, and took a slug from hers.

Dana smiled, but didn't touch her glass.

"If you'd prefer, it can be forced down your throat later," Brandon said.

She was going to throw up. It was only a question of *when.*

"Your prerogative," he said. "Ultimately, it's going down you."

Dana ignored him, and he made a sound that might have indicated amusement, or might have been disgust.

No one spoke for a few minutes, and the ticking of the grandfather clock seemed very loud. It was going on to three-thirty now, and she really hoped that Valerie was down on Park Avenue getting nervous, and would decide to call the police earlier than planned.

Next to her, she saw Peggy's free hand clench a few more times, and glanced over enough to see that she was, in complete silence, gasping for breath. Her face was very pale, and she was sitting so rigidly that she was trembling.

A thing that almost no one in the world knew about Margaret Woodruff was that, occasionally, during moments of extreme stress, she was prone to attacks of anxiety-induced asthma.

"Do you have it with you?" Dana asked.

Peggy nodded a tight nod.

All right, then. No problem. Dana turned to Brandon. "Don't panic, Mitch, okay? She's going to reach into her bag for a second, and take out her inhaler."

"The hell she is," he said.

Christ, she really hated him. "I know it's hard for you, Mitch," Dana said, "but try to be a human being for a second. It'll be a nice change of pace."

He scowled at her. "I hope they make it *bad* for you, Dana. I really do."

He was beneath contempt. In every way. Dana nodded. "Fine. Whatever makes you happy. But she's going into her bag now."

Peggy waited a few seconds, and then, slowly, extended her hand towards the coffee table. She fumbled with the drawstring at the top of her bag and reached inside, coming out with a small yellow inhaler. She shot a couple of quick sprays into her mouth, and then put it away, blinking hard.

"You all right?" Dana asked.

Peggy gave her an unconvincing nod, and drank some Scotch. Drank quite a lot of Scotch, actually.

Brandon looked over at his wife, who was as quiet and tense as everyone else in the room. "There's no need for you to stay in here. I don't think you should be involved."

"For better or worse," she said, and there was so much bitterness in her voice that Dana was *very* glad that she didn't know any of the intimate details of their marriage.

Felix, lying on the rug by the fireplace, whined, and Mrs. Brandon reached down to give him a pat.

"That's often an Aryan thing," Peggy remarked, gulping away at her drink, and pouring herself another. "Liking animals, hating people."

Oh. Okay. Any justification not to like animals, right? Dana grinned, and drank some Scotch without thinking. It tasted pretty damn okay, and she drank some more.

Mrs. Brandon stopped patting Felix, and looked at her husband again. "How long?" she asked, in a low voice.

He glanced at his watch. "Half an hour. Forty-five minutes, maybe."

Mrs. Brandon nodded, and they all sat there, in silence.

It was three-thirty.

By four o'clock, Peggy was smashed. And—oddly—chatty. *Incredibly* chatty. Endlessly so. The Brandons had broken down and poured drinks of their own, and everyone was sipping Scotch and watching everyone else. Mostly, though, the rest of them were watching *Peggy.*

"This, this whole Information Superhighway thing," Peggy said, slouching back against the plump couch cushions and gesturing expansively. "I don't like it. I don't even, really, know what it means, in the long run, but—I don't like it."

Dana smiled, and took a gulp of her drink. If death was going to be the end result of all this, prior mental obliteration might be a wise choice. It was clearly the one Peggy had made.

"Nutrasweet," Peggy said. "I don't like Nutrasweet, either. Never have. It's dangerous. It's *sick."*

Jesus, she *liked* Peggy, and she wasn't sure if she could handle any more of these "Pronouncements." The fact that Brandon hadn't shot her yet might be an indication of astonishing self-control on his part.

Peggy looked over at her, drunkenly. "It's important to recognize the years of one's prime, always remember that."

Right.

"I'm half in the bag, Dana," Peggy said.

Dana nodded. "At *least* half."

"Which reminds me," Peggy said, and topped off her glass.

Across the room, the Brandons exchanged strained glances. Mrs. Brandon looked pointedly at the clock, and her husband shrugged.

"Any minute now," he said.

She nodded, and hunched her shoulders.

Were they all enjoying themselves yet?

"So," Peggy said. "Where was I?"

Christ almighty. Dana couldn't help sighing—and she heard the Brandons sigh, too. The *dog* might even have sighed.

"Velcro," Peggy said. "It bugs me."

Given the opportunity, Dana would consider pulling the trigger herself.

"Let me tell you why," Peggy said.

All right, all right, the clock was ticking. Dana tuned her out, trying to come up with a way out of this. Sitting and waiting for their killers to arrive was beginning to lose its already minuscule charm.

She looked at the fireplace, where the last logs were still flickering. Fire. She looked at the Scotch bottle. Alcohol. Hmmm. Somewhere in here, there was a plan. She should maybe refine it—but there was always the fear of reading too cerebral. There was also plain, *ordinary* fear to consider. In her favor, everyone's guard was down at the moment. Numbed by a verbal drug that answered to Peggy.

The only thing she had to decide was whether to push *off* on her bad knee—or *land* on it. Either posed potential problems. But she should probably land on it. That way, at least, she'd have momentum on her side. Gravity. Yeah. What the hell. She'd go out in a blaze of glory.

Without thinking anymore—logic and good sense had no place

in this—she leaned forward to refill her glass, lethargically, as though her reactions had slowed so much that she wasn't sure what she was doing. Then she held the bottle up.

"Anyone else?" she asked. "No?" She picked up her drink, and then threw it—hard, side-arm—into the fireplace. As the flames spurted up, she grabbed the bottle and lunged over the coffee table. From some reason, Peggy—a little late, a little uncertain—was throwing *her* glass at the fireplace, but Dana consciously ignored that, landing on the other side of the table with all of her weight on her weak leg. Her knee buckled, and she felt something tear, but she kept her weight going forward and swung the bottle at Brandon's wrist as he rose halfway to his feet. She connected—game, set, and match!—and knocked the gun out of his hand.

As the .45 went skidding across the floor, they both went after it at once, Brandon slamming her down with a tackle so hard that it jarred all the way through her. She couldn't think at first, but then she twisted around to face him before he could pin her down, trying to fight back.

He was swearing—for that matter, she was, too—and he was so much bigger that she was already getting the worst of this. She had played sports; she knew goddamn well that if she let doubt creep into her mind, even for a second, she would be—his hand smashed across against her face, and she punched back with everything she had, savagely glad when she heard him groan.

He stared down at her—they both stared—and then his fist came swinging towards her again. She got her arm up just in time, and was able to block most of the impact, although she heard a weak groan of her own burst out.

The gun. She had to get the goddamn gun. She managed to break partway free, but then something hit her rib cage with so much crushing force that she sagged down, and he yanked her roughly back again.

The bottle. He had hit her with the Scotch bottle, and—he was going to do it again.

She managed to get her arms down to protect her ribs, realizing—too late—as he raised the bottle, that that's what he wanted, that he was going to go for her face next, that—her face.

Her *head.*

Oh, Christ.

Twenty-seven

"Don't even *think* about it," an unrecognizably lethal voice said.

They both looked up to see Peggy standing there with the fireplace poker, holding it like an awkward, but *dangerous,* baseball player.

Brandon's hand tightened on the Scotch bottle, and Peggy hefted the poker all the more threateningly.

"I'm drunk," she said. "And I don't like you."

Dana took advantage of his split second of uncertainty to squirm free far enough to grab the gun and then point it at him. "*I* don't like you, either," she said.

Brandon frowned, but then let the bottle drop out of his hand.

"Get off me, you son of a bitch," Dana said, pointing the gun at his face. *His* face, this time.

He got up, very cautious, and Dana followed, the gun shaking so much that she was having trouble controlling it. Peggy was standing perpendicular to them, waving the poker back and forth, poised to swing at the slightest provocation.

Mrs. Brandon was standing just beyond them, bent over in obvious, if dignified, pain, and Dana looked at Peggy.

"It's only her arm," Peggy said in a flat, cold voice. "She'll recover. I purposely missed her elbow, even."

Good Christ. Dana swallowed, and hung on to the gun with shaking hands.

Brandon crouched, maybe about to spring, and she aimed the gun at him.

"Don't," she said, then glanced at Peggy. "Why did you throw your glass?"

Peggy looked irritated. "I thought it was a symbolic gesture—I didn't know you had a *plan."* She also blinked, and then went to put the poker away, drunk enough to knock over the entire fire stand—which was so loud that they all cringed. "Sorry," she said, after a pause, and then clumsily set the tools back up.

Okay. Okay. Her ribs hurt. Her left leg wasn't holding her up right. Okay. She aimed the gun at the Brandons, taking slow deep breaths. Okay. Okay.

"The police," Peggy said. "We need the police."

Right. Dana nodded. "Please don't move," she said to the Brandons.

Peggy paused in the act of dialing. "What if they *do* move?"

They all stared at her.

"Just call the police," Dana said.

"All right," Peggy said, "but I might also point out that you and I hate and despise guns, and it seems a contradiction for you to be standing there holding one."

Impeccable timing, as ever. Dana nodded stiffly. "Thanks for the input. Now, call the goddamn police."

Peggy nodded back, already waiting for someone to pick up. "I just—oh, yes, Operator, I need the police, it's an emergency." She paused to listen, and then scowled. "Someone with a *gun,* that a good enough emergency for you?" She stopped to listen again. "The Livingston Building, on Park. We're in the penthouse. They'd better hurry." Abruptly, she hung up the phone. "I'm serious, Dana. Put the gun down."

What the hell was this? Dana shook her head. "No, see, we've turned the tables, Peggy—and that's good."

"We also have standards," Peggy said. "Let's try to live up to them."

Screw their standards. Principles, morals—all of it was out the window, as far as she was concerned. Under the circumstances.

"I'm not kidding, Dana," Peggy said, taking a step toward her.

Dana was *very* tempted to swing the gun in that direction. Give her a scare. But, with monumental self-discipline, she looked at the Brandons instead. "What do you think—treachery, or wisdom?" she asked, and then answered before they could. "Yeah, treachery was my feeling, too."

The Brandons, although obviously unnerved—and busy plotting—were also watching this entire exchange as though it were a very bizarre tennis match.

"Dana," Peggy said.

This wasn't a time to be reasonable. It just wasn't. "I didn't enjoy having a group of men beat me up," Dana said, just as quietly. "I didn't enjoy it at all."

Peggy nodded. "I know. But don't let him do that to you. We are *not* going to be like them, no matter what."

Dana looked at her, and then at Mrs. Brandon, who was clutching her arm in extreme, soundless pain.

"That's different, you were in immediate peril." Then Peggy frowned. "Also, I lost my head."

Dana shifted her position, felt her leg give out, and quickly shifted back. Her ribs were throbbing, and holding up the gun was hard work. It seemed to weigh about ten pounds. "He's going to get away with it," she said. "I mean, he's rich. They *always* get away with it. Once the lawyers show up—"

"The police are on their way," Peggy said. "It's out of our hands now."

Yeah. Exactly. "Is that enough for you?" Dana asked.

Peggy nodded, looking, for the first time all night, exhausted. "It's going to have be, isn't it?"

Dana let out her breath, winced, and kept holding on to the gun. She had worked awfully hard, and she was damned if she was going to let—

"Dana, I know you're tired," Peggy said. "You're angry, you're in pain, you're *drunk.*" She paused. "Could be a bad combination."

Dana thought about that—thought about it hard—and then

looked down at the gun. She hated guns. Always had. Hated having it in her hand.

Hated how much she wanted to blow him away.

"How's this thing open?" she asked.

"I'll do it," Brandon said without missing a beat.

Yeah. Right. Dana ignored him, trying to unload the gun. She succeeded, finally, and the clip came popping out.

"Careful," Peggy said. "One could still be chambered."

It could? Dana looked at the gun apprehensively. "How do I tell?"

"Do I look like an NRA member?" Peggy asked.

Well—they *were* targeting women these days. She looked at the gun some more and then shrugged, putting it down on the coffee table.

Brandon moved into action, shoving her out of the way and grabbing it.

"Do something smart," Dana said, shoving back. "Go find your passports."

As he started to point the gun at her, there was a loud pounding on the front door—so loud that they could hear it easily.

"Hey! Open up!" a male voice yelled. "Police! Open up right now!"

Brandon smiled at her. "Who do you think they'll arrest? The frightened homeowners, or the hoodlums who held them captive?"

Tough call.

"He makes a good point," Peggy said.

"An excellent point," Mrs. Brandon said, through pain-gritted teeth.

Yes, she was tired. She was very, very tired. Dana sat down on the couch as Brandon went off to answer the door, his smile confident now.

"This is going to be complicated," Peggy said.

Dana looked up at the grandfather clock and saw that it was now four thirty-five. "Is it ever," she said.

As Brandon led several officers into the room, Mrs. Brandon suddenly became a complete basket case, collapsing in tears.

"Oh, thank God you're here," she said. "These—these *animals*—broke into our home! They assaulted me, terrorized us for hours—I want them arrested, and I want to press full charges!"

One of the cops moved to comfort her, while the others surrounded Dana and Peggy. More officers were arriving, and it was starting to get crowded. Confusing.

"All right, you two, up against the wall!" one of the officers ordered. "Right now!"

Peggy looked over. "This is the part where we assume the position?"

This was *not* the part where they started making wisecracks at nervous cops holding loaded weapons. "Just do it," Dana said, putting her hands up, and limping over toward the wall.

One of the cops frowned, and then pointed at her. "Hey! You do that dumb diaper commercial, don't you?"

Guilty. Dana nodded.

"It'll make *anyone* feel like a king," Peggy said, already leaning against the wall.

In the silence that followed as everyone looked over to see if they recognized her, there was an audible click behind the couch.

Oh, *yes.* And—if her reading on the law was at all accurate—it was admissible, even. "Love that auto reverse," Dana said, and then grinned at Brandon. "Better go call your lawyers, you son of a bitch, because I think we got you."

She wasn't surprised when he didn't grin back.

After that, an already complicated situation became all the more so. Various levels of police brass arrived, and then Brandon's lawyers started showing up. Lots of lawyers. Including partners who had been rousted out of bed, not just associates. Mrs. Brandon—lucky her—had been taken off to Lenox Hill for X-rays.

No one seemed to be sure how to handle this, and Dana and Peggy were ushered—under guard—to the kitchen, where they sat at the butcher block table, as the Brandons' very nervous maid brewed a huge pot of coffee. Two officers were posted at the door, watching every move they made.

Peggy had already called the law firm her family had kept on retainer for the last thirty years, so more partners and associates were likely to join the jurisprudence glut in the apartment any time now. The only call Dana had made was to ask Craig if he would please walk Bert again this morning. He had said fine, as long as she returned to the Cloisters with him sometime very soon—and *also* rented *The Mirror Has Two Faces.*

Although he would probably have to wait until after she got out on bail.

She and Peggy sat without speaking, not quite meeting each other's eyes, either. In a funny way, there was something embarrassingly intimate about almost getting killed together.

"Are you as close to stormy tears as I am?" Dana asked finally.

Peggy nodded, her hands wrapped around one of the cups of coffee the Brandons' maid had nicely set in front of them. She had stumbled off to the bathroom—female police officer in tow—twice so far and, as far as Dana knew, thrown up both times.

They sat there.

"I was afraid of you tonight," Peggy said. "And I was *terrified* of me."

No, Dana hadn't particularly enjoyed seeing murder in her best friend's eyes—and her friend probably hadn't liked seeing it reflected right back at her. There were things that were *too* personal, no matter how close you were.

Had been?

Still were. She hoped.

"Would you really have done it?" Peggy asked.

Killed him. Yes. Dana shrugged without looking at her. "Would you?"

Peggy didn't answer. Which, of course, *was* an answer.

Dana glanced at the door, where the two cops—a light-skinned Latino man and an African-American woman—were frowning at them suspiciously. "Relax," she said. "Regardless of how it may seem right now, we're the good guys in this."

Neither cop responded, or even made eye contact.

It was exhausting to think of how many hours it was going to take to straighten all of this out.

Another police officer—a sergeant—came into the kitchen

and looked them over for a minute. He didn't seem impressed. "There's some hooker downstairs, claiming she's with you," he said. "That true?"

Oh, probably. "Does this hooker have astoundingly good dental work?" Dana asked. Dental work Dana happened to know Valerie was still paying off on her credit cards, a year and a half later.

The sergeant thought about that, then nodded.

"Yeah, she's with us," Dana said. "Go ahead and send her up, please."

Peggy raised her head from her arms. "Valerie?"

Seemed like a safe bet, yeah.

They sat there for another few minutes, too tired to talk.

Peggy sipped some coffee, lifting it to her mouth with quivering hands. "I really hated hurting that woman, Dana."

Which probably had more to do with why she kept throwing up, than the alcohol.

"If you hadn't," Dana said, "I would be lying in there right now, with a crushed skull."

Peggy shuddered.

Okay, but it was true. "Thanks, by the way," Dana said.

Peggy smiled weakly. "I'm not the idiot who dove at a loaded gun."

And tore her stupid cartilage, in the clumsy process. Dana shrugged, and then felt her rib cage experimentally. Were they going to make her go straight to the precinct house, or would she get to stop at the hospital first? Maybe she could get some of Peggy's lawyers to insist.

An apparition with frightfully teased red hair, too much makeup, a tight sequined sweater, a leather miniskirt, and some of those high-heeled jelly sandals appeared in the doorway.

"Did someone call for an escort?" Valerie asked, and winked lasciviously at the male cop. "Hiya, big boy. Want to see the town with me?"

He ignored her.

Once again, the outfit, the walk, the accent—all of it was perfect. A work of art.

"You two look like hell," Valerie said, and took a seat at the table. She pulled out—a prop?—a pack of cigarettes, lit two, and handed one to Dana.

"I'll have one, too, please," Peggy said.

Hell had just become thickly encased in ice.

Valerie shrugged, gave her the one she already had in her mouth, and lit a third.

Dana couldn't help feeling like a very bad influence as they all puffed away.

"You have another black eye," Valerie said to her.

Dana nodded.

"Does it hurt?" Valerie asked.

Dana nodded.

"I have an acquisitions meeting, *and* an author lunch today," Peggy said, and then shook her head. "If I cancel at the last minute, he'll be blocked for a month."

Dana and Valerie thought about that, and they all kept smoking.

"You should see how many reporters there are outside," Valerie said. "Already. It's completely nuts."

Peggy lowered her cigarette and looked at both of them seriously. "None of us are *ever,* at any point in time, going to discuss this situation with *any* member of the media, for *any* reason. Clear? I want you both to promise."

Not the sort of promise that required arm-twisting. "What if they report that you're a thespian?" Dana asked. "You don't want me to correct that?"

Valerie looked puzzled.

"I'll just learn to live with it," Peggy said, unsmiling.

Horrors.

Then, Peggy lifted an eyebrow at her. "Why haven't you called your lawyer yet?"

Perhaps because she didn't have one? Although someone she knew from Brown *had* gone on to become a public defender. In Houston. Dana shrugged. "What lawyer?"

"I think you should call him, too," Valerie said.

Kevin? No way. He would be *far* too morally outraged about

all of this. About her. "He couldn't represent me, anyway," Dana said. "He's a prosecutor, remember? Conflict of interest."

Peggy and Valerie looked at her with great pity.

"Do it," Valerie said. "Not to be your lawyer, just to be social. He sounds like the kind of guy who'd be upset if he had to hear about this on New York One."

The local twenty-four-hour station, to which Dana was somewhat addicted. Dana shook her head. "It's six in the morning. I don't want to wake him up."

"The man was shoveling your walk at *eight,* on his day *off,"* Valerie said.

Not the behavior of a slug-a-bed, true.

Peggy nodded. "Pick up the phone and dial, before we lose patience with you."

It would be too cruel to ask if her response would be to brandish—and perhaps *swing*—a fire poker. Or, would she select a weapon at hand instead—a large butcher knife, say?

Besides, now that they'd brought it up, she was a little curious about what his reaction would be. Better she should know, before she forgot, and became smitten. Dana shrugged, and limped over to the wall phone.

The cops at the door didn't like this. At all.

"I'm making a call," she said to them. Firmly. "You two should just be smart and keep your heads down. There's going to be a lot of bad career-breaking stuff flying around here today. It's also going to be multi-jurisdictional." *Hard Copy* would probably weigh in, too. "Let the brass take the heat."

The cops exchanged glances, but didn't move to stop her.

Good. She didn't know his phone number by heart, so she had to call Information, first. The phone rang twice, and then he picked up, sounding wide awake. His voice was so crisp and decisive that he must have expected the call to be business-related.

"Hi," Dana said. "I hope I'm not calling too early."

"Oh." He sounded more tentative now. "Dana. Uh, hi. I mean, no, I'm up."

Yes. She had figured that out.

"And, uh, I guess you are, too," he said.

So it would seem, yeah.

"I, uh, I had a really good time the other night," he said. "I guess I probably should have called you yesterday—um, right?—but, well, I figured—I mean, I'm never really sure when to—" He stopped. "It's really early, Dana. What's going on?"

She should think of something better than "all hell's breaking loose." "Well, it was a late night."

"You all right?" he asked. "You seem sort of—"

"A *rogue* night," she said.

There was a short silence on the other end. "I see," he said. "That doesn't sound too good."

It wasn't. "Anyway," she took a deep breath, "here's the thing. I was just thinking about you, and—"

Peggy and Valerie made "get to the point" motions at her.

Were the three of them Frick, and Frack—and *Frock*—now?

"Things got a little complicated," Dana said into the telephone, "but—" She should just show some gumption here. "Anyway. If I'm out of lockup by Friday, I was wondering if you maybe—" it was *hard* to ask someone for a date, it really was, especially this early in the morning—"Would you like to go to another movie?" Except, they *did* live in New York, after all. There were all sorts of entertainment options. "Or—maybe go hear some jazz, or see a show, or—" Why wasn't he saying anything? "A date. Would you like to go on a date?"

Silence.

"With me, I mean," she elaborated. "In case I didn't make that aspect of it clear."

More silence.

"Lockup?" he asked.

Yes, an incisive mind could always cut right to the heart of the matter. She looked over at the table, where Valerie seemed to be trying to teach Peggy how to blow smoke rings—even though Valerie didn't really know how to do it either. "I'm at the Brandons' penthouse, and I guess we're all going over to the Nineteenth Precinct any time now. It's—well—probably going to be a topic of conversation in New York City law enforcement today."

The pause that followed was extremely brief.

"You need help?" he asked.

Good answer.

Twenty-eight

Lawyers, lawyers, lawyers, as far as the eye could see. More police officers—most of whom appeared to be lieutenants, and captains, and inspectors—had also crowded into the kitchen, and it was very noisy. When Kevin showed up, very dignified and official in a nice wool suit, more people seemed to know him than she would have guessed, and she noticed that while he looked like an attorney, he *moved* like a cop. A somewhat brusque, alert, tightly-wrapped cop.

There were lots of people in the room who seemed to have titles like "Deputy Chief" and "Borough Commander," and as he paused to talk to some of them, Dana was very aware of how intently Peggy and Valerie were checking him out. Peggy had even stopped consulting her *own* lawyers for a minute.

"He's kind of big," Valerie said, sounding dubious.

Yeah. So?

"Shouldn't he have come over to see how you were first?" Peggy asked.

They were *most* unsatisfactory sidekicks, that's all there was to it. Dana slouched down, trying to decide if her knee hurt more than her shoulder. At the moment, it seemed like a toss-up.

"We're kidding," Valerie said.

Peggy frowned. "Sort of."

When he finally headed toward them, one of the other officers—a precinct captain, maybe?—moved to block his path.

"Wait a minute, Gallagher," he said. "I want to make sure they've been fully Mirandized and advised before we—"

Kevin shook his head. "If that's where you're going with this, Chuck, trust me—you're backing the wrong horse." He continued over to the table, taking in all three of them with one swift glance before focusing on Dana. "Who hit you?"

Oh, right. The black eye. She grinned, and pointed at Peggy—who was not amused. So, she pointed at Valerie, who *was* amused.

Kevin let out his breath. "Why do I have a feeling I'm going to regret ever having gone to the Abbey Pub that night?"

Because he was—psychic, maybe?

"Okay," he said, and set his briefcase down. "Okay. Anyone make any statements?"

They all—including Peggy's entire legal entourage—frowned at him.

He must have decided to take that as a no, because he nodded. "Okay. Good. Don't start. Let's try to keep whatever's happened here from getting any worse."

Had attorney-client privilege just set in? She, personally, would have preferred boyfriend-girlfriend privilege. Or, at any rate, something less *gruff.*

Valerie put her hand out. "Hi. I'm one of Dana's accomplices. We met back when we were both working on the Deuce."

Dana grinned again—both because Kevin looked speechless for a few seconds, and because it was true. "Theatre Row," she said. "She means Theatre Row." Which was also, of course, on 42nd Street.

"I knew that," Kevin said, but blinked anyway.

Yeah. Sure. "Want some coffee?" Dana asked.

"Very much," he said, and helped himself to her mug.

Well, okay. At least *that* smacked of boyfriend-girlfriend.

"Who the hell are you?" one of the partners representing Peggy wanted to know.

"I'm their lawyer," Kevin said, equally pugnacious. "Who the hell are you?"

One of the other partners—this one, female—glared at him. "*We're* their lawyers."

"Oh, yeah? Well, I'm working pro bono," Kevin said. "Top that one, why don't you."

Upon which, Peggy sighed, and looked over at Dana. "It's going to be a long day, isn't it."

Very long.

At some point after they got to the precinct house—mostly because of Kevin's blustering—they were downgraded from suspects, to material witnesses. Which still didn't mean that they could go home, or that Dana had been allowed to go to the hospital yet, but the conversations became considerably less verbally assaultive.

Until Peggy's father showed up, of course.

One of the cops had given Dana some Advil, but she must have looked pretty terrible, because one of the associates slipped her a Percocet, too. Since, among other things, she'd been up all night, shortly thereafter she stopped making much sense, and it was decided that she should be escorted to the nearest emergency room, and have some long-overdue X-rays.

"Look," Kevin said, "I have to get down to the office for a while before my boss has apoplexy, but your friend from the Deuce said she'd go with you. If it's okay, maybe I'll come by and see you later?"

Dana looked at him blankly. "What?"

"Right," he said, and touched her face for a second before straightening up.

"Are you going to sling your arm around my shoulders, and then I can help you off, like in a war movie?" Valerie asked.

How totally not cool. Dana shook her head, and cautiously put weight on her extremely swollen knee. Her leg trembled, but held her up. More or less.

One of the captains—she couldn't remember his name—was frowning at her, and she frowned back.

"Do me a favor," she said, "and tell me not to leave town. It'll really make my day."

"Shut up, Dana," Kevin said.

Right. She looked over at Peggy, who was in the middle of her best foot-tapping, watch-checking routine while, across the room, Mr. Woodruff and his legal coterie railed away at anyone within earshot. Brandon and his people were almost certainly doing the same thing, elsewhere in the precinct house.

"You owe me *big* for this," Peggy said grimly.

Yeah, yeah, yeah.

There seemed to be something of a crowd outside, but she and Valerie were ushered into a squad car and driven away before anyone really had a chance to bother them.

Then, at the emergency room, of course, there was another interminable wait, and Valerie was having almost as much trouble staying awake as she was.

"I'm going to have to call my parents," Dana said. "Before they hear about this on the news or something."

Valerie nodded, sipping her third cup of vending machine coffee, and loosening the strap on one of her jelly sandals.

"What am I going to tell them?" Dana asked. How was she even going to *start?*

"You'll figure something out," Valerie said cheerfully. "I mean, you went to Brown."

So she had. For all the good it was currently doing her. Dana drank some of her own coffee, then frowned. "This tastes really weird."

"That's because it's chicken soup," Valerie said. "I pushed the wrong button, and I figured you were so out of it, you wouldn't notice."

Oh. And it was *lousy* chicken soup.

After more waiting, she ended up being sent down to have an MRI—although that also involved waiting. Lots of it. While wearing a hideous little hospital gown in the middle of a public corridor.

"I should dress like this more often," Valerie said, and showed her an array of cards. "Look at all the phone numbers people gave me. Two of the associates, even."

"Are you going to go out with any of them?" Dana asked.

Valerie shook her head. "Men who think women should look like hookers? No way. It's still flattering, though."

It was, indeed.

She was dozing off again, when Valerie nudged her.

"Here comes another jerky cop," she said. "I thought they were going to leave us alone until tomorrow."

Dana looked up, and saw Molly Saperstein hurrying down the hall. "No, it's okay. That's a firefighter, not a cop."

Valerie frowned. "You sure?"

Well, the FDNY patch on her sweater was kind of a dead give-away.

"You're hard to track down," Molly said, slightly out of breath. "The desk sergeant sent me to the wrong hospital, even."

How unsurprising. Dana gestured toward Valerie. "This is Valerie. We met at Central Booking."

"Oh, come on," Valerie said. "You can admit you're my dealer."

Molly looked uneasy, but shook her hand, anyway. "Uh, nice to meet you," she said, and then sat down on Dana's other side. "Are you okay? Did you break anything this time?"

"I think it's just cartilage," Dana said. And maybe her ribs and shoulder again.

"And got a lovely shiner to boot," Valerie said.

Yes. Quite lovely.

They sat there.

"Word on the street is that you're a hero," Molly said.

Not quite. Dana shook her head.

"Okay, but with the possible exception of the red caps, you made thousands of new friends today," Molly said.

That many? Dana opened her eyes. "Oh, yeah?"

Molly nodded. "From this point on, I think the New York City Fire Department is collectively on your side."

Which sounded nice, but—"The convictions might not be very good," Dana said. Especially not with all that expensive legal talent at work. "Kevin said Brandon'll probably end up pleading to some sort of lesser conspiracy charge, and then *maybe* play minimum-security tennis for eighteen months." In fact, with all of the pleas, and deals, and turning state's evidence that had been going on all day, the likelihood of any of it even going to *trial* was very slim.

Court TV would be greatly disappointed.

Molly shrugged. "That's better than it was yesterday. And I heard the underlings are all starting to beg for immunity, so who knows?"

Yeah. In the end, probably months from now, in some convoluted way, maybe justice *would* be served. Maybe. "I picked his head security guy out of a lineup, and they're going to prosecute him for assault," Dana said. Attempted murder would be more satisfying, but aggravated assault would do. And she very much hoped that they would get the other guys from the van, too.

Molly nodded. "It works for me." Then, she looked at Dana. "What are *you* going to do now?"

"Disneyland," Valerie said from Dana's other side. "What else?"

Dana grinned. For someone who hadn't gotten any sleep, Valerie was pretty damn perky.

"Seriously," Molly said.

What was she going to do? Be a super? Call Terence and start auditioning frantically? Go ahead and enroll at John Jay? Take an NYPD exam?

"I'm going to have an MRI," Dana said.

Molly laughed. "Sounds good."

The upshot of the MRI was that arthroscopy and a short stay at the Hospital for Special Surgery were in her very near future. However, for the time being, she was sent home taped, and splinted, and Ace-bandaged, with a brand-new prescription for pain pills.

"When I went by your building before," Molly said, as the three of them rode across the park in a taxi, "there were some reporters waiting around."

Great.

"Can I make a lot of outrageous comments, tell them my name is Margaret Woodruff, and make sure they spell it right?" Valerie asked.

Not if she valued her life. "Don't worry, I have all my keys, so we can go in around the corner," Dana said. "Where I take the trash out."

It was an elementary sort of ruse, but the reporters—there *were* quite a few of them—were caught off-guard, and they made it inside—Dana very awkward on her crutches—before they were even really caught on film.

They ran into Paul, the yuppie account executive who lived in 4H, on the elevator.

"Did you have to go and get arrested? This is *very* inconvenient," he said, sounding nothing if not piqued. "How long are those people going to be out there?"

Dana shrugged, which hurt her shoulder. "Until something more interesting happens, I guess."

He pursed his lips, and looked them over, making it clear that he thought they were quite a motley little crew—and brought down the standards of the building. "Yeah, well, if they're not gone by tomorrow, I'm calling the landlord."

Yeah. Fine. Whatever.

"*And* one of the lights on my bathroom mirror burned out this morning," he said, as the doors opened on the fourth floor.

What a nightmare for him. Smiling would have taken too much effort, so Dana just nodded. "I'll be sure and get right on that, Paul."

"Well, I hope so," he said, and got off the elevator.

The doors closed.

"Does he tip well?" Valerie asked.

Not even *remotely* well. Dana shook her head.

When they got to her floor, she saw someone familiar slouching against her door, half-asleep, wearing what had once been her army jacket. He heard them coming, and scrambled up.

"It's about *time,* lady," he said. "I was getting all worried and stuff."

Bert must be worried, too, because he had started barking.

Dana started to unlock her door, the keys feeling very heavy. "How'd you get in?"

Travis motioned toward the door next to hers. "That weird artist lady. I helped her carry a bunch of stuff."

Okay. Why not. Unlocking her door seemed increasingly challenging, and she let Molly do it for her.

"Some real thin guy was up here a few minutes ago, making like he was going to steal your dog and all," Travis said. "But, don't worry, I scared him off."

Poor Craig. She was going to owe him a *passel* of favors, by the time all of this was over. Joan Crawford videos would probably be added to the deal.

"The phone was ringing way a lot of times, too," Travis said.

No doubt. She looked at Molly. "This is Travis. He lived in Harrison." She turned to Travis. "Molly's engine company was the first one to get there that night."

"Oh," Travis said, and then thought about that. "Is she the fire lady who was rescuing all those people?"

Dana nodded, and Molly avoided their eyes, bending down to pat Bert and the cats.

"She isn't very *tall,*" Travis said, sounding critical.

No. She wasn't.

"I'll take Bert out," Valerie said. "Then, can we order up some food? I'm starved."

Dana nodded. Yes. Food would be good. Sleep would be even better—but, for now, food would do.

As Valerie left with Bert, Travis leaned closer.

"Don't tell her," he said, lowering his voice, "but she looked lots prettier, the other time I met her."

Dana laughed, and maneuvered over to the kitchen table, sitting down with an effort. What a very long night and day it had been.

Travis sat down across from her, looking very happy. "So, I guess you like, solved it and stuff, hunh?"

Dana nodded, and patted Edith. "Looks that way, yeah."

"Wow, pretty excellent," Travis said, and then grinned at her. "So, can I start getting bad grades again?"

He was probably kidding, but—"Don't even *think* about it," Dana said.

His grin widened, and he dug into one of the army jacket pockets, handing her a crumpled paper.

A math test, with a bright red 93, and "Good work!" written across the top.

"Pretty okay, hunh?" he said.

Yes. It was pretty okay. She smiled back at him, so exhausted that it was hard to see straight.

The telephone rang, and Molly answered it.

"Sure, just a minute, please," she said, and lowered the receiver. "It's your mother, Dana."

Her mother. Who made a habit of following New York news on the radio, whenever she could pick it up.

Ouch.

Had Maria Von Trapp—or Julie Andrews—once said something about the beginning being the very best place to start? She reached out for the phone, and then lifted it to her ear.

"Hi, Mom," she said, and then couldn't help laughing. "What's up?"